W9-BQZ-448

PRAISE FOR *THE LAST OF THE STANFIELDS*

"Marc Levy's eighteenth novel, an excellent vintage, has all the potential to be this summer's bestseller."

—*L'Express*

"A gripping thriller that plunges into the folds of family secrets and the human soul."

—Europe 1

"Marc Levy is the master of modern romanticism . . . *The Last of the Stanfields* is a novel you simply can't put down."

—*Entrée Libre*

"A mystery that draws you in and won't let go."

—RTL

"A winding hunt for truth . . . What is Marc Levy's profession? Expert story weaver."

—*Le Parisien*

"[*The Last of the Stanfields*] is a free dive into the depths of family secrets under a single guiding question: How well do we know our loved ones?"

—*Le Figaro*

"Edge-of-your-seat suspenseful. A success. We highly recommend."

—France Inter, *La Bande Originale*

"A magnificent gallery of female characters, not to mention a search for truth that's riddled with plot twists."

—RTL

"Suspenseful and unpredictable, [*The Last of the Stanfields*] brings you characters you won't want to leave."

—Aufeminin.com

"Marc Levy's new novel shows his mastery from start to finish. Impressive."

—RTL

"Marc Levy delivers a beautiful novel about love and family . . . Levy is an expert at teaching us to never doubt the existence of goodness and forgiveness."

—France Info

"Suspense of a magnificent caliber, tangible and moving."

—France Info

"Marc Levy leads the reader to discover a staggering family secret."

—*Le Parisien*

"Marc Levy has always been interested in family secrets. But this time he outdoes himself."

—Josyane Savigneau, writer for *Le Monde*

"An enthralling mystery that revolves around an unexpected family secret."

—Aufeminin.com

"Full of emotion and suspense: a breathtaking treasure hunt."

—*Web TV Culture*

"A real page-turner. You won't be able to put it down."

—Passion Bouquins

"A gripping plot, a winding mystery that leads to an unsuspected family secret."

—Femina Suisse

"A family saga done well."

—Ouest France

"Right from the start, you won't be able to put down *The Last of the Stanfields!*"

—Aufeminin.com

"An absorbing saga . . . the author holds a steady hand crafting a plot that is richly historic, artistic, and—of course—romantic. What's more, his writing is better than ever and his dialogue is on point."

—L'Express

ALSO BY MARC LEVY

If Only It Were True
All Those Things We Never Said
Replay
P.S. from Paris

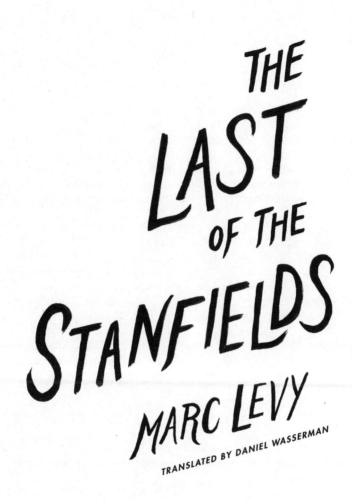

THE LAST OF THE STANFIELDS

MARC LEVY

TRANSLATED BY DANIEL WASSERMAN

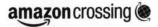

amazon crossing

Text copyright © 2017 by Marc Levy
Translation copyright © 2019 by Daniel Wasserman
All rights reserved.

Previously published as *La dernière des Stanfield* by Éditions Robert Laffont, in France in 2017. Translated from French by Daniel Wasserman. First published in English by AmazonCrossing in 2019.

Published by AmazonCrossing, Seattle

www.apub.com

Amazon, the Amazon logo, and AmazonCrossing are trademarks of Amazon.com, Inc., or its affiliates.

ISBN-13: 9781503959125 (hardcover)
ISBN-10: 1503959120 (hardcover)
ISBN-13: 9781503904057 (paperback)
ISBN-10: 1503904059 (paperback)

Cover design by Kimberly Glyder

Printed in the United States of America

First edition

To Louis, Georges, Cléa, and Pauline

"There are three sides to every story:
your side, my side, and the truth.
And no one is lying."
Robert Evans

1

ELEANOR-RIGBY

October 2016, London

My name is Eleanor-Rigby Donovan.

The first name may ring a bell. My parents were huge fans of the Beatles and the song "Eleanor Rigby."

Back in the 1960s (my father hates it when I point out that he grew up in the previous century), rock fans were split into two very distinct groups: you were either a Rolling Stones fan or a Beatles fan. For reasons beyond me, it was inconceivable to like both.

My parents were seventeen when they got together for the first time, in a London pub not too far from Abbey Road. All eyes in the room were glued to an international broadcast of a Beatles concert, everyone singing along to "All You Need Is Love." With seven hundred million viewers looking on, the moment marked the beginning of a decades-long love story.

And yet they fell out of touch just a few years later. Life, always full of surprises, reunited them under rather odd circumstances in their late twenties. And so it was that I was conceived a full thirteen years after their first kiss. They sure took their time.

My father's sense of humor knows no limits—it's how he won my mother's heart, as the story goes—and so, when registering my birth, he decided to call me Eleanor-Rigby.

"We listened to that song around the clock while we were creating you," he confided to me one day in explanation.

I had absolutely no interest in knowing this particular fact and even less in picturing it. As for my childhood, I could go on and on about how miserable it was, but that would be a lie, and I'm a terrible liar. Like every family, mine is dysfunctional. Here as well, we find two distinct groups: families who admit it, and families who don't and go on pretending. Our family falls into the first category: dysfunctional but happy, perhaps too happy at times. It was impossible to say anything serious at home without being made fun of. There's an overriding will amongst my kin to take everything lightly, even when the consequences are serious. And, I have to admit, while I was growing up it often drove me up the wall. Each of my parents insisted the other was responsible for the lunacy that permeated all conversations, meals, and gatherings throughout my childhood. And I wasn't the only one driven crazy, either. My big brother, Michel (born twenty minutes before me), and my little sister, Maggie, had to deal with it as well.

Maggie—named for "Maggie Mae," the seventh song on the A-side of *Let It Be*—has a strong personality and a heart bigger than anything, and yet she's completely selfish when it comes to the little things. The two aren't mutually exclusive. If you have a serious problem, she'll always be there for you. Don't feel like getting into a car at four in the morning with two buddies too drunk to drive? She'll steal Dad's keys, hop into his old Austin, and drive all the way across town in her pajamas to pick you up. Then, she'll drop your friends off at their doorstep, but only after giving them a good scolding, of course, despite the fact that they're two years older than she is.

But try grabbing a slice of toast from her plate at breakfast and she'll give your forearm something to remember. Don't hold your breath for her to leave you a drop of milk in the fridge either. Why my parents have always treated her like a princess is a mystery. From the start, Mum harbored an unhealthy level of admiration for her—the baby—and thought she was destined for great things. Maggie was going to be a lawyer or a doctor, or even both, savior of widow and orphan alike, eradicating world hunger. In short, she was the golden child, and the entire family had to keep watch over her, and her future.

My twin brother, Michel, is named for the seventh song on the A-side of *Rubber Soul*—though on the album, of course, it's Michelle, the female version of the name. The radiographer didn't see his willy during the ultrasound. Apparently, the two of us were too closely bound for the doctor to make it out. *Errare humanum est.* Then: big surprise during the delivery. But the name had already been chosen, and changing it was out of the question. Dad simply dropped the *l* and the *e*, and my brother spent the first three years of his life in a bedroom with pink walls and an Alice in Wonderland mural, and the rest of his life explaining to everyone that he wasn't French. One visit to a shortsighted radiographer can yield some truly unexpected consequences.

Those whose high level of education rivals their own hypocrisy tend to fidget uncomfortably as they explain that Michel is "special." Prejudice is the prerogative of people convinced they know everything. The world Michel inhabits is blind to violence, pettiness, hypocrisy, injustice, and malice. To doctors, his world is full of disorder. But for Michel, every last thing and every last thought has its proper place. His world is so spontaneous and sincere that I sometimes think we're the ones who are "special." These same doctors have never been able to confirm whether it's Asperger's or if Michel is just different. Maybe the truth isn't that simple.

Michel is an incredibly sweet man, a true wellspring of common sense and an endless source of laughter. If I'm the terrible liar, Michel's weakness is that he can't keep from telling the truth, saying the first thing that pops into his head. Michel waited until he was four years old to start speaking. While queuing up in the supermarket, he opened his mouth to ask a woman in a wheelchair where she'd found her "carriage." Overcome with emotion at hearing her son finally utter a complete sentence, Mum swept him into her arms for a kiss before turning beetroot red with embarrassment. And that was only the beginning . . .

My parents were deeply in love from the very first night they got back together. As with all couples, there were some wintry patches when things ran cold. But they always made up and never failed to treat each other with the utmost respect and admiration. I once asked, after a particularly rough breakup of my own, just how they managed to stay in love for a whole lifetime. My father replied, "The key to lasting love is knowing how to give."

My mother died last year in the middle of a dinner out with my father. The waiter had just brought out dessert—rum baba, my mum's favorite—when she suddenly dropped facedown in a mound of whipped cream. The paramedics couldn't revive her.

Dad went to great lengths not to weigh us down with the pain of his loss, knowing that each of us was suffering in our own way. Michel kept trying to call Mum every morning, and my father would invariably explain that she couldn't come to the phone.

Two days after we buried Mum, Dad gathered us all around the kitchen table and declared that wallowing in misery would be strictly prohibited from that point forward. Mum's death should in no way ruin the close-knit, joyful family that my parents had painstakingly built over the years. The next day, he left us a note on the refrigerator door. *My sweet children, all parents die eventually, and it'll be your turn one day, too, so enjoy the day. Love, Dad.* A "logical point," as my brother would say; don't waste a single moment feeling sorry for yourself. When your mother kicks the bucket by doing a face-plant into her rum baba, it certainly puts things into perspective.

Every time I'm asked what I do for a living, I get to sit back and watch people turn green with envy. I write for *National Geographic*, and am paid a salary—a meager one, but still—to travel, take photos, and write about the world's diversity. The strange part is that it took traveling to the ends of the earth for me to realize that what I was looking for was right there in front of me the whole time. All I had to do was open my eyes and start noticing the wonder of the world outside my front door.

It's not as glamorous as it sounds. Imagine spending all your time on planes. Or sleeping three hundred nights of the year in hotels, sometimes comfortably, but more often *un*comfortably due to budget restrictions. Imagine writing your articles aboard bumpy buses, and nearly dying of pure joy at the sight of a clean shower. In a job like mine, once you finally make it home, all you want to do is put your feet up and sink into the sofa, not budging an inch, with a TV dinner in front of you and your family close at hand.

My love life has been a handful of flings and short-lived relationships, as rare as they are fleeting. Traveling constantly is like being condemned to singledom for life. My longest relationship was with a *Washington Post* reporter. It lasted about two years, though I had wanted it to go on longer. What a lovely feat of self-delusion it was. We shot emails back and forth and tried to tell ourselves we were "close" without ever having spent more than three days in a row in each other's company. All in all, the time we spent together over two years added up to just over two months. Our hearts would flutter wildly every time we reunited, and again when we said goodbye. Eventually, the palpitations got to be too much, and we had to call it quits.

While my life was already anything but banal next to most of my friends' lives, things took a turn for the truly extraordinary one morning when I opened my post.

My father had come to pick me up at the airport after an assignment in Costa Rica. I've been told that thirty-five is a little old to be so attached to my father. Although I'm fine when I'm away, as soon as I come home and see my father's face in the sea of people waiting at arrivals, I instantly revert to the sweet bliss of childhood. Try as I might, it's useless to fight off that feeling.

My father had certainly aged since Mum died. His hair looked thinner and his belly rounder, and there was something heavy-footed about his stride. And yet he was still just as wonderful, dignified, brilliant, and wacky as ever. For me, nothing was quite as comforting as burying my face in Dad's neck when he wrapped me in a big bear hug. Call me a daddy's girl all you want, but I was happy to be one as long as I could.

Not only had the trip to Central America been utterly exhausting, but I'd spent the whole way back crammed between two sleeping passengers whose heads bobbed and lolled onto my shoulders every time we hit turbulence. Seeing my tired and wrinkled face as I washed up back at my dad's flat, I could understand how they might have mistaken me for a pillow. Michel came over for dinner and my sister joined us halfway through the meal. My heart leapt back and forth between the happiness of being all together again, and a strong desire for some time alone in my childhood bedroom. While I hadn't officially lived there since I was twenty years old, in truth, I'd never really left. I rented a studio flat on Old Brompton Road, on the west side of London—rented solely on principle and out of pride, since I almost never slept there. On the rare occasions when I was back in England, I preferred staying under my father's roof, right where I grew up.

The day after that particular trip, I did stop by my studio to check my post. There, amid the myriad bills and junk mail, I discovered a strange letter addressed in elegant and ornate cursive handwriting, with flourishes and thick and thin lines, as though it had been written a century ago.

The letter inside revealed parts of the secret my mother had kept from her family for years. It hinted at something hidden among her belongings that could help shed light on the person she once was. But the anonymous letter writer—the "poison-pen," as I immediately began to think of him—didn't stop there. The letter seemed to imply that

Mum had taken part in a masterful crime committed thirty-six years ago. The letter gave no further details, but there was enough information given to be alarming, and it just didn't add up. First off, thirty-six years ago put us in the year leading up to my own birth—it was difficult to imagine a woman pregnant with twins as a criminal mastermind, let alone my kind, rational mother . . . The anonymous letter called on me to seek out the truth, to follow a trail which would take me to the other side of the world. Lastly, the poison-pen implored me to destroy the letter after reading, and not to mention its existence to anyone—especially not Maggie or my father.

How in hell did this stranger know so much about my family, down to my sister's name? This was also rather alarming.

I had just buried my mother the previous spring and was far from finished with the grieving process. I knew my sister would have never played such a cruel joke on me, and it didn't seem likely that my brother would even be capable of fabricating a story like that. Flipping through my address book, I couldn't find a single person who would ever dream of doing such a thing.

So . . . think about it. What would you have done in my place? Well, you'd probably have made the same mistake that I was about to.

2

SALLY-ANNE

October 1980, Baltimore

Sally-Anne left the loft and peered down the steep stairwell.

One hundred and twenty steps to the ground floor. It was a harrowing descent, down three dark and dingy levels with exposed light bulbs casting halos of light into the abyss. Those stairs were a death trap. The way down was treacherous, and the way up a grueling climb. Sally-Anne endured both, morning and night. The freight elevator had long since died, its rusty gate swallowed up in the dingy landscape of dust and brick.

As she exited the front door of the building, Sally-Anne was blinded by the bright sunlight reflecting off the wooden docks, like always. Old redbrick warehouses lined the street. Tall cranes loomed at the end of a jetty, battered constantly by sea winds as they stood forever awaiting cargo ships that would never enter the decaying port. The neighborhood was abandoned and untouched, not yet gentrified by canny developers. Only a motley grab bag of young people had chosen to settle there: budding artists, musicians, writers, the destitute, as well as trust-fund babies, whose dreams and creativity were nourished often in illicit ways. The nearest corner store was a ten-minute motorcycle ride up the road.

Sally-Anne's Triumph Bonneville was a veritable monster: 650 cubic centimeters capable of rocketing forward at more than a hundred miles an hour, should the driver be crazy enough to hazard such speeds. The blue-and-white fuel tank had been banged up a bit, a souvenir of a memorable crash back when Sally-Anne was still learning to tame the beast.

A few days before, Sally-Anne's parents had told her to leave the city and go see the world. Her mother had scrawled cold, hard numbers onto a check, then had carefully torn it from the checkbook with manicured hands—carefully tearing her daughter from her own home—and handed it to Sally-Anne.

Sally-Anne had considered blowing the money on booze and other debauchery. But she soon became consumed with a thirst for revenge, enraged at being forced into exile for a crime she didn't commit. She resolved to achieve a level of success that would make her parents rue the day they had ever turned their backs on her. Although it certainly was an ambitious undertaking, she was armed with a brilliant mind, breathtaking beauty, and an address book teeming with useful contacts.

Success in her family was measured by dollars in the bank and possessions that could be put on display. Sally-Anne was never short on cash, but that wasn't what interested her. What Sally-Anne loved was people. She laughed at how much it appalled her family to see her shun high society and go mingle with those on the other side of the tracks. She may have had her faults, but Sally-Anne had scores of heartfelt friendships.

The azure sky above made it hard to imagine it had rained throughout the night. On a motorcycle like hers, a slick road was a merciless thing. Feeling the warmth of the engine humming beneath her, Sally-Anne reveled in the Triumph's speed as it swallowed the asphalt in front of it. The wind whipping at her face filled her with a sense of boundless freedom.

She caught sight of the phone booth in the distance, standing alone at an intersection in the middle of no-man's-land, and pushed back her glove to check the time on her watch. Shifting down a few gears and tightening her grip on the hand brake, Sally-Anne expertly steered the Triumph up onto the sidewalk and lowered the kickstand. She approached the pay phone, eager to confirm that her accomplice was on schedule.

Five rings? It shouldn't have taken that long. Sally-Anne's throat tightened, but relaxed when May picked up at last.

"Everything okay?" Sally-Anne asked.

"Yes," May answered tersely.

"I'm on my way. I just wanted to make sure you're ready."

"I'd better be. It's too late to back out now, isn't it?"

"And why would we want to do that?" asked Sally-Anne.

A laundry list of reasons leapt to May's mind. The stakes were too high, and none of it seemed worth the risk. What good was vengeance if it did nothing to change the past, to erase what had happened? And what if their plan went off the rails and the two of them actually got caught? It would be too much to bear. Nonetheless, May would have taken any risk for Sally-Anne, no matter how great. And so, she stayed silent.

"Just don't be late," Sally-Anne insisted.

A police car came cruising around the corner and Sally-Anne's heart froze. She knew she had to keep her fears at bay; otherwise, how in the world would she be able to go through with it? She had done nothing wrong, at least not yet. Her motorcycle was parked legally, and using a pay phone wasn't a crime. The cruiser carried on past, allowing just enough time for Sally-Anne to catch the officer throwing a sleazy look her way. *Give me a break!* she thought as she hung up the receiver.

She glanced at her watch once more and did the math in her head. Twenty minutes until she was at the Stanfield estate's front door. Sixty until she was off the property. Ninety minutes in all until she was safely back home. In the span of a mere ninety minutes, both their lives would change forever. With that thought in mind, Sally-Anne mounted the Triumph, kick-started the engine, and zipped down the road.

On the other side of the city, May slipped her jacket on. She checked that the lockpick was still there, wrapped in tissue in her right-hand pocket, and paid the locksmith for it on her way out. As she stepped out of the building, May was hit by a harsh blast of cold air. The wind made the bare branches of the poplars creak above, sending shivers down her spine. She pulled her collar up around her neck and walked a bit faster.

May boarded a crosstown bus and used the window as a mirror, pulling her hair back into a bun that she secured with bobby pins. Two rows ahead, a man was playing Chet Baker on a little boom box in his lap, his head swaying and oscillating with the slow rhythm of "My Funny Valentine." Another man seated nearby ruffled his newspaper in retaliation. "It's just the most beautiful song I've ever heard," the man with the boom box murmured to his irate neighbor.

May found the song more sad than beautiful, though the truth was probably somewhere between the two. She got off the bus six stops later, arriving at the foot of the hill without a moment to spare. Sally-Anne was there waiting for her on the bike, a second helmet in hand. She gestured for May to hop on board. Soon after, the engine roared to life, and the Triumph sped off into the distance.

3

Eleanor-Rigby

October 2016, Beckenham, outside London

It seemed to be a normal night like any other, but nothing would ever be normal again. Maggie leaned against the doorframe of her living room with an unlit cigarette between her fingers, as though sparking it up would somehow make all the insanity real.

I was sitting at the living-room table, fidgeting with nerves. I had the letter clutched in my hands as though it were some sort of sacred relic or talisman.

"Read it again," Maggie ordered.

"Read it again, *please*," I corrected, for good form.

"Right. Remind me who exactly showed up on whose doorstep in the middle of the night? So, come on, cut the crap . . . *please*."

How was it that jobless Maggie could afford a one-bedroom flat, while I could barely find enough rent for a studio, even with a full-time job? I figured she had to have been getting some help from our parents. And with Mum out of the picture, that meant she must have roped Dad into her shenanigans now as well, which was the part that really irked me. One day I'd muster the courage to ask the question point-blank at a family meal . . .

That's right, I thought to myself. *One day I'll have the guts to stand up to my little sister, and put her in her place once and for all.* The thought intermingled with all the others zig-zagging around my head, keeping my mind from the letter that Maggie had ordered me to read for her again.

"Cat got your tongue, Rigby?"

I couldn't stand it when Maggie butchered my name by leaving out the Eleanor part, and my lovely sister knew this all too well. Aside from our unconditional sisterly love, there has never been anything simple about our relationship. As kids, we would only go as far as yanking each other's hair, but our clashes grew fiercer the older we got. When the fighting got too intense, Michel would bury his face in his hands, as though our nastiness had unleashed some evil that turned our poor brother into a suffering martyr. An immediate ceasefire would commence, both of us having long since forgotten why we were fighting in the first place. We'd throw our arms around each other in a giddy little circle dance to convince Michel it was only a game from the start.

Maggie wanted to be like me, a calm redhead with an unassuming appearance who never let anything get to her—or at least not as far as she could see. As for me, I always dreamt of being strikingly beautiful like my younger sister, or having her thick-skinned nerve, not to mention the head of curly black hair that would have spared me years of teasing at school. Every exchange between the two of us had the potential to spiral into conflict. But as soon as our parents or anyone else started mucking about with one of us, the other would come running, ready to go to war in defense of her sister.

I sighed and reread the letter aloud for Maggie.

Dear Eleanor,
I hope you don't mind that I've abridged your name,
but hyphenated monikers run a bit long for my taste,
even when they are as elegant as yours. But I digress.

My opinion about your name is not why I'm writing to you today.

I'm sure the sudden death of your mother seemed like a profound injustice. She was meant to grow to a ripe old age and die in her bed, surrounded by children and grandchildren, the family for whom she sacrificed so much. Your mother was a brilliant and remarkable woman, capable of great good . . . and great evil.

Until now, you have only known the good.

This is the natural order of things: all we can ever see of our parents is what they wish to show us, how we in turn choose to see them. It's easy to forget that they had a whole life before us. The life of which I speak was theirs and theirs only, a life with all of its dreams and fantasies, as well as the tormented hardship of youth . . .

They, too, had to break free of their chains. The question is: How did they do it?

Your mother, for instance, walked away from an extraordinary fortune thirty-six years ago. However, that fortune was not an inheritance. So, then, how did she come by it? Did she find it? Or . . . did she steal it? Why else would she have left it behind? There are so many unanswered questions, should you decide to seek the truth. But I would caution you: you will need to conduct your research skillfully. As you might imagine, a woman as shrewd as your mother would not bury her most intimate secrets somewhere they would be easy to find. As soon as you lay your hands on the proof that will back up my claims—for undoubtedly, your first reaction will be utter disbelief—you will need to find me. But not before the time comes, as I live on the other side of the world. Until then, take some time to think it over. You've much to do. Best get started straightaway.

I hope you'll forgive me for leaving this letter unsigned. It's not out of cowardice, I assure you, but rather for your own good that I remain anonymous. I'd caution against telling anyone about this letter— most of all Maggie and your father. Destroy it as soon as you've finished reading it. Keeping it will serve no purpose.

Please believe me when I say that I wish you nothing but the best, and hope you will accept my much-belated condolences.

"Pretty diabolical," I remarked. "No way of gleaning a single detail, if it was written by a man or a woman, nothing."

"Whoever wrote it is demented, that much I can tell you. The only sane thing in there is where it says to destroy the stupid thing."

"It also says not to tell anyone about it, most of all you."

"You were right to ignore that advice."

"You . . . and Dad."

"Hold on—there's no way you're telling Dad. I'm not letting you worry him with your sketchy web of crap."

"Would you just stop it! Always telling me what to do and what not to do. I'm the oldest!"

"What, you're one year older so you're somehow blessed with superior intelligence? In that case, you wouldn't have come running over here to show me the stupid letter in the first place."

"I didn't come running," I corrected her. "I received it the day before yesterday."

Maggie pulled up a chair and sat opposite me. I slid the letter across the table and watched my sister run her fingers across the surface of the paper, admiring the lavish stock.

"Don't tell me you actually believe this rubbish," she said with a sigh.

"I don't know what I believe. But why take the time to write the thing if it was all just made up?"

"Because there's a nutter on every corner, ready to do anything and everything to hurt people."

"No one's out there trying to hurt me. Boring as it may seem to you, I actually don't go around making enemies."

"What about some guy whose heart you broke?"

"If only! My love life is a barren wasteland, remember?"

"What about that reporter you were seeing?"

"He'd never be capable of anything this despicable. What's more, we left things on good terms."

"So, how exactly does this creepy letter writer know about me?"

"He seems to know a lot more than that. He says don't tell Maggie, don't tell Dad, but doesn't mention Michel. So, that means—"

"It means he knew you wouldn't risk traumatizing our brother by dragging him into this whole mess," Maggie said, fidgeting with her lighter on the table. "So, the poison-pen must know exactly what he's like. I have to admit that is a little unsettling."

"Agreed. What do we do?" I asked, noting with silent amusement that Maggie had picked up on my nickname for the letter writer.

"Nothing. We do nothing. It's the best way not to be baited into his twisted little game. We put this piece of rubbish where it belongs, and forget the whole thing."

"Can you imagine Mum being rich when she was young? The letter said 'a fortune,' which doesn't make any sense at all. If she had been rich, why did we always have so much trouble making ends meet?"

"Come on, don't exaggerate. It's not like we were living in poverty; we had everything we needed!" said Maggie, her temper rising.

"*You* may have had everything you needed, but there was a whole lot going on that you didn't know about."

"Like what?"

"Scrounging before payday, for example. You think Mum put in all those extra hours tutoring just for the hell of it? And all those weekends Dad spent editing manuscripts?"

"He worked in publishing and Mum was a teacher. I always thought that was just part of their jobs."

"You thought wrong. Everything after the workday was extra. And when they sent us to summer camp, they didn't just run off to the Bahamas. They worked in the summers, too. Mum even did shifts at the front desk of a hospital."

"*Our* mum?" Maggie uttered in shock.

"Three summers in a row, when you were thirteen, fourteen, and fifteen."

"And why were you told about this and not me?"

"Because I asked. See, who would have thought? Maybe one year does make a difference."

That shut Maggie up for a moment, however fleetingly.

"No." She shook her head. "No way. Mum sitting on some secret stash of money? It just doesn't hold water."

"The letter said 'fortune.' That might not necessarily mean money."

"Fine. If not money, what was all that stuff about this mysterious fortune not being inherited?"

"Good point. The poison-pen also said we'd have to be skillful to find proof . . . Maybe there's hidden meaning to the choice of words."

"Sure, could be. But that's a whole lot of maybes. Just throw the stupid letter away, forget you ever saw it."

"Right, sure! You don't fool me for a second. I give it two days before you run over to Dad's and ransack the place."

Maggie flicked her lighter and lit up her cigarette at last, taking a nice long drag and puffing a cloud of smoke up toward the ceiling.

"Fine," she conceded. "We'll invite everyone here for dinner tomorrow. You grill the food, I'll grill Dad and get some answers just to be sure, but I know it's a total waste of time."

"Perfect. We can order pizza or something and question Dad together. But we'll have to be careful; Michel will be there."

4

RAY

October 2016, Croydon, south of London

Ray wondered why his kids couldn't just come to his place for dinner. As much as he loved seeing them, he was a homebody and far too old to change that now. No matter, he thought, as he took a herringbone blazer from the wardrobe. He could pick up Michel in the old Austin, which he hardly ever drove these days, ever since a Tesco Express had opened within walking distance.

Ray was under doctor's orders to get in fifteen minutes of walking per day at the very minimum to keep his joints moving. Truth be told, he didn't care all that much about that these days. He really didn't know what to do with his body anymore, now that he was a widower. Nevertheless, he checked his reflection in the mirror, pulled in his stomach, and slicked back his hair.

Ray wasn't too bothered by aging, but he did miss the thick mane of hair he'd had as a younger man. With the countless millions the government spent on pointless wars, it was a wonder they couldn't do something useful, like discover a way to grow back hair. If he could travel back in time to his thirties, he would convince his wife to apply her scientific skills to growing back hair instead of working as a chemistry teacher. She would have found the magic formula, making a fortune so that the couple could coast through their golden years, living it up in palaces the whole world over.

Ray had a change of heart and grabbed his gabardine coat instead. On second thoughts, his wife hadn't made it to their golden years, and globetrotting alone as a widower would be absolutely unbearable. And why travel at all if you're a homebody?

Tonight would mark the first time Maggie had invited them over to her place. Why was that? Could it be she planned to announce her engagement? Ray immediately wondered if he could still fit into his dinner jacket. Worst-case scenario, he would go on a diet, which meant they'd have to leave him enough time to lose five or six pounds. Ten at most. He was in pretty good shape, apart from a few soft edges here and there. It was nothing he couldn't handle. Problem was, Ray wouldn't put it past Maggie to tie the knot the very next weekend, what with her lack of patience. What in the world would he offer them as a wedding gift? Noticing the grayish bags under his eyes, Ray pulled the skin under his right eye a bit tighter with his finger. The puffiness did disappear, but he looked ridiculous. Maybe he should just stick a couple of pieces of tape under his eyes. That would crack everybody up. Ray tested out the look and made funny faces in the mirror, laughing to himself. Feeling chirpy, he snatched up his baseball cap, jingled his car keys in the palm of his hand, and popped out of the door with a sprightly gait that belied his age.

Ray's trusty old Austin, with its dusty aroma, was timeworn and elegant, just like a collector's car. His neighbor claimed an A60 estate wasn't an estate at all, but Ray knew the man was only jealous. Good luck finding such a handsome rosewood-effect dashboard these days. Even the clock on the dash was a vaunted relic. The Austin was already used when he acquired it all the way back in . . . Good lord. What year was it? Before the twins were born; had to be, of course. After all, Ray had used the Austin to pick up his future wife at the railway station when they were finally reunited. Incredible to think that this vehicle had been part of their lives all that time! How many miles had they racked up in this one car? 224,653, to be exact—make that 224,654 by the time he got to Michel's place. Not a collector's car? Ray chuckled. His neighbor was an idiot.

It was impossible for Ray to even glance at the passenger seat without being haunted by his wife's ghost. He could picture her perfectly, sitting there, twisting herself into knots trying to put on her seat belt. She always had a hard time adjusting the damn thing, and would regularly accuse Ray of having shortened it as a prank, gaslighting her with the idea she had put on weight. In truth, he *had* pulled the prank two, maybe three times. No more than that. Okay, maybe a little more, come to think of it.

Ray had even often thought it would be nice to be buried in the Austin. But then he thought about how much room it would take up—that wouldn't be very eco-friendly . . .

After pulling up in front of Michel's place and honking the horn a couple of times, Ray cut the engine and gazed through the window at the faces of the passersby on the shimmering pavement outside. Complain all you want about the English rain, Ray knew of no other country as green as his homeland.

A passing older couple caught Ray's attention, the husband clearly not big on smiling, much less laughing. If there was a god, *this* guy would have lost his wife, not Ray. The world certainly was one messed-up place. Good lord. Why did it take Michel so long to get out of the door? Of course, Ray knew why. Michel first had to check that everything was in its right place, verify that the gas wasn't on (even if he hadn't used the cooker in ages), double-check that all lights were off (except the one in his bedroom, which was kept on at all times), and make sure the fridge was closed. Speaking of the kitchen, the sink was in rough shape. Ray thought he would come over and replace it one day soon while Michel was at work; he'd be sure not to tell his son a thing until the repair had been completed.

When Michel at last emerged, Ray opened the door for him, and his son slid into the passenger seat. After a quick hug, Michel put on his seat belt and folded his hands snugly in his lap, his eyes fixed on the road as Ray started the car. A full two traffic lights later, the young man finally spoke.

"I'm very happy that we're going to have dinner together, but it's quite strange that the setting is Maggie's flat."

"And what's so strange about that, my boy?" Ray asked.

"Maggie doesn't cook. Therefore, it's strange."

"As I understand it, she's going to order pizza. It'll be a proper party."

"Ah. Well, that factor does make it less odd . . . but still odd, nonetheless," Michel declared, his gaze drawn to a lovely young woman crossing the street.

"Not bad!" Ray whistled.

"Granted. She is a bit out of proportion, strictly speaking," Michel muttered.

"You kidding me? She's gorgeous!"

"The average height for a female as of 2016 is five foot six. That woman is at least six foot one, well above average, with particularly elongated lower extremities."

"Whatever you say, old man. But if I were your age, I'd probably appreciate those type of proportions."

"As a matter of fact, I tend to prefer women who are . . . well . . ."

"Shorter?"

"Yes, well put. Shorter."

"Well, whatever floats your boat, son."

"I don't quite see what flotation has to do with it."

"It's an expression, Michel. It means 'to each his own.' When it comes to women, everyone has different preferences."

"Ah, yes. That seems like a logical conclusion to me. The initial expression didn't make any sense at all, but the second is something of which I have seen proof."

As the Austin moved into heavier traffic, typically fine English rain began to fall. The asphalt was shimmery and slick within minutes.

"My personal theory is that I think your sister is going to announce she's getting married."

"Which sister? I have two."

"Maggie, I think."

"Ah. And what makes you think that?"

"Call it fatherly instinct. Like a sixth sense. And, Michel? I tell you this now for a specific reason. I need you to understand this is good news, so when she makes the announcement, you know that the right response would be to show her that you are happy to hear it."

"Ah. Why is that?"

"Because if you don't, it'll make your sister sad. When people tell you something they're happy about, they expect you to share and demonstrate that happiness in return."

"Ah. But why is that?"

"Because it's one way for you to show them you love them."

"I understand. And getting married is good news?"

"Well, my boy, that is a complicated question. But generally speaking, yes."

"And will her future husband be in attendance?"

"Maybe. You really never can tell, with your sister."

"Which sister? I have two."

"I'm well aware, Michel. After all, I am the one who brought your two sisters into being—and your mother helped, I suppose."

"And Mum will not be in attendance."

"No, my boy. Your mother will not be there. And you know why."

"Yes, I do know why. It's because she is dead."

"There you have it. It's because she is dead."

Michel gazed out the window before turning to face his father.

"And what about the two of you? Was it good news when you got married?"

"Wonderful news! If I could do it all over again, I'd marry her even sooner. So, it stands to reason it'll be good news for Maggie as well. After all, happy marriages run in our family."

"Ah. I'm not sure that trait can be considered genetic. I'll have to confirm tomorrow at the university."

"What about you, Michel? Are you happy about Maggie?" Ray asked softly.

"Yes, I think so . . . I am happy knowing that Maggie is going to get married, and more so now that I know it'll be a happy marriage because that runs in our family, as you say . . . but I admit I am a bit scared of meeting her future husband."

"What are you afraid of?"

"Well, I simply hope that the two of us will get on."

"You already know each other, Michel. You know, good old Fred? Tall chap, nice guy. We've had dinner a few times at his pub. At least, I'm assuming he's the one your sister is going to marry. But who knows—it's Maggie."

"It's a shame that Mum can't be there with you to celebrate the good news that her daughter is going to get married."

"And which daughter might that be?" Ray replied with a wink and a grin. "We've got two."

Michel chewed on this for a moment, then returned his father's smile.

5

May

October 1980, Baltimore

The motorcycle roared its way up the hill. Whenever Sally-Anne twisted the throttle, dust streamed out from behind the back wheel. She had just a few more bends to go before the manor came into view. May was able to make out the limits of the Stanfield estate even from a distance, with the finials of elegant black wrought-iron railings forming an imperfect circle around the sprawling grounds. Her grip on Sally-Anne's waist got tighter as they caught sight of the manor, tight enough to make Sally-Anne turn around and shout over the wind with a devil-may-care smile.

"Hey, you're not the only one who's scared shitless, but that's what makes it such an exciting adventure, isn't it?"

The rumble and purr of the Triumph drowned out most of what she said. May could only make out "scared shitless" and "exciting," which did properly describe the mixed emotions she was feeling at that moment. She and Sally-Anne were fully in sync with each other.

Sally-Anne downshifted and tilted toward the pavement as she whipped around the last hairpin bend, hugging the tight curve before picking up speed again as it straightened out. Her masterful control of the Triumph would have turned any biker green with envy.

As they entered the home stretch, the manor stood out starkly at the top of the hill, its pretentious columns reigning over the entire valley. Such ostentatious and gaudy luxury was typically reserved for upstarts and the nouveau riche, yet the Stanfields were one of the oldest and most venerable families in the city, playing a major role in Baltimore life from its very founding. It was whispered that the family had amassed their fortune on the backs of slaves farming their lands. The rumor was contested by others, however, who claimed the esteemed Stanfield clan was among the first to have set slaves free, and that certain family members would have been ready to pay any price for their liberty—even in blood. The truth varied depending on whom you asked, and in what neighborhood.

Sally-Anne slowed the Triumph to a stop in the employee parking area, cut the engine, and lifted her helmet to just above her ears. As May stepped off the bike, Sally-Anne gestured across the way.

"The service entrance is straight ahead. Introduce yourself using the accent we practiced, and tell them you have an appointment with Miss Verdier."

"Couldn't she somehow still be inside?"

"Not unless she has the ability to be in two places at once. See the lady walking toward the black Ford right now, right over there? Miss Verdier, in the flesh. Like I told you, she takes her break at eleven in the morning every day like clockwork, jumping into her pretty little car and zipping into town for a nice lunch-break massage . . . and other things, if you know what I mean."

"You know, you never fully explained how you know all this."

"Well, when I said I've been following her closely for the past few weeks, I meant *closely*. Believe me, I know Miss Verdier a little too well at this point."

"No. Even you wouldn't have gone that far . . ."

"My dear, it is neither the time nor the place for such sordid details. Just take my word for it: Miss Verdier has a tough time getting off, which gives us a full forty-five minutes before she enjoys her little daily orgasm, knocks back a BLT and a Coke, and comes waltzing back in here. So, get moving. You know the plan by heart; we've run through it a hundred times. You've got this."

But May wouldn't budge. Sensing her hesitation, Sally-Anne drew her close and whispered into her ear how stunning she looked and promised that everything would be fine. Sally-Anne looked on from the parking lot as May crossed the road and made her way to the service entrance, where hired help brought in newspapers, fancy food, beverages, and flowers, as well as the spoils from Mrs. Stanfield's or her son's shopping runs to the city.

When the butler came to greet her, May gave the cover story, perfectly playing the part of a well-educated young jobseeker. The phony British accent that Sally-Anne had advised May to adopt worked brilliantly—its natural authority was so intimidating that she was granted entry, no questions asked. The butler could see she had arrived early, and there was no way he was going to ask someone like her to wait in the foyer. He led May straight up to a small study on the second floor . . . all just as Sally-Anne had predicted.

The man contritely offered May a seat, assuring her that Mr. Stanfield's secretary had only stepped out for a moment and would be back shortly. He asked if May would like a glass of water, but she politely declined. The butler gracefully took his leave, and May found herself alone in the little study, just next door to Miss Verdier's office.

The study was furnished with a pedestal table and two velvet armchairs that perfectly matched the plush curtains. An Aubusson rug covered the dark oak floors, and a small crystal chandelier hung above the wood-paneled walls.

May checked the timing. Meeting the butler, climbing the stairs, and walking the long corridor to the study . . . ten minutes in all.

Another thirty-five minutes before the sex-obsessed secretary came back. Normally, the thought of her at that massage parlor downtown would have cracked May up, like it had when Sally-Anne first described Miss Verdier's lunch-break escapades. But now that May was about to enter the woman's office and commit an actual crime, the whole thing felt a lot less amusing. Getting caught in the act by Miss Verdier was not an option. May had to be long gone by the time she returned. If the police were called, it wouldn't take long for them to connect the dots, and the charge would be far more serious than simple trespassing . . .

Don't think like that, not now. May's throat was dry. She was really wishing she had taken that glass of water, but it was too late now. She went through the steps in her head: *Rise. Walk to the connecting door. Turn the handle and slip inside undetected.*

She did exactly that, and was amazed by her own nerve. She felt like she was a robot programmed for this one specific task.

Once inside, she closed the door softly behind her. May knew that even the slightest noise would give her away. There was a good chance that the master of the house was sitting in the adjoining room at that very moment, fully aware that his assistant would not be at her desk at this time of day.

May did a full scan of her surroundings, stunned by the modern aesthetic of the room, in sharp contrast to everything else she'd seen inside the manor. A reproduction of a Miró painting graced the wall across from an elegant pale wooden desk. On second thought, maybe it wasn't a reproduction at all. No time to dwell on it. She softly eased the chair back from the desk and crouched in front of the desk drawers, then slipped the lockpick out of her pocket and carefully unwrapped it.

May had practiced picking the lock on an identical set of drawers over a hundred times, honing the skill so that there would be no trace of her intrusion. Sally-Anne's locksmith friend had explained to them that it was a Yale tumbler lock and helped them find the right tool for the job straightaway: a steep-angled pick with a half-diamond tip.

With a wide angle at the end and a narrow base, the pick was as easy to insert as it was to remove. May remembered her lessons: avoid scratching the inside, or else risk leaving behind telltale iron scrapings that could block the mechanism and serve as proof of the forced entry. Hold the handle horizontally with a firm grip opposite the barrel and slowly insert the hook. Feel for the pins and apply measured pressure to each, lifting them without causing the least bit of damage. When she felt the first pin reach the precise point, May slowly advanced the tip of the hook to lift the second, then moved on to the third. She held her breath and slowly turned the lock rotor until she at last felt a sweet release. Her newly acquired skills paid off: the lock on the drawer yielded.

May would still have to complete the final step, closing the lock and removing the pick, both of which required great precision and a delicate touch. Careful to avoid nudging the tool, she slid the drawer open and explored its contents.

Eyeglasses, face powder, a hairbrush, lipstick, a bottle of hand cream . . . The *list*, where was the goddamn list? Jackpot: a stack of papers. May slid out the stack and began leafing through it, studying each sheet in turn. At last, she found it. Her pulse quickened as she thought about all she was risking just to add two names to a guest list.

"Stay cool, May," she whispered to herself. "Stay cool. You're almost there."

May took a quick glance at the clock on the wall. Another fifteen minutes in the safety zone. Unless . . . Miss Verdier somehow happened to get off quicker today.

Don't think like that. She wouldn't go all that way just to be stingy with herself and stop at foreplay. After all, if she were pressed for time, she would have skipped the masseur and done the job herself, wouldn't she?

May looked at the typewriter on the desk, a classic Underwood. She slipped the guest list between the roller and the paper rest and turned the platen knob. The paper disappeared beneath the roller and reemerged on the other side.

All that was left was to type out two additions to the list, one false name for Sally-Anne and one for May herself, as well as the PO box they had opened the week before at the main post office as contact information. The guest list would undoubtedly come under heavy scrutiny after the crime took place as the police sought out the guilty parties. And when they did, the search would yield nothing but a pair of fake names and an untraceable PO box. May typed in the first name with the utmost care, using a gentle touch on the keys to stifle the rattling of the type hammers against the ribbon. She barely breathed as she pulled the carriage return lever with the same delicate care, trying as hard as she could to avoid even the slightest jingle of the bell as the paper slid up to the next line. It jingled anyway. May's heart nearly stopped.

"Miss Verdier, is that you? Are you back already?" called a voice from over in the next room. May froze, paralyzed with fear. Then, without making a sound, she lowered herself carefully to the ground and curled into a fetal position under the desk, hidden from view. She stayed completely motionless, listening to the approaching footsteps. The door creaked open and Mr. Stanfield poked his head into the office.

"Miss Verdier?"

He found the office empty and spotless, as usual. Mr. Stanfield scanned the room, not giving the typewriter a second glance, which was lucky considering that Miss Verdier—clearly the epitome of orderliness—would never have left on a break with a sheet of paper still in the roller. Mr. Stanfield shrugged. "I must be hearing things," he mumbled, and closed the door.

After he left, it took May several minutes to get her hands to stop shaking, but her whole body was trembling, too. She had never been so terrified.

The incessant ticking of the clock on the wall brought her back to reality. Ten minutes left at most. Ten short minutes to type out the second name and the fake PO box, all while keeping perfectly quiet. Then: replace the paper in the stack, slide the stack back in the drawer, lock the drawer, remove the lockpick, and escape the sprawling manor before the secretary got back. May was behind schedule. She should have already been back with Sally-Anne, who must have been losing her mind at that very moment, out in the parking lot . . .

Concentrate, goddamn it! You don't have a second to lose.

May began typing, one key after another, wincing at the tapping noise of each letter hitting the page. If the old geezer heard keys rattle or the bell ring again, there was no way he would be satisfied with just a quick little once-over like the last time.

There, done. Turn the roller, slip out the paper, put it exactly as it was within the stack. Keep tapping the papers until they're packed perfectly tight—do it down on the carpet to keep totally silent. Next, slide the neat little stack back into the drawer, push it all the way in there, just where you found it. *Easy now, easy.* Close the drawer. Turn the lockpick and don't even breathe; just listen for the sound of pins clicking into place. Ignore your throbbing temples, the sweat on your brow. Just one more millimeter to go. *You can do this, you* have *to do this . . .*

Be cool, May. Be cool. If you can't get the lockpick out, you're done for.

After a few attempts, May succeeded, slipped the pick out, and clenched it in her clammy palm. She slid the tool into her pocket and used the tissue to wipe the sweat from her hands and forehead. If the butler saw her sweating, he would surely suspect something.

May slipped through the connecting door into the small study, straightened her jacket, and exited out into the long corridor. Every step felt like an eternity, with May praying she wouldn't cross paths with anyone. She reached the staircase and began the climb down, treading lightly to avoid any attention. All the while, she tried to keep calm and measured in the event she ran into the butler and had to explain that she could wait for Miss Verdier no longer and would have to come back another time.

But her luck held: the foyer was deserted. May reached the service door and stepped outside, her heart still hammering inside her chest. Sally-Anne hadn't budged an inch, watching from the very same spot astride the Triumph. For an awful moment, May thought her legs wouldn't move another step. But they did, carrying her all the way to the parking lot. Sally-Anne handed May her helmet. May mounted the motorbike, the engine roared, and they were on the move again.

As the bike rounded the sharp curve once more, they passed Miss Verdier's Ford on its way back to the estate. Sally-Anne caught a glimpse of the driver, all fresh, aglow with a naughty little smile on her face. She matched it with her own devilish grin, albeit for entirely different reasons.

6

ELEANOR-RIGBY

October 2016, Beckenham

We had already been sitting around the table for a half hour and Maggie had yet to announce her engagement to Fred, the strapping young lad who ran a gastropub in Primrose Hill.

Michel couldn't have been more thrilled. First of all, he got to watch our father be so happy and excited he could hardly sit still, all fidgety, barely eating. The fact that Dad wasn't ravaging his pizza meant he had a lot on his mind, and Michel knew it was because he must have been wondering if he had been wrong about Maggie marrying Fred. But Michel was relieved that it seemed our father was wrong, because the engagement had been worrying him the whole way over. He didn't actually like good old Fred as much as he had claimed. Fred made Michel uncomfortable. There was something about his kindness that felt forced and insincere. Michel detected an underlying sense of superiority that was off-putting.

Michel had enjoyed the food at Fred's pub, but his appetite for food was nothing compared to his ravenous appetite for books at the library. Michel knew nearly every title by heart and had memorized them alphabetically, which perhaps wasn't all that extraordinary considering it was his responsibility to sort them into the proper order to begin with. Michel enjoyed his job at the library, where silence reigned. He couldn't have found a more tranquil place to work. Most library visitors were pleasant enough, and helping them find what they were looking for as quickly as possible gave Michel a proud sense of purpose. The only part that bothered him was seeing the books sitting abandoned on the tables at the end of the day. On the other hand, if library visitors were less messy, Michel would have less work to do. It was very logical.

Before the library, Michel had worked in a laboratory, a position he landed after receiving high marks in his final exams at university. Michel had a knack for chemistry, and the periodic table of the elements felt like a second language to him. Yet his promising career quickly came to an end when his enthusiasm for experimenting with all the endless combinations of chemicals at his disposal became a safety issue. Dad had howled at the injustice and cursed Michel's narrow-minded employers, but there was nothing to be done. After a period of seclusion at home, Michel decided to get back to work. He connected with Vera Morton, manager of a small local library, who told Michel she was willing to give him a chance. He solemnly vowed to never let her down. The speed and accessibility of the internet had caused library attendance to drop to the point where a whole day might go by without anyone walking through the door. Michel took advantage of the time to read, mainly works on chemistry and biographies.

As I quietly observed my father throughout the meal, Maggie delivered a constant stream of nonsense that certainly didn't justify hogging the spotlight. Her blabbering didn't sit well at all with Michel, who suspected she had the jitters about the impending announcement that he was dreading. When Maggie sat down across from Dad and took his hand in her own, Michel interpreted the out-of-character move as an attempt to reassure him. Maggie certainly wasn't the touchy-feely type. Every time Michel went to hug her, she would make a fuss and accuse him of smothering her. Michel was careful not to, and had concluded that it was just a strategy to cut short any physical contact. Because logically, what kind of sister wouldn't want to hug her own brother?

Maggie's show of affection caught Dad off guard, and he held his breath and waited for the big news to drop. Maggie getting engaged was a given, of course. What had Dad on the edge of his seat was *when* the marriage would take place.

"Okay, darling. That's enough. If I listen to you babble for one more minute, the anxiety might kill me. Tell us: When's the big day? If you ask me, three months would be ideal. Two per month is reasonable, since as you know they're not so easy to shed at my age!"

"I'm sorry," Maggie replied. "But what are you talking about?"

"All the pounds I've got to lose to fit into the old dinner jacket!" our father exclaimed, slapping his belly.

I looked to Maggie, but she seemed equally perplexed. Michel swooped in to save the day.

"He means: for the wedding. The dinner jacket for your wedding," he explained with a sigh.

"That's why you called us all here tonight, isn't it?" Dad said, smug and satisfied. "Where is the old chap anyway?"

"Who's that?" Maggie asked, once more looking to Michel.

"Good old Fred," he replied drily.

"Okay. I say give it a half hour, and if you two are still talking nonsense, we'll take you to the hospital," said Maggie.

"Good lord, Maggie, we'll be taking *you* to the hospital if you keep on like this. What is up with you? Forget the whole thing. I'll just wear my suit. It always was a bit large for me, so as long as I can keep my breathing to a minimum, I should be able to close the jacket. Though it is brown. They say you shouldn't wear brown to a wedding, but I'll tell you what else they say: desperate times call for desperate measures. After all, this is England, not Las Vegas, so if we don't have time to get all our ducks in a row, that's just the way it is, and we can leave it at that."

Once more, my sister and I exchanged a dumbstruck look, until the sheer absurdity of the moment made me burst out laughing. It was an uncontrollable fit that soon proved contagious. Dad was the only one to hold out, but he never could resist a good case of the giggles and was soon in stitches with the rest of us. By the time Maggie managed to catch her breath, sighing and wiping the tears from her eyes, Fred's unexpected arrival caused everyone to burst out laughing once more. Good old Fred's bewildered look was the icing on the cake.

My father cleared his throat. "So, how about you tell me just *what* we are doing here if the two of you aren't getting married?"

The word made Fred freeze halfway through taking off his jacket. Maggie saw his worried eyes and blurted out, "Don't worry!"

"Dad, everybody . . . We are gathered here for the sheer pleasure of being together," I interjected, trying not to sell it too hard.

"As far as reasons to gather, that one is far more commonplace," Michel stated. "From a statistical point of view, so I've been told."

"I don't see why we couldn't have done this at home," Dad grumbled.

"Well, we would have missed out on all these laughs," Maggie insisted, and then went in for the kill. "Can I ask you a question? Was Mum well-off when you met her?"

"At seventeen?"

"No, later. When you got back together."

"Not at seventeen, not at thirty, not ever! She didn't even have change to get the bus from the railway station when I picked her up . . . you know, when we *reunited*," he added, choosing his words carefully. "Just think, if your mother had been a few pence richer that night when she got off that train, she might have never even called me. You know, it's high time I confessed something to you kids. Fred, since you're not officially part of the family yet, I'd ask that you keep it to yourself."

"Confess? Confess what?" I asked.

"If you save the questions till the end, you'll find out. Children, your mother and I may have somewhat embellished the circumstances under which our relationship was rekindled. Truth is, your mother did not just miraculously reappear, hopelessly and desperately in love with me, after being spontaneously struck with the epiphany that I was her one true love, despite that being how we may have described it, from time to time."

"Always described it, *every* time," Michel corrected.

"Fine, every time, I grant you that. Truth of the matter is, when your mother came home to England, she didn't have anywhere to stay. I was the only person she knew around here. She looked up my name in the telephone directory from a phone box. This was before the internet, mind you, so that was the way we found people back in those days. Donovans were few and far between in Croydon. The only other one in the whole damn phone book was a sixty-eight-year-old woman—never married, no children, for those of you keeping track. Anyway, you can imagine my shock at hearing your mother's voice on the other end of the line.

"It was the end of autumn, but already cold enough to chill you to the bone. I remember what she said like it was yesterday. 'Ray, you'd have every reason to hang up on me right here and now, but you're all I've got, and I just don't know where else to turn.' What in the world does one do when a woman says, 'You're all I've got'? I knew at that very moment that destiny had brought us back together, this time for good. I leapt into the Austin—yes, indeed, the very same one parked outside right now, don't give me that look, it's still running just fine, thank you very much—and went to pick up your mother. Now, I've every reason to believe it was the right choice, seeing as I'm lucky enough to find myself thirty-six years later sharing a hysterical pizza night with my three wonderful children and my not-quite-yet son-in-law."

Silence. The three of us siblings exchanged looks around the table until Dad cleared his throat and declared, "Maybe it's time I took Michel home."

"Wait—why did Mum say you had reason to hang up on her?" I cut in.

"Some other time, sweetheart, if you don't mind. Stirring up all these old memories takes its toll on me, and I prefer to leave tonight on a happy note, such as our little giggle session, rather than open up a can of worms."

"So, the first time you got together, when you two were teenagers, she was the one who left you?" I insisted.

"He said *another time*," Maggie jumped in before our father could respond.

"Yes, exactly," Michel chimed in. "But it may be . . . more complicated than it seems," he added, pointing a finger in the air, as though hoping to snag his thoughts out of thin air before they fluttered away—one of his many peculiar habits. Everyone waited quietly, as always, for Michel to complete his thought.

"While Dad did express a preference to say no more on the subject this evening, 'some other time' could imply that he might be willing to reconsider, as long as it's . . . *some other time*."

"Yeah, thanks, we got it, Michel," Maggie said.

With everything crystal clear, Michel rose from his chair and put on his trench coat. He kissed me on the cheek, gave Fred's hand a flimsy little squeeze, and then pulled Maggie in for a tight hug. Desperate times called for desperate measures, after all. Michel whispered his congratulations into her ear.

"Congratulations for what?" my sister whispered back to him.

"For not being engaged to Fred," Michel replied.

On the way home in the Austin, not a word was exchanged between father and son until they pulled up to the curb outside Michel's place. Ray reached to open Michel's door, then stopped to look his son right in the eye and spoke in a voice as gentle as could be.

"You won't tell them anything, will you? Understand: it should be me who tells them. One day."

Michel looked right back at his father.

"You can sleep easy, Dad. No need to open up a can of worms. I'm pretty sure fishermen buy them in bags nowadays, anyway. I'll verify that tomorrow at the library."

With that, he hugged his father and slipped out of the Austin. Ray hung around a few moments, waiting until his son had safely entered the building, before starting the engine and driving away.

7

ELEANOR-RIGBY

October 2016, Beckenham

I stood up from the table and left the kitchen, opting to give Fred and Maggie their privacy. After the couple had been holed up in there for a solid ten minutes, I decided it was time to leave. I entered to find Fred drying glasses with a tea towel and Maggie sitting on the counter with her legs crossed, puffing at a cigarette near the window. My sister offered to call a taxi for me, but I politely declined, explaining it would cost a small fortune to get home from Beckenham. I'd be better off taking the train home.

"I thought you were going to Dad's," Maggie said with a sneer. "Decided not to stay at his place?"

"I thought he might want to be alone tonight. It forces me to revisit my London life, anyway, which has been long overdue."

"Well, I think you've got the right idea," Fred offered, with a clap of his hands. "Beckenham, Croydon . . . too far out in the sticks."

"Whereas Primrose Hill is too far *from* the sticks, not to mention way too posh," replied Maggie, flicking her cigarette butt right into the dishwater, where it landed with a hiss.

"I think I'll leave you two to whisper sweet nothings in peace," I said with a sigh, slipping on my jacket, but my sister stopped me.

"Fred would be delighted to drop you off at the station, what with his awesome car and all. Or, Fred, why not take her all the way to London? Then you could spend the night in your precious little Primrose Hill."

I flashed my sister an admonishing look. How could she be so nasty and still be the one with the boyfriend, whereas it seemed that I, being nothing less than kindness incarnate, was doomed to be single forever? Just one more mystery to unravel.

"You want a lift, Elby?" Fred offered, but Maggie snagged the tea towel he was folding straight out of his hands and threw it in the washing hamper.

"Insider tip: nobody but Michel is allowed to butcher my sister's name like that. She hates it. Anyway, I need some air, so I'll walk her to the train."

Maggie grabbed a sweater and led me by the arm out into the street. The streetlamps washed the pavement with an orange glow, illuminating row upon row of modest brick-built Victorian houses, mainly two, and never more than three, stories high.

As we crossed the junction into the shopping district, everything became brighter and livelier. Maggie waved to the Syrian owner of the twenty-four-hour corner shop. There was a launderette next to a kebab joint, followed by an Indian restaurant that could seat no more than two at a time. A former video store was entirely boarded up and covered with posters, most of which had been ripped to shreds. Ahead, we plunged back into darkness as we strolled along the gates of a park. Soon after, the air was filled with the metallic, urine-smelling odor of the platform, which cleared as we entered the station.

"Something wrong?" Maggie asked.

"Why do you stay with Fred when you spend all your time pecking away at him? What's the point?"

"*Pecking away.* You know, sometimes, I ask myself where it is you get all these expressions from. Anyway, what's the use in putting up with a man, if you can't peck away at him from time to time?"

"If that's how relationships go, maybe I should just stay single."

"Ah, I wasn't aware you had a choice in the matter."

"Touché! Thanks—only a major bitch would say something like that."

"Flattery will get you everywhere, my dear. Anyway, on a more important note, we failed pretty miserably at getting anything out of Dad tonight, huh?"

"Well, at least we didn't have to slave away in the kitchen. And we got some good laughs out of it. What do you think got into him tonight with the whole wedding thing? You think he's already itching for grandkids?" I suggested.

Maggie stopped short and began to hum under her breath.

"Eenie meenie miney mo, catch a tiger by the toe. If he squeals, let him go, eenie meenie miney mo!" Maggie's finger landed on me. "Sorry, sister. Looks like you're stuck with it. Personally, I have zero desire to have kids."

"With Fred or just in general?"

"At least we were able to answer the burning question of the night: Mum was as broke as ever when she got back together with Dad."

"Maybe. But the whole night did raise a load of new questions," I countered.

"No need to make a fuss, in any event. Mum gave Dad the push when they were young and then came back ten years later with her tail between her legs."

"Seems to me the truth may be a bit more complicated than that."

"Ah. Maybe you should give up traveling and devote yourself to sentimental investigative journalism."

"Good lord, your sarcasm never fails to slay me. I'm talking about Mum and Dad here, about the over-the-top weirdness of the letter I received, all the shadowy parts of their histories. The lies they told us. You don't have the slightest interest in learning more about your own parents? Or are you too busy thinking about yourself?"

"Well, touché right back at you, Elby. Only a real bitch would say something like that."

"You know, we could also interpret Mum showing up penniless as actually corroborating the poison-pen's story."

"Sure. Because everyone who's penniless must have walked away from some massive fortune."

"Like you'd even know. You've never been penniless, thanks to our parents constantly coddling you."

"Ah, poor Rigby. Should everybody join in, or you want to keep singing that same sad old song all by yourself? Maggie, Maggie, Maggie. Last out of the cradle, first in line for pampering, the whole family always bends over backwards just for her. You know, don't forget who has the studio in London and who lives in the suburbs an hour away. Don't forget who goes gallivanting across the globe and who stays behind to take care of Dad and Michel."

"I don't want to fight, Maggie. I just want your help in getting to the bottom of this. Whoever sent this letter did it with a purpose. Even if everything in it is completely baseless, there has to be some kind of motive behind all this. So: Who sent us the letter, and why?"

"Sent *you* the letter! Don't forget, you weren't even supposed to tell me about it to begin with."

"Unless, maybe, just maybe, the poison-pen knows me well enough to know I'd tell you anyway. What if that's just what he wanted?"

"Well, if that was the plan, he definitely went about it the right way. Look, enough beating around the bush. I can hear that little cry-for-help thing in your voice, so you win, I'll help. First step: invite Dad out to lunch this week, somewhere near Chelsea. He may moan about having to go that far away, but he'll say yes for the excuse to take the Austin out for a spin. Try to find a place with good parking, since there's no way he'd risk leaving it on the street, which cracks me up every time, but hey, let's focus on the task at hand. I have spare keys to his flat. As soon as the coast is clear, I'll go in and have a look around."

As queasy as the notion of tricking my father made me, I couldn't think of a better idea, so I accepted my sister's offer.

It was already late, and the station was empty, the two of us the only ones on the platform as we waited for the train. According to the departures board, a Southeastern train to Orpington was due shortly. I'd have to change at Bromley for a train to Victoria, then get the tube to South Kensington and walk another ten minutes to get home.

Maggie sighed. "You know what I'd like to do right now? Hop on that train with you. A proper sleepover at my sister's place in London. Slip into bed with you and just chat the night away."

"You know I'd love to, except . . . Fred will wonder where you are."

The train roared into view at the end of the platform, brakes squealing as it came to a stop. The doors opened, but not a single passenger stepped out. When the long whistle sounded to announce departure was imminent, Maggie nudged me forward.

"Come on, Rigby! Move it or you'll miss your train!"

After we exchanged a knowing glance, I boarded the train and disappeared into the night.

◆　◆　◆

Fred was waiting for Maggie in bed, eyes glued to an old episode of *Fawlty Towers*. The lovers' quarrel was no match for John Cleese, and the couple soon found themselves roaring with laughter at the endless antics of England's reigning lord of the absurd.

"Okay, maybe you don't want to get married, but what about moving into my place?" Fred asked.

"Ha! Come on, *I'm* the one who doesn't want to get married? Don't be a hypocrite. I saw your face when my dad said the M-word."

"And I saw you wasted no time in setting the record straight."

"Look, Michel and my dad are both right here. London's just too far away for me to keep an eye on them."

"Your brother is a grown man, and your father has led the life he wanted. Isn't it time you started living yours to the fullest?"

Maggie grabbed the remote and shut off the TV. She straddled Fred and took off her T-shirt, looking him straight in the eye.

"What? Why are you giving me that look?" he asked.

"Because we've been together two whole years and it's the first time I've realized that I know next to nothing about you—your life, your family. You've never introduced me, never talked about them at all. Meanwhile, you're a leading expert on all things Maggie, the whole family . . . I don't know where you grew up, where you went to college, *if* you went to college."

"Right. Because you never asked."

"That's not true! You just always get dodgy and elusive when I ask about your past."

"Well, here's the thing," he said, brushing his lips across her bare breasts. "Sometimes a man has other priorities. But if you insist, I'll tell all . . . everything, my whole life story, in full detail . . . I was born thirty-nine years ago in London . . ."

Fred slipped lower as he spoke, making a trail of kisses down Maggie's stomach.

"Okay, you win, I see your point," Maggie murmured, her breath quickening. "Stop talking. Now."

8

Keith

October 1980, Baltimore

Shafts of moonlight streamed into the loft through the skylights, filled with little specks of floating dust. May slept soundly, the folds of the bedsheets hugging tightly to the curves of her body. Seated at the foot of the bed, Sally-Anne studied her and watched her breathe. At that very moment, the rising and falling of May's chest was the only thing she cared about in the world. They could have been the last two people on earth, the whole of the universe contained within that loft.

One hour earlier, visions of the past had jolted Sally-Anne awake. Familiar faces glared down at her in judgment—frozen, expressionless, and unforgiving—while she sat, immobile, on an empty stage. So much of Sally-Anne's character came from these judging faces, from a youth spent learning everything, without ever being taught.

Can two broken souls fix each other? Sally-Anne wondered. Would one person's pain cancel out the other's, or would it simply be piled on top of it?

"What time is it?" May groaned, her face buried in the pillow.

"Four in the morning, maybe a bit later."

"What's on your mind, what are you thinking about?"

"About us."

"Good things or bad?"

"Go back to sleep."

"You think I can sleep with you gawking at me like that?"

Sally-Anne slipped on her boots and grabbed her leather jacket off the back of a chair. May sighed.

"I don't like it when you ride at night."

"Don't worry. I'll be nice and careful."

"That'd be a first. Stay. I'll make you a cup of tea," May insisted. She rose and draped a sheet over her naked body, crossing their living space. The kitchen nook was little more than a sad-looking portable gas stove, a handful of mismatched plates and glasses, and two porcelain mugs on a wooden table near a tiny sink.

Holding the sheet with one hand, May struggled awkwardly to make the tea. She filled the kettle, stood on her tiptoes, fumbled for the tin box full of Lipton teabags, plucked two sugar cubes from a terra-cotta pot, and struck a match to light the gas stove. Sally-Anne didn't lift a finger.

"Well, don't come rushing in to help me!"

"I was waiting to see if you could manage with only one hand," Sally-Anne replied, grinning playfully. May shrugged and let the sheet drop to the ground.

"Be a dear and put it back on the bed. I can't stand dusty sheets."

After pouring tea for them both, May came back to sit cross-legged on the mattress.

"We've received the invitations," Sally-Anne revealed.

"When?"

"Yesterday. I stopped by the post office to have a look, and there they were."

"And you didn't think of telling me sooner?"

"We were having a good time, and I thought you'd spend the rest of the night thinking about it."

"A good time? All these piss-poor political conversations are tedious at best and unbearable at worst. The guys we've been running with lately are a pain in the ass, going on and on about changing the world when all they do is get stoned. So, sorry to say, I wasn't exactly having the night of my life to begin with. Can I see them?"

Sally-Anne reached into her jacket pocket and casually tossed the invitations onto the bed. May tore through one of the envelopes, noting, as she did, the surface of the elegant paper and admiring the embossed letters bearing her fake name. But then her eyes fell on the date of the party . . . only two weeks away. The women would be decked out in extravagant gowns and their finest jewelry. All the men would be wearing absurdly over-the-top costumes, aside from a handful of grumpy older guests in simple tuxedos and domino masks, refusing to play along.

"I've never been so excited about a masquerade ball in my entire life," May snickered.

"My dear, you never cease to amaze me. I thought seeing the invitations would make you anxious."

"Well, you thought wrong. That was the old me. Just setting foot in that house again changed everything. As we left the estate, I promised myself I was never going to let those people scare me again."

"May . . ."

"You know what? Go out and wander the night, or come to bed with me . . . Just make up your mind. I'm tired."

Sally-Anne picked up the dropped bedsheet and draped it over May. Then she quickly undressed and stretched out naked on the mattress next to her. She gazed at May with the same playful grin.

"What is it now?" asked May.

"Nothing. Just noticing how cute you are when you're vindictive."

May was silent for a moment. "I want to tell you something. It's personal, I'm just speaking for myself here, but you should know. I'll never let them take me alive."

"What the hell does that mean?"

"You know exactly what it means. And life is too short to look back, or dwell on sadness or regret."

"Hey, look me in the eye. You're making a huge mistake here, May. If it's just revenge you're after, it gives them way too much power, too much importance. Think of it this way: we're simply taking something from people who didn't deserve it in the first place."

Sally-Anne knew what she was talking about. She had known that crowd all her life, those who had everything handed to them from the cradle to the grave. Their high standing allowed them to help themselves to what others had to beg for, to find pleasure where others could only find hope. Some in those superior circles used disdain to elicit the envy and admiration of ordinary people. It was the epitome of cruel behavior—using rejection as a means of seduction, as a strategy to make one seem more desirable.

Sally-Anne had changed her whole life to distance herself from those people—where she lived, how she looked, right down to sacrificing her very long hair for a boyish pixie cut. At that time, she stopped obsessing over boys and started obsessing over noble causes. The country known as the "land of the free" had let slavery thrive and condoned years of segregation. Now, a full sixteen years after the Civil Rights Act of 1964 had been passed, attitudes and mind-sets had scarcely budged. Women were now following the black community in the fight for equal rights, which would undoubtedly be a long and painstaking struggle. Sally-Anne and May had been exemplary soldiers on the front line, working at a daily newspaper. As researchers, they had already hit the glass ceiling for women in their field. Despite their positions and low pay-grade, the women would regularly write articles. Their arrogant male counterparts would then swoop in, sign off on the work as their own, and send it off to print.

May was the more talented journalist of the two, with a natural instinct for hunting down inflammatory subject matter. She never failed to push the privileged to their limits, striving to shake the earth beneath their feet. She relentlessly spoke out when powerful entities dragged along too slowly, delaying the implementation of promised reforms.

Earlier in the year, she had started digging into stories about influential lobbies that lined the pockets of senators in order to curb the passage of anti-corruption laws. She shone a light on anti-pollution laws that powerful companies were laughing off, thirsty for profit and ready to destroy the environment. May denounced arms deals that were prioritized over education for the poor. She spoke out against reforms that sought justice in name rather than in action. She had even launched an extraordinary investigation in her free time to expose a mining company that was shamelessly dumping toxic waste into a river, polluting the water source for an entire town. May traveled to the area herself and discovered that local leaders, including the board of directors of the company, the mayor, and even the governor, were well aware of the travesty and stood to profit from the situation. May managed to amass hard evidence on the facts and root causes of the pollution, and of its negative impact on public health. She had exposed hair-raising breaches of security and corruption running rampant through the upper levels of city and state governance. But when she submitted the article to her editor in chief, he ordered her to stick to the research assigned by her superiors. The man literally tossed May's article into the trash, told her to get him a cup of coffee, and reminded her not to be stingy with the sugar.

May held back the tears and refused to give in. Sally-Anne consoled her. Revenge, she explained, was a dish best served *lukewarm*; contrary to popular belief, it is far less satisfying cold. That very night, toward the end of spring, a new project emerged out of nowhere, one that would come to change the course of their lives. The idea was born in the most unlikely of places: a cheap Italian restaurant, where they had gathered with their friends for dinner.

"We're going to start a newspaper, one with real investigative journalism at its core, with no censorship, that will print the whole truth, speak truth to power," Sally-Anne declared, to no one in particular.

May, seeing the tepid reaction from their friends, stepped in without missing a beat. She clambered onto the table, more than a little tipsy, and suddenly had everyone's undivided attention.

"The reporters on staff . . . will all be *women*," she said, raising her glass. "Male employees will be limited to secondary roles, such as secretarial staff, switchboard, or archives."

"Except that would be doing exactly what we're trying to stop," Sally-Anne countered. "Staff reporters should be hired solely on qualifications, with zero regard for gender, skin color, or religion."

"Great idea."

They began drawing up plans for their project right then and there, surrounded by their ragtag group of inebriated friends at the hole-in-the-wall Italian restaurant. First and foremost, the plan for the newsroom was drawn on a cocktail napkin. Rhonda, the oldest of the group and a junior accountant at Procter & Gamble (and rumored to have a history of attending Black Panther meetings), offered up her professional expertise. She began to sketch out the strategy for an operating account. She also drew up a list of posts to fill, the pay scale, and cost estimates for premises, overhead, supplies, and field expenses. She promised to calculate the cost of paper, printing, and shipping, and the margin that had to be allocated to distributors and dealers. In exchange for these services rendered, Rhonda was gunning for the title of CFO.

Their friend Keith shook his head and cut in. "Let's assume that your project does somehow scrape together funding—which, mind you, is not at all a given—no one would ever print your rag, much less sell it. An investigative newspaper run by women?"

Keith was a strapping young man, built like a bear with a square jaw and intense blue eyes. Sally-Anne found him attractive, and had had a fling with him for a few short weeks before losing interest. Keith, however, was pining to get back into bed with her. Beneath his hardened shell was a willing lover with soft hands who gave Sally-Anne just what she wanted. But no matter how adept they might be between the sheets, Sally-Anne never grew attached to men. After six weeks, she would get sick of their antics and move on. Keith, however, had also managed to catch May's eye, a fact that had not escaped Sally-Anne.

May suspected that Sally-Anne had broken things off with Keith just to clear the way for her to have a turn. "You can have him; he's all yours," Sally-Anne had declared, having returned home one morning after leaving him high and dry. May balked at being next in line after Sally-Anne, and got an earful from her lover in response.

"Come on! Get your kicks wherever you can. Don't hesitate when an opportunity presents itself. Worry about the consequences later. Believe me, if you don't, you'll end up either bored silly, or becoming boring yourself, or both," she concluded, before ducking off to the shower. May could see straight through Sally-Anne's self-proclaimed rebel veneer into the arrogance that lay beneath.

Whenever May and Keith made eye contact, she had to struggle not to picture the dalliances that Sally-Anne had recounted to her from time to time. Tonight, however, when Keith mocked their project, May delivered a comeback that left him speechless.

"We'll find our funding all right, and while you're sitting on your lazy ass reading *our* paper, you can take your cynicism and shove it."

The group sniggered in response, partly because it was the first time anyone had dared humiliate the pretty boy in public. Everyone watched as Keith rose from his seat, walked all the way around the table, and leaned over to apologize into May's ear.

"You're absolutely right. I hope you'll count me among your very first subscribers."

On a carpenter's wages, Keith was barely scraping by and could afford little more than the bare necessities. And yet, he dug into the pocket of his jeans and laid a ten-dollar bill before May. "There, you can put me down for some shares in your paper," he added before walking straight out of the restaurant, leaving everyone flabbergasted.

May ignored her friends' looks and darted out onto the dark street after Keith, waving his ten-dollar bill and calling after him.

"Hey! You really think you can become a shareholder just with this? This'll barely buy you the first few issues."

"Well, then consider it an advance toward my subscription."

May watched as Keith continued on his way, and then she stepped back into the restaurant, more resolute than ever. She would show them. First and foremost, she would prove it to herself. She would prove once and for all just how far she was willing to go. While Sally-Anne and May shared the same vision, it was for very different reasons, but their fates were now intimately bound. All that remained was finding the money to make the newspaper a reality, even if no one else would ever want it to see the light of day. That night, neither of them had even the faintest notion that bringing their dream to life would hinge upon a sinister crime.

May tried to chase away the memories of the wild drunken night that started everything. She wrapped the bedsheet around her shoulders and turned away. Sally-Anne moved in bed beside her and held her close as she drifted off to sleep.

9

ELEANOR-RIGBY

October 2016, Croydon

Maggie turned the key and found the flat door unlocked. As she opened the door, she could imagine a burglar already inside, pilfering away. She couldn't count how many times she had begged her father to lock his front door when he went out, only to receive the same stock response every time: he had been living there forever and never had any issues.

She hung her coat on a hook and moved down the hall, completely writing off the kitchen; Mum would never choose her husband's favorite room as a hiding place. The task was so daunting, Maggie had to cut corners. Why waste time on something so pointless? It was a lost cause from the start. But, no matter. Best to tackle the master bedroom, then the bathroom and toilet—or maybe start with the loo, in the hope of finding a secret compartment or a trapdoor. She decided to leave the front door unlocked. All her father would do if he found her sneaking about would be to pat her on the shoulder, smile, and say, "Always expecting the worst, Maggie! Why snoop around when you could just ask?"

Just then, a hand actually *did* land on Maggie's shoulder, and she cried out with shock. She turned to find her father staring right back at her with wide eyes.

"Well, what in the world are you doing in here?" he asked. "I didn't hear the doorbell."

"I, uh . . . I . . ." she stammered.

"Yes, you . . . ?"

"I thought you were out to lunch with Elby."

"I certainly was supposed to be, but wouldn't you know it, the Austin is being finicky. The old girl just won't start! I'll have to go have a look under the bonnet, see where the trouble is . . ."

"She could have at least let me know," Maggie growled under her breath.

"The Austin?"

"Elby!"

"Eleanor-Rigby should have at least let you know that my car broke down?" he asked with a kindhearted laugh. "Always picking fights with your sister. You know, I wish you two would cut it out. I can't stand watching you squabble. I've been waiting thirty years for the pair of you to grow up and act like adults. And rest assured, this is the very same lecture I give her every time she, uh, well . . ."

"Every time she what?"

"Oh, nothing." Ray sighed. "Would you please just tell me why you're here in the first place, darling?"

"I came . . . looking for some papers."

"Come along now, let's continue this in the kitchen over sandwiches. See? Even after my day takes a sour turn, I still get to have lunch with one of my daughters, and everything's right as rain in the end. Come to think of it, it'd be best if you don't mention this to your sister. If she starts thinking I lied about the Austin so I could grab lunch with you instead of her . . . Well, then . . ." Ray cringed, as though the sky could fall at any moment. He clearly wanted to avoid causing the dramatic episode of the week. He then opened the fridge and took out ingredients for a bare-bones meal, recruiting his daughter to help set the table.

"So. What's the matter, pet? Are you broke? If you need a bit of money, all you have to do is ask."

"It's nothing. Nothing's the matter. I just need to get my hands on . . . my birth certificate," Maggie improvised, without a clue where that idea had come from.

"Aha!" Ray exclaimed, face beaming.

"Aha what?" Maggie replied, trying to stay calm and act normal.

"Think about it. All of a sudden you show up, absolutely *needing* to get your hands on your birth certificate. I bet you figured I'd leave lunch with Elby around 2:30 p.m., knowing just how long it would take to get back home with all these damn traffic jams. To think that these politicians throw billions into the wind, decade upon decade, and they still haven't found a way to fix the common traffic jam! And here we are in the twenty-first century. I say they should all be kicked to the curb, the good-for-nothings . . ."

"Dad? You're rambling."

"I am not! Just reiterating my point of view. Anyway, don't change the subject. Clearly you deduced that lunch would give you enough time to get in and out well before 4 p.m. Come on, admit it!"

Without a clue to what he was driving at, Maggie chose to stay mum.

"Aha!" her father repeated with a hearty guffaw.

Maggie buried her face in her hands, with elbows planted on the table. "There are times when I talk to you and I feel like I'm stuck in the middle of a Monty Python sketch."

"Well, if you're trying to make fun of me, the joke's on you, because I take that as a compliment. The only thing I find insulting is that you think I still don't know what you came here for. Best hurry. Town hall closes at four o'clock, now doesn't it?" Dad chuckled with a sly wink.

"Possibly. What would you have me doing at the town hall?"

"All right, it seems I'm to believe you're redecorating your place, and you're so very grateful to have come into this world that you've decided to hang your birth certificate on the living room wall? A 'logical choice,' Maggie, as Michel would say! Now, enough messing about. I'm sorry for being tactless, bringing up your engagement in front of your brother and sister. But now that we're alone, you can tell me the truth."

"The truth? I have zero interest in getting married, and the thought never even crossed my mind. I swear, Dad. There's no wedding. Get the idea out of your head."

Father observed daughter with quiet, wary eyes, then slid the plate of freshly made sandwiches her way. "Eat. You're too skinny. You look like death warmed up."

Maggie bit into the white bread, happy for an end to the conversation. Dad watched her chewing, then, proving once more that he couldn't handle more than a millisecond of silence, said, "What's so urgent that you need to get your hands on your birth certificate right now?"

"It was . . . my bank. They're doing some kind of check on my account status or something," Maggie improvised.

"So you need to take out a loan? Turns out I wasn't so far off the mark after all—you *do* need money. It's like a sixth sense with my daughters. If you were hard up for cash, why didn't you come to me? Those banks will bleed you dry with interest rates, but if they owe *you* a single penny, suddenly money magically loses all value!"

"What makes you say that? Do you mean that your bank once owed *you* money?" asked Maggie, hoping she had uncovered some telltale morsel of information about her mother's alleged fortune.

Her hopes were soon dashed when Dad explained that he had only been talking about his retirement fund. "Thousands of pounds saved that didn't yield a single thing," he explained with a sigh. "And why is it that you need a loan? Are you in debt or something?"

"Dad, forget about it, I was just trying to negotiate my overdraft limits, and that's it. You make the tiniest request, and then, boom, you have to produce a mountain of paperwork! Speaking of which: Do you have any idea where Mum kept stuff like that, administrative papers and what-have-you?"

"More than an idea! I'm the one who's in charge of that around these parts. Your mother was allergic to paperwork, you could say. I could go and fetch them for you, if you like."

"Don't bother. Just tell me where they are and—"

The doorbell rang, cutting Maggie off. Ray had no clue who it could be; he certainly wasn't expecting anybody, and the postman had already been there that morning. When he swung open the door, he was dumbstruck once again.

"You? Good lord, did you really come all the way here?" Dad looked astonished to see me.

"What's it look like? I dropped by the office and borrowed a car. The traffic was a nightmare!"

"I was just telling your sister the same thing."

"Maggie? Is she here?"

"She is. But don't think for a second that my car breaking down was some kind of excuse to have lunch with her instead of you! It's the oddest thing, she just popped up all discreet and such, hoping I wasn't about, all so she could—"

"Could what?" I asked, trying not to sound too panicked.

"Well, if you ever let me finish a sentence, I'd tell you. She was looking for paperwork. Apparently, she's applying for a loan at the bank. Your little sister's got a bit of a hole in the pocket, see."

Right on cue, Maggie stepped into the hallway, glaring angrily, but I had come prepared. "Before you open your mouth to say something you'll later regret, take a look at your mobile. I left you ten voicemails."

Maggie retreated to the kitchen and dug through her purse, discovering her iPhone was in silent mode. She quickly realized I'd attempted to warn her over and over.

"You know, I may gripe about the Austin, but I should be singing its praises for this double surprise," said Dad. "All that's missing is Michel knocking at my door. I'll go see what's hanging around in the fridge. Had I known, I would've stocked up!"

With Dad relieved that he was in the clear for his car breaking down, I sat down at the table with Maggie. She gave me a reassuring nod to show that we were in the clear, too; Dad didn't suspect a thing. As soon as our father stepped out of sight, Maggie grabbed her phone once more and laughed out loud upon checking the screen.

"I can't believe my eyes, Rigby! You actually texted 'Abort Mission' three times! Talk about watching too much TV!"

Dad returned to the kitchen with a document in hand.

"Strictly speaking, it's not *exactly* a birth certificate, but rather a printed section of our family tree. One validated by a Mormon notary public, no less! This should appease that banker of yours . . ."

I managed to snatch the paper from him and glance over it.

"Well, that certainly is weird," I said, as my father fiddled with the switch on the electric kettle and cursed under his breath. "It says here you and Mum didn't get married until after we were born."

"Does it now?" he mumbled absently.

"It certainly does! It's written right here. You're honestly telling us you don't remember the date of your own wedding?"

"Before you, after you—what difference does it make? We were in love then and stayed that way until the day she died, as far as I know. I'm still in love with her to this day, for what it's worth."

"But the way you always told it, you got hitched right after you reunited."

"So what? So the truth was a bit more complicated than the stories we told while putting you kids to bed at night."

"What do you mean by more complicated?"

"And here we go again with the third degree! Really, Elby. You should have been a detective instead of a journalist," he grumbled, at last yanking the plug out of the wall and wrapping it around the kettle. "Of course. How fitting. My trusty old kettle decides to give up the ghost. No car this morning, and now it's no tea. I must be cursed." Dad grabbed a saucepan, filled it with water, and set it down on the hob. "Either of you have any idea how long it takes to boil cold water?" My sister and I both shrugged and shook our heads. "Neither do I, but it looks like we're about to find out," he said, peeking at the wall clock.

"What do you mean by more complicated?" I repeated.

My father sighed. "The first few weeks after we got back together were a bit tricky. It took time for her to adjust to her new life out in the sticks. Believe it or not, back then this wasn't the most joyful place to settle down."

Maggie scoffed. "Back then?"

"Hey, my hometown was nothing to write home about, either. Look, back then I had to work long hours at the office and she had yet to find work herself, so your mother was feeling quite alone, sort of just walking in circles around the flat. But she was a fighter, all right. She signed up for some courses, found some short-term work, and hey presto, she was a teaching assistant and later a teacher. Add a pregnancy on to that—the sheer joy of becoming a parent notwithstanding—and, well, it all takes a toll. You have no idea what that's like, but hopefully one day you will! Anyway, without the means to buy a proper wedding dress or a ring, or any of that razzle-dazzle that everyone expects, we waited a bit before taking our vows. There's the honest truth. Does that satisfy your curiosity?"

"So, Mum got pregnant how long after you got back together? How far into the second chapter of your romance?"

"Nice choice of words. I suppose you could say your mother hated the mere mention of that first chapter. Ten whole years had passed, ten years of life, ten years of becoming a new person. So, your mother really loathed the young woman she once was, to the point where she would actually get jealous that I had been in love with the 'past her.' She couldn't understand how one man could have loved two drastically different people. Of course, it never occurred to her that I could have become a drastically different person myself! Of course not. Well, truth be told, I really didn't change all that much, so maybe she was right. Your mother lived in the present. She rarely looked ahead to the future, and she considered the past to be dead and gone. The two chapters of our story were night and day for her, Old and New Testament, if you will. Two tellings, which never agreed on the coming of the Messiah."

"So, does that make you the Messiah in her story, Dad?" Maggie guffawed.

"One minute, twelve seconds," he said, eyes fixed on the boiling water and flatly ignoring the wisecrack. He turned off the gas and served the tea.

"That sure is quick. One minute, twelve seconds to get Mum pregnant? That must be a world record," I persisted.

After adding a splash of milk to his tea, Dad studied us each in turn. "I love you both, no doubt about that. I love you two more than anything on earth, aside from your brother of course. But, good lord, you can be a pain sometimes! Mum got pregnant very quickly, just a few months after we got back together. Do you want to know how much you and your brother weighed at birth, Elby? Well, believe it or not, *you* were the heavier one. So there!"

This made Maggie laugh out loud, puffing out her cheeks and imitating fat baby Eleanor-Rigby until Dad brought her down to size.

"Not so fast, Maggie. You weighed more than both of them com-bined! All right, now that all your prying has ruined my mood, I think I'll have a little stroll through the cemetery. Care to come with?"

Maggie hadn't been back to the grave once since the funeral. Seeing Mum's name on the gravestone was more than she could handle.

"You know what? Scratch that," my father said, reading her face. A father, after all, picks up on such things. "Don't take it the wrong way, but I should go alone, clear my head." With that, Dad downed the rest of his tea, put the mug in the sink, and planted a kiss on each of our foreheads, taking his leave. Then he paused in the doorway and called back to us, "Don't forget to lock the door on your way out, Maggie," before walking out of the flat with a smile on his face.

10

ELEANOR-RIGBY

October 2016, Croydon

We waited just long enough to ensure our father was really gone before taking up a thorough search of the premises. We cut the bathroom from the list, knowing it was far too improbable a hiding place. Maggie scoured the hallway cupboard from top to bottom like a forensics expert, but found no trapdoor or secret compartment. As I was finishing combing through the master bedroom, Maggie ducked back into the kitchen and had a look at our family tree.

"Totally fine, enjoy a nice break, don't worry one second about helping me!" I called out sarcastically.

"I didn't get any help from you for my rooms, as far as I know," Maggie shot back. "You're not done yet?"

I sulked back into the kitchen, tail between my legs. "I looked everywhere and couldn't find a single thing. I even tapped the entire wall looking for hollow spots. Nothing. Nada."

"You didn't find anything, Elby, because there's nothing to find. The letter is full of shit. Fun as this has been, it's time to call it a day."

"Try to think like Mum here. If you were her, where would you hide your stash?"

"Why hide it in the first place, and not just spend it on your family?"

"Well, say it wasn't money but something she couldn't do anything with? I mean, think about it. What if she was a drug dealer when she was young? Everybody was on drugs in the seventies and eighties."

"Like I said, Elby: you watch far too much TV. And I don't mean to burst your bubble, but a lot of people are on drugs today, too. You extend your London visit much longer, and I might need to start taking some myself."

"Out of the three of us, Mum was closest to Michel."

"Brilliant observation. If that's an attempt at making me jealous, it's downright pathetic."

"It's not pathetic, it's the truth. I only mention it because if Mum had some kind of secret she was keeping from Dad, then Michel is the next most likely person she would tell."

"If you want to keep this up and be pigheaded about it on your own, go ahead, but don't even think about dragging Michel into this."

"I don't take orders from anyone, least of all you! You know what? Screw it. I'm going to see him right now. He may be your brother but he's my twin!"

"Yeah, well . . . it's not like you're identical!" Maggie spluttered as I stormed right out of the apartment. She came rushing after me, and the two of us raced down the stairs and out of the front door.

The pavements outside were blanketed in crimson, the fallen leaves remnants of an October with especially bitter winds. I love the feeling of dry leaves crunching underfoot, and the scent of autumn mixed with rain. I slipped behind the wheel of the car I had borrowed from one of my coworkers, and turned on the engine before Maggie had even made it inside.

We didn't exchange a word throughout the entire drive, save one small exchange in which I told Maggie I was glad she was starting to take the anonymous letter seriously. After all, why else had she come along? Maggie insisted she was only trying to protect Michel from his evil twin sister's wanton lunacy.

I found a parking spot and headed towards the library. The lobby was empty, and the varnished cherrywood counter that looked like it was pulled from some forgotten century was unattended. There were only two full-time employees at the library: the manager, Vera Morton, and Michel. Aside from a cleaning woman who came to dust the shelves twice a week, that was it.

As we entered the lobby, Vera came out to greet us, her face lighting up as soon as she recognized Maggie. Vera was a lot more complex than a first glance might suggest. She could have been an absolute knockout if she didn't go to such lengths to disappear into the crowd. The sparkle of her blue lapis eyes was dulled by a pair of round glasses, complete with greasy fingerprint smudges on the lenses, and her hair was pulled back with a simple elastic band. Her choice of attire was equally unappealing. She looked sober as a judge in a mud-colored jumper two sizes too large, with matching moccasins and socks to complete a kind of variations-on-beige ensemble.

"I trust everything is all right?" Vera asked.

"Oh, right as rain," I replied.

"Well, that is quite a relief. I was worried that you had some sort of bad news to relay. After all, it's only once in a blue moon we're lucky enough to be graced by your presence."

I couldn't think of another person I knew who talked like that these days. Maggie made up a story about us being nearby and deciding to stop by to pay our brother a visit. Watching Vera, I couldn't help but notice a slight flush rising in her cheeks every time she heard Michel's name. Maybe Vera's heart was beating faster beneath that mud-colored jumper . . .

You couldn't blame her, after all. You throw two fish into the same bowl for eight hours a day, with sporadic visits from schoolchildren serving as the only other form of interaction? It's no big surprise that they might begin to consider each other the best possible specimens humanity had available. That said, it did seem that Vera could be harboring some real feelings for my brother, begging the question: Was the feeling mutual?

The young manager of the crumbling establishment was overjoyed to lead us across the library towards the reading room, where we found Michel alone at a table with his nose buried in a book. Despite Michel being the only soul in the room, Vera still whispered to him as though the place were full of visitors. Libraries must be like churches, I thought to myself, where believer and nonbeliever alike must employ the same hushed tones.

My brother looked up in shock to find his two sisters staring back at him. He promptly closed the book he had been reading and returned it to its proper place before coming back to join us.

"We were just in the area and thought we'd stop by to give you a hug," Maggie declared.

"Ah, that's odd. You always tend to avoid our hugs. But, by all means." With that, Michel extended two stiff arms and stood awkwardly awaiting a hug from his sister.

"I meant that . . . figuratively," Maggie explained. "Come join us for a cup of tea. If you're able to get away, that is."

Vera cut in to answer on his behalf. "Of course he can. It's a particularly slow day. Go on, Michel," she said, her cheeks once more suffering a mini roseola attack. "I can close the library on my own."

"Ah. But I do still have a few books to put away."

"Oh, I'm sure those old books would be delighted to spend the night on top of each other . . . I mean, you know, in *piles*," she said, the reddish hue intensifying by the second.

With that, Michel reached out and shook Vera's hand, jostling it awkwardly like an old bike pump. "In that case, thank you very much," he said. "I'll be sure to work a bit extra to make up for it tomorrow."

"Thank you. That won't be necessary. Have a lovely evening, Michel," she added, her cheeks full-on scarlet now.

Since hushed tones seemed to be official library policy, I bent over to Maggie and whispered in her ear, pointing out Vera's behavior. Maggie rolled her eyes and led Michel out.

The three of us ducked into a tearoom. It was on the ground floor of a modest yellow-brick building dating back to the seventies, its bay window covered in posters and fliers. In a neighborhood that seemed especially slow to change with the times, the establishment was a vestige of the suburb's industrial past. With no table service, Maggie went up to the counter and ordered Earl Grey with a heap of scones, generously leaving me the opportunity to pay the bill. The three of us sat down on plastic chairs around a Formica table.

"Has something happened to Dad?" asked Michel in a calm, measured tone.

I quickly assured him Dad was fine. Michel sipped his tea and turned to Maggie. "Are you here to announce you're marrying Fred?"

"Come on! Just because we've stopped by to see you doesn't mean there's some kind of major drama afoot," she said.

Michel pondered this for a moment, then cracked an exaggerated smile to let us know he liked her choice of words.

"I figured, for once I get to stay in London for more than two seconds," I added. "So, why not come see my brother? And I invited Maggie to come along, too."

"So, Michel," asked Maggie, cutting straight to it. "Did Mum happen to tell you a secret, one just for you?"

"That's a peculiar question. I haven't spoken to her in ages, and neither have you."

"I meant . . . you know, before."

"Let's say that she did," he said, nodding his head. "Then I wouldn't be able to tell you about it. A logical point, wouldn't you say?"

"I'm not asking you *what* she said, just *if* she told you a secret."

"No," Michel confirmed sternly.

"See?" said Maggie, throwing a smug look my way.

"She didn't tell me *a* secret; she told me many," Michel clarified. Maggie and I looked at each other. "Am I allowed to have another scone?" he asked, and Maggie slid the plate over.

"Why would she tell you and not us?"

"Because she knew I wouldn't say anything."

"Even to your sisters?"

"Most of all to my sisters. When the two of you fight, you'll say any thought that comes into your head, even things that aren't true. While you both have many virtues, of course, knowing how to control what you say when you're angry is not one of them." Michel seemed pleased with his well-reasoned point.

I placed a soft hand on Michel's forearm and looked deep into his eyes with nothing but tenderness and love.

"You know that we miss her just as much as you do."

"Considering there's no specific metric to prove such a thing, would it be safe to assume that's just a manner of speaking?"

"No, Michel," I continued. "I mean what I'm saying. She was our mother as much as she was yours."

"Indeed."

"If you know something that we don't, it's not exactly fair to keep it to yourself, do you see what we mean?" Maggie pleaded.

Michel looked my way, unsure. I nodded to tell him it was okay to talk, but all he did was dip another scone into his tea and devour it in two huge bites.

"What did she tell you?" I insisted.

"Nothing, she didn't tell me anything."

"Then what's the secret, Michel?"

"I meant to say, the secret . . . wasn't anything she *said*, per se."

"Then what was it?"

"I don't think I'm allowed to tell you."

"Michel, I don't think Mum knew that she would be gone so soon, and so unexpectedly. I'm sure she would have wanted us to share everything with each other."

"Possibly. But I'd have to find some way of verifying that with her."

"Right, except you can't. So, you're just going to have to rely on your judgment, and your judgment only."

After downing the rest of his tea in one gulp, Michel put his cup back in the saucer with a trembling hand, shaking his head, his eyes lost and frantic—all signs of an impending attack. I stroked his neck and spoke soothingly and deliberately, hoping to calm my twin brother down.

"You don't have to say anything now. I'm sure Mum would have wanted you to think things through. After all, that's why she entrusted her secret to you. Do you want another scone, love?"

"I don't think that would be reasonable. But perhaps. To mark the occasion of all three of us being together."

"Right when I had decided not to get up again," Maggie muttered before making a round-trip to the counter. She set one last scone down in front of Michel and returned to her seat.

"Let's change the subject, huh?" said Maggie, her voice gentle. "How about you tell us about your life at work?"

"It's quite similar to my life at home."

"Sure, sure. But not everything, right?"

"How about your manager?" I asked innocently. "You two seem . . . *close.*"

Michel looked up in doubt. "Just to verify . . . 'close' is a manner of speaking, I suppose."

"Indeed, or call it an observation."

"Yes, we are quite often 'close,' in terms of proximity, which is to be expected since speaking in anything above a whisper is strictly prohibited at the library."

"So I noticed."

"In that case, you should understand why we are often close."

"She seems to really enjoy your company." I could feel Maggie glaring at me for raising the subject. "Don't look at me like that, Maggie. I'm allowed to talk to my brother without having you judge my every word."

"Are you two going to argue?" Michel asked.

"No, not today," Maggie assured him.

"I'll tell you one thing that fascinates me about you two," Michel began, while dabbing the corners of his mouth carefully with a napkin. "Most of the time, what you say makes no sense. Yet, you seem to understand each other better than most of the people I've observed, at least when you're not fighting. If that's what it means to be 'close,' then yes, I suppose we are. I hope that answers your question, Elby. Your real question."

"I'd say it does, love. And if you happen to need any advice, you know . . . girl stuff? I'm right here for you, anytime."

"Thank you," he said. "Thank you, Elby. Even though you're not 'right here' very often, you can always come back, unlike Mum. Which is very reassuring."

"This time, I'll be right here for a while. At least, I think."

"Until your magazine sends you to study giraffes in a faraway land? How is it that you care more about people you don't even know than about your own family?"

If anyone else on earth aside from my brother had asked that question, I might have been able to give an honest answer. At the beginning, I set off to see the world, scouring the globe in search of hope, something I was sorely lacking at the age of twenty. I wanted to break away from a life that was mapped out in advance. I was desperate to avoid being boxed in to the type of life my mother had led, the same sort of path that Maggie seemed to have no qualms about pursuing. I had to leave my family to learn to love them again. Because in spite of all the love around me, I found suburban life to be suffocating and unbearable.

"I was just fascinated by all the diversity in the world," I replied. "I left to try to learn more about all the things that make people different from each other. Does that make sense?"

"No. Not very logical, I must say. After all, I myself am different from the others. And yet, that wasn't enough for you."

"You're not different, Michel. We're twins, and you're the person I feel closest to in the whole wide world."

"You know . . . if I'm intruding, just let me know," Maggie said, rolling her eyes.

Michel studied each of us in turn. He took a deep breath and laid his hands on the table, ready to get something off his chest, a secret that had been weighing heavily on him.

"I do feel . . . *close* to Vera," he whispered, short of breath.

11

THE *INDEPENDENT*

June to September 1980, Baltimore

Ever since that drunken night at the end of spring, May and Sally-Anne had devoted every waking hour to the newspaper, body and soul. They spent the entire summer working on the project, with the exception of one short Sunday at the beach.

First, a great paper had to have a great name. May took the first stab, drawing inspiration from Robert Stack's portrayal of Eliot Ness in old reruns of *The Untouchables*. Even though it was a bit dated, the show still ran late at night on ABC. At first, Sally-Anne thought May's idea was a joke. Not only was the name pretentious, but she could already hear the lewd jokes some men would make. A newspaper run by women could never be called *The Untouchables*.

Sally-Anne found an abandoned warehouse on the docks that she planned to transform into the paper's newsroom, and got Keith to help with the renovation. On a particularly hot July afternoon, Sally-Anne stood admiring their muscled friend's physique as he lent them a hand with the work.

Sally-Anne had declared that all the warehouse really needed was a new coat of paint. Keith took the time for a thorough walk-through and found she had vastly underestimated the scope of the work. What was more, they had an absurdly small budget for the project. This was all the more absurd, Keith observed, considering that Sally-Anne's family wasn't exactly strapped for cash.

What Keith didn't know was that behind the facade of carefree temptress, Sally-Anne lived by an unshakably strong moral code. As far back as she could remember, long before her teenage years, she had known she was different from her family, as illustrated in a tale she recounted to Keith and May.

Sally-Anne had once told her teacher that she had so little in common with her father, and even less with her mother, that she sometimes wondered if she had been switched at birth. Her observation was rewarded with a long lecture, in which the teacher berated the brazen young lady for being so judgmental of parents who were models of success. Sally-Anne thought the only success anyone could credit her parents with was managing to cling to their inheritance, compromising their principles and telling unforgivable lies in the process.

Suddenly, it clicked. Keith's offhand remark had triggered an idea, a common ground that both women could wholeheartedly unite on: they didn't owe anyone a single thing. Thus, the name the *Independent* seemed to be a perfect fit for the paper.

"Well, lovely as that sounds, without any resources, this is going to be one mammoth undertaking," Keith exclaimed. "The window frames are all eaten through with salt. The hardwood floor is such a mess you can actually fit your whole hand between the planks! I'm not sure even Superman could get that boiler up and running, and this shit-hole hasn't had electricity in ages."

"There are only two types of men in this world," Sally-Anne replied with a chiding smile. "Men with problems and men with solutions."

Sally-Anne had learned out of sheer necessity—and often when dealing with men—that she sometimes had to put her ethics on hold. The deed was done: Keith had walked straight into Sally-Anne's trap.

Watching the man leap back into his work with an extra dose of fervor and energy almost made May feel sorry for him. But it was for a good cause, after all.

Keith certainly hadn't been born with a silver spoon in his mouth, and his rugged upbringing had required him to be resourceful and make do with what he had. On the first Sunday he came to work, Keith tried to pull a cable from the main circuit breaker. It was after dark by the time he finally reconnected it, and the task had required a perilous climb to access the transformer on an electrical pole outside. It had taken him all day and a good part of the night. But in the end, they had electricity.

In the days that followed, Keith spent all his free time at the warehouse. Within a week, he had begun to consider the project a personal challenge. Keith would cart in truckloads of wood scraps he had collected at work, to use on the window frames, and decided to completely redo the hardwood floor from scratch. While the scheme was hard to keep under wraps and did not go unnoticed by his employer, his talent as a carpenter kept him from getting fired. By the end of the first week, Keith at last came to his senses, realizing that the task was far too vast for him to tackle on his own. He pulled together a scrappy little work crew consisting of friends who came aboard after they were treated to a few meals prepared by May and Sally-Anne. Apprentice plumbers, masons, painters, and locksmiths came in turn, to take care of the boiler and the pipework, to remove the cast-iron radiators, repair the decrepit walls, and deal with every last inch of rust-covered metal in the space. Nor did May and Sally-Anne sit around twiddling their thumbs. When they weren't busy bringing drinks and snacks to Keith's ragtag crew, they would help drill, hammer, paint . . . whatever needed doing.

There, in that lively, boisterous atmosphere, a subtle love triangle was unfolding. It was a bizarre game of seduction, with one player skilled, another sincere, and the third clueless.

Keith was growing on May more and more every day, and she found herself quietly watching everything he did and listening carefully every time he spoke. She made sure to be in the right place at the right time to lend him a helping hand. Their short exchanges, between his hammering and her vigorous painting, made it clear to May that Keith's mind was just as appealing as his body. Meanwhile, Keith's eyes would always drift back toward Sally-Anne, who was intentionally keeping him at arm's length. May eventually began to believe that Keith might be helping out just for the chance to get close to Sally-Anne again, but she kept her suspicions to herself.

◆ ◆ ◆

One month in, the game changed again when Keith started to pick up on Sally-Anne's strategy. He decided to ask May out for dinner, taking her to an Indian restaurant on Cold Spring Lane. That he would choose such an exotic cuisine came as a surprise to his date. At the end of the meal, Keith suggested he accompany May back to the warehouse so he could put a second coat of varnish on the main door.

"That way, I can let it dry overnight and jump right to the next step first thing tomorrow," he explained.

May once more thanked Keith for everything he had done for them. *Did I do it for them . . . or for her?* he thought to himself as he grabbed his car keys and led May out to his pickup.

"Feel free to put on some music if you want," Keith said as they cruised along.

May reached out to turn on the radio, slyly hiking her skirt halfway up her thigh in the process. Her milky skin, impossibly smooth and peppered with freckles, came in and out of view with the light of every streetlamp they drove past, drawing Keith's gaze every time without fail. It wasn't long before his hand followed suit.

May felt a rush of electricity from his touch, like heat was radiating straight from his palm. After they parked, Keith let May lead the way up the warehouse stairs, his desire growing with each step of the steep climb.

May entered the warehouse and called out Sally-Anne's name, secretly hoping she would be out. She could just picture Sally-Anne at some random bar on the other side of town, surrounded by young men undressing her with their eyes, or young women who either loved her or hated her, or both.

As soon as they were sure the coast was clear, Keith made a move straight for May. She backed up coyly and pressed herself against the window with a come-hither smile. Keith pursued, running a hand through May's hair and closing in for a passionate kiss. She had been envisioning this moment for weeks, yet it was more tender and less frenzied than she had imagined. The nape of Keith's neck smelled of wood and turpentine. His hands sent chills down her spine. He explored every last inch of her face, and May nibbled softly at his pioneering fingertips. Keith pulled her to him by the waist and opened her blouse, kissing her breasts as she unbuttoned her jeans. She could feel him pressing against her, leaving no doubt in her mind: Keith was all hers.

May knew she was cheating on Sally-Anne for the first time, but Sally-Anne's grab-it-while-it's-there approach to life seemed to allow room for Keith and others. In any case, she was helpless to resist. Meanwhile, at that very moment, Sally-Anne was sitting outside the warehouse on her motorcycle, calmly watching the window with May's bare back pressed against it. Sally-Anne didn't avert her eyes once, watching every movement, gazing at the small of May's back as it curved each time Keith thrust. That particular dance was quite familiar to Sally-Anne, having experienced it firsthand herself. She could still recall how Keith felt inside her and the salty tang of his skin.

"Go ahead and enjoy, darling. Don't hold back, you're not doing anything wrong. He's my gift to you. I just hope you don't mind if I borrow him back from time to time, when the mood strikes me."

With that, Sally-Anne started up the Triumph. She zoomed away / with her helmet off, wind blasting through her hair, in search of some company somewhere out in that dark night.

◆ ◆ ◆

By mid-August, the lion's share of the work was complete, and it was clear that Sally-Anne's bet had paid off. The warehouse may not have been as good as new, like she had promised, but at the very least it had been given "one hell of a face-lift," as Keith put it. The new look clearly pleased May and Sally-Anne, who leapt on Keith and showered him with kisses.

The two had even taken advantage of the renovation to add a little bedroom nook for workers. Everything was in place, and they could now start putting what little money they had left into the paper itself. Although Keith and his crew had made the best of recycled and found materials, Sally-Anne and May had still had to invest most of their savings into the renovation.

By the end of the month, they had skimmed and scraped together enough to acquire some cheap furniture and secondhand equipment. May found half a dozen typewriters thrown into a trash heap by an insurance company that had upgraded to IBM Selectrics. Sally-Anne went on a charm offensive of mythical proportions and got a great deal on a collection of secondhand equipment: an old mimeograph machine (a poor man's printing press), a pair of tape recorders, a light box for the photo studio, six chairs, and a velvet sofa. She scored the entire package for next to nothing, which was important considering they had next to nothing when September rolled around.

Early one Sunday morning, May decided to go to mass, as she did from time to time. Her faith was one of the only things from her past she hadn't completely left behind, and yet she still felt guilty every time she set foot in a church. She hadn't come to ask God for forgiveness; she had come to get away from it all, even if only for an hour. She refrained from prayer, as it would have been an insult to the others in attendance. May looked out over the congregation, wondering about the lives of the people gathered in the pews. She watched children yawning their way through litanies, and tried to imagine which couples truly loved each other and which were only sharing the same bed. May was troubled. As exhilarating as it was for her to be living life with such freedom, it came with its own anxiety, and she feared loneliness above all.

The night before, Sally-Anne had come home late from a charity gala that had bored her to tears. She had only attended to try and convince a young entrepreneur to invest in the *Independent*. Sally-Anne didn't find the man quite attractive enough to venture outside the realm of the professional into less constrained territory.

The young businessman had listened politely to her pitch, but raised a few concerns. The challenge arose from trying to generate profits from a newspaper lacking any kind of national scope. Since television had started sucking all the oxygen from advertising budgets, print was barely profitable these days. This trend only seemed to be on the rise, so the businessman had to wonder if print media's days were numbered. Despite Sally-Anne's intelligent and compelling counterarguments, she simply couldn't get the man to budge, and he was ultimately unconvinced the project had enough profit potential to warrant investment. She stressed that there were other benefits beyond the bottom line. The country was in dire need of newspapers that were independent and not in the pockets of the rich and powerful. Out of sheer courtesy, the businessman committed to supporting the *Independent* in the second round of investment, so long as the paper had a successful first year. Sally-Anne ended up returning home late at night, still fuming, and her rage only intensified when she found May and Keith sleeping side by side in the bed. It was her bed, too. She toyed with the idea of slipping under the covers with them, but ultimately opted for the sofa.

The next morning, Sally-Anne awoke to the sound of May leaving the loft and discovered that Keith was still sleeping soundly across the way. Hovering in the entrance to the loft, Sally-Anne watched Keith's chest rise and fall in a steady rhythm. Even when unmoving and sprawled out on the mattress, the man exuded pure strength. His skin was divine, enticing her to explore the hair on his chest. She pulled Keith's discarded shirt off the ground and pressed it to her face, taking in his distinctive scent.

If May had gone to church—and where else would she be headed this early on a Sunday morning?—she wouldn't be back for another two hours, and Sally-Anne wouldn't need nearly that long. She took off her T-shirt, slid down her panties, and climbed on top of Keith's sleeping form. In one of nature's great mysteries, the dawn transforms men into creatures of pure, uncontrollable desire. When he awoke to find Sally-Anne's lips exploring his stomach, Keith didn't put up much of a fight, and soon they were both enjoying the delights of an early-morning encounter. Afterwards, Sally-Anne rose, carrying her undergarments, and Keith climbed into the shower with her. While the two got dressed, they promptly agreed that none of it had ever even happened.

◆ ◆ ◆

Eight days later, a miracle occurred at the bank. Rhonda Clark, their friend who was the assistant accountant at Procter & Gamble, dreamt of one day becoming financial director. She also knew that a woman attaining such a post at a multinational corporation was akin to scaling Mount Olympus in flip-flops. Rhonda had already set up an operating account for the newspaper that covered all the bases. She created budgets so detailed they accounted for every last paper clip, with thorough two-year projections of advertising revenue versus cash flow, calculating just what was needed to keep the paper up and running. She bound the report with a nice plastic cover as the final touch. Then the big day arrived: a meeting with Rhonda's husband, the manager of a Corporate Bank of Baltimore branch, who was set to review their application for a line of credit.

Mr. Clark, who had been married to Rhonda for fifteen years, was a small man with a friendly sparkle in his eyes and a smile that was positively disarming. He possessed such charm and warmth that he seemed completely exempt from normal beauty standards. Cynics might have whispered that Mr. Clark already knew just how serious and thorough his wife's projections were, since questioning their quality would have cost him more than a few nights' sleeping on the couch.

"Let me begin with a question, if I might," he said, peering at Sally-Anne over his glasses. "If my establishment were to become your lender, would you ever write an article that runs counter to our interests?"

As May began to answer, she was cut off by a sharp kick in the shin from Sally-Anne. "Actually, I have a question of my own, before we get to yours," Sally-Anne asked. "This bank, insofar as being one possible source of financing for our paper, obviously wouldn't have any current issues with integrity, correct?"

"That goes without saying," replied Mr. Clark. "And while we're speaking so candidly, let me say that a project like this takes a lot of nerve. I really do admire your ambition. The fact is, a certain person, who shall remain nameless, has been talking my ear off about it every night. I can now see what all the fuss is about."

With that, Mr. Clark opened his desk drawer and took out a form, which he passed to Sally-Anne.

"I've no doubt you'll fill out this official loan request quickly. As soon as it's complete, come back to see me. That way I can present your application personally at the credit committee meeting. This step is little more than a formality; I'm overseeing your application myself.

We'll open an initial line of credit of twenty-five thousand dollars with a repayment duration of two years. By that point, since the paper will have achieved, or hopefully surpassed, its financial goals spectacularly, I hope that you will consider choosing our establishment for all your banking needs."

Mr. Clark shook their hands and walked them out of the office. As they stepped out of the bank, Sally-Anne and May were so ecstatic that they practically leapt into each other's arms even as they were thanking him. The two women were positively beside themselves as they made their way down the block.

"We're really gonna make this happen, aren't we?" Sally-Anne said, still coming to grips with what had transpired.

"Yeah, I think it's for real, I really do. Twenty-five thousand dollars is no joke, you know! We'll be able to hire two secretaries, a telex operator, maybe even a receptionist . . . Of course, down the line, we'll have to hire all women to cover graphic design and editing, photography and political reporting, the culture beat, and one or two reporters at large."

"Just women? I thought we'd decided on equal treatment."

"True. You're right, we should hire men, too. Just imagine how euphoric it would feel to say, 'Frank, honey, go and fetch me that file I asked for, will you?'" May mimed hanging up a telephone. "'John? Be a dear and fix me a cup of coffee,'" she continued, batting her eyelashes condescendingly at her imaginary assistant. "'Boy oh boy, those sure are some very flattering slacks, Robert. They really make your ass look fantastic!' That would be something else."

Cynics might have speculated that Mr. Clark would have never have approved the loan if he hadn't been married to Rhonda. But they would have been dead wrong. The manager of the Corporate Bank of Baltimore branch was keenly aware of who Sally-Anne was, and more importantly, who her family was. The Stanfields were major stockholders at the bank. He knew they would never allow outstanding debts there, not in a thousand years. Regardless of the success or failure of the newspaper, the bank's investment was safe.

Cynics might have argued that Mr. Clark had been wrong to give the green light so quickly, and that it was far too early for the two women to be celebrating. Maybe on this front, the cynics would have been right. Just a few days later, a bank employee discovered the application prior to the credit committee meeting. He immediately picked up the phone and made a call to none other than Hanna Stanfield, Sally-Anne's mother.

12

GEORGE-HARRISON

October 2016, Eastern Townships, Quebec

My name is George-Harrison Collins. Every time people start giving me a hard time about my first name, I tell them I heard enough taunting back in the schoolyard to last me a lifetime. The funny thing is, I didn't even listen to the Beatles growing up. My mother was more of a Stones fan. She refused to give any explanation of her choice for my name. It was just one of her many mysteries that I never could quite unravel.

I was born in Magog, and haven't lived anywhere outside the Eastern Townships of Quebec in the thirty-five years since. The scenery here is breathtaking, and the winters long and brutal. Spring pops up like a light at the end of the tunnel as everything wakes up again, followed by scorching summers that light up the woods and make the lakes sparkle.

Khalil Gibran wrote: *But memory is an autumn leaf that murmurs a while in the wind and then is heard no more.* While nearly all my most cherished memories revolve around my mother, her own memory was now languishing in the desolation of a permanent autumn.

From the time I turned twenty, she pushed me to leave home and go out on my own. "This town is way too small for you!" she would say. "Go see the world." But I defied her wishes. The truth is, there's nowhere else I could think of living. My heart belongs to the Canadian forests, and there is nothing better than living out among the maple trees. After all, I am a carpenter.

Back when her mind was still sharp and her sense of humor even sharper, my mother would always say I was like an old man, driving around in my silly old pickup. I had to admit I did spend the lion's share of my time in the workshop, alone. Working with wood can be truly magical. It makes you feel like you can transform matter itself. I first wanted to be a carpenter after reading *Pinocchio*. That Geppetto really got me thinking: if he could create a son with his bare hands, maybe I could use wood to create the father I had never known. I stopped believing in fairy tales as I grew up, but I never stopped believing in the magic of my chosen trade. The things I make go on to become part of people's lives. Tables for family dinners and unforgettable evenings, beds where couples make love, beds where children lie dreaming or staring up at the ceiling in wonder, bookshelves that house all the important books a person will ever read. I wouldn't have it any other way.

One morning in October, I found myself in the middle of a tough job, wrestling with a drawer slide for a chest. The wood had come from planks that weren't nearly seasoned enough. The slightest misstep and they'd split apart, which had already happened twenty times over. I was furious that the precious maple was rebelling against my touch. When the mailman arrived and broke my concentration, I admit I was a bit gruff with him. He interrupted me, and for what? All I ever got in the mail was bills and other paperwork from bureaucracies that eat away at life like termites.

Yet that day, he came bearing something else entirely: an anonymous letter. The beautiful handwriting on the envelope gave no hint as to the identity of the sender. I tore open the envelope and sat down to read it.

Dear George,

I hope you don't mind that I've abridged your name, but hyphenated monikers run a bit long for my taste, even when they are as dignified as yours. But I digress. My opinion about your name is not why I'm writing to you today.

I can't even begin to fathom how difficult it must be to watch your own mother slip away right before your eyes, day after day.

Your mother was a talented and courageous woman. But she was other things, as well. All we can ever see of our parents is what they wish to show us, and we in turn must choose how to see what we've been shown. And how easy it is to forget that they had a whole life before us. The life of which I speak was theirs and theirs only, a life with all of its dreams and fantasies, as well as the tormented hardship of youth . . .

Your mother, too, had to break free of her chains. The question is: How?

Did she ever tell you the truth about your father, the man you never knew? How did he meet your mother? Why would he abandon you? There are still so many questions. To uncover the truth, you need to go out and find the answers. Should you decide to do so, I would caution you to conduct your research skill-fully. As you might imagine, someone as shrewd as your mother would not simply bury her most intimate secrets somewhere they would be easy to find. As soon as you lay your hands on the proof that will back up my claims—for undoubtedly, your first reaction will *be utter disbelief—you will need to venture out to come and find me.*

But not until the time comes ... Until then, take some time to think it over. You've much to do. Best get started straightaway.

I hope you'll forgive me for leaving this letter unsigned. It's not out of cowardice, I assure you, but rather for your own good that I remain anonymous. I'd caution against telling anyone about this letter. You'd be wise to destroy it as soon as you've finished reading it. Keeping it will serve no purpose.

Take my words to heart: I wish nothing but the best for you and your mother.

Without hesitation, I crushed the letter in my fist and threw it across the room. Who in the world would send something like that? For what purpose? How did he know so much about my mother's health? The whole thing was so full of mysteries, I didn't even know where to begin. It was impossible to concentrate, a serious problem when working with saws, hand planes, and chisels. I decided to put away my tools and head out. I threw on my jacket and leapt behind the wheel of my pickup.

Two hours later, I pulled up to the gates of the nursing home where my mother had lived for the past two years. It was a stately building perched on a modest little hill in the middle of a large park. Thick, broad-leafed ivy crept up the facade of the building, which seemed to make the structure come to life whenever the wind blew. The care workers were kindhearted people struggling to attend to residents who all suffered from the same affliction. It was the same condition, but the expression of the disease was dramatically different in each patient.

Take my mother's next-door neighbor, Mr. Gauthier. The poor guy had spent the last five years rereading the same page of a book he never got any closer to finishing. He would come back to page 201 again and again, stuck in a loop all through the day reading the very same passage, and bursting out laughing at the end every time. "Ha! What a riot! Oh, that really is something!" he'd repeat.

Mrs. Lapique was stuck in her own loop, an unending game of solitaire—which tried the patience of any sane person watching—in which she would deal the cards facedown and simply stare at them, not even bothering to flip them over. From time to time, she would graze the surface of a card with trembling hand, murmur something inaudible through a timid little smile, then draw back her finger and leave the card unturned. Then she would gather up all the cards and start all over again: graze the surface of a card with trembling hand, murmur something inaudible through a timid little smile, then draw back her finger and leave the card unturned.

Sixty-seven patients in all lived at the New Age Residence, spending their days drifting about like a throng of ghosts, wholly unaware that their lives had already passed them by.

My mother was both a hardheaded woman and a hopeless romantic. Love was her drug of choice, and her habit could sometimes spin out of control, like with any other drug. Countless times I would come home from school to find a strange man in the house with Mom. They would awkwardly pat me on the shoulder and ask me how I was doing, with sheepish looks on their faces . . . How was I *doing*? As well as any kid who loved his mother but loathed her "suitors." Without exception, these men would disappear later that night or the next morning. But my mother would never leave me.

I can't exactly say what came over me that day the letter arrived. From the moment I read it, I felt anger welling up inside me, a feeling buried away so deep I had forgotten it was even there. I longed for the possibility that the all-consuming disease that afflicted the residents would take just one day off, even for the briefest of interludes, kindly taking a bow and shuffling offstage for a moment's relief. Mr. Gauthier would actually flip to page 202 and find the new page depressing. Mrs. Lapique's trembling hand would actually steady and flip over a card, revealing the king of hearts in all his glory. And my mom would actually be able to answer my questions.

I caught sight of her as I entered the space and she smiled at me, one small gesture she still had within her capacity. The subject I had come to raise with her was, as a rule, completely off-limits. On my tenth birthday, I had flatly refused her gift and thrown a massive tantrum in hopes she'd finally tell me who my father was. Did he really flee like a thief in the night just before my birth? Why didn't he want me in the first place? But my mother's own tantrum trumped mine, and she swore up and down that she would refuse to even speak to me if I ever dared ask that kind of question again. The fight stormed all through that week, with neither of us uttering a single word to each other. Finally, the following Sunday morning, on the way out of the grocery store, Mom hoisted me up into her arms, hugged me tenderly, and covered me with kisses.

"I forgive you," she declared with a sigh.

Only my mother had the confidence and the nerve to forgive somebody else for something that was her fault to begin with. My mother was guilty of staying silent and keeping me in the dark, and it was a heavy burden to bear, living under such a shroud of mystery. I tried asking a few more times over the years, but it never worked. If my mother didn't fly into a rage at the first mention, she would leave in a fit of tears, casting aspersions, lamenting that nothing was ever good enough for me, and that I never failed to rub her face in it, despite all the sacrifices she had made. Finally, at eighteen, I gave up asking. After all, I already knew all that I needed to know. If my father had wanted to meet me, he would have come knocking at our front door by then.

The strange letter must have given me some nerve, because I walked straight into the nursing home, looked my mother dead in the eye, and asked the big questions point-blank.

"Why did he leave us? Did he ever come to see me? Was he one of the men who came during the day to jump your bones while I was at school?"

I instantly felt terrible talking to my mother that way. We definitely got in a lot of fights, but I had never disrespected her like that. It wouldn't have even crossed my mind to speak to her so harshly when she still had all her wits about her. Had I been dumb enough to try back then, there would have been hell to pay.

"Looks like snow," my mother said. Her eyes drifted to a nearby table, where a care worker had just finished clearing up Mrs. Lapique's cards and was now pushing the old woman down the hall in her wheelchair. "They made our walks shorter, which means it won't be long before first snow. What are you doing for Christmas?"

"It's October, Mom. Christmas is in two months, and I'll be right here with you."

"Oh, no you won't!" she protested. "I can't stand turkey! Let's do Christmas in spring. You can take me to that restaurant I like. What's it called? You know the one, down by the river?"

The river she was referring to was actually a lake, and the restaurant was a little snack bar that served croissants and sandwiches. Despite all that, I nodded along in agreement. Even if I was still livid, upsetting her would be pointless. She gestured down at my thumb, which was bandaged, the result of a small cut I got a couple of days before.

"You hurt yourself, honey."

"It's nothing," I replied.

"Don't you have to work today?"

My mother's mind was perpetually floating in a very special place on the outskirts of reality. She was capable of carrying on the semblance of a conversation for a few short minutes, as long it was limited to small talk. Then, without warning, her mind would start to stray and she'd begin babbling nonsense.

"Melanie didn't come with you today?"

Melanie and I had broken up two years before when my isolated lifestyle—which had originally attracted her—lost all its charm. After five years living with me on and off, Melanie simply took her things and waltzed out the door, leaving behind nothing but a note on the kitchen table. Her message was short and sweet. *You're a bear deep in the woods,* it said.

Women really are something else. How is it they're able to sometimes say more with one sentence than a man can get out in an entire monologue?

"You're going to have to buy me an umbrella, you know," Mom continued, her eyes scanning the ceiling. Then Mr. Gauthier burst into a fit of laughter that made me flinch, cackling away from a nearby chair.

"He sure is one pain in the ass. You know that I once stole it? That book of his? I didn't find it the least bit funny. So, I gave it back to the old bum. The nurse promised me he'd be dead by New Year's. I cannot wait!"

"That doesn't sound like something the nurse would promise."

"Well, she did! She sure did," my mother insisted. "Go ask Melanie if you don't take my word for it. Where'd she duck off to anyway?"

It was starting to get dark, which meant there wasn't much time left before I'd have to start the drive home. I felt ridiculous having bothered my mother for what I knew to be a lost cause. With a two-hour drive ahead of me, and a whole chest of drawers to finish making by the end of the week, it was time to call it a day. I took Mom by the arm and led her back toward the dining room. Along the way, we crossed paths with a pretty nurse, who gave me a sweet, compassionate smile. What was a pretty girl like that doing in a place like this, constantly surrounded by death? My eyes were drawn to the woman's breasts. I could just picture her, later tonight, describing her long day to some lucky guy before they made love. Why couldn't that lucky guy be me? I wondered how it would feel to sleep by her side, to discover what she smelled like, the touch of her skin . . .

Then my mother chuckled and shattered the vision. "If Melanie could see you now! Anyway, you're barking up the wrong tree," she said under her breath. "She's impossible to please, if you catch my drift. Don't ask how I know, I just do. Full stop!"

Mom may have lost her mind, but she had managed to hang on to her obsession with always being right, down to her favorite catchphrase, "full stop": an odd Britishism in her otherwise North American vocabulary.

She took a seat in front of her dinner and peered down at the plate with blatant disdain, gesturing with her hand that it was time for me to go. I leaned down and she offered me her cheek for a kiss. Her freckles had long since disappeared, replaced by age spots and wrinkles.

Considering that October day's particularly strange start, it was more than fitting that it should end with another twist. My mother drew me in close, her grip stronger than usual, and whispered right into my ear.

"He didn't *leave us*, honey. He never even knew."

My heart started beating faster—faster even than the time I slipped and nearly lost my hand to a circular saw. For a moment, I told myself she couldn't possibly be lucid.

She quickly proved me wrong.

"He never knew what?" I asked.

"That you even existed, my darling."

I stared deep into my mother's eyes, not even daring to breathe as I waited for more . . . and then the moment passed.

"Go on, get out of here," she muttered, lost again. "Snow's on its way, first snow is coming . . ."

Across the way, Mr. Gauthier was howling with laughter again. Mom tilted her head upwards, looking to the ceiling of the dining hall, her eyes sparkling and full of wonder as though stargazing on a summer night.

My mind was made up. I had no idea how, but I knew once and for all: I was going to find my father.

13

ELEANOR-RIGBY

October 2016, Croydon

While Maggie had more or less decided to ignore the whole thing, I was more determined than ever to find the truth behind the anonymous letter. I lay stretched out on my bed, rereading the letter aloud in a hushed voice, at times speaking right to the author as though he could somehow hear me.

Your mother was a brilliant and remarkable woman, capable of great good . . . and great evil. Until now, you have only known the good. "What exactly do you mean, good and evil?" I said, gnawing at the end of my pencil. I sat up and jotted down in a note, *The "evil" must have been before I was born.*

As I glanced over what I'd written, it suddenly hit me that I knew next to nothing about my mother's life before she had children. All I knew came from little anecdotes my parents told, basically snapshots from their "first chapter," and their conflicting accounts of why they eventually split up. Then, the story jumps years ahead to the night my mother came knocking at Dad's door again.

But when it came to that ten-year gap between the first and second chapters, I was completely in the dark. I set the letter down on the bed, my mind running in circles. I had been rather young at age thirty-four when I lost my mother, but I knew in my heart that I could have got to know her better if I had tried harder. I had no excuse. I never learned a single thing about her teens or twenties. As much as it now hurt to admit, I just never asked her enough questions. Were we similar at similar ages? How much had we had in common? My mother and I shared the same eyes, facial expressions, and temperament, but that didn't necessarily mean we were similar.

Before the letter, I never took the time to question my relationship with my mother. I certainly felt close to her. No matter the distance, I had managed to call her, even from the other side of the world. And after I gave her that laptop for Christmas, not a week went by without a video chat. But what did we even talk about, with our faces side by side on-screen? I couldn't think of a single lasting conversation. Mum would ask about everything happening in my life and my trips around the world. But it often stressed me out to hear how much she worried about me, so I must have sounded evasive at times or, worse, wasted precious time chatting about the weather in classic British fashion.

I thought back to Michel's blunt question as he gobbled down his scone in that drab tearoom. How was it that I cared more about people I didn't even know than about my own family? The question stung more than a slap in the face.

Come on, Elby! How the hell did you let so much of your life pass by without finding out who your own mother really was? Was it out of respect, or because you were scared? Or was it just simple negligence? Of course, the thought that she would be snatched away so suddenly never even crossed your mind. You told yourself you'd ask someday. But someday never came. And now she was gone.

I was surprised to find tears welling up in my eyes. I'm not the emotional type. Well, at least not *that* emotional.

I only knew your good side. How is it that I had to get a letter from an anonymous shit with weird riddles about your bad side to finally be interested in you? Maybe that's why you kept so many secrets: you didn't want to share them with your selfish brat of a daughter. My friends used to get so jealous when I bragged that you were my best friend and I could trust you completely and unconditionally. I knew I could tell you anything. *Anything.*

But you couldn't tell me a thing, because every time I knocked at your door, all our time together was reserved for me, and never for you. I thought of the countless times you took me to school in the morning and then picked me up at night. And the countless times you were cleaning or taking care of everything for us kids. I could *hear* you out there, while I lay in bed, all alone in my room, and I never bothered to venture out and show any interest in you. So proud, with my books and my passion. But the story of your life remained sealed and unread, and now I was left only with blank pages.

Just then, I heard the door to my childhood bedroom creak open, and I turned to find my father staring at me from the hallway.

"Oh, hello, dear. I thought you were at your studio."

"Well, I just wanted to . . . I don't know what I wanted."

Dad came and sat on the edge of the bed.

"The comfort of home, perhaps. What's got you down, sweet pea?"

"Nothing, everything's okay," I assured him.

"Come now. Those eyes of yours are way too red for 'okay.' Problems in your love life? Something about a man?"

"A . . . *what?*"

"You know, I myself was single for a long time. I recall that being the worst period of my entire life. I was always so afraid of being alone."

"Well, how do you cope with it, now?"

"I'm not alone, I'm a widower. It's not the same thing, not at all. And I have you children."

"Do Maggie and Michel come to see you often when I'm not here?"

"I should hope so, as you're not often here! Anyway, I have dinner with your brother every Thursday. Maggie comes to check on me two or three times a week, never for all that long because she is a busy woman, after all. Busy with what, I don't have a clue . . . But you asked about being lonely? I can tell you, even when you're far away, you're always with me. All I need to do is think of your mother, or one of you kids, and the loneliness just skitters away like a thief in the night."

"I don't believe you."

"You got me. I was lying. How about you tell me what's really got you down?"

"What was Mum doing before she came back to England? Where was she?"

"And there you have it! Silly me, thinking you came because missed your old man so much," said Dad, teasing me as always. Then he gave a weary sigh. "I really can't tell you much, love. She wasn't fond of talk-ing about that period of her life. You know that daft saying—I suppose they're all daft, come to think of it—that the apple doesn't fall far from the tree? Maybe that one's not so daft when it comes to you two. Like mother, like daughter. Truth is, your mother actually had a bit of a career . . . in journalism."

That certainly was a bit of a bombshell. Mum had been a chemistry teacher.

"Your mother excelled in chemistry when she was at university. Then we both abandoned that path around the same time, and she became a journalist. Don't ask me how or why, I never understood the whole thing. When she came back and got pregnant with you and your brother, it didn't take long for us to see my salary alone wasn't going to cut it. She hunted around for a journalism job for a few weeks, but the bigger her belly grew, the quicker those doors would swing shut in her face. The best offer she got was to be the secretary of an editorial board, working for peanuts. Of course, she was livid at the very notion! That a woman—much less a pregnant one—wasn't fit to be offered a *real* job. And that type of rage just won't do when you've got a bun in the oven, much less two. When she finally came to her senses and realized she had to calm down, she decided to return to her first love. Or rather 'loves,' I should say—besides me, of course," Dad added with a wink. "In the run-up to you two being born, she took courses by correspondence to complete her chemistry degree, which you already know. Studying between bouts of morning sickness, she managed to pass. As soon as you were old enough to be away from her, she became a teaching assistant, then did her PGCE to become a full-on science teacher. Your mother was passionate about children. She couldn't get enough of them. I would have liked to have been twelve years old forever just to get to hang around with her all day and be the teacher's pet."

Dad went quiet and ran his hand through his hair, a nervous habit of his on the rare occasion he actually let the conversation veer towards anything deep.

"Elby. I've told you a hundred times: Don't be sad when you think of her. Think back to the special moments you two shared together. How much she loved you, how close you were. Close enough to even make your own father jealous at times, I'll admit. Whether she's dead or not, they can't take that away from you."

Before he even finished his sentence, I had burst into tears and curled up in his arms. *Sure, right. You're not the emotional type, not at all. Just keep telling yourself that.*

"Well, safe to say I've done a great job of cheering you up. Give me another chance, will you? I know just the remedy for this type of heartache. Come on, now! Let's go," my father said, taking me by the hand. "The old Austin is fit as a fiddle once more, so what do you say we splurge on some ice cream, yeah? And I've got news for you, little lady: Croydon now has its very own Ben & Jerry's! If that's not good news, I don't know what is. And now that your sister's wedding is off, to hell with fitting into my dinner jacket!"

"So . . . what newspaper did she work for?" I asked, licking melted chocolate ice cream from my spoon.

"I really don't feel like talking about all that," my father replied, without looking up from his own massive portion of ice cream.

"Why is that?"

"Because I don't want you getting any ideas."

"If you really think you're getting off that easily, then you don't know your own daughter at all."

"Elby, I have to tell you right off: one word of any of this to your brother or sister, and you and I are going to have some real issues."

"Hey, when you call me Elby, I know you mean business."

"Her newspaper was called the *Independent*."

I threw my father a dubious look. Knowing him, he could be pulling my leg just to see how far he could take the joke.

"The *Independent*? The daily paper with some of the most talented voices in journalism today? Which section? Culture? Economy? Hold up, I know . . . the science desk!" I gasped, laughing, emphasizing the ludicrousness of it all.

"It was the Metro section. You know, social issues."

"Are you sure we're talking about the same woman?"

"She was quite keen on politics, and had an exceptional knack for editorials. And you can wipe that snide look off your face, young lady. It's the absolute truth."

"Nice lesson in humility, right? Considering I only write travel chronicles, essentially just hyped-up tourist recommendations."

"Now, don't you start! It's not like any particular subject is more important than another. You transport your readers to distant lands that they'll never set foot in. It's the stuff that dreams are made of! And every single one of your articles is a call for tolerance, which is all too rare these days. You need proof your work is important? Flip open the *Daily Mail*. One glance at that rubbish is all you'll need. Don't belittle what you do, my dear."

"You wouldn't be trying to say . . . you're *proud* of me, would you?"

"Why, because you don't know that already?"

"You never talk about my work."

"Well, maybe that's because . . . because your bloody work keeps you so far away from me! Look, let me buy you another ice cream."

"Dad's favorite antidepressant, results guaranteed," I said with a smile, running my finger along the rim of the bowl and savoring every last drop. "But this stuff has got to be a thousand calories per spoonful, so it might be just a little over-the-top."

"What's wrong with a little over-the-top once in a while? You've got to live sometimes, take a risk or two. Start with the banana split. It's over-the-top in all the right ways!"

Dad came back carting two immense glass bowls, overflowing with perfect banana slices held captive in a prison of absurdly rich ice cream, covered in steaming hot caramel. Delicious as it looked, I was busy tapping away on my smartphone in a frenzy.

"Is that the magazine?" he asked.

"No. I'm digging around for articles by Mum, but I can't find any. It doesn't make any sense. All the big papers have put their archives online, and the *Independent* only puts out a digital edition these days, anyway, so you'd think there'd be something."

My father cleared his throat. "You won't find a thing written by your mother in there."

"What, she didn't use her real name for the byline?"

"No, she did . . . but you've got the wrong *Independent*. The one I mean is from way back when."

"I don't understand. There was another *Independent*?"

"It was a weekly paper. Very short run. See, I might've left out . . . The fact is, your mother actually *started* the paper herself, along with a motley crew of her pals, all mad as hatters, just like her."

"Wait, wait, wait. Mum . . . started her own newspaper?" I repeated, my voice rising. "And you two never thought to mention it? Not even when your own daughter became a journalist?"

"No, it never really occurred to us," my father said. "What's so awful about that? You don't have to make a fuss about it."

"Don't have to make a fuss? Typical. Of course. Never make a fuss in our family. I break my leg. Don't make a fuss. I could have fallen to my death from that roof, and you'd have stood over my dead body saying, 'Don't make a fuss, Elby! You'll be right as rain soon!'"

"Oh, good lord! You were six years old! What was I supposed to do, give you a look of sheer terror and tell you we'd have to amputate?"

"Great. There it is. You found a way to make everything all cheeky and fun again. *This is serious.* Tell me why you kept it from me."

"Because I didn't want you getting any ideas. Remember our daft saying from before, about apples falling . . . ? The one that's not so daft in your case? I knew you'd stop at nothing to impress your mother. If we had told you she had founded a weekly paper, I can't imagine what you'd have done. Run around covering war zones? Or, even worse, try to top your mother, create your very own paper?"

"You make that sound like such a terrible thing!"

"It would have been! That shitty little rag of a newspaper ruined your mother! Financially and emotionally. Quite a price to pay, even for one's dream. Now, for goodness' sake, let's move on before you make me order a third ice cream and I end up in the back of an ambulance."

"Unbelievable," I scoffed. "For once, you're the melodramatic one. This is a historic moment."

"I'm not being melodramatic. Fact is, I'm a bit diabetic."

"What? Since when are you a diabetic?"

"I said 'a bit' diabetic. How long has it been now?" Dad feigned counting on his fingers, breaking into a snide little smile. "Twenty years, give or take a few."

I buried my face in my hands, furious. "You have got to be kidding me. It's like the bloody house of secrets!"

"Come now, Elby. Don't blow things out of proportion. Did you expect me to pin my medical chart to the kitchen wall? Why did you think your mother always gave me such hell every time I tried to get my hands on a packet of biscuits?"

With that, I confiscated my father's ice cream and asked him to drop me off at the station, using the excuse that I had to rush back to London for work.

I hate lying, especially to him. The moment I boarded the train, I took out my phone and called an archivist from the magazine. I had a huge favor to ask.

14

Eleanor-Rigby

October 2016, London

Back at my studio, I sat cross-legged on the couch watching *Absolutely Fabulous*, about to start my third bag of crisps.

Not only was the show a cult classic, but it also happened to serve a vital public service for certain members of society. Take, for example, a woman who might be home alone stuffing her face on a Friday night, feeling guilty about having opened a bottle of wine that she would almost certainly drink all by herself, made all the worse considering the bottle was a gift from a friend who came for dinner, back in the days when she still had friends over for dinner.

Or, another example, picked at random: a woman who catches a look at herself naked in the mirror after stepping out of the shower and feels that it's absolutely absurd that she's still single . . . and then makes the critical error of lingering too long in front of said mirror, and realizes maybe it's not so absurd after all.

For that woman, and others like her, *Ab Fab*'s Patsy and Edina were absolute lifesavers. Genuine saints. Late at night, they come to your rescue, easing your drunken shame by showing you that it could be worse, and giving you another strong dose of reality the next day when your morning hangover reminds you that real life is nothing like TV.

In this episode, Edina and Saffy—her daughter—are arguing, which reminded me of all the fights I had with my own mum. In walks Saffy's grandma, who calms everything down. I never knew my grandparents, and never would, since Mum grew up in an orphanage. The fog around her backstory suddenly seemed to have grown a lot thicker in light of current events. Struck with a thought, I rushed over to grab the troubling letter from my bag.

All we can ever see of our parents is what they wish to show us . . .

But Mum never wanted to show us a single thing.

As I held the letter in my hand, I had a closer look at the stamp on the envelope. I nearly slapped my forehead—what an awful detective I was! The stamp bore an image of the Queen, but the color was different—it wasn't an English stamp at all. Squinting, I could make out a word written in tiny letters beneath Her Majesty's glowing smile: *Canada.* Of course. How could I have missed it? The postmark said Montreal, and it had been right there under my nose the whole time. It begged the question: Just who was this poison-pen writing to me from the other side of the world?

It was only the first of many questions.

The next day, I was flipping through a magazine and watching my laundry in the washing machine spinning around in a dizzying dance when I received a call from the archivist friend I'd contacted. She hadn't found a single trace of a weekly *Independent* in all of England. Thinking of the stamp, I asked her to extend her search to the other side of the Atlantic.

One hour later, I opened up my postbox down in the lobby and made another discovery. There, standing out amongst the fliers and ads, was a second letter. I recognized the beautiful handwriting immediately. I stumbled out of the lobby—straight by a worried neighbor, who told me I looked pale—and returned to the flat, still light-headed as I tore the envelope open.

It contained nothing more than a single sheet of lined paper bearing a short and cryptic message:

October 22, 7 p.m. Sailor's Hideaway, Baltimore.

It was the nineteenth. That left less than three days.

I began rushing about, throwing my toiletry bag and other essentials pell-mell into a carry-on bag before realizing I hadn't even bought a ticket yet. I ran to my computer, hunted down a last-minute ticket, and hit "Buy Now." *Insufficient funds.* Shit. With my heart racing in my chest, I called Maggie up in the hope she could lend me the cash.

"About that . . ." I could hear her wincing. "It turns out there's some truth to the story I told Dad about problems with overdraft at the bank." Being an absolute expert on all my sister's shortcomings, I knew for a fact she wasn't a cheapskate, so I took her at her word.

"How about you tell me why you need two thousand pounds so desperately?" she asked. "Are you in deep shit or something?"

I told Maggie about the strange new letter. She immediately flew off the handle and started ranting and raving about what a mistake it was. What the hell was I thinking, putting myself at the mercy of a lunatic, just to get kidnapped and murdered and have my ravaged corpse thrown into the sea? Why else would the poison-pen set up a nighttime encounter at a place called Sailor's Hideaway?

Maggie has a wild imagination that concocts outlandish things, most of which tend to be macabre. My counterargument far from convinced her: If a maniac were really trying to lure in his prey, wouldn't he lay the traps a bit closer to home? It seemed like a whole lot of trouble making his victim cross the ocean, with perfectly decent murder victims just next door. *A logical point.*

"Aha!" Maggie exclaimed. "Not so fast. You disappear so far from home, there's a better chance no one would ever realize."

"It's not like the poison-pen asked to meet in the middle of the woods somewhere," I pointed out. "It's Baltimore!"

Maggie went silent and gave up. She knew me well enough to know that I had made up my mind and would stop at nothing to see this through.

"What about asking your magazine for an advance on travel expenses? Isn't traveling part of your job, or am I a blubbering imbecile?"

I was the blubbering imbecile, to use her beautifully poetic words. The thought hadn't crossed my mind. I hung up on my sister midsentence and called my editor in chief. By the time he picked up, I had already contrived an angle for the article. The magazine was long overdue for a feature on Baltimore. After all, the city had some intense urban renewal underway, not to mention one of the largest commercial ports on the East Coast. We could also do a sidebar on Johns Hopkins University (the article was writing itself—thanks, Wikipedia!). Why not highlight the Reginald F. Lewis Museum, a center for African American history?

When I paused, my editor grunted out his indifference, not quite sold on the pitch. "Baltimore isn't exactly sexy stuff, you know."

"Oh, I beg to differ. It's sexy, all right. And undiscovered."

Another grunt, but with a little more interest this time. "Let's say you're right. Why Baltimore, out of the blue?"

"Because no one knows about it, and I'm out to remedy that!"

Right in the nick of time, I made a serendipitous discovery at the bottom of the screen, the perfect weapon for a masterful coup de grace. My boss had a well-documented Edgar Allan Poe obsession, and since the illustrious poet had been kind enough to make Baltimore his final resting place, I pitched using Poe to tie the feature together, complete with a perfectly pompous title: *Baltimore and the Last Days of Edgar Allan Poe.*

Before I even got to "Poe," my boss had burst out laughing. I couldn't blame him.

"Easy, tiger," he said, composing himself. "How about you just stick with the economic resurgence angle, how far the city has come and all that, how it's growing into an appealing destination for students. Engage with locals, take the city's pulse. The elections are just a few weeks away, and I'm not convinced Trump is going to get the epic ass-whooping all the polls are predicting. So, fine. I'll sign off on a one-week assignment. Accounting will send your funds through tomorrow. And take a nice snapshot of Edgar Allan Poe's tombstone for me, will you? You never know."

Under normal circumstances, I would have literally jumped for joy at having convinced my editor to green-light a story I came up with all on my own. But not tonight. While my job was entirely built on leaping into the unknown, I had a sinking feeling that this trip would uncover things of a whole different nature. And for once, my courage was faltering.

In any event, I couldn't leave England without saying goodbye to my family. Seeing Maggie was pointless; she would just berate me again and do everything within her power to change my mind. I had a feeling Dad wouldn't take the news very well either, considering I had promised to stay in London longer this time around. But I was most concerned about telling Michel. Even though it was already late, I called him and asked if I could drop by.

"You . . . want to come here? Why?"

My silence told Michel everything he needed to know. He sighed. "When are you leaving?" he asked.

"Tomorrow, an early-afternoon flight."

"Will you be gone for a long time?"

"No. I'll be back soon, I promise. A week, ten days at the most."

"Are you hungry? I can go down to the corner shop and buy us something for dinner, for example."

"That sounds great. You and I are long overdue for a one-on-one."

Just after getting off the phone, Michel turned to Vera Morton and announced that his sister was on her way.

"Would you be very cross if we were to share this meal that you've prepared with my sister?" Michel asked Vera.

"No, not in the least bit. It's just that I hadn't really thought she'd find out about us like this."

While the way Michel spoke could sometimes lack subtlety, his eyes were a dead giveaway. Vera instantly understood. She grabbed her jacket, checked over the table, and returned the wineglasses to the cabinet. After all, Michel would have never thought to put those out on his own. Everything now sorted, Vera took her leave.

I rang the doorbell, and my brother appeared in the doorway, wearing a kitchen apron, of all things. Without a word, he ushered me into the living room, where the surprises just kept on coming. I never imagined he'd go to such trouble for me. He slipped into the kitchen and returned with a piping-hot casserole that he placed carefully on a trivet. I sat down and lifted the lid. Steam wafted up toward my nose, and my stomach growled in response.

"Since when do you know how to cook?"

"Unless I'm mistaken, this marks the first time you've ever visited before leaving. Or should I say, before leaving in such a hurry. Thus, I thought long and hard after receiving your call, and naturally concluded that something was wrong, something you didn't wish to speak of on the telephone. And that's why you have come. A logical analysis."

"Sure, but even a logical analysis can be wrong. Especially with a sister as complicated as yours."

"Yes, that's correct. And yet—"

"And yet," I interjected, "everything is *fine*, love. I just wanted to spend some time with you."

Michel stared up at the light fixture hanging above us and took a deep breath. "And yet . . . you didn't want Dad or Maggie to hear what you have to tell me. There's something wrong with your logic."

"My advice for the duration of the evening is not to dig too deep for logic, because I can assure you there's none to be found here. But don't let that bother you. I came because I have a secret to tell you. You weren't totally off the mark; I'm not really leaving for a story, even if I did manage to bill the whole thing to the magazine—which, I admit, wasn't the most honest thing to do, but it's for a good cause. And I'll still write the dumb story, or at least I'll try."

"None of that makes any sense. *Where* exactly is it that you're not going for your magazine?"

"Baltimore."

Michel rubbed his chin. "Intriguing. Cecilius Calvert, second Baron Baltimore, was the first governor of the Maryland colony. Did you know there is a coastal city in southwestern Ireland of the same name? Why not simply go to that Baltimore? It's far closer."

"I didn't know any of that. Remind me—how do you know so much?"

"I read often. Books, mostly."

"Well, I'll never understand how you manage to remember so much."

"How could I forget something, if I've read it?"

"Most people do. But, hey—you're not most people."

"Is that a good thing?"

"Of course it is, just like I tell you every time."

Michel served me a nice chicken wing from the casserole dish, opting for a thigh himself, then looked me in the eye and waited for more.

"I'm leaving . . . on a search to find Mum," I told him.

"That's wonderful, although I'm afraid your search could be fruitless, as I'm rather convinced she's not in Baltimore. In fact, no one really knows where dead people go. Certainly not into the sky; it could never support the weight. For my part, I favor the theory of an alternate dimension. Are you familiar with the alternate dimension theory?"

I laid my hand on Michel's forearm to cut the tangent short, staring right at him so he would listen to my every word.

"It was just a manner of speaking. I'm leaving on a search to find Mum's past."

"Why, did she lose it?"

"No, but she lied about it. She never told us much about her youth."

"That's probably precisely the way she wanted it. I don't believe it's a very good idea to go against her wishes."

"I miss her as much as you do. But I'm a woman, so I need to know who my mother really was . . . to finally be able to grow up, or at least to be able to understand who I really am."

"You're my twin sister," he said, as though the answer was clear as day. "Why Baltimore?"

"I'm supposed to meet somebody there."

"Someone who knew her?"

"I assume so."

"And you, do you know this someone?"

"No, I don't have a clue who it is."

I told my brother about the letter without revealing any of its specific contents. I didn't want to worry him, and I knew it didn't take much to knock Michel off-balance. Instead, I concocted a beautiful little fantasy, using the art of embellishment that I had come to master as a professional necessity.

"So, if I understand correctly," he began, forefinger raised in his signature way, "you will depart for a distant city in hopes of meeting someone you do not know. Someone who, as you claim, is supposed to tell you things you don't know about your own mother, things that will help you know who you are . . . . I'm beginning to understand why my doctor is so eager to meet you."

My brother's deadpan humor always caught me off guard. Michel paused for a moment, then rose to his feet, dead serious now.

"Mum worked in Baltimore," he said, dropping the bomb and then departing for the kitchen with our dishes in hand.

I leapt to my feet and followed my brother, joining him as he began washing the dishes.

"How do you know that?" I asked.

"Because she told me that was the place where she spent the happiest days of her life."

"What a lovely message to give her own child!"

"I made the same observation, but she was quick to clarify: happiest days *before* we were born."

"Michel, please. I'm begging you here. Tell me everything Mum told you."

"She was in love with somebody there," he said matter-of-factly as he handed me a tea towel. "Although she never specifically admitted it. On the rare occasions she mentioned Baltimore, she seemed rather sad. As she claimed to have spent some of the happiest days of her life there—albeit, prior to our birth—this was not a very logical connection. I therefore deduced that perhaps she suffered from nostalgia, and in all the books I've read, such contradictions seem to always involve a love story."

"She never mentioned a name?"

"She never mentioned anything, as you would know from my prior statement, had you been listening carefully."

Michel put away the rest of the dishes and took off his apron.

"I must sleep now, or else tomorrow I'll be tired and I won't perform my tasks adequately. Don't tell Dad about this. I entrusted you with this secret because you have confided in me as well. It was in the spirit of equal exchange. And even though the rest is just mere conjecture— conjecture that I am fully confident about, but nonetheless—I fear that

Dad's feelings might be hurt. Men always feel worse knowing their wife loved another before them, rather than not knowing it at all. Or at least, that's the case in the majority of books I've read. It seems far-fetched that such a trend would come solely from the imaginations of writers, wouldn't you say?"

My brother had started nervously nodding his head. I knew any more questions might push him over the edge, so I decided to drop it for the night. His yawns told me it was time to go. I waited in the living room as he ducked off—for what seemed like ages—to retrieve my jacket. When at last he returned, he seemed to have calmed down. He draped my coat around my shoulders with a tender look in his eyes that let me know he wanted a hug. I took my brother in my arms and held him tight.

I promised I would call from Baltimore to give him a full report on the city, and, of course, to fill him in on anything I uncovered about Mum. It was a bald-faced lie. I had no way of knowing if I would find any answers at all. Everything now rested on a critical encounter with an anonymous correspondent. The outlook was pretty grim.

The next morning, I called Dad with a major favor to ask: I needed him to give Maggie the news that I was heading off.

"Well, you certainly have got some nerve asking me something like that!"

I had to admit, sometimes cowardice can lead to pure genius. I could almost hear the sad smile on my father's face as we spoke. Just like Michel, he had started by asking where I was headed and if I would be gone for a long time—the exact set of questions I was always asked before my trips. I told my dad how much I would miss him and apologized for not being able to say goodbye face-to-face. My flight was too early, especially considering I still had to drop by the office to get the ticket. This, of course, was just another lie. Plane tickets had gone electronic a long time ago. The truth was, I didn't have the heart to look him in the eye and feed him some half-baked story, especially knowing how hard he'd grill me about why I was really leaving in such a hurry.

I called Maggie during the cab ride to Heathrow, letting her know from the start that I'd hang up if she started to lecture me. She made me promise to keep her informed on all my discoveries. As always, traffic was bumper-to-bumper around the airport, and the last stretch was so bad I began to fear I would miss my flight. As we pulled in, I could tell it was going to be tight.

On your marks, get set, go! I leapt from the taxi, scrambled across the terminal, ran up the escalator two steps at a time, begged for forgiveness again and again as I cut to the front of the line, and made it to the security check with "last call for boarding" flashing ominously in red on-screen next to my flight number.

I rushed toward the X-ray scanner and dropped my keys and iPhone onto a tray. Then, as I rummaged through my jacket pocket, I was shocked as my fingers landed on a worn leather pouch. I had never seen it before and didn't have a clue how it got there. I had definitely been running too fast for even someone sneaky to slip anything in. There was no time to figure it out. I took off my shoes, finally made it through the metal detectors, snatched up my things, pushed my way past several more people, and took off running again. As my gate came into view, I shouted an impassioned plea to the flight attendant at the ticket scanner, panting and nearly collapsing as I apologetically handed over my boarding pass. Then, I tore down the gangway like a madwoman. The overhead compartment was jam-packed, and cramming my bag inside took the very last ounce of energy I had left. I slumped into my seat, completely knackered.

As the doors closed and we readied for takeoff, I fastened my seat belt and finally had a closer look at the mysterious pouch in my pocket. I found an old envelope inside, yellowed with age, along with a little note Michel had scribbled out for me.

Elby,

This pouch belonged to Mum. It originally contained a necklace, which I removed and replaced with this old letter. The letter was originally kept in a wooden box, which also belonged to Mum. As you might imagine, the dimensions of the box were so large, it would never have fit inside the pocket of your jacket. Mum gave me the wooden box to make sure Dad didn't find it while they were repainting their flat. There are many other letters inside the wooden box. This one was at the top of the stack. I promised Mum I'd never read them. I never have. You did not make any such promise, so you may do what you wish. When you come back, if you haven't yet found what you're looking for, I will give you the other letters. Be careful. I will miss you. Actually, I'd like to tell you something that for reasons I cannot quite grasp I am unable to tell you face-to-face, that in fact, I miss you all the time.

Signed,

Your brother

I put away Michel's note and had a closer look at the old envelope, confirming a hunch. The letter had been postmarked in Montreal.

15

May

September 1980, Baltimore

May had spent the entire evening poring over résumés and cover letters. The project had to be kept under wraps as long as possible, so all outreach had to be through unconventional means. They had to pique the interest of journalists, copy editors, librarians, and designers, all without drawing any unwanted attention.

By the time midnight rolled around, there was still no sign of Sally-Anne, and May began to feel antsy. At three in the morning, when she saw Keith drop her off down on the sidewalk below, she was positively livid. To think those two were out living it up while May slaved away late into the night.

She heard Sally-Anne come into the room, slide into bed beside her, and ask how she was doing. May rolled over and turned her back to her, pretending she was asleep.

The silent treatment carried over into the next morning. May tore open job applications, blatantly ignoring Sally-Anne, even after she had gone to the trouble of fixing them both breakfast.

"Will you stop it already, May? I'm supposed to be the trust-fund baby, and you're the one pouting like a spoilt child. You know I love you more than anybody. I just . . . also enjoy men. Does that make me a bad person? Keith is gorgeous, he's strong—all with that surprisingly soft touch—and we're both hooked on him. So what? What's wrong with just sharing him? Men do it all the time. Why can't we? I highly doubt that Keith is bothered by the arrangement. Who the hell is still bothering with monogamy at all these days anyway?"

"I am!"

"Really. Are you now?"

May avoided her eyes, aware of her own hypocrisy.

"And if you try to tell me you're actually *in love* with him, I'll laugh in your face," Sally-Anne continued. "Honestly, I'd prefer hearing about the ways he makes you come."

"Enough already. I don't need lectures from you on morality, Sally-Anne. I may not be a saint, and I'm certainly not blind to our society's mores, I just choose not to live by them. So, as much as you might not want to hear it, I'm actually more progressive than you because I still choose to believe in true love."

"Please don't tell me you're talking about Keith! I mean, don't get me wrong. It's not every day you find a man that attentive, that's for sure. The fact is, you threw yourself at him because he's great in bed, *full stop*, to borrow your catchphrase. Now, can we please just stop fighting? Let me buy you lunch. I've got the perfect spot. There's this brand-new oyster bar that just opened on the waterfront called Sailor's Hideaway. They get oysters in fresh from Maine every morning, and they are to die for."

"Is that where you two went for dinner last night?"

"Damn! I totally forgot," Sally-Anne said with a groan, her face falling. "I have to have lunch with my brother. Listen, if you still love me at all, even a little? Come with me. No one gets under my skin like he does."

"Then why are you having lunch with him?"

"He asked to see me. I don't have a choice."

"I'll hitch a ride with you into the city, but as for your sibling date, you're on your own."

◆ ◆ ◆

They didn't even make it out the door until past one o'clock. May had put some makeup on, having agreed to at least meet the brother, and Sally-Anne teased her incessantly for it. Then they roared away on the Triumph, not slowing even once before coming to a screeching halt in front of the Baltimore Country Club.

The valet raised his eyebrows, admiring both the bike and its riders. The doorman bowed extra low for Sally-Anne, and May watched with surprise at the respect she was shown at every turn, totally in awe of the opulent surroundings. An elegant maître d' popped up to accompany the two women, and they continued down lavishly decorated corridors beneath portraits of high-society men in ornate gilded frames, until they at last entered the dining room. The maître d' led them to the Stanfield table—reserved year-round exclusively for the family—where Sally-Anne's brother, Edward, sat waiting. He sighed as his sister approached, not even bothering to look up from his newspaper.

"Late as usual. Vintage Sally-Anne."

"Nice to see you, too," she replied.

Edward looked up at last and noticed May hovering behind his sister. "Aren't you going to introduce me to your friend?"

"Oh, she's quite capable of introducing herself, believe it or not," Sally-Anne replied coolly.

Edward rose to his feet and bowed, kissing May's hand. She smiled, blushing at the old-fashioned greeting, and fought hard not to burst out laughing. The silky-smooth etiquette was jarring compared to how he had greeted his sister. And yet, May had to admit, she found the chivalry sweet.

"I'll duck out and let you two catch up," May said, embarrassed.

"I wouldn't dream of it!" Edward said. "Please join us, we'd be delighted. Besides, who knows? With a bit of luck, having you here might help keep the lunchtime fisticuffs at bay." Grinning playfully, he pulled out a chair for her.

"Wow, is it really that bad between you two?" asked May.

"Like oil and water," Sally-Anne said.

"The pair of you are behaving like children, you know. You should be grateful instead of acting like spoiled brats. I used to wish I had a brother."

"Not this one, sweetheart." Sally-Anne sighed. "Believe me!"

"Jab at me all you like, you're just going to make your friend more uncomfortable." Still smiling, Edward leaned in and studied them closely. "So, what exactly are you two ladies up to? It must be salacious, considering this is the very first I've heard of you."

"Why would you have heard of her?" Sally-Anne asked. "Are you trying to tell me you people still actually sit around discussing me? I thought my name hadn't even been uttered inside that house in ages."

"You thought wrong, dear sister. You'd know, if you actually deigned to visit your own family from time to time."

"Nice try, but I'm not buying it."

May cleared her throat, coughing into her own hand.

"We're business partners," she began, stopping abruptly as she received a sharp kick from Sally-Anne under the table.

"*Partners?*" repeated Edward.

"In a manner of speaking; we work in the same department," Sally-Anne corrected.

"Don't tell me you're still at the *Sun*?" Edward scoffed.

"And where else would I be?"

"I've been asking myself that same question. Considering I heard you quit the paper at the start of summer."

"Well, you heard wrong," May interjected. "Your sister has made herself indispensable in the newsroom. As a matter of fact, she might even get bumped up to reporter one of these days."

"Imagine that! I certainly didn't mean to spread unfounded rumors. That's very impressive. And how about you, May? What do you do at the *Sun*?"

The meal quickly shifted into a getting-to-know-you session as Edward peppered May with endless questions. Sally-Anne was unbothered by her brother's curiosity. At the very least, May was drawing attention away from her, thus sparing Sally-Anne a considerable amount of scrutiny and drivel. Sally-Anne wasn't fooled at all by these quarterly lunches with Edward; she knew that they were intel-gathering missions for the Stanfield clan. Edward was a dirty little mole, a double agent working for their mother. After all, Hanna Stanfield had far too much pride for a face-to-face investigation into her daughter's "decadent lifestyle." Hence the convenient coincidence that every time Sally-Anne came to the country club, the Stanfield matriarch was nowhere to be found, a marked break from her daily routine.

As Edward motioned to a waiter for more coffee, he casually asked if May was fond of the theater. A renowned company would be premiering Harold Pinter's *Betrayal* in Baltimore the following evening, hot on the heels of a New York run that had wowed critics and audiences. "It is an absolute masterpiece, an experience not to be missed under any circumstances," Edward declared. He explained that a friend had given him tickets for a pair of amazing seats at the premiere, but he had no one to accompany him.

"Does this mean you're all done with that blonde?" Sally-Anne asked innocently. "She was a knockout. What was her name again? You know who I'm talking about . . . Zimmer's daughter?"

"Jennifer and I decided to take some time apart to see where we really stand going forward," Edward replied with utmost gravity and sincerity. "Everything was moving a bit too fast."

"What a pity. That must have come as such a disappointment to our poor mother. Jennifer was quite rich, after all."

"That's quite enough, Sally-Anne. No need to be rude."

Edward signaled for the bill and quickly scrawled his signature, charging the meal to the family account, before rising to his feet.

"Tomorrow night, seven o'clock sharp. I'll be waiting for you in the lobby by the ticket booth. Don't forget: I'm counting on you," he told May, then bowed once more to kiss her hand.

Edward then turned and gave his sister a cold, obligatory peck on the cheek. As soon as he walked out, Sally-Anne waved the waiter over and ordered two cognacs.

"Don't even think about going!" she warned May, swirling the amber liquid around in her glass.

May sighed. "Did it even occur to you how many years of scraping and saving it would take for me to get to see Pinter onstage? I can't even afford the nosebleeds."

"I'm telling you: it's a rotten idea. Even the name of the play is no mistake, I guarantee."

"You don't have to be so dramatic about it. It's one night."

"Don't underestimate my brother. He'll play you. It's his very favorite pastime, and he's a master at it. He takes down way bigger game without breaking a sweat, so if you want to keep a shred of your dignity, stay the hell away from him."

"Dignity? Who said anything about dignity?" May replied, giving Sally-Anne a nice little elbow to the ribs.

◆ ◆ ◆

The next day, May luxuriated in the bath before her date with Edward. Sally-Anne entered and sat down on the edge of the bathtub, a cigarette between her lips. She stared wordlessly at May, and the silence felt interminable.

"Don't start with the looks again!" May said. "I'll come home right after the curtain call. I promise."

"We'll see about that. But you can't say I didn't warn you. Just don't forget: not a word to Edward about the paper."

"Oh, I know. My shin got that memo yesterday. What exactly went down between you two? You never talk about him. I almost forgot you even had a brother. I don't understand why you—"

"Because they're all complete frauds, every last one of them. The glory of the Stanfields . . . is nothing but a tall tale. It's all smoke and mirrors. My mother is like a queen reigning over an empire of lies, with my father as her spineless stooge."

"Don't you think that's going a little overboard? Your dad is a war hero."

"I don't remember ever telling you that."

"You didn't. Someone else did."

"Who?"

"I heard it around. People talk." May hesitated a moment, then sighed and gave in. "Fine. You really want to know? After we . . . became intimate, I did some research on you here and there. Don't be mad. It is our job, after all! Comes with the territory, right? You could even think of it as a compliment; it shows just how interested I was in you. In any event, I never heard one bad thing about your parents, least of all your father. The man is widely admired. He's a perfect success story."

"He's not who you think he is. And that success was my mother's, not his. She paid dearly for it, more than you could know."

"What does that mean?"

"Sorry, darlin'. We may be 'intimate,' but we're not quite there yet," said Sally-Anne, closing the lid on the conversation.

May sat up in the bathtub and took Sally-Anne's hand, gradually guiding it to her bare breasts. She titled her head upwards and kissed her passionately.

"You're trying to tell me that's not intimate enough for you?"

But Sally-Anne pushed her away softly. "Brother and sister in the same night? Wouldn't that be a little uncouth, my sweet May?"

With that, Sally-Anne walked out of the bathroom, grabbed her jacket, and left the loft.

Sally-Anne, May would learn, had been right about everything.

◆ ◆ ◆

It was an exquisite night, in which everything unfolded magically. The play exceeded all expectations: an astounding tour de force with remarkable performances. Far from a vaudeville piece charting the escapades of a couple in an extramarital affair, the play revolved around the importance of what was left unsaid. The subject matter hit rather close to home for May, who couldn't help but think of the double life she had been leading for the past few months. In their love triangle, the secret lover was clearly Keith. In that case, who exactly was the betrayed, Sally-Anne or May?

All at once, May was filled with a sudden, desperate urge for something *normal*. It was like a breath of fresh air to spend the evening with a man who made proper conversation without swearing like a sailor, and wore an actual suit instead of work clothes. Just one night in classier company, away from the rough cast of characters running rampant through her life.

Her friends would always ask to bum cigarettes, while tonight it was Edward who offered her one from his own pack. Silly as it seemed, even the fact that he used a proper lighter—and an expensive one at that—left an impression on May. Edward lit her cigarette like a proper gentleman, leaning in close with the flame. He politely asked where she'd like to go for dinner, treating her with respect instead of making the decision for her. Ironically enough, May ended up choosing Sailor's Hideaway. A fitting choice, as despite Edward's charm, Sally-Anne was still very much on May's mind, and in her heart.

With unfinished wood floors, tables, and chairs, and waitstaff wearing fishmongers' aprons, Sailor's Hideaway was obviously nothing like the restaurants Edward frequented. He put up with all of it, to the great delight of his date. When May saw that Edward ate his oysters with a fork, she opened another and brought it up to his lips.

"Smell that, take it in," she said with a smile. "You've got to relish the taste, right in the salt water itself. It's amazing, you'll see."

Edward did as she asked, savoring the flavor. "Okay, you're right, I have to admit. It's better that way."

"And now, a sip of white wine—tell me that's not the most amazing combination."

"How in the world did you ever find this place?" Edward asked.

"I live around the corner."

"So, this is how you spend your evenings. I certainly do envy you."

"How does a man like you end up envying someone like me?"

"The life you lead," he said, with a sweeping gesture around the space. "It's freedom. Everything is simple, full of joy."

"I take it you spend your nights in a prison? Or maybe the morgue?" May asked.

"You can poke fun at me all you want, but that's not so far from the truth. The establishments I frequent can be fairly grim, the patrons stilted and cold."

"Like you?"

Edward looked May in the eye.

"Yes, like me," he replied evenly, then leaned in closer. "Would you mind if I asked you a favor?"

"Ask. And we'll see if I mind."

"Would you consider helping me? To change myself."

May studied her date, finding his vulnerability endearing. But all at once she came to her senses and burst out laughing.

"Give me a break!"

"Am I that ridiculous?"

"Sally-Anne warned me about you, but I think you're even more dangerous than she let on."

"My sister can be judgmental," Edward said. "But listen. I have a confession to make. As long as you promise not to tell Sally-Anne."

"Fine. I would spit in my palm, but I don't want to embarrass you."

"The way things are between the two of us is entirely my fault. I envy my sister almost as much as I admire her. She certainly is braver than me. After all, she broke free from her chains and ran away."

"Sally-Anne has her flaws, too."

"Hers are exceptions; mine are the rule."

"I, me, mine. Four times total in the last thirty seconds."

"I rest my case. You see just how serious the situation is, how much I need you?"

May resisted the urge to roll her eyes. "And just what could I do to help such a deeply unhappy man?"

"You can't call a man unhappy . . . when he doesn't even understand what happiness is."

Not even the greatest masters of the art of seduction would have been able to come up with such a line. May's last defenses soon yielded to her nurturing instincts. She led Edward down to the waterfront and kissed him at the end of a long dock.

It was as though Sally-Anne's words were ringing out from a distance over the calm waters . . .

"They're all complete frauds, every last one of them. The glory of the Stanfields . . . is nothing but a tall tale. It's all smoke and mirrors."

16

Robert Stanfield

March 1944, Hawkinge Airfield, Kent

It was a perfect night for flying. The twinkling stars cast just enough light for visual flight, while the glow of the crescent moon was weak enough to obscure the Lysander's dark frame, improving its chances of crossing enemy lines undetected. As the two-passenger plane was prepared for takeoff on the dirt runway, Robert Stanfield checked and rechecked his harnesses from the back seat. He heard the radial engine sputter to life and make the propellers spin, first choppy, then steady. As the mechanic pulled out the chocks, the small plane lurched forward with a jolt and started rolling down the runway.

The Royal Air Force base, located just seven miles west of Dover, had played a vital role during the Dunkirk evacuation of 1940, aiding in the emergency airlift of soldiers from the battlefield. It continued to be a crucial operations base until the 91st Squadron abandoned the site for Westhampnett. Now, it served solely as a refueling station for aircraft traveling long distances over France.

Special Agent Stanfield had landed in England two months earlier, after a risky transatlantic crossing. German submarines prowled the waters like steel sharks, ready to torpedo any prey that crossed in front of their periscopes.

From the moment Robert set foot on British soil, he had worked hard to master the French language, just one part of the intensive sixty-day training regime for his mission. Over those long weeks, his superiors thoroughly tested his aptitude. He memorized the drop zone's geography and topography, the names of surrounding villages, and colloquial expressions he could use to charm the locals. Robert also committed key players to memory, keeping careful tabs on who could be trusted and who might be playing both sides.

The previous evening, around dusk, an officer had knocked on the young agent's door. Robert had packed up his gear, including fake ID, transit papers, revolver, and a map of the Montauban area.

The three-hour flight would push the Lysander to the limits of its radius of action, all six hundred miles, as planned, provided the weather didn't change along the way.

Robert's mission was not to wage war, but rather to prepare for it. The Allied Forces were keeping their disembarkation plans shrouded in absolute secrecy. Once Allied troops had advanced into the heart of the French theater, one key condition for victory would be to supply the supporting forces with weapons and munitions. For months, the English had been airdropping equipment, which the French Resistance then had to stealthily recover and hide.

Stanfield was assigned to serve as liaison officer. His mission was to make contact with a local Resistance leader and acquire crucial intel in order to map out the warehouse locations. The mission would run for one month, at which point a second Lysander would come and take Robert back to England.

Robert's fate had been sealed one evening at a Washington, DC, gala dinner in the winter of 1943. His parents had come to mingle with other wealthy American families being solicited for contributions to the war effort. While the Stanfields were eager to maintain appearances, at that point their riches had all but disappeared. Robert's father, who was afflicted with an all-consuming gambling addiction, had squandered the entire family fortune. Yet the proud family carried on their lavish life-style, living far beyond their means and racking up crippling debts that dug them deeper into financial ruin. Robert was twenty-eight years old at the time. He was well aware of the consequences of his father's reck-lessness, which strained their relationship to a breaking point. Robert harbored dreams of saving the family, restoring the Stanfields to their former glory and wealth.

That night, as Robert was scanning the faces of the guests around the table, he noticed an understated man, slight of frame, with a gaunt face and receding hairline. It was Edward Wood, British ambassador and the Earl of Halifax, who found himself sidelined by Churchill and Roosevelt's habit of direct communication. Wood hadn't stopped star-ing at Robert throughout the entire meal, including during the inau-gural address. Everything that night was exquisite: the grand hall, the gleaming china, the impeccably dressed women, the heaping platters of delicacies, the magnificent address. Yet Wood was transfixed by Robert, because his own son had been about the same age when he'd died in the war one year earlier. Eventually, the two began speaking at their table in hushed tones about the war effort.

"I'm not talking about giving money," Robert whispered to the older man. "I'm talking about devoting myself to the cause."

"Then enlist. Isn't that what people your age do?" Wood asked.

"Not in families like mine, not with my parents. I managed to avoid the draft due to some obscure, made-up medical issue. My father's doing, I've no doubt."

"Assuming that's true, that he could exert such influence, you shouldn't hold it against him. I'm sure your father simply acted out of fear of losing his son. Quite a burden to bear, watching one's children go away to war."

"And what of the child's burden? Being branded a coward. Is that somehow better?"

"Ah, to be young again. Such intensity, such idealism. It is truly commendable. But do you have any notion of what war is, my boy? I railed against the march of war with every fiber of my being. I even went to Hitler personally in hopes of averting the conflict."

"You met Hitler? The man himself?"

"Indeed, I did. Although 'man' may be too lofty a title for such a creature. Actually, Hitler came to greet me on the doorstep of the house where I was staying, and like a fool, I went to hand him my coat, mistaking him for the butler! Imagine that. It was very nearly a massive diplomatic incident, caused by yours truly!" he snickered.

The Earl of Halifax certainly was an elusive and complex figure. He viewed racism and nationalism as two natural forces that weren't necessarily immoral in nature. When in service to His Majesty as the Viceroy of India, Wood had had all members of the Indian Congress arrested, and even threw Gandhi behind bars. While Wood was a bigot, an arch-conservative, and a staunch supporter of Chamberlain, he refused any level of compromise with the Third Reich, and even turned down the post of prime minister, contending that Churchill was a better choice to lead Britain through its darkest hour.

"Perhaps we should continue this conversation in private, if you're interested," Wood told the young man at the end of the meal. "Come to my office, and I'll see what I can do for you."

A few days later, the ambassador greeted Robert in Washington and connected him with a friend working in the secret service.

By Christmas Eve, Robert was aboard a cargo ship set for distant lands, watching Baltimore's twinkling lights fade into the distance.

The Lysander had been torn apart by a storm over Limousin, and now the pilot was barely able to maintain trajectory. With the propeller seriously damaged, it was a dangerous gamble to try and maintain altitude above the canopy of clouds. Yet dropping any lower would expose them to a whole host of other dangers. Agent Stanfield wasn't faring much better than the plane. He clutched his harness so tightly his knuckles were white, and his stomach dropped every time they hit an air pocket. The leading edges of the wings were so battered, they seemed ready to tear at any moment. The pilot had no choice but to seek refuge at lower altitude, the outcome inevitable. The Lysander plummeted a thousand feet through the thick curtain of rain, the needle on the fuel gauge quivering frantically. Suddenly, the motor sputtered and died altogether just another thousand feet above the ground, leaving seconds to maneuver a crash-landing.

The pilot jerked the plane toward a flat strip of land near a patch of woods. The wheels first grazed the surface of the wet marsh, then took a nosedive straight into it. The propeller, still spinning, shattered as it hit the ground, and the plane's tail was thrust up into the air. Robert felt himself being thrown forward, slamming hard in his seat as the plane flipped. He was the lucky one. The canopy over the cockpit was crushed flat on impact, killing the pilot instantly. Robert was miraculously unharmed, aside from a deep gash on his face and intense bruises from the harness. But he wasn't safe yet. Upside down, Robert felt gas dripping onto him from the fuel tank below the seat.

He finally managed to fight his way out of the wreckage and crawled through the torrential downpour, barely making it to the small patch of woods before losing consciousness.

The next day, local villagers stumbled upon what was left of the Lysander. They buried the pilot, set the fuselage ablaze, and dispatched a search party to look for any survivors. They found Robert Stanfield unconscious at the foot of a tree. The young man was taken to a farm, where he could rest and receive medical care. A country doctor revived him and dressed his wounds. The following night, Robert was driven to a hunting lodge deep in the woods, a safe house that the Resistance used as a weapons cache. There, in a tunnel below the hunting lodge, of all places, was where Robert first met Sam Goldstein. He and his sixteen-year-old daughter had been hiding there for the past six months. Hanna Goldstein had red hair, fair skin, and piercing blue eyes with the hardened glint of a prizefighter's—a young woman so stunning, she made time stand still.

17

George-Harrison

October 2016, Eastern Townships, Quebec

I wrapped the chest of drawers in blankets and loaded it into my pickup, strapping it down so it would be safe for the trip. Magog is a picturesque little town just north of Lake Memphremagog, where everyone knows each other and life flows in rhythm with the seasons. The boon of summer tourism keeps the whole town afloat for the rest of the year. The lake tapers down to a narrow point, and the southern half extends across the border into the United States. In the heyday of Prohibition, ships carrying forbidden cargo would glide across those waters, protected by the night. Imagine that!

Pierre Tremblay was my most loyal customer, the owner of an antique store specializing in rustic furniture. If you know what you're doing, there are plenty of ways to make furniture appear older than it is. A few strategically placed chisel marks here, some light blowtorch work there, a dash of the right acid and varnish in the right spots. You could add a hundred years in a day.

If a hesitant customer wanted to know how old something was, Pierre always muttered something like "turn of the century." It wasn't technically a lie, since he never said *what* century.

One look at my latest creation, and Pierre slapped my shoulder and delivered his favorite words of praise. "What can I say? GH, you're a class act!" Sure. A class act at fraud. But he was careful to leave that last part out, and I was grateful for the omission. I did feel an occasional pang of guilt when I would have dinner at La Mère Denise and hear Denise herself bragging about the "authentic touch" her newly acquired antique bookcase added to the restaurant. Given that she had bought her bookcase from Pierre, I knew it was about as authentic as a three-dollar bill.

Pierre would swear up and down with good cheer and utter sincerity that his scam benefited all parties involved, customers included. Every time I objected to his methods, he'd use his favorite catchphrase: "I'm a dealer of dreams, and dreams are ageless." I've known Pierre forever. I used to walk past his store every day as a snot-nosed kid on the way home from school. I always thought he might have had a thing for my mother. He always complimented her on her clothes or her new haircut, and his wife always gave him the stink-eye whenever Mom and I crossed paths with them in town. Old Pierre helped get my carpentry business off the ground—he was the very first person to entrust me with a commission for a piece. I couldn't have been more grateful.

"What's got you all grumpy today?" he asked, looking me over.

"It's that damn chest. It took a couple of sleepless nights to get it done."

"Right! The chest, of course. How about telling me what really happened? You get in a spat with that blonde of yours?"

"I wish. I've been having a bit of a dry spell since Melanie left."

"Don't worry about it. She wasn't the sharpest tool in the shed anyway, truth be told. So, it's business and not romance that's got you down . . . What, are you broke? I know we didn't have the greatest season this year. If you're hard up, I can commission a set of table and chairs. I'm sure I can manage to sell them before the end of winter. What am I talking about? I can do better. How about you make me a pair of antique sleds, like seriously old ones? I found mock-ups for these hundred-year-old models. We'll make a killing at Christmas, no doubt about it!"

Pierre hurried off giddily to the back and returned with a book that he beckoned me to look over. His sleigh mock-ups dated back to the nineteenth century. I could tell at a glance it would be a lot more work than he thought. But I humored the man, taking the book with me and promising to take a closer look.

"GH, I've known you since you were just a wee little tyke. So, how about you quit messing around and tell me what's got you down?"

I tried to avoid his eyes and moved toward the door, but he was right. Pierre knew me far too well, and I just couldn't lie to him.

"I got a . . . funny little letter in the mail, Pierre."

"Couldn't be that funny, if it's got you all twisted up in knots. Come on, let's get out of here. You can tell me about it over a hot meal."

Seated at La Mère Denise, I read the letter to Pierre.

"Who sent it? Sounds like one hell of a busybody," he said.

"No clue. See for yourself, it's unsigned."

"Well, whoever it is, they sure put a lot of funny ideas in your head."

"You know, I'm just so sick and tired of secrets, and things 'better left unsaid'! I just want to know who my father is, once and for all."

"If he wanted to meet you, GH, don't you think he would have come? After all these years . . ."

"It's not that simple. I went to see Mom."

"Ah, yikes. As bad as ever, I take it?"

"She comes and goes, it never gets any easier. But she told me something—*confessed* something—that I can't stop thinking about."

I let Pierre in on what my mother had said back at the home.

"And she was in her right mind when she said that?"

"Certainly seemed to be."

Pierre looked at me for a moment, then took a deep breath. "Well, I know your mom would rap my knuckles and then some for doing this, but there's something I've got to tell you, kid. Something that's been weighing on me for a long time now. Now, you've got to remember, your mother already had a bun in the oven when she first arrived in Magog. That bun, of course, was you. As you can imagine, it was tough for her to fit in. She wasn't from around here, and back then when a woman had a baby without a father . . . Well, let's just say it didn't happen as often as it does nowadays. She was a knockout, and folks sometimes thought she was gallivanting around, you know, looking for trouble. Most of all, it was the women that didn't exactly take a shine to her, out of jealousy. But she had some grit to her, and she was so friendly that people appreciated her more month by month.

"You helped a lot in that regard. People saw the way she was bringing you up, and you were always such a polite little fella, which sure as hell isn't the case for every kid running around with skinned knees. You must have been, I don't know, about one year old, when this tall man came rolling into town, just poking around, asking for your mother. He seemed nice enough, especially with the big old goofy ears he had on him. Eventually, someone pointed him in the right direction, and he headed for your place. When I found out what was happening, I rushed over to make sure he didn't mean you two any harm. My wife warned me not to meddle where I wasn't wanted, but of course I didn't listen. When I got to your place, I got a little peek in through the window, enough to see that your mother was deep in conversation with him. Everything seemed cordial enough, but I hung around for a bit to make sure. As for him? He didn't leave until the next morning. The guy hit the road, never came back. Hard to imagine someone coming that far for one night, then taking off quicker than you can say 'goofy ears.'

"It didn't make sense; he must have had a serious reason to come all that way. There was nothing of value at your place, just some random furniture I sold to your mother, some cheap dishes, and a crappy second-rate painting hanging on the wall. I may not be a genius, but you don't have to be Sherlock Holmes to figure out what he came all that way for. It was your mother. And you. So, I'm telling you this now because, as you can imagine, I'd always wondered if he hadn't come there . . . to find you."

"How did you know he came from far away?"

"The license plate on his car. Of course, I can't remember it now after all this time. I did jot it down in my cash book, which maybe I could dig up. But I remember this much: it was from the state of Maryland. I wish I had more to tell you, but that's all I know."

"What was he like, this guy?"

"A big fellow. Nice-looking face. That's all I could really make out through the window. But he certainly was pining for your mother, that's for sure. Even from that far, I could see his eyes were fixed on her. At one point, he seemed to want to go upstairs, and your mother actually blocked his path. But he had manners. He gave up on it and plopped down in a chair in your living room. From that point on, I could only make out his shoulders and shoes."

"Do you really think you could dig it up? The license plate number?"

"I certainly can try, but finding one scrap of paper from more than thirty years ago is a long shot. Anyway, I'm not so sure it would make a whole lot of difference. But, hey, you never know."

I paid for the meal, treating Pierre, and we left the restaurant. He apologized for not having told me everything sooner. My only regret was not learning about it back when Mom was still all there. I promised to return his book as soon as I had figured out those sleigh diagrams. It was as good a way as any of letting him know there were no hard feelings.

As it turned out, I didn't have time to dwell on any of it. When I got back, I found a second letter there waiting for me in my mailbox. Same handwriting on the envelope, with nothing but a sheet of lined paper inside listing a time and place.

October 22, 7 p.m. Sailor's Hideaway, Baltimore.

October 22? That was less than two days from now.

18

Robert Stanfield

April 1944, outside Montauban

Robert had been waiting and waiting for the chance to be introduced to the local head of the Resistance. Every day, the villagers gave him a new excuse. Current mission preparation was limiting the brigade's operational vicinity. Enemy activity made any unnecessary movement too risky. The local leader was busy with other liaison officers in need of his attention . . .

Robert had already witnessed firsthand the lack of coordination between French and English forces. At times, he would receive orders from one side that flatly contradicted the other. Decoding the complex and tangled chain of command from the other side of the Channel was no small feat, and Robert found it no less complicated now that he was on the ground. One night, he was driven up a bumpy trail through the woods to check out a case of Sten submachine guns. Another night, he met a trio of local farmers-turned-partisans with only two guns between the three of them. It was a far cry from the type of intel and tallies his superiors were seeking, and Robert was beginning to wonder what the hell he was doing there. In the two weeks since the crash, he had only managed to mark down three pitiful little *X*s on his map, and only one of them actually constituted a real weapons cache—the very hunting lodge Robert had occupied since his first night. The remote outpost had arms and munitions stashed in a tunnel that had been dug into the bottom of the cellar.

Robert's only break from the constant boredom was the Goldsteins. Sam was a highly cultured and passionate man, and their lengthy conversations were a fascinating diversion for Robert. Yet, his daughter stubbornly refused to exchange a single word with him. After a brief period of getting to know each other, Robert and Sam soon became inseparable, whiling away the long afternoons discussing the past and the future. Sam insisted on staying hopeful, more out of concern for his daughter's morale than out of any deep-seated conviction. Every night, Radio London would broadcast coded messages, telling listeners that the arrival of the Allied Forces was imminent. Sam would assure his daughter the war would soon end. "Soon! Soon, peaceful days will come again, you'll see."

Robert was the first of the two to bare his soul. He opened up to Sam about his family and how he had acted against their wishes in joining the war effort. Things with his parents had been so tense that Robert had gone without even saying goodbye.

One day, Robert tried to strike up a conversation with Hanna and was met with only dead silence, as the girl simply carried on with her reading. Sam discreetly beckoned Robert to follow him outside. They sat down side by side on a tree stump and smoked a cigarette, in what had become a daily ritual for the two men. After a short while, Sam broke the silence.

"Don't take it personally. Hanna . . . she protects herself by staying silent, and I should tell you why. Not because you deserve an explanation, but because I think I might lose my mind if I don't tell somebody what happened. We had managed to acquire forged papers, which cost a fortune, and no one in the village knew we were Jews—just city dwellers from Lyon who had decided to move out to the countryside. We led a quiet life, my wife and Hanna and I, discreet, just like everybody else. I always told Hanna, the best way to avoid being discovered was to stay hidden in plain sight.

"On the same day that the Resistance took over the post office, another group was out there tearing up train tracks. Now, there was this enemy convoy passing through, you know, motorcycle sidecars and all, not far from the tracks. So, the Resistance attacked, hitting the convoy with grenades from the embankments along the road. Boom! No survivors. The two efforts weren't coordinated, but because they happened simultaneously, German command planned a brutal retaliation. An SS squadron marched into the village the next day, accompanied by local militiamen. They arrested villagers at random, killing some on the spot, slaughtering others in the middle of the schoolyard.

"My wife . . . had gone out to the farm next door in search of eggs. Eggs. They hanged her, along with ten others, and left them dangling from a telegraph pole. Hanna and I stayed home, with the doors locked. When the Germans left, those militia bastards, in their *eminent kindness*, allowed us to recover the bodies. Some of the sons of bitches went as far as to actually lend us a hand cutting them down. We buried Hanna's mother. Members of the Resistance feared the Germans might strike again. That night, they came to get us out of there. We've been hiding here ever since."

Sam was trembling. "Tell me about Baltimore," he managed to get out as he lit another cigarette. "I've never been. Back in the thirties, we often traveled to New York. Hanna was obsessed with the Empire State Building. She was there even for the opening, at the tender age of three."

"Unbelievable!" Robert exclaimed. "I was there myself, at the opening. My parents dragged me along. I guess I was maybe fifteen, sixteen years old? To think we could have run into each other. What brought you to New York? Are you in real estate?"

"Oh, no. I'm an art dealer. Or at least, I was. My clientele included some of the top American art collectors, most of whom are located in

New York," Sam explained, with more than a hint of pride. "Of course, the Depression hit everyone pretty hard, but I still managed to do business with galleries like the Findlay, the Wildenstein, and the Perl. On my last trip, in the summer of '37, I sold a Monet to Mr. Rothschild himself. Wildenstein had made the introduction, and then I noticed a stunning piece by Edward Hopper that I simply had to purchase myself. Let me tell you, my boy: it cost an arm and a leg, but it was love at first sight. The painting is of a young woman, a girl really, sitting in a chair looking out the window. I always thought she looked so much like my Hanna. Soon as I got my hands on it, I promised myself I would never sell it. When the time comes, it will be handed down to my daughter so she can one day pass it on to her own children. It's meant to always stay in our family. My legacy. The Hopper is something I know will be around long after I'm gone. To think how happy and proud I was about bringing it back here to France. So very stupid. Had I known, even for a second, what was coming . . . I'd have stayed in New York."

"So, you were a rich art dealer."

He nodded. "*Were* being the operative word."

"What happened to your paintings? Did you still have them at the start of the war?"

"That's another story for another day," he said with a sigh. "I should get back; Hanna doesn't like being left alone this long."

Weeks passed. Robert at last found his place in the brigade. At times, he would even hop on a bicycle and ride across the countryside with important messages to deliver. One night, he filled in for a partisan who was missing and drove a pickup carrying two cases of grenades. Another night, he joined a small crew setting up runway lights for a makeshift landing strip. Two planes arrived that night, one carrying a Brit and the other an American. Shaking hands with a fellow American made

Robert homesick, especially since they only had time for a few quick pleasantries. The American was promptly received by handlers Robert had never met, and then disappeared into the night. He remained in the dark about his compatriot's mission.

But aside from those brief moments of action, Robert spent most of his time pacing around the hunting lodge. Every night, he would sit on that same tree stump next to Sam. The art dealer would bum a cigarette and ask about the day's mission. The fact that Robert had come so far from home to be embroiled in a conflict that was completely foreign to him seemed to make Sam feel indebted to the young American.

A real friendship was forming between the two. The art dealer was a great listener, one Robert could trust completely. Sam listened to him in a way that his own father never did.

"So, my boy, have you got somebody waiting for you back home in Baltimore?" Sam asked one day, and it didn't take long for Robert to understand what Sam was getting at. "Come on, the ladies must be all over you!"

"I'm no Don Juan, Sam. I never was much of a ladies' man, and the truth is, I haven't been with that many women in my life."

"Well, what about the current one? Have you got a photograph?"

Robert reached for his wallet, and his fake ID fell to the ground in the process. Sam picked it up and had a look.

"Robert *Marchand*? You're posing as a Frenchman? With your accent? I sure hope you never actually have to *use* that name. And if you do, pretend you're a mute, or deaf, or something."

"I didn't think my accent was that bad."

"However bad you think it is, my friend, it's worse. So, all right then, where's this girl?"

Robert took back his ID and slid the photo to Sam.

"Well, well, she's a knockout! What's her name?"

"No idea. I found this photograph on the gangway of the ship I took across the pond, so I just slipped it into my wallet. I have no idea why. Maybe it helps somehow, pretending there is somebody waiting for me back home. I'm a walking cliché."

Sam squinted his eyes at the smiling face on the photo.

"I say . . . Lucy Tolliver. Twenty-two years old, volunteer army nurse, Dad was an electrician, Mom was a housewife, she's an only child . . ."

"Great. So apparently we're both walking clichés."

"Careful not to get attached to this face. It's not a meaningless thing. There's no lie without a bit of truth to it, especially when you lie to yourself. When I was a schoolboy, my parents were very strict. So, I invented a best friend, sort of as a way to get back at them. Of course, my friend's parents were far laxer than mine. He wasn't forced to keep his mouth shut at the dinner table. His bedtime? Much later than mine. And he only had to do homework when he felt like it. I even made him Catholic in an attempt to annoy my mother, as, of course, his parents didn't make him keep the Sabbath. Long and the short of it is, Max was allowed to do everything I wasn't, and as a result, boy oh boy did he thrive on such freedom! I was a child, I couldn't see any other reason for my own shortcomings and failures than my authoritarian parents.

"Mother wasn't fooled by the whole thing for very long, but she let me dig myself deeper and deeper into my fantasy. And for an entire school year, my imaginary friend had a whole life of his own. Mother would ask for regular updates on how he was doing. If I dreamt up a sore throat for Max? She would slip a honey candy into my backpack. She would sometimes give me twice as much food for my snack, just so I could share with Max. Then one day, for reasons that still escape me after all these years, I was complaining about something or other, going on and on about how great Max's parents were, and my mother decided to call my bluff: she invited Max over to our place for lunch! After all this time and how much she'd heard about him, it was only natural she'd want to meet her son's very best friend in the world, this marvelous boy, this Max . . ."

"What did you do?"

Sam winced. "There was an accident! Poor Max ended up getting tragically crushed beneath a trolleybus."

Robert whistled. "That's a pretty drastic move!"

"Granted. But I was in quite a bind, and I couldn't think of anything else to get me out of it. Want to know the icing on the cake, the most absurd part? I actually felt like I'd lost a friend that day. It took me two months to get over his 'passing,' and even longer to fill the void left by losing him. I still think of him from time to time, even now. Point is: you can never really get rid of a lie you've convinced yourself is true. Food for thought. Anyway, it's late. We'd better continue this conversation tomorrow."

"Sorry to say I won't be here tomorrow, Sam. I'm heading off on a mission, and this time it seems like it might be something serious."

"Oh? What's it all about?"

"I'm afraid I can't tell you that. But I need to ask a favor, in the event I don't make it back."

"Get out of here! You'll make it back just fine. Forget your favor."

"Sam, please. If anything happens to me, my one wish is to be buried back home."

"And how in the world do you think that *I* could make something like that happen?" asked the art dealer.

"When things calm down, when peaceful days come again, I know you'll find a way."

"And if I'm not around then? If I don't live to see these peaceful days?"

"Well, then you can consider yourself released from your promise."

"Careful now: I haven't made any promise."

"Oh yes you have. Maybe not with words, but your eyes sure did."

"You're not following me. You didn't think I'd want anything in return? This is Sam Goldstein you're talking to, my boy! My condition is as follows: should some ill twist of fate befall me before you, take Hanna with you back to Baltimore. And don't tell me I drive a hard bargain. You and I both know your end of the deal is much sweeter. You get to take a cruise with my lovely daughter, and I with your coffin!"

After a laugh and a nod, the two men sealed the deal with a firm handshake.

As it turned out, Robert did make it back from his mission just fine, and May 1944 came and went with no Lysander arriving to take him back to England. By early June, the war had escalated even further. Stranded and seemingly forgotten, Robert grew more and more involved with the Resistance.

With the arrival of the Allied Forces imminent, the partisans began emerging from the shadows. Armed Resistance fighters rose out of nowhere to strike the enemy. The beaches of Normandy were a world away, and even with Allied Forces on the march, peaceful days weren't coming nearly as quickly as Sam and Robert had hoped. Backed into a corner, the Germans began lashing out, their crackdowns increasing in severity. The most fanatical members of the local militias had yet to surrender, and instead doubled down on their relentless hunt for Resistance fighters.

One night, an enemy patrol of local militiamen came dangerously close to discovering the hunting lodge. Lookouts spotted them approaching through the forest and raised the alarm. Sam and Hanna ran to hide in the cellar while the partisan crew stationed themselves at the windows, guns in hand.

With tension mounting, Sam came up and begged Robert to join them in the cellar. Once below, Sam led Robert to a wall of some twenty-odd crates that had been stacked up to mask the secret tunnel leading to the weapons cache. The men moved aside boxes until there was a large enough gap for Hanna to slip through. The tunnel was nearly ten meters long, with sufficient space for Hanna to hide for a short time. But she refused.

"Not without you, Papa!" Hanna pleaded. "I won't be locked up in there without you."

"Do as I say, Hanna! You mustn't question me. You know what you're responsible for now. You have to do the right thing."

Sam hugged his daughter close, then began stacking up the crates once more to close the gap. Robert stood watching in shock. It was the very first time he had heard Hanna speak a single word, and the mere sound of her voice had left him dumbstruck.

"Well, are you just going to stand there gawking or are you going to lend a hand?"

"Sam, don't be crazy! Get into the damn hole with your daughter, and let me seal the two of you up in there."

"No. Not this time, I refuse. I've spent too long burrowing down here like a frightened animal. If the good guys are taking on the enemy, I plan to join in and fight by their side."

Once the crates were back in place, Sam and Robert climbed back up to ground level, and each took position at a window with a Sten submachine gun in hand.

"You know how to use that thing?" Robert asked.

"Well, you don't have to be a genius, do you? Let me guess: Pull the trigger?"

This made a nearby partisan snicker. "You hold it like this, by the magazine, old man, or all you'll end up doing is shooting a bunch of holes in the ceiling," he said. "That thing's got a hair trigger, so hold on tight. You do so much as hiccup, you'll set it off!"

They could hear the militiamen stalking through the forest outside, the sound of their footsteps marking their approach. The partisans were tightwire tense, barely even breathing as they waited to open fire on a pack of faceless enemies. Just then, the militiamen abruptly departed, and everyone sighed with relief. They had never even set foot on the path leading toward the hunting lodge.

Crisis averted, Sam and Robert went down to free Hanna from her hiding place. The girl immediately stormed up the stairs and disappeared into her room. Robert started to follow, but Sam stopped him with a hand on his arm. He dragged his American friend down into the dark tunnel, came to a sudden stop, and sparked up a lighter. Robert squinted as his eyes adjusted to the light.

"I got the idea from watching the partisans dig away down here, hiding their weapons," the art dealer whispered. "See this wooden post?" he asked, running his hand over one of the thick beams holding up the tunnel. "I've used it as my very own hiding spot."

In the glow of the flickering flame, Sam slid out part of the wooden beam and waved Robert in for a closer look. A deep hole had been dug into the wall behind, and Robert could make out some kind of a tube hidden within, the flames reflecting off its metal surface.

"I rolled them inside the cylinder and hid it here where they would be safe," Sam said. "Whatever fate befalls the two of us, they must never get into German hands."

Robert watched entranced as Sam slid the wooden beam back into place.

"Manet, Cézanne, Delacroix, Fragonard, Renoir, Ingres, Degas, Corot, Rembrandt. And of course, my precious Hopper. The ten most beautiful paintings from my entire collection . . . the spoils of a life's work. Priceless masterpieces. *Priceless.* Enough to ensure Hanna's entire future."

"Who else knows about this?"

"Only you, my boy. Now, don't you forget our little deal . . ."

19

ELEANOR-RIGBY

October 2016, en route to Baltimore

As the plane glided over Scotland, I gazed out of the window to where the coastline met the rolling waves, the rest of the land still hidden under the wing. I had kept the leather pouch in my lap since take-off, clutching it tensely as though it were some sort of precious relic. The leather was cracked, and the cord slack and worn with age. I had explored every last inch of the pouch, putting off the most important part. I was terrified to actually read the letter.

I thought about Michel writing that note and slipping the pouch into my jacket, all in secret. It must have weighed very heavily on him. Strangely enough, it actually gave me hope to know that my brother had strayed—even the tiniest bit—from the straight and narrow. It was crazy to think that lying and sneaking around had actually brought him one step closer to "normal."

As I finally took the letter from the pouch, I was struck by the scent of my mother's unique perfume on the envelope. I had to wonder: Just how long did she hold on to this mysterious letter? Closing my eyes, I pictured my mother opening the envelope and reading the message within, just as I was doing now . . .

My darling Sally-Anne,

First, I must tell you that this will be my final letter, even if it's the last thing I want. This annual tradition has been so important to me—a much-needed escape from the crushing loneliness of my daily life. But you don't need me to tell you about loneliness.

I often ask myself: How could two people's lives be so utterly destroyed by one single, tragic mistake? Do you believe that kind of rotten luck is passed down from one generation to the next, like a curse?

I can just hear you teasing me for rambling, going on one of my tangents. How very clever of you. Well, it's true. I'm losing my mind, darling. The guillotine dropped yesterday at the doctor's office. I watched as that stuffed shirt studied my brain scan, his doughy face all soft with compassion, desperately trying to avoid looking me in the eye. That bastard doctor couldn't even tell me how long it'll be before I forget who he is! The most absurd part is that the disease won't claim my life, just eat away at my memory. I don't know if that's a blessing or a curse. I'm keeping my chin up, as always. But I am terrified, darling. I want you to remember me as the woman I was, no matter what happens, not a decrepit old loon rambling away in a total fog. And that, my love, is why this will be my final letter.

So many memories that will be wiped away in time, yet they are still crystal clear in my mind. I see us riding through the wind on your motorcycle. I see those wild days and nights. I see our newspaper and the loft where I spent some of the happiest days of my youth . . . God knows I loved you. So much. I have loved you every day since and will keep on loving you until my dying day.

Who knows? Had we stayed together, maybe that love would have eventually turned to hate, as it happens with so many couples left to weather the storm of time . . . Maybe that's the one silver lining to our story.

You resolved to put the past behind you, my darling. I have always respected that choice. But we've all got to go sometime, even you. And I can't help but think back to what we stole. So, I am begging you, my love. Do not let such a precious treasure dwell in darkness and fade from memory. Bring it back into the light where it rightly belongs, no matter the cost. You know that Sam would have wanted it that way.

It's time to forgive the dead, my love. Bitterness left to fester doesn't help anyone, and clinging to vengeance comes at such a heavy cost.

Tomorrow, I will set foot in my new home, one which I'll never leave. Maybe I could have enjoyed my freedom a bit longer, but the burden would be too great on my son. So, I've decided to pretend—if I act crazier than I am, he'll be free of that burden and free of any guilt. It's the least I can do in light of the sacrifices he's made for me.

To think of all the suffering we've caused. I would have never thought that love could take such cruel turns. And yet, I do still love you. I have always loved you.

Think of me from time to time—not the person writing these words today, but the fiery young woman with whom you shared so many dreams. All those dreams, my love . . . when the impossible was within our grasp, close enough to touch . . .

Still Independent, and your most faithful accomplice,

May

I read the letter over again, start to finish. The first pieces of a cryptic puzzle were falling into place right before my eyes. Mum did launch a weekly paper, it seemed—but not in England.

Who in the world was this woman calling her "my love"? Why did Mum never mention her, not even once? The loneliness part escaped me completely. What act could Mum have committed to ruin the rest of her life? So many unanswered questions. The treasure. Sam. The suffering she mentioned. The talk of tragedy and vengeance that was completely shrouded in mystery. What did she mean, "forgive the dead"? Forgive whom, for what?

I resolved to find this mysterious May, wherever she was. I hoped—albeit selfishly—that her condition had not worsened too much in the years since she wrote the letter. Then it hit me. I flipped over the envelope in a frenzy, cursing myself for not thinking of it sooner. The *stamp*. It was the same as the one from the anonymous letter. Could May have written it during a momentary lapse of reason? No, she couldn't be the poison-pen. The handwriting didn't match at all.

Three years had passed since May's letter. Even if her mind had deteriorated, the son she mentioned might be able to provide some answers. I thought of the sacrifice she had alluded to. Did he grow up knowing his mother's mysterious past, or was it kept secret from him as it was from us? I wondered what he looked like and tried to figure out how old he must be.

I glanced at my watch, anxious for the plane to arrive in Baltimore at last. I had to be patient. Still six hours to go.

◆ ◆ ◆

When we finally landed, I was questioned by an immigration officer about the purpose of my visit. I flashed my press card, explaining to the man that I worked for a prestigious publication, and had come to give his fair city its moment in the sun. No reaction. The officer had been stationed in Baltimore for only two years. He was a Charleston native, and didn't think much of his adopted city. Nevertheless, he stamped my passport and wished me well.

An hour later, I checked into a cheap little hotel two blocks from Sailor's Hideaway and settled into my room. I thought of those other letters Michel had mentioned. It was already too late in the UK for me to call him, eager as I was to learn more. I longed to find answers to all the questions that were still haunting me and had kept me awake throughout the entire flight. In the meantime, I decided to go wandering along the pier.

I came upon Sailor's Hideaway and pressed my face to the window for a view of the space. With the rendezvous still a day away, I felt like a spy lurking about, come to case the joint. The interior was old-fashioned, to say the least, with rustic wooden tables and floor, and scores of old framed photos lining a wall. Above the counter between the dining area and the kitchen was a large blackboard with choices from the menu on display: oysters, various shellfish, and the daily special sauce.

The restaurant's patrons seemed a bit more modern than the decor, for the most part, a mix of lively young city dwellers crowded around large tables. My stomach began to growl. I had eaten almost nothing since London, so I decided to head inside for a bite. The hostess seated me at a table against the wall.

In all the countries I've ever visited across the globe, I've noticed that restaurants never seem to appreciate the solo diner—hence my table with a lovely view of the wall in all its glory. Luckily, this particular wall was lined with faded photos, vestiges of a past long forgotten. They were all of the same group of friends, probably around the same age as me, drinking and enjoying a night out. The young people seemed wild and giddy, with a life of freedom I could only imagine. As my envy swelled into full-blown jealousy, I decided to get over it by mocking their outdated looks and over-the-top attire. The guys looked absurd in grotesque bell-bottoms, and the women's hairstyles were just as bad.

Clearly moderation wasn't in fashion back then. Each of them had a drink in one hand and a cigarette in the other, and their glazed looks made me think they were puffing away at more than just tobacco.

My eyes drifted from frame to frame, until one particular photo caught my attention. I rose from my seat and leaned in for a closer look. Two women were locked in a passionate kiss, one of whom I had never laid eyes on before. But the other . . .

My heart began thumping at a hundred miles an hour. The other woman in the photo—not yet thirty years old, looking far younger than I had ever seen her—was my very own mother.

20

SALLY-ANNE

September 1980, Baltimore

With the night already in full swing, Sally-Anne traipsed about Sailor's Hideaway with a magnum champagne bottle in hand. May winked at her from the bar, and Sally-Anne blew back a kiss, zig-zagging toward her and filling up champagne flutes along the way.

"You don't slow down with that champagne, you're gonna blow all our money on one party!" May warned.

"Darling! We got the green light. The bank approved our loan! I think we can afford to splurge for one night."

All formal steps to register the new publication had already been taken, and the lease for the warehouse transferred into the paper's name. The newsroom was fully staffed with an impressive roster of journalists, all of whom were gathered now for the official baptism of the *Independent*. Joan, who was in charge of graphic design, had created a new typeface for the paper that the whole team was buzzing about, and she'd gone with sophisticated Caslon italics for the nameplate. With a month left before the first issue, May was working hard to bring her feature article up to date, the very same investigative report her former boss had refused to publish.

As for Sally-Anne, she had an entirely different target in her cross-hairs: a sprawling tale of fraud and scandal, how a formerly wealthy and renowned family rose back to prominence in the aftermath of the war. As she took another sip of champagne, Sally-Anne savored the sweet taste of revenge that had gotten stronger over the course of almost two decades.

The two women were too drunk by the end of the night to ride Sally-Anne's Triumph, and accepted Keith's offer to drive them back home to the loft.

◆　◆　◆

Two days later, the whole staff shuffled in at eight in the morning for the paper's first editorial meeting. As each new team member settled in at their workstation, Keith took a moment to admire his own handiwork before leaving for his day job.

They started by reviewing each of the current leading story pitches, which were posted on a large board in clear view of the entire team. There was a rumor in town that city officials had accepted bribes in exchange for a shady deal that would award a public works outfit from a neighboring state with a plum contract. Sally-Anne insisted they would need far more than unsubstantiated rumors to go to print. The *Independent* was no tabloid rag; the paper had to maintain an irreproachable standard of ethics.

Another writer suggested an article on the lopsided allocation of funds in the budget, with education getting the short end of the stick. Schools in impoverished neighborhoods were subject to steep cuts, while funding for schools in higher-income, generally white neighborhoods seemed to be untouched.

"True, but that's not really much of a scoop, is it?" said Sally-Anne, sighing. "Everybody knows about that, it's just that nobody gives a damn, at least nobody whose vote matters."

"Well, I'm pretty sure families in the poor neighborhoods still give a damn," May quickly responded. "The mayor plans to center his reelection bid on safety. While he's out there vowing to put a stop to all the violence, he's leading the charge on creating new ghettos. So, why not tackle the story from that vantage point? Shine a light on the incoherence of his policy and all its consequences."

Everyone agreed May's angle might have legs, and the story was added to the short list. The meeting came to a close just before noon, with a daunting amount of work remaining before the first edition could go to print. Sally-Anne jumped onto her motorcycle and rode across town to the bank. After all, she would have to write everyone's paychecks by the end of the week.

After waiting forever at the teller window, Sally-Anne was told the checks she had ordered were nowhere to be found. More troubling, there was no account listed under the paper's name. She asked to see Mr. Clark, but the teller insisted he was in a meeting. In response, Sally-Anne barged straight into the bank's administrative area and whipped open the door to Mr. Clark's office without knocking. The man's warmth and charm had evaporated. Mr. Clark, with downcast eyes, explained regretfully that there was a problem.

"What kind of problem?"

"I'm so sorry, Miss Stanfield. Believe me, I did everything I could. But the committee rejected your loan application."

"No, that isn't possible! You promised me that money!"

"I'm not the only one who decides here. There are scores of loan managers who—"

"Listen to me. We both know my family has a large stake in this bank. So, I suggest you do something, unless you want to try explaining to your boss why you lost the Stanfield account."

Mr. Clark motioned Sally-Anne to close the door and take a seat.

"Look, I'm counting on your discretion. My job is on the line. Normally, I wouldn't be able to tell you a word about any of this, but since my own wife is mixed up in it, I may as well. I'll have to tell Rhonda eventually, unless I want to find my things out on the sidewalk when I get home tonight. And as soon as I tell her, she'll turn around and tell you, so you may as well hear it from the horse's mouth. The members of the committee got cold feet. They were scared your mother would be upset."

Sally-Anne sat bolt upright in her chair, white with shock. "You're not suggesting that my mother would have actually intervened? To prevent me from getting funding for my newspaper? Who would have told her about it at all?"

"It wasn't me, I can tell you that much. My best guess? There was a loan manager at the hearing who spoke out quite forcefully to make sure your loan was rejected. It could have been him."

"And what about client confidentiality? Is there even a shred of morality in this place?"

"Keep your voice down, please. You have to believe me. I am truly sorry for all of this. But you know your mother better than I do, and you should know neither of us stand a chance against her."

"Maybe you don't, but there's no way in hell I'm taking this lying down. This isn't over. Not by a long shot."

Sally-Anne rose and stormed out of Mr. Clark's office without looking back, breaking into a run as soon as she got out the front door of the bank. By the time she reached her motorcycle, she had to stop, doubling over in pain from the rage in the pit of her stomach. She waited a few seconds for the spasms to pass, then leapt onto the bike and roared down the road.

Fifteen minutes later, she pulled into the parking lot of the country club, stormed inside, and stomped down the corridor to the dining room, where Hanna Stanfield was dining with a pair of well-to-do ladies. Sally-Anne walked right up to the table and glared at her mother, enraged.

"Tell your two parakeets to find somewhere else to squawk. We have to talk. Right now."

Hanna Stanfield let out a heavy sigh of apology. "Please forgive my daughter. Despite her age, she still hasn't grown out of her teenage angst, and rotten manners are how she wages her rebellion."

The two women exchanged a sympathetic look with Hanna, then rose and nodded politely, far too "elegant" to cause a scene. The maître d', who had followed along skittishly during Sally-Anne's dramatic entrance and had been hovering nearby ever since, led the women to a nearby table. Everyone in the room had turned to watch, and the man was positively mortified by the entire incident.

"Well? Sit down," Hanna commanded. "But I'd caution you to change your tone, young lady. I won't sit here and be disrespected."

"How could you do something like this? It wasn't enough to exile me?"

"Ah, the exaggerations! The drama! To think of the education we gave you, only to watch you throw it all away. And, might I add, your homecoming was contingent upon maintaining a harmonious relationship with the family. You, my darling, agreed not to cause trouble. That was the condition for receiving help from your father and me. If you don't live up to your end of the bargain, you suffer the consequences."

"Exactly what have you been helping me with? Banishing me from my own family?"

"You thought that plum job at the *Sun* just fell into your lap, based on charm alone? You came back from London with nothing, not even a diploma. Eight years, princess, whiling away your youth and having a jolly good time at our expense. And just what have you accomplished since then? Drinking yourself silly night after night, prowling around town in vulgar clothes on your precious motorcycle? Not to mention your . . . *entanglements*. Is a little discretion really too much to ask? Your brother said you even had the gall to bring that girl here to the club!"

"'That girl' has a name; it's May. I guess I shouldn't be surprised that Edward would go running to Mama to brag about his latest conquest."

"*His* conquest? I thought she was yours. As far as I'm concerned, all the better he snatched the girl away from you. Had I asked you to cut short that shameful 'relationship,' I've no doubt you would have disobeyed me, as always."

Sally-Anne balked. "Impossible. You're not saying it was *you* who sent Edward? Even he wouldn't stoop so low as to—"

"To act responsibly? To adhere to his mother's wishes? You have done nothing but drag our reputation through the mud time and time again. When will it end? To think of this latest blow. Associating our good name with that little rag of a tabloid . . . You must be out of your mind!"

"Me? You treat people like they're marionettes, whose strings you can pull whenever you please."

"People are free to do as they wish."

"To think of the woman you once were. Is there even an ounce of her left? Or are you nothing but bitterness and resentment stuffed into an empty shell?"

"Darling. By the time I was your age, I had already survived the unspeakable. I had worked endlessly and restored my father's name and legacy to its full glory. Just how do you plan to live up to your name? What have you achieved, what gives *you* the right to judge *me*? Have you ever once done good for the people around you? All you've brought is pain and sorrow."

"You've got it all wrong. I love with all my heart, and I'm loved for who I am, not for what I represent."

"You love? Tell me, who is it you love? A husband? Children you're raising, a family you've built? All you love is having those pitiful souls orbit around you. You have no values, no sense of morality."

"Oh, please, don't talk to me about morality. Your whole life is built on a lie. And how dare you bring my grandfather into this! As far as I can see, I'm the only one who hasn't betrayed his memory."

Hanna burst out laughing in response. "My poor darling, you are so very far off the mark. You're not like us, Sally-Anne, and you've never wanted to be. Let me be crystal clear: I'm not your enemy, so long as you don't cross me. But I won't sit by while you destroy what took me a lifetime to build."

With that, Hanna opened her purse and took out a pen and checkbook. "Since money is what you're after, you don't have to borrow from a bank." Hanna finished writing the check, tore it from the book, and held it out to her daughter. "But don't be foolish enough to spend a penny of it on your newspaper. That rag will never see the light of day—you'd just as well throw the check out the window. I know exactly what you planned to do with that paper. For once, I implore you, try not to be so utterly selfish. All your efforts and persistence won't change a single thing for the big players in this city. But it *will* hurt our clientele. You were looking for twenty-five thousand dollars. This is half, which should be more than enough. Now, please leave us in peace. Why not go abroad again, darling? It's a fine notion. Go see the world. A nice long trip is just what you need to open your eyes. Return to London if you wish, wherever you want, just stop meddling in our affairs. Your father and I are on the brink of a major sale, which should close in the next two months, and the profits will be used to finance his campaign. Perhaps you haven't heard, since our lives seem to be of such little interest to you, but your father's friends have been pushing him to run for governor. I trust you will keep quiet and not cause any disturbances, at least not until after he announces his candidacy. I hope I have made myself clear."

Sally-Anne grabbed the check and stuffed it into her jacket pocket.

"And for the love of God," her mother added, "start by buying yourself some proper attire."

Sally-Anne rose to her feet, shooting daggers with her eyes.

"What do you think my grandfather would say if he could see you now? I'll ask you one more time: Is she gone forever? His daughter? The young girl you once were? All I can do is pray she'll come back one day, when you finally realize no one can live a lie forever."

21

George-Harrison

October 2016, Baltimore

I drove all night in the pouring rain and got to Baltimore exhausted.
After checking into a hotel near the waterfront, I peered down the alley
from the window of my room, filled with dread at the thought of what
I might discover in the mysterious meeting that was to take place that
night. I decided to take a nap, and woke up a few hours later. It was
late morning, and I set out to explore the city. Walking past all those
souvenir shops only reminded me that I had no one waiting for me back
home. I still missed Melanie from time to time, and that day I missed
her terribly. But then something back at the hotel made me forget all
about her.

A young woman was asking a question at the front desk. Her rough,
scratchy voice immediately drew me in, not least because of her English
accent, which was pretty charming. As I waited patiently behind her, I
played a little guessing game I'd made up. The game was to figure out
what brought her all the way here. It wasn't like Baltimore was a particularly appealing tourist destination, especially in late October. Maybe
work? She could be traveling for business, maybe for a conference. The

convention center wasn't all that far away. But why not stay at a hotel for business travelers in that case? Could she be here visiting family?

"Yes, you'll get the busy signal if you don't hit 9 for an outside line," the receptionist explained. "Then dial 0-1-1 to call international."

She was traveling alone, so maybe she had to call and check in with her husband—or boyfriend, rather, judging by the lack of ring. Next, she asked how much a taxi to Johns Hopkins University would cost. Bingo! A clue. She had to be a professor—English literature, I'd have bet money on it—living at the hotel until her official accommodation was organized for the semester.

Just then, she turned around to face me.

"So sorry. I'll just be one more minute."

"Don't worry about it," I replied. "I've got time."

"Is that why you've been staring straight at me since you walked in? In case you didn't notice, there's a huge mirror behind the front desk, so I can stare right back at you."

"Then I'm the one who should be saying sorry. It's not what you think, honestly. It's just my weird way of killing time. I like to guess what people do for a living."

"Really. What did you come up with for me?"

"Professor. English literature. And you've just landed a position at Johns Hopkins."

"Impressive. But wrong on all counts," she said, extending her hand. "Eleanor-Rigby Donovan, journalist. *National Geographic.*"

"George-Harrison," I replied, shaking her hand.

"Well, isn't that clever! Are you always so quick with comebacks?"

"Sorry, you lost me."

"Eleanor Rigby . . . George Harrison . . . still don't see it?"

"I guess not. What's so funny about it?"

"The Beatles! I'm the title of a song, you're the guitarist?"

"Believe it or not, I don't know that song. I never really got into them. Neither did my mom, actually. She was all about the Stones."

"Lucky you. And lucky me, meeting a real-life George Harrison. I think my own mother would have got quite a kick out of that. Anyway. Duty calls."

With that, she walked straight out, and it was my turn to approach the front desk. As I retrieved my room key, the receptionist seemed to be fighting back laughter, having followed every word of my exchange with Eleanor Rigby.

I took the elevator and stepped into my hotel room, all with a bit of a spring in my step. I felt better than I had in ages.

◆　◆　◆

Now it's my turn, George Harrison. With fifteen minutes to kill in the back of a taxi, I took a stab at his little guessing game.

What brought him to Baltimore? In a pair of jeans with worn leather boots and loose-fitting jumper, he didn't strike me as a businessman, and the hotel didn't seem geared toward that kind of guest to begin with. Hmm. Musician? A musician with a name like George Harrison? No way. That's like being a contemporary painter named Rembrandt . . . unless he was just messing with me by calling himself that. Quite a cheeky sense of humor, I had to admit. There's a thought. A painter? Would a painter come show his work in Baltimore? Plus, I didn't spot a single speck of paint anywhere on him. What else could he be? He didn't seem tortured enough to be a filmmaker. Why was I so set on him being an artist?

Definitely not a reporter, or else he would have mentioned it when I brought up the magazine. *Eleanor-Rigby Donovan, journalist.* I must have come on strong. I can't imagine why I felt the need to impress him in the first place. Unless . . . forget it. Was he in town to visit his mother? He did mention her. But that still doesn't tell me what he does for a living. Why bother trying to unravel the mystery? Well . . . what if we crossed paths again in the lobby, and I just nailed him with the right guess? He'd be speechless! Okay. Interesting thought. But why bother trying to leave him speechless? Well . . . what if it was because I *wanted* to?

No harm in that, after all.

The Johns Hopkins public relations guy gave me loads of info for the article and let me take some pictures of the campus. The lighting was so striking that I decided to head into town to take some more. Best to move ahead with the assignment, since it was the entire justification for the trip.

I had butterflies in my stomach as I returned to the hotel. I realized I didn't know how I would recognize my contact at Sailor's Hideaway later that night. This, of course, assumed the rendezvous was real, and not just part of a sprawling scavenger hunt or enormous hoax that I'd willingly bought into.

Did the poison-pen really drag me all the way here just so I could see that photo of my mother, proving the validity of his allegations? If that were the case, why set such a specific time to meet? Why go so far as to set up a rendezvous—just so a single photo would be right in front of my face? Wouldn't sending a copy have been easier? Although I did have to admit, discovering it the way I did had definitely intensified the dramatic effect.

I was getting sick and tired of rehashing the same questions again, all the while trying to ignore the little voice in my head that kept reminding me just how frightened I was. I decided to make my way to Sailor's Hideaway a bit earlier than necessary, hoping to get a lead on whoever would step through that door to meet me.

◆ ◆ ◆

I walked in and asked for a table for two.

"Do you have a reservation?" the hostess asked. I always found it amusing when they asked that question in a half-empty restaurant.

"No . . . not that I know of," I replied warily.

"Name?"

"Eleanor-Rigby."

"Well, what do you know? Looks like we do have you in here." Her words made my blood run cold. "Right this way, please."

The hostess led me to the very same table beneath the photo. As we approached, I decided to improvise. I asked for a different table, pointing to one with a clear view of the door. For once, I would be one step ahead, thwarting the plans of the puppeteer who had pulled all the strings for quite some time. Now, all I had to do was wait for my poison-pen to walk in and sit down at the table originally assigned to me and then, well . . . from that point, I had no idea. I would cross that bridge when I came to it.

I got settled at the table and ordered a Pimm's. After all, you can take the girl out of England . . . A couple walked in at approximately 6:55, most likely on their first date, judging by their awkward body language. At 6:57, two young women entered and chose a spot at the bar, neither seeming much like a conspirator. When 7:00 rolled around, there was still no one who fit the bill. Then, at 7:10, the door flew open and good old "George Harrison" from the hotel lobby burst in and rushed up to the hostess. Even though he was completely out of breath and disheveled, he looked a bit more presentable than earlier. I watched as he tucked his shirt into his trousers, straightened out his jacket, and ran his hand through his unkempt hair. He still hadn't noticed me.

For reasons I couldn't quite explain, I found his presence reassuring. I chalked it up to the feeling you get when you see a familiar face in a cold and unfamiliar setting. I kept my eyes glued to George Harrison, wishing I had a newspaper to hide behind to help me spy on him. I could just hear Maggie telling me again that I watch too much TV. Then, to my great surprise, another waitress led George Harrison right to the table reserved under my name! I watched breathlessly as he took his seat, while the voice in my head urged me to think things through before taking any action.

As far as I could see, there were two explanations. The most likely: George Harrison was the poison-pen himself, in the flesh. It fit perfectly. He was staying at the same hotel, and was now eating at the same restaurant. His performance in the lobby had been flawless, having totally convinced me that he didn't recognize me in the slightest. Somehow, the idea hadn't occurred to me during my guessing game in the cab. Yet, I heard the little voice in my head pushing another explanation: he simply wanted to have dinner at the closest decent spot, and the waitress led him to that table because it was free again. When the *real* poison-pen showed up, the hostess would surely lead him straight to me. I couldn't say for certain which of the two possibilities frightened me more.

I watched him quietly for a full ten minutes, during which he checked his watch incessantly, sighing every time he did. He never once glanced at the menu. It was clear: he was waiting for someone. And that someone was me!

Suddenly, he rose and approached my table.

"Well, look who's spying now. You've been staring at me since I walked in. And I didn't even need a mirror to tell me that."

"Uh-huh" was all I got out, just a faint grumble.

"Are you waiting for somebody?" George Harrison asked. I didn't say a word. "That . . . wasn't a trick question," he continued, chuckling.

"Maybe I am. It depends," I ventured, not letting my guard down.

"Oh, I get it," he said, wiping the smile off his face.

"You get what?"

"Somebody stood you up."

"Funny, I thought you were waiting for someone yourself."

"Actually, I'm worried somebody may have been waiting for me and then left because I was late," he said, eyes on his watch once more.

George Harrison scratched his forehead, a habit I've observed in men when something is troubling them. My own go-to tic is twisting and twirling my hair around my index finger. Who was I to judge?

"I drove the whole night to be here for this, only to pass out like a fool in my hotel room. I overslept," he said with a sigh.

"Call her and apologize."

"I would if I knew how."

"Oh, I get it."

"Get what?"

"Not a very smooth move, showing up late for a blind date. But let me set your mind at ease: *you* were the one who got here first. I've been here for a half hour and haven't seen anyone who fits the bill, unless you pick up your women in pairs, in which case, your dates are seated at the bar." He still looked troubled.

"I'm sorry. I shouldn't tease. I didn't mean anything by it. Bottom line: your date never came, so either she's the one running late, or . . . *you've* been stood up."

"Fair enough. Since it seems I'm not the only one who got left high and dry, any chance I could sit down with you for a bit while I wait?"

I glanced at my watch. It was seven thirty.

"Sure, I suppose. Why not?"

George Harrison took a seat, appearing just as uncomfortable as I was. He flagged down the waitress and asked me what I was drinking.

"Pimm's," I said.

"Any good?"

"Yes. But quite sweet."

"I think I'll go with a beer. And you?"

"The same, please."

"Meaning . . . a beer?"

"No, another Pimm's. Please."

He took a breath. "So . . . what brings you to Baltimore?"

"Can't you try something a bit more original? Maybe a question you don't know the answer to?"

"Ha! And I'm the one who's supposed to be good with comebacks? This round goes to you, hands down."

"Now . . . your real name isn't George Harrison, is it? Admit it, you're an actor!"

"Actor? Me?" he said, laughing. "Never heard that one before. Does that mean you ripped off my favorite game?" He had a charming laugh. I had to give him points for that.

"Maybe. Maybe I did."

"What else did you come up with?"

"I had painter, musician, filmmaker . . ."

"That sure is a lot of hats for one man to wear! Impressive, but wrong. I'm a carpenter. And George Harrison Collins is absolutely my real name. Sorry if that comes as a disappointment."

"Disappointment? Not at all. It just means . . . you're not as funny as I had hoped."

"Well, isn't that sweet."

"Oh, no. I didn't mean it like that."

"Don't I get a second chance?"

"Afraid not, it's a bit late for that. You came here on a date and now you're hitting on me? I may be alone, but I'm nobody's plan B."

"Who said I was here on a date?"

"Okay, that point goes to you, but you're still losing."

"Can't we call it a draw and stop keeping score? Anyway, for your information, I was not hitting on you, thank you very much. But just out of curiosity, since you're obviously very fixated on first names: What's his name? The guy who stood you up? You can trust me, you know. One plan B to another."

"Fine, let's call it a draw."

"So, backing up. What brings you to Baltimore?"

"An article for my magazine. And you?"

"My father."

"That's who you're waiting for?"

"Sort of. It's who I had hoped would show up."

"I have to admit that's pretty bad, getting stood up by your own father. My dad would never dream of doing that. But couldn't he just be running late?"

"I've been waiting for him for thirty-five years. I think 'late' might be a bit of an understatement."

"Wow, that's awful. I really am sorry."

"Why are you sorry? It's not your fault."

"Well, I am nonetheless. I lost my mother last year and I know how much it hurts . . . to be missing a parent."

"Let's change the subject. Life is too short to dwell on pointless things like sadness and regret."

"Well said."

"I can't take credit. My mother liked to say that. But enough about me. Your turn. What are you going to write about Baltimore?"

Moment of truth, Elby. Make a choice: Do you trust this man or not?

"Your lips are moving," he said, "but no words are coming out."

"You said you drove all night. Where were you coming from?"

"Magog. It's a small city about an hour outside Montreal, in the Eastern Townships."

"I know where Magog is," I replied coldly.

"Of course you do. Writing for *National Geographic* must take you to the ends of the earth and back," he continued, without noticing my change in tone. "It's a beautiful area, huh? I don't know what time of year you visited, but the scenery changes so dramatically, it's almost like a different place depending on the season."

"Yet . . . *still in Canada* . . . am I right?"

George Harrison just gaped at me like I was a total idiot.

"Yeah, sure . . . I guess," he stammered. That clinched it. There was no longer any doubt in my mind.

"And how about the Canadian postal service? Is it top-notch?"

"Sure, I mean . . . I really don't get much in the mail except bills."

"Really? And what about the things you *send*?"

"I'm really sorry, but I just don't know why you're asking me this."

"Let's just say I'm trying to figure out what you're playing at. Maybe it's time you explained yourself."

"Did I say something to offend you? I really didn't mean to. Maybe it's best I head back to my own table."

I must have been face-to-face with the world's best actor. Or, a modern-day Machiavelli.

"Great idea," I told him. "In fact, I'll come along. There's something I'd like to show you."

I crossed the space quickly and sat right down at the table, facing the wall, leaving "George Harrison" no time to think things through. He looked at me, perplexed, and then strode over to join me.

"I admit, your little story about growing up without a father really tugged at my heartstrings," I said. "You'd have to be a stone not to be moved by that, and even more so to make it up. Now, look at that photo. Are you really going to try and tell me running into each other, first at the hotel and now here, was a coincidence? How? When that's my *mother* you're looking at!"

George Harrison glanced at the photo and went pale as a sheet. He went in for a closer look, unable to get a single word out.

"Well?" I persisted, raising my voice.

"There, right next to your mother," he finally managed. "That's mine . . . *my* mother."

He turned back to me, his face a combination of confusion and mistrust.

"Who are you? What do you want from me?" he whispered.

"I was going to ask you the same question."

George Harrison dug into the inner pocket of his jacket and took out an envelope, which he laid on the table. I immediately recognized the handwriting.

"I don't know what it is you're accusing me of, but go ahead and read this," he said, tapping the envelope softly. "Read it and you'll see why I drove the whole night to get here."

I unfolded the letter and read, hardly breathing. As soon as I finished, I took my own letter from my bag and handed it to George Harrison—or rather, George-Harrison. He looked as shocked and afraid as I was, and went another shade paler by the time he finished reading. We studied each other silently. The staring contest went on until the waitress finally came back, wanting to know if we would be dining together . . . and if we had finally settled on a table. *Yes* . . . and *yes*.

"When did you receive that letter?" George-Harrison asked.

"It came around ten days ago, followed by another about a week later telling me to come here."

"I got mine around the same time, same story."

"I'm still not sure who you are, George-Harrison."

"But I know who *you* are, Eleanor-Rigby. I didn't until now, because my mother never called you by name."

"Your mother . . . talked about me?"

"Well, not you in particular. Your family. Every time she scolded me, she'd say, 'My friend's children in England would never talk back to their mother like that!' Those kids, they always had perfect table manners. They would clean their rooms, they never whined when their mother asked them to do something, and, of course, they were model students . . . Basically, everything I screwed up as a kid, your family did well."

"Then your mother didn't really know my family at all."

"Who would pull a dirty trick like this? And . . . why?"

"I still have no way of knowing it isn't you."

"I could say the same for you."

"Right, just a question of perspective, I suppose," I admitted. "There's no way for either of us to know exactly what's running through the other's head. And we both have reasons not to trust each other."

"Are you sure? If you ask me, that's why we're here in the first place."

"What does that mean?"

"Like I said, our mothers knew each other. My mother mentioned yours many times."

"But mine didn't mention yours."

"That's a shame. But it doesn't change anything. This photo shows them getting along very well—like partners in crime, even. I'll bet that the person behind this whole thing wanted us to see that. Together."

"Wanted us to see it so we would have a reason to trust each other? I'd say that's a bit of a stretch, but fine. Why would the poison-pen want us to trust each other?"

"Poison-pen. That's good. I don't know. To save time, I guess?"

"The fact that you can understand such twisted reasoning doesn't exactly cry innocence, you know."

"Granted, but maybe it does cry . . . intelligence?" he asked.

"Sure, with a nice dash of modesty on top."

"Someone is messing with us. Why, I have no idea. But we have a way better chance of unmasking him if we join forces."

"Well, don't you think the poison-pen would see that coming?"

"Yes, I do. But it's a risk he chose to take."

"Why *he* and not *she*?" Even though I'd been assuming it was a man as well, I didn't want him to know that.

"Good point."

"Whatever happened to trusting each other? I'm the one who brought it up in the first place."

"Which definitely cries sincerity, or at least proves you're smart."

"Smarter than you, you mean?"

Once again, our eyes locked, and we studied each other for what felt like ages. And once again, we were saved by the bell as the waitress arrived to take our orders. George-Harrison asked for a lobster roll, never taking his eyes off mine. I was too engrossed in the stare down to think up something original to order, so I ordered the same.

22

May

October 1980, Baltimore

May had tried three times to get hold of Edward, to no avail.

Their second date had been just as magical as the first. Even though she still had feelings for Sally-Anne, May was falling for Edward. And judging by his tender care and thoughtfulness, he seemed to feel the same way. May was showing Edward a whole new world, one that was beginning to grow on him. It was like *Pygmalion* in reverse—the girl who came from nothing was the teacher; the privileged man, the student.

And so what if Sally-Anne was upset? She had been in a blind fury at everyone for days now, so May's actions didn't seem to make a whole lot of difference. At the editorial meeting, Sally-Anne had rebuffed the entire team, shutting down any ideas they pitched and picking fights at every turn. It had come as a relief when she'd ended the meeting early.

The source of all that rage was a mystery. If Sally-Anne enjoyed Keith so much, she should have been happy to have him all to herself. May could see the whole situation pretty clearly. Sally-Anne couldn't bear May being involved with Edward, and seeing him shower her with attention while he ignored his own sister disgusted her. But May saw no reason to feel guilty about any of it. She hadn't tried to seduce Edward; he was the one tripping over himself to win her over. Sally-Anne had it all wrong that Edward would chew May up and spit her out once he'd gotten what he wanted. After that passionate kiss on their first date, Edward had walked May to her door and said good night. Two days later, he had treated her to an unforgettable meal at an expensive restaurant. As they sat down, May had peered in wonder at the rows of cutlery, and Edward had softly clued her in: "Work your way from the outside in, one at a time."

The day after that, they went shopping and bought each other gifts. Edward draped a ravishing scarf around her shoulders, while May bought him a striking leather wallet. He slipped the wallet into the inner pocket of his suit jacket and patted his heart.

"I'll keep it right here."

Edward had even driven May out to Kent Island for the weekend. He had treated her to a lush suite in a sprawling manor atop a dune facing the sea. They spent most of that weekend making love. She had never been spoiled so thoroughly. May's only regret was not being able to share her newfound joy with her closest friend. Despite Sally-Anne's juvenile and selfish behavior, May still had sympathy for her and felt she understood. Nonetheless, there was no way Sally-Anne's pigheaded, jealous attitude could last. There was nothing shallow or selfish about this budding love story. May resolved to find a way to get the siblings to patch things up. A brother and a sister were meant to get along. She was convinced the two of them could make it work.

May wanted to build trust with Edward, so she decided to take the first step herself during that weekend on Kent Island. She told him about the newspaper as they walked arm in arm along the beach.

"It may still be only a pipe dream for now," she lied. "But the two of us are going nowhere at the *Sun*. Our managers are chauvinists who think the only thing women are good for is serving coffee, and that we should all just stick to research."

Edward seemed appalled by that notion, and asked May more about the dream project. What type of editorial point of view did they envision? She walked Edward through the broad strokes and he was nothing but encouraging, praising her fearlessness and hard work in the quest for truth. But nonetheless, Edward advised her to be cautious. Exposing corruption, abuse of power, and partisan politics came at great risk. If she didn't tread lightly, sooner or later she would end up drawing the wrath of the powerful.

"I grew up with those people, and I know just what they're capable of," he warned her.

Edward's words reminded May that with all the important people he knew, he might be a good connection for the paper, at least eventually. Despite all his admirable qualities, she could tell he worried too much about appearances, a weakness she'd found in so many men. May knew she had to be patient and wait for the right moment, and she was sure Edward would certainly rise to the task and help them.

"I just hope you're not getting used by my sister. With the chip she has on her shoulder, it's no surprise she would launch something like this."

"Just what happened between you two?" asked May.

"Sally-Anne blames me for not taking her side. She's been waging an endless war against our parents since we were teenagers. I find her hostility toward them as unfair as it is unbearable. I know Mother isn't always easy. She may seem harsh, but after going through what she did when she was young . . . I know it makes me sound stuffy, but I actually admire my parents. And not only because they've been so successful. They both suffered terrible hardship. My mother certainly didn't grow up with a silver spoon in her mouth. When she came to America, she was penniless, her parents dead and buried. I never met my maternal grandparents; they were Jews in hiding, murdered by the Nazis before I was born. Mother made it out alive thanks to her sheer courage and my father's heroism. That's why I just can't accept the way Sally judges them so harshly. I've always tried to smooth things out between them. I tried to protect my sister, from herself most of all . . . all her rage and excess . . . nothing ever stopped her from doing just as she pleased. In the end, I gave up."

"Well, she certainly still loves you very deeply," May lied.

"Oh, I highly doubt that."

"When she talks about you, you can hear in her voice how much she admires you."

"Darling, that's very thoughtful to say, but I don't believe it for one second. Sally-Anne thinks only of herself. She has such hatred for her own family . . . There's nothing but bitterness in her heart."

"If you think that, you don't know her at all. Not really. You think *I'm* thoughtful? Sally-Anne's the queen of thoughtful! She spends all her time thinking about other people. Sure, she was born into money. She could have just put her feet up and enjoyed the easy life, but she didn't. She *chose* not to. Yeah, she's rebellious, but always for noble causes, all against the injustice of the world."

"If I didn't know better, I'd say you were in love with her, the way you talk."

"Please, Edward, don't be silly."

"Very well, then," he sighed. "Message received. Don't speak ill of my sister, or else run the risk of getting my head bit off."

May took Edward by the arm and led him back to the manor.

"Let's head back inside," she said. "I'm thirsty, and I think we should get drunk. I can't stand Sundays. I wish this weekend would never end."

"Not to worry, dear. It's far from the last."

"Of course. As long as we take it slow. I got the message loud and clear, what you said about . . . what was her name again? Zimmer, was that it? I don't know anything about her, but I know I don't want us to end the same way. Do you still have feelings for her?"

"Ha! Oh, you women and the traps you set for us. If I say no, I'm a swine. If I say yes, I'm *king* of the swine. I think you've got the right idea: enjoy what life has given us, without rushing to ask questions, especially about past romantic entanglements. Which reminds me: you haven't told me a thing about yours."

"That's because there's nothing to tell."

The couple entered the manor and settled into the smoking room for a nice cozy drink, the fire crackling in the fireplace. May ordered a glass of champagne, while Edward opted for bourbon.

Around sunset, they returned to the room and packed their bags. May stopped halfway through and took a long look around the room. She had slept so soundly in that massive four-poster bed, gazing up at the silk canopy the next morning with Edward sleeping softly beside her. She'd opened the thick window curtains, and the sunlight streamed in over a gorgeous room-service breakfast. May savored the divine sensation of walking barefoot on the Persian rug. She never wanted to leave.

"Can't we stay until tomorrow?" she asked Edward as he folded his things. "I just can't imagine walking back into that loft tonight."

"Sorry to say, I have to work early tomorrow, darling. But since we'll get in late in any event, why not spend the night at my place?"

"Under the same roof as your parents? In their home?"

"It's more of an estate, really. I have my own quarters, May. Believe me, we can stay there and not cross paths with them at all."

"Even tomorrow morning?"

"We can leave through the service door—there's nothing to worry about, honestly."

They made incredible time in Edward's Aston Martin on the way back. The car smelled of leather, and the roar of the engine was exciting.

"Would you promise me something?" May said.

"I have to know *what* first, my dear. I'm a man of my word, and I don't take promises lightly."

"I want you to make up with her."

"With Sally-Anne? It's true there's some tension there, but there's nothing specific to reconcile."

"No. I mean all of you, the whole Stanfield family. Sally-Anne would never take the first step, and neither would your mother. It has to be you. Help them make peace."

Edward slowed the car and looked at May, a broad smile on his face.

"I can't promise it will work . . . but I can promise you now that I will try. I will try my very best."

May leaned in and kissed Edward, then pulled away, telling him to keep his eyes on the road. She rolled down the window and breathed in deeply. With her hair blowing in the wind, May closed her eyes and felt something close to happiness.

23

ELEANOR-RIGBY

October 2016, Baltimore

We parted ways out on the landing, both of us waving good night from the doorways to our own rooms. Lying on top of my bed, all I had to do was close my eyes and I could picture Maggie asking me:

All right, genius. Now what?

And since I was clueless as to the answer, I decided to call her. Dial 9, then 011, just like the lady at the front desk said—as if I had never been abroad before!

My sister picked up straightaway. "Jesus! You have any idea what time it is here?" Maggie grumbled, her voice hoarse and scratchy.

"I'm sorry if I woke you both up, but it just couldn't wait."

"It's just me; Fred stayed in Primrose Hill," she replied, with a long, drawn-out yawn. "It was crazy busy last night, and he closed too late to make his way over here."

"Good for him, if his restaurant can drum up that kind of business."

"Oh yeah, la-di-da. When my boyfriend's on cloud nine because of a full house at the pub, I get to sleep alone. But when things go south and he's down in the dumps, I get him all to myself. Who could possibly ask for anything more? Anyhow, I'm guessing you didn't ring me at five in the morning to hear me gripe about Fred."

There was no arguing with that logic. Despite having been woken up ridiculously early, Maggie listened intently to the latest in the family saga: the letter Michel slipped in my pocket, the picture on the wall at Sailor's Hideaway, the woman with whom Mum had a relationship thirty-six years ago, and most of all, the encounter with George-Harrison and all that followed. The story was so riveting, Maggie didn't interrupt, not even once.

"What does he look like, this carpenter?"

"Don't tell me that's the first question that comes to mind."

"Even if it was, it shouldn't stop you from answering it."

I laid out a vague description of the man.

"So . . . you're saying he's hot. And George-Harrison is his real name?"

"Well, I didn't make him show me his driving license or anything, but that was the name on the letter. I took him at his word."

"So I see. Considering our mothers were so close, you really think the names are a coincidence?"

"The two of us are pretty much the same age. There could be something there, maybe."

"I'd call it more than a maybe. She did call Mum 'my love' in that letter, in case you missed it. Although that could be because she had already started losing her marbles. You know, I can't picture Mum roaring down the road on a motorcycle, not for the life of me. The same lady who put on her seat belt religiously every time she got into the Austin? Can you see her as a biker chick?"

"Honestly, that's the last thing on my mind right now. I'm having more trouble picturing her as a thief! And I'd like to know more about what they stole, what this whole 'tragedy' was all about . . ."

"Well, it does seem to give the anonymous letter some credence."

"Yeah, some parts of it are starting to make some sense. The shadowy parts of Mum's past, her relationship with George-Harrison's mother, the mysterious fortune she once had, but didn't inherit, and, of course, the *Independent*."

"What's that?"

"It's the newspaper Mum launched with her friend May—George-Harrison's mother. Dad can fill you in on some of the details."

"Are you sure this is *our* mother we're talking about here?"

"I had the same exact reaction when I heard."

"And this 'precious treasure' thing. Did this George-Harrison person have any info on that?"

"No. That was a total surprise to him. He said the letter from his mother was the first time he had ever heard of it. Apparently, there are other letters out there as well. She and Mum went back and forth for years and years."

"And what if he's been playing you from the start? I mean, the sequence of events that brought you two together contains a hell of a lot of coincidences. What if he's your poison-pen?"

"Why go to such trouble?"

"To bring together all the puzzle pieces! Years of correspondence, you said. Let's say he already has all of Mum's letters and wants to get his hands on his mother's, too. The poison-pen encouraged us to find proof of his claims, didn't he? There you have it!"

"I don't buy it. If you'd seen how dumbstruck he looked at the sight of that photo in Sailor's Hideaway . . . not to mention, *he* received an anonymous letter of his own."

"Which he could have absolutely written himself. And why was he so shocked at the picture if he knew about all the letter writing?"

"He didn't know about that; I learned about it from Michel. And you have to make sure not to tell him any of this. I promised I would keep it a secret. I've been trying to get in touch with him—I've called him at least ten times since I got here. I want him to send me the rest of those letters."

"Jesus. Why are there so many bloody secrets in this family, and why am I always the last to know? Dad tells you about Mum's newspaper, Michel tells you about these letters, and no one tells me anything. Do I have the plague or something?"

"Dad didn't mean to tell me a thing. We were out for ice cream and he just sort of ended up with his foot in his mouth."

"Ice cream? Unbelievable," my sister sulked. "If you say it was Ben & Jerry's, I am hanging up, I swear."

"As for Michel, I went to see him the night before I left. I don't even know why he slipped the letter into my jacket pocket."

"Great. You run over to say goodbye to Michel in person, and you say goodbye to me through Dad . . . Isn't that sweet! I'm surprised you even bothered calling me for help."

"Come on. You've already helped a ton by telling me to keep my guard up with George-Harrison."

"Damn right you should! If our mothers really do have some buried treasure out there, you'd better find it before that clown does. Especially considering that my bank won't budge on the overdraft thing."

"If you want to make sure you have money in the bank, you could just try getting a job."

"I can't do everything! I'm going back to college."

"At thirty-five?"

"Excuse me? Thirty-four! Anyway. Are you going to see him again, or what?"

"Tomorrow morning, for breakfast."

"Oh, no . . ." she groaned. "Elby, don't you dare fall in love with this guy!"

"Hang on. First off, he's not my type. Second, I don't trust him one bit. Not yet."

"First off, I don't believe you. Second, you trust everyone. So, for the last time, do not get involved, at least not until we've got to the bottom of this whole mess."

Maggie made me promise to call every day to keep her up to speed, and she in return promised not to say anything to Michel. After we hung up, it took a long time for me to fall asleep. I tossed and turned late into the night.

◆　◆　◆

When I went downstairs the next morning, George-Harrison was already there, waiting for me in the hotel lobby. The dining area in the hotel looked especially grim, so I hopped into George-Harrison's pickup and we went out for breakfast.

"What type of carpenter are you?" I asked to break the ice.

"Type? It's not like there are that many to choose from."

"Sure there are. Some build houses, some make furniture, or maybe . . ."

"When you talk about building houses, it's more construction than carpentry . . . You know, maybe I just don't have a father at all."

"What's that got to do with carpentry?"

"Nothing, absolutely nothing. But I stayed up all night thinking about my mother's letter. She calls your mom 'my love.' What if my father was an anonymous donor—or not anonymous, who's to say?—and the tragedy they keep mentioning was me being born?"

"Tragedy might be pushing it. Tragically dramatic, maybe. And while it's true that you're . . . easy enough on the eyes, a 'treasure' that must be brought back into the light? Don't flatter yourself."

I burst out laughing at my own joke and instantly felt bad about it. The whole thing seemed to really bother him. At the next red light, George-Harrison turned to face me, his face pale and serious.

"It doesn't bother you at all to think of our mothers being . . . so close?"

"How 'close' they were doesn't seem to be what's eating at you, since you're so carefully avoiding saying what you really mean. And if the thought of them as more than friends bugs you so much, maybe you need to think about why that is. Not to mention . . . it might not even be true! By the time your mum wrote that letter . . . she was already, you know . . ."

"Batshit crazy?"

"You really have to finish all my sentences? Look, after a certain age, communicating gets harder. And between love and friendship, things can get mixed up. Let's play your theory out, and you'll see it doesn't fit. Imagine our mothers were in love and decided to have a child together through an anonymous donor. Your mum gets pregnant—and mine just abandons her?"

"What is it about this that doesn't fit?" he asked, as a car honked behind us.

"Hey, step on it, will you? Don't you hear the beeping behind you? I know men are no good at multitasking, but listening and driving at the same time isn't exactly brain surgery. Even my dad can pull that off, and no one's more easily distracted than him."

George-Harrison stepped on the accelerator and crossed the junction, then quickly pulled over to the side of the road.

"How old are you?" I asked him.

"Thirty-five."

"Date of birth?"

"July 4, 1981."

"Well, then—there you have it. Your theory doesn't work. My mother was already back in England when your mother got pregnant with you, by my calculations."

"Men are no good at multitasking, huh? What else do you have against men?"

"Are you planning on parking, or are we just going sit here with the engine on?"

"We're parked, right in front of the place where we're having breakfast. Come on. A cup of coffee would do you a world of good."

◆ ◆ ◆

Without glancing at the menu, George-Harrison ordered eggs Benedict with extra toast, extra bacon, and a large orange juice. Something about that made me smile. I stuck with just tea, figuring I could scavenge some toast. There was no earthly way he would actually clean his plate.

"Since it turns out that I'm not the tragic mistake my mother was referring to," he said, with a crooked grin, "just what do you think she meant? I'm guessing your mother never mentioned—"

"My mother never talked about that period of her life, and we knew better than to ask questions. She was an orphan and there was a lot of pain in her past. We tried to tread lightly, out of respect. Or, to tell you the truth, maybe it was more out of fear than respect."

"Fear of what?"

"Of . . . pulling back the curtain and finding something else there."

"Like what? I don't understand."

"Something other than her children. And how about you? What do you know of your mother's past?"

"I know she was born in Oklahoma, that her dad was a mechanic and her mother was a housewife. My grandfather was as tough as nails, and a bit stingy when it came to affection. Mom told me that he would never hug or touch any of his kids, using all the grease and grit on his hands as an excuse, not wanting to get dirt on them. The only thing tougher than him was growing up in Oklahoma. Maybe people didn't really know how to . . . show their feelings to their kids that well back in those days. Mom took off to New York when she was still young, her head buzzing with all the books she'd read as a kid. She made it sound like books were the best part of her childhood. She got a job as a secretary at a publishing house and went to night school for journalism at NYU. I know she applied to every newspaper up and down the East Coast and got work as an archivist. Then she left the United States and started a new life in Montreal—right around the time she had me."

"Did you know she lived in Baltimore in the late seventies?"

"No, not at all. She only talked about New York. But if I asked even the slightest thing about the period just before she had me, she would clam up or lash out and we'd end up at each other's throats. Where exactly are you going with this?"

"I don't really know, just a tangent."

"Is the treasure what you're after?"

"I didn't even know it existed until about halfway through the flight over here. Crazy as it may sound, I found your mother's letter in my jacket pocket while I was going through security."

"Well, if your poison-pen can manage to slip a letter in your pocket, you should turn around and go look for him in London."

"The poison-pen didn't slip me the letter—my brother did. And what are *you* after in all this?"

"I just want to find my father, like I told you."

"Any idea where to find the letters my mother wrote to yours?"

"Not a clue. Maybe they're gone. How about the rest of the letters from my mom?"

"Same story," I fibbed. "No clue where to find them, or if they even still exist. And to be honest, I have no clue about what to do next either."

A long silence followed, with both of us staring down at the table, until George-Harrison asked me to sit tight for a minute and got up. He went outside and I caught sight of him through the window opening the door to his pickup. If he hadn't left his jacket behind, I would've been afraid he was about to make a run for it. But he came back soon after, sat down, and slid a framed picture onto the table—the photo of our mothers from Sailor's Hideaway.

"The owner doesn't know the first thing about any of the photos on the walls. They were already hanging there when he bought the place. The kitchen is the only part that ever got updated. Aside from a fresh coat of paint, the rest of the place hasn't changed."

"Is this supposed to be a lead?" I asked, sighing with exasperation.

George-Harrison put two other photos in front of me. "These were taken that same night. Look. You can clearly make out the faces of two other people."

"How did you even manage to steal those? I didn't see a thing."

"You really assume the worst about people, don't you? I went back last night. I don't know about you, but I couldn't get to sleep. When I got there, the owner was closing up, and I explained that it was my mother up there on the wall."

"So, he just took it down and gave it to you, throwing in two more as a bonus, all because you batted your eyelashes?"

"You flatter me," he said. "Truth is, I offered him twenty bucks and didn't really have to twist his arm. He told me he's renovating the main space this winter. Remind me—what's the name of that newspaper?"

"The *Independent.*"

"Well, I guess that's as good a place as any to start. If the paper was published in Baltimore, there's gotta be something out there."

"I've already done some serious digging online, and couldn't find a single trace."

"Isn't there some kind of archive where old newspapers would be stored? You're a journalist, shouldn't you know this kind of thing?"

I was. And I should. Yet my first thought was of Michel. "The public library! If there's even one copy out there, that's where we'd find it. Just the masthead alone could be a gold mine . . ."

"Remind me what a masthead is again?"

"It's usually on the editorial page, where you can find all the editing and publishing credits."

We climbed back into the pickup, and George-Harrison waited behind the wheel while I dug up the address.

"Four hundred Cathedral Street," I said, scanning the screen on my iPhone, smiling at what I read.

"What's got you so chirpy all of a sudden?"

"Just the library we're headed to. It has a whole collection of Edgar Allan Poe stuff, original editions donated by his family."

"And that's a good thing?"

"Maybe not for you, but for me? Definitely. Step on it!"

We got to the library in no time and strode right up to the front desk. Unfortunately, it quickly became clear that the woman working there had no idea how to navigate the maze of books and archives for something so specific. But I knew someone who might. I glanced at my watch—still just three in the afternoon in Croydon. Vera picked up straightaway, faithfully stationed at her post as always. After some polite small talk, she offered to go and get Michel, but I told her not to bother; she was the one I was calling for. Vera was flattered and eager to help. I told her I needed to know how the archives would be organized at a library like hers, or at a similar one that was a bit larger. Specifically, how one would go about finding a weekly newspaper published in the late seventies.

"For that, your best bet is microfiche," she explained. "That's how newspapers were archived in those days."

I would have kissed her, had we been in the same time zone.

"Are you sure you don't wish to speak to Michel? I know he'd be delighted to hear your voice. Ah, and here he comes right now. Just a moment, please."

I heard a muffled exchange, and then my brother came on the line. "Although you never checked in with me, I am aware that you arrived safely. I tracked down all the flight information and verified that no plane has crashed since your departure."

"Well, there you have it, that's one way to find out I'm still alive and kicking," I replied. "I actually did try calling you a few times, but you never picked up."

"That makes perfect sense. Mobile phones are strictly prohibited within the library. And I tend to keep mine off when I'm at home."

I took a few steps away from George-Harrison until I was sure he couldn't listen in to our conversation. "I read the letter you gave me," I told my brother.

"I do not wish to speak of it. I believe that was the arrangement."

"And I do intend to respect that, but you did mention a box where other letters could be found."

"Yes, thirty, to be exact."

"Assuming you're not willing to read those to me over the phone, would you consider sending them here?"

"No. I was given specific orders from Mum to always keep them close at hand."

"Damn it, Michel! Mum's dead. And I need those letters."

"Why is that?"

"Look. You were the one who said I care more about people I don't even know than my own family. I'm trying to change that, Michel."

I could hear Michel's breathing quicken, a telltale sign he was headed for an attack. And it was all my fault; logic was a critical component of his approach to decision-making, and irrational notions could derail his entire thought process. The decision I was forcing him to make represented a major dilemma—to help his sister set the past right, he would have to betray his mother.

I was mortified at the idea that I may have triggered a meltdown, especially since there was no way to help from so far away. I could just picture my brother trembling and moaning, burying his face in his hands . . . I had no right to push him that way, especially not when he was at work, next to the one woman he felt close to—or at least "in a manner of speaking," as Michel would have said. I wanted to take it back, to never have gone so far, but it was too late. I heard Vera prying the phone away from him.

"I'm sorry to cut in on your conversation," she said softly. "But if you wouldn't mind . . . I need Michel to locate a couple of reference books over in the main section."

I felt ashamed. Vera showed that she was undeniably far more kind-hearted and sound of judgment with Michel than his own sister was. I thanked her sheepishly and apologized for all of it.

"Don't worry, it'll be okay," she reassured me. "And don't think twice about reaching out; I'd be delighted to lend a hand, so let me know if there's anything else you need."

There was. What I needed was for Vera to convince Michel to send the letters, or to read them to me herself over the phone. But that was far too much to ask. I thought about asking Maggie, but there was no way to do it without Michel learning that I had betrayed his trust by telling her about the letters. I said goodbye to Vera and hung up. I found George-Harrison waiting out in the front hall and joined him to walk back to the library assistant.

"Could you please point us to the microfiche archives?" I asked.

"Of course," the assistant said. "I'll just have to see your credentials first. Are you a student, lecturer, or researcher?"

I flashed my press card, hoping it would do the trick. The girl studied the card warily, until George-Harrison cut in, dropping a smooth compliment about her outfit. Then, he went in for the kill, boldly asking what time she got off and if she wanted to join him for a drink.

"Oh, you're not together?" the assistant asked, blushing.

"Her? And me? No way! Not at all," replied George-Harrison.

The girl ripped out a pair of passes from a pad. She seemed almost embarrassed on my behalf.

"The archive you're looking for is on the lower level. Take the stairs at the back of the room, as quietly as you can, please. Show these passes to the attendant."

As we crossed the large room, I noticed that the library was quite different from the one back in Croydon. Aside from dwarfing it in size, it featured cubicles with cutting-edge technology that would have made Vera turn green with envy, and probably would have put my brother out of a job. The library was packed. Students and researchers sat with eyes glued to computer monitors, and the sound of fingers tapping restlessly on keyboards echoed through the space like a platoon of scrabbling rodents.

George-Harrison and I sat down in front of a machine from a whole other era. It had a broad black screen above a clear platen. I recognized the clunky apparatus from old movies, but had never laid my eyes on one in real life. The archive assistant went searching through a series of cabinets and returned with a cellophane sheet containing eight images so small you could hide them in the palm of your hand.

"Jeez, that's what I call a short run! There's only one edition," the assistant remarked, as he slid the sheet onto the platen and pushed it under the lens reader. The *Independent*'s brilliant logo flashed to life on the black screen. The edition was dated October 15, 1980. I held my breath and scrolled through the eight pages one by one.

The lead stories focused on the presidential campaign that had been in full swing at the time. For several weeks, the sitting American president and his upstart challenger had been entrenched in a brutal war of words. Reagan ridiculed Carter's pacifist mind-set, while Carter accused Reagan of pushing dangerous right-wing extremism and filling his speeches with none-too-subtle references that stoked hatred and racism. "Let's Make America Great Again" was the former California governor's campaign slogan, with the central promise of restoring power to states that had long been abused by Washington.

George-Harrison reminded me how that election had ended. That campaign message wound up propelling Reagan and the Republicans to victory, and they seized both the White House and Congress in a huge electoral landslide.

"Let's hope that formula doesn't work again this time, or else this country's headed for a Trump victory," I grumbled.

"No way; it'll never happen," George-Harrison insisted. "The guy has no credibility. He doesn't stand a chance."

I continued searching through the pages, from one controversial story to the next. One article exposed the consequences of welfare benefit cuts, which had a devastating effect on the poorest in the nation, with 30 percent of the population already living below the poverty line. Another reported on the US Air Force's part in a disastrous accident in which a ballistic missile exploded in its silo and contaminated an entire town. A third covered the arrest of a journalist who had refused to reveal her sources for an article on a controversial parental custody dispute. The last page featured culture highlights. *Evita* won a Tony for Best Musical. Coppola was presenting a Godard film in New York. Ken Follett had climbed to the top of the bestseller list, and Elizabeth Taylor was finally making her Broadway debut at the age of forty-seven.

I had reached the end of the issue without finding anything that even resembled a masthead. I went back through each slide, inspecting page numbers to ensure none were missing. No luck. No masthead. The writers and editors of the newspaper hadn't wanted their names published. The byline for each article was a set of initials instead of a full name.

"What's your last name again?" I asked George-Harrison.

"Collins."

I scanned the screen and pointed out an article. "See that story? The one about runoff from a factory polluting a river, contaminating the drinking water . . . Are those your mother's initials?" George-Harrison squinted at the letters *MC* on-screen and nodded.

"Great," I sighed. "Except I don't see one article written by my mum."

"Are you sure she was involved in the writing? I mean, you don't have to be a doctor to run a health clinic, right?"

"Right, I suppose," I replied, lost amid all these riddles. I went back through the issue and took pictures of each page with my phone, hoping to read every last word of the newspaper in the calm of my hotel room. A strange sensation had come over me, as though my mother's reassuring presence was there, as though she were giving her blessing to keep digging.

"So? What do we do now?" asked George-Harrison.

"I have no idea, not yet. But at least we've got proof the *Independent* was real. We'll have to roll up our sleeves and do some more digging. We're on the hunt for any lead, however flimsy, on people who knew them, maybe an employee of the paper, something like that."

"How can we identify anybody if none of the articles are signed?"

A twisted idea leapt to mind, which happened so often that I didn't think entertaining one more would do any harm. From even the most cursory reading of the *Independent*, it was easy to see a clear and consistent editorial line. It was a paper built on investigative journalism.

I called over the assistant—who I noticed had the same pallid complexion as the microfiches and really needed to get more sun, but that was neither here nor there—and requested all issues of the *Baltimore Sun* from October 12 to 19 of that year.

"What are you up to?" asked George-Harrison.

"Are you familiar with the saying 'When in Rome, do as the Romans do'?" I asked.

I knew from personal experience, if you're writing a feature, you have to get out in the field. So, I put myself in the shoes of the *Independent*'s staff. Where would they have gone for a scoop on the local bigwigs—politicians, socialites, professors, or any other high-society types? Certainly where those sorts of people were most likely to be found: official ceremonies, high-society gatherings, events like that. I figured the society pages of the *Baltimore Sun* from that period would be full of articles with photos of such events. With a little luck, maybe I could find the right photo with the right caption, and maybe I could identify attendees who were actually there as reporters. After all, that was exactly what I would have done.

24

Michel and Vera

October 2016, Croydon

Vera opened the fridge door and peered inside. Everything was in its place: vegetables in the drawers, dairy on top, and a thin strip of netting covering the middle shelf. She sighed as she caught sight of her own reflection on the microwave door, and decided to let down her hair and take off her glasses. Stepping into the living room, she found Michel laying a tablecloth, his eyes glued to the TV, avoiding Vera's.

"Is something wrong?" she asked, but received no response. She came closer, sitting on the armrest of a chair and letting out another sigh. "Michel. Why give just one letter and keep the rest?"

"To do my part. To help, without betraying Mum."

"Fine. But why now?" she asked. "I know you had something specific in mind. You never leave anything to chance."

"Ah, that is because I've never found substantial proof that chance really exists. I wanted to give my sister hope so she would continue her quest. I am quite certain Maggie would have tried to dissuade her. Despite Elby's claims to the contrary, our younger sister exerts a special level of influence over her."

"Wouldn't it just have been simpler to tell her everything?"

"Perhaps, but that would not be a logical choice. Imagine I did find a way to get around my promise, which in and of itself would be by chance . . . if I could move forward for that one reason . . . Even so, anything I could tell her would be biased."

"I don't see why that would be the case," Vera protested.

"When I'm doing research and I question the veracity of any of the facts, I seek out other sources to back them up. That way the story becomes my own, in a way. But if I hear the same story with a personal perspective that includes the intonations and feelings of the narrator, then the story becomes someone else's interpretation, not my own. No matter how accurate that account may be, in such cases the story will never be my own. Elby must find her own truth and not simply have my truth handed to her. I want to give her every possible chance to discover it on her own. And this sort of thing takes time to accept. Letting my sister chart her own course to the truth increases the likelihood that she will achieve that level of acceptance."

"Do you really believe that?"

"It's not so easy, accepting that you've been lied to all your life."

"But you've moved on and learned to forgive, haven't you?"

"No. I have simply learned to accept. It's not the same thing."

25

Eleanor-Rigby

October 2016, Baltimore

We ended up spending all day at the library. The next day, I took a break from all the research to buy a book of papers released by the estate of Edgar Allan Poe, a gift which I was sure would make my editor in chief overjoyed.

Back at the library, George-Harrison and I went through every last article in those eight issues of the *Baltimore Sun* with a fine-tooth comb. We were on the hunt for even the slightest clue that would help push our investigation forward. I found one article on the mayor's development plans, which described an initiative to revitalize the waterfront district. He hoped to convert parts of it into a holiday resort that would attract more tourists. The new convention center, which had opened a few months earlier, had already attracted droves of business visitors. I read another story about what to watch for in the upcoming presidential debate scheduled for the twenty-first. The *Sun* also described a confrontation between Baltimore's mayor and the owner of the Colts. The team owner was enraged by the lack of funding for repairs to the stadium, which was clearly in a state of neglect. He even threatened to move his franchise elsewhere. I moved on to another article describing a fire on the seventeenth of the month that had ravaged portions of Old Town, including a college campus and a Presbyterian church.

The Culture pages featured some great photos of the Who (or "the Sub-Beatles," as my father called them) performing at a local concert venue. At the time, Baltimore's punk, hard rock, and metal music scene was thriving. I wished I had been around in those days, just to breathe in all that freedom.

Just then, something caught my eye. "Hold on a minute," I told George-Harrison. "Go back, just a bit . . ."

George-Harrison used the wheel to scroll back through the microfiche until we reached the page in question. An enormous photo of a masquerade ball took up half the page, of guests decked out in elaborate costumes. But it was the caption that caught my attention.

All the stars turned out looking their very best for an extravagant party celebrating Edward Stanfield's engagement.

"Stanfield," I said, eyes fixing on the name. "There was something about them in the *Independent* as well."

"You're right, that does ring a bell," said George-Harrison, with a deep yawn. "But I can't remember what the story was about."

The assistant was nowhere to be found, and we couldn't get our hands on the *Independent* microfiche again without his help. Luckily, I had taken photos of the pages so I could reread the entire issue later. George-Harrison rubbed his tired eyes, both of us exhausted from staring at that screen for hours on end.

The night before, we had gone out to eat at a quaint little place overlooking the harbor, and I got to learn more about George-Harrison. He told me all about his carpentry studio and his ability to "age" furniture—which was a total scam, no matter what he said—but he became very reserved when I asked about his mother.

Several times I thought he might be coming on to me. Not only did he hang on my every word, laughing—or at least cracking a smile—at all my jokes, but he seemed to get a real kick out of hearing about my family, and he even said he'd love to meet them one day. No one would say something like that without implying something more. But he was wasting his time. First off, he wasn't my type. Second, I had resolved to heed my sister's advice.

The way the night ended only proved that my instincts had been totally spot-on.

◆ ◆ ◆

George-Harrison

I was totally down in the dumps and didn't want to hear another word about her damn family. I made the mistake of asking her about herself, just to be polite and to reciprocate after enduring her own getting-to-know-you game of twenty questions. I wasn't going to fall into her trap by acting self-centered and confirming her negative stereotype of men. In hindsight, it would have been worth the risk, because once she started talking, she didn't stop.

I learned all about her diabetic father with his crummy old jalopy and his Beatles obsession . . . Then the sister she always fought with, and her sister's boyfriend, who ran a gastropub . . . Her brother's crush on a fellow librarian . . . I had already wasted all day reading old newspapers only to now be trapped listening to an endless monologue about her family.

"I must be boring you," she said, after an eternity.

"Are you kidding? Not at all," I replied, courteous as could be. "It sounds like there's never a dull moment with you guys. I bet it would be a real blast meeting a family like yours. Or better yet, have you ever considered renting them out?"

"I know I'm blabbing on and on. I just miss them."

"By all means, go ahead, don't stop on my account."

"If you ever come to England, I can introduce you to them."

Whoa. Was she actually coming on to me? No one would propose such a thing, really, without implying something more.

"Sounds like a plan," I replied. "Who knows where the investigation might lead?"

"I imagine it'll lead to Canada sooner or later, since that's where all the anonymous letters came from."

"The first ones, sure. But the second one I received had a Baltimore postmark."

"Why would the poison-pen go to all that trouble? He could have just sent them from the same place."

"Maybe to cover his tracks? Or maybe he just likes to travel."

"You think he's here in Baltimore right now, as we speak? There's something extremely unsettling about that, don't you think?"

"Nope, not at all. We have no idea what his intentions are, so why should we be scared?"

"Because . . . we have no idea what his intentions are."

She had a point. I took another stab at it.

"Okay. Intentions. The poison-pen wanted us to end up together, and here we are."

"Sure, for starters. He also wanted us to learn that our mothers knew each other, and here we are. He also wanted you to search for your long-lost father, and here you are," Eleanor-Rigby said, rattling off points that were hard to deny.

"Well, I've always wanted to find my father, letter or no letter."

"Yeah, but receiving the letter was the catalyst, the whole reason you're here right now. But that's not the real issue. The real issue is: *Why* did he orchestrate all this? To what end?"

"Are you actually asking me? Or do you already know the answer?"

She leaned across the table, coming closer, and looked deep into my eyes. That was it—she was *definitely* coming on to me, no doubt about it. I hadn't been with anyone since Melanie, and lord knows I'm not exactly a master of seduction, but I found something off-putting about a woman being so forward.

"Money," she said coolly. "The poison-pen wants us to find the money our mothers stole."

"Who said it was money they stole?"

"Are you actually asking me? Or do you already know the answer?"

"How could I know the answer to that?"

"I don't know, you tell me!"

"So, you still don't trust me?"

"Come on, honestly? You must have at least thought it might be me who wrote the letter. The idea never even crossed your mind?"

"No, it didn't. I guess my mind's not quite that twisted. I'm going to bed. If you're still suspicious of me tomorrow morning, if you still think I might be a big enough bastard to pull something like this off—well, then we'll have to go our separate ways and start investigating on our own."

"Great idea," she shot back, rising to her feet before I could.

Well, that settled that. She *definitely* hadn't been coming on to me. I paid the bill and walked straight out.

Back in my hotel room, I fell asleep feeling exhausted, irritated, and generally gloomy. I figured a good night's sleep would clear my head. Once more, I figured wrong.

◆ ◆ ◆

Eleanor-Rigby

Not only was he an absolute swine with an abysmal sense of humor, but he had the nerve to walk out on me! Granted, he did treat me to dinner, which was classy on his part. And maybe I had gone a little bit too far . . . but that didn't make him any less infuriating. Maggie would have told me that the only time a guy runs away like a thief in the night is if he has something to hide. And, might I add, he wasn't doing himself any favors in the honesty department with the whole furniture-aging scheme. Or maybe I had it backwards. Maybe he truly had been offended by my insinuations, which might be because he was innocent.

I returned to the hotel, thinking a good night's sleep might clear my head. After emailing the photos of the microfiches to myself, I opened them on my laptop and sat cross-legged on the bed to read the newspaper pages. Just then, I remembered the note I had jotted down about that photo of the masquerade ball. I looked over the scrap of paper, found the article, and started reading.

> The Stanfields, headed by matriarch Hanna Stanfield, are one of Baltimore's most powerful families. Hanna's husband, Robert, a war hero who served in World War II, owes the family's success to his wife, who is credited with making the Stanfields one of the country's leading art dealers.

> In a few days' time, the Stanfields will hold an exclusive auction for the upper echelon of the art world, presenting masterpieces by La Tour (estimated at $600,000), Degas (estimated at $450,000) and Vermeer (estimated at $1,000,000) to buyers from all over the world.

> Robert Stanfield met Hanna Goldstein in 1944, while the war was still raging, in her native France. Robert returned to the States with Hanna, and having fallen out of grace with his father, the couple first settled in New York.

> In 1948, the Hanna Stanfield Gallery opened its doors on the prestigious Madison Avenue. Hanna started

building the business with a number of pieces that she had inherited, which helped the burgeoning gallery break into the art market and prosper for years to come. Hanna Stanfield was no stranger to the art world. Her father, Sam Goldstein, was a renowned art dealer, with a clientele that included the Rockefellers and the Wildensteins, before he became a victim of the Nazi regime.

The Hanna Stanfield Gallery quickly rose to prominence. After the tragic loss of Robert's parents in a car accident, Robert and Hanna settled the family's debts and made the move to Baltimore in 1950. Hanna set her sights on buying back the family estate, acquiring mortgages that had been seized by local banks.

The sales continued rolling in and the Stanfield empire grew considerably. In 1951, the gallery opened a second location in Washington, DC, followed by a third in Boston in 1952. The Stanfield fortune continued to grow as the family branched out from the art world into real estate. They played a vital role in constructing one of Baltimore's top golf courses. Hanna made a donation to help renovate the Greater Baltimore Medical Center, a sum so generous that the hospital named a wing after her father, Sam Goldstein. The family is also heavily invested in the large-scale renovation of the waterfront district, working hand in glove with City Hall. The Stanfields have also contributed to the construction of the new convention center, one of the city's current flagship projects.

However, since the private lives and moral fiber of public figures are of great importance to our readers, we
believe that Robert Stanfield's upcoming run for governor warrants a second look at this prestigious family's
background. Many questions remain regarding Robert
Stanfield's acts of heroism during wartime, none of
which have ever been confirmed by the Department
of Military Affairs. Equally important are the mysterious circumstances under which Hanna inherited her
father's vaunted art collection.

The true story of how these precious works of art
made it to the US has never fully been brought to light.
Questions remain regarding the exact location where
Sam Goldstein hid his collection during the dark days
of the war, as well as how the precious bounty was
kept out of enemy hands. Many Jewish families were
systematically robbed by Nazi forces during this period. Who hid the paintings away? What middlemen
helped the Goldsteins? How did the paintings end up
in Hanna Stanfield's possession? These secrets have
been safely guarded for years, and their answers are
still shrouded in mystery as the family seeks to exert
influence beyond the city limits and gain a foothold in
state government.

—S

While I didn't know who the author was, my professional instincts
left little doubt: it was a hit job, written with express intent to harm
the subjects. Although the allegations and innuendoes might not have
caused a great stir today, I imagined that it might have been different for

that kind of family in the early eighties. I did some digging online and found a press release about Robert Stanfield withdrawing his candidacy for governor following a terrible accident—*a tragedy* that had befallen his family. The rest of the paper provided no more details. I knew I needed to find out more about what this tragedy was.

26

ROBERT STANFIELD

June 1944

Early morning, before dawn, with the dark of night fading bit by bit, two Resistance fighters struggled to stay awake as they kept watch outside the hunting lodge. The surrounding woods were quiet, and there was not a soul in sight.

The safe house, which held the weapons cache, was not especially large, but it was comfortable enough. The living room on the ground floor also served as a rustic kitchen, with a countertop and a stone fireplace, while a trapdoor further down led to the cellar. The bedroom Sam and his daughter shared was down to the right, and Robert's room was to the left. Upstairs, five Resistance fighters were snoring away in the attic-turned-barracks. At five in the morning, Robert rose from bed and shaved in front of the little mirror in the kitchen. As he packed up his gear, his partner, Titon, the Italian member of the crew, was watching.

"Don't take your gun," Titon advised. "If we get stopped, they'll search us, and we need to pass as local farmers."

"Good luck with that!" Maurice snickered from the kitchen. "He's got a mighty strange accent for a local farmer. If you two get stopped, have him hand over his papers, but don't let him say a word."

"Hurry up," another member of the crew urged. "The factory opens its doors at six o'clock. You'll need to walk in with the workers; that's the only way to get in unnoticed."

Titon and Robert's mission was to infiltrate the cartridge factory.

"Go to the manager at the workshop, and give him this message: 'There were doves flying overhead this morning.' He'll give you a haversack full of what you'll need."

"Then what?" asked Titon.

"Then, you blend in with the others and discreetly insert the rigs under the assembly lines." The rigs were gutter pipes they had swiped from a scrapyard and modified to suit their needs. Bolted end-caps had been added to each side, and each had a hole for a fuse leading to Ablonite charges to pass through. The explosives had been scavenged by sympathetic miners from a nearby quarry.

"At noon, the workers will head to the courtyard for a break. You two light the fuses. You'll have two minutes before the explosion, and then you take advantage of the chaos to get out."

Robert and Titon served themselves soup from a large pot hanging in the hearth above coals still burning from the night before. They needed to get something in their stomachs; they wouldn't be back at the hunting lodge until after nightfall.

Sam Goldstein and his daughter stepped out of their room. Hanna leaned against the doorframe silently, while Sam came up to shake Robert's hand. "Be careful," he whispered, pulling Robert in for a tight hug. "I am hoping to never have to hold up my end of our deal."

Hanna watched, still walled up in her world of silence. Robert waved at her, then grabbed his gear and followed Titon outside. They made their way down the path through the woods and hopped onto a tandem bicycle that lay awaiting them, Titon in front and Robert behind. Titon asked Robert if there was something going on between him and the Jewish girl. Everyone noticed the way she looked at him.

"Well, she's a bit young, don't you think?" said Robert.

"Il cuore pien di dibolesses," sighed Titon in his native tongue, a patois from Treviso.

"Sorry, what does that mean?"

"It means it's a shame to see a child's heart so full of sorrow. But you, you're American. Why do you come to fight so far from home?" asked Titon.

"I'm not exactly sure. To rebel against my father, I guess. My heart was full of romantic ideals."

"Ah, so you're a fool, then? There's nothing romantic about war."

"What about you? Didn't you come from far away to fight?"

"I was born here. My parents arrived in '25. But to the French, I'll always be a foreigner. They don't like us all that much. I've always found them to be quite an odd people. Our parents showered us with affection, but the French never even kiss their children. When I was growing up, I thought it meant they didn't love them, but it's simply that they don't know how to express their feelings."

"If they have so many flaws, why do you fight for them?"

"I fight fascists wherever they are. And next time someone asks you that question, you should say the same thing; you'll be better off."

Ten kilometers later, they ran straight into French militiamen at a crossroads and were stopped for questioning. Robert handed over the papers and Titon did the talking, just as planned. He explained that they were workers on their way to the factory. Titon begged the ranking officer to let them go on their way, explaining that their foreman would dock their pay if they were even a minute late.

One of the soldiers approached Robert. "What's the matter with you? Cat got your tongue?"

Titon spoke for Robert: "He's deaf and dumb." The officer ordered the two men to dismount the bike.

As Robert swung his leg over the bike, the officer shoved him hard, knocking him down. Caught off guard, Robert cursed loudly. Their cover was blown. Everyone froze. Then all hell broke loose.

Even outnumbered four to two, the partisans weren't about to go quietly. Titon lunged at the ranking officer and struck him down with a fierce right hook, while Robert wrestled another to the ground. The third soldier kicked Robert in the ribs, knocking the air out of him, then stunned him with a boot to the chin.

Titon leaped in to push the man off Robert, landing a solid uppercut, when shots suddenly rang out. The fourth soldier had drawn his gun and fired three shots, killing Titon instantly. The soldiers dragged his corpse off into a ditch, leaving a long trail of blood on the road. They handcuffed Robert, threw him into the back of their van, and took him straight to the police station.

Robert's clothes were torn off and he was tied to a chair, naked. Three militiamen kept watch over him. Another prisoner, a woman who had been tortured, was hunched over on the ground, writhing in pain. Robert had never seen such brutality. The filth and the stench of blood mixed with urine were entirely new to him. One of the militiamen strode over to Robert and gave him two thunderous slaps across the face, knocking the chair straight over. The two other men set Robert upright once more so the militiaman could rear back and strike him again. This game lasted a full hour. Not a single question was asked. Robert fainted twice, both times brought back to consciousness by a bucket of ice water thrown over him.

Next, as the men dragged Robert toward a small cell, they passed another prisoner huddled on a straw mattress, his torso and legs covered in wounds. Robert looked at the man long and hard, until the militiaman barked, "You two know each other?"

The Resistance fighter threw Robert a surreptitious glance, silently pleading with him not to reveal their connection.

At noon, Robert was brought back to the torture room for another round of beatings. The blows rained down on him, until a policeman strolled into the room and ordered the militiamen to stand down and leave.

"My name is Inspector Vallier," he said. "Allow me to express my regret for the treatment that you have been forced to endure here. We thought you were English . . . but you're American, are you not? I don't have a thing against Americans. On the contrary—Gary Cooper, John Wayne . . . doesn't get any better than that! My wife fancies Fred Astaire, who is maybe a little effeminate for me, but I have to admit, the man sure knows how to move those feet!"

Vallier did a quick little dance move, clearly trying to lighten the tension still hanging over the room.

"Now, I am a curious man by nature—call it an occupational hazard. So, I have to wonder: What on earth is an American doing riding a tandem bicycle with a terrorist? Don't answer, not yet. First, let me share two hypotheses with you, two explanations that spring to mind. First: you were hitchhiking, this scum picked you up, and you had no idea he was a traitor. The second explanation is that you were *working* with him. Of course, the two don't carry the same consequences. Don't speak, please, not yet. I'm still working it out in my head. Ah, there. You see, it just doesn't fit. Why ride a tandem bike alone? But let's say he did . . . he just happens to run into a hitchhiker? You see, it doesn't add up, which is unfortunate. Because if my colleagues make this same connection, I honestly wouldn't know what to tell them. You'd be at their mercy. It seems we still have a little while before they're done with their lunch break. So, I'll let you in on a little secret.

"There are two doors out of this police station. One leads to the courtyard, where you will be shot. Our court system is far too overloaded with our own terrorists as it is. And anyway, an American working with an enemy of the state on French soil wouldn't be entitled to a trial. Foreign agents are subject to military punishment. So, think carefully about the story you're about to tell me. You're young, you have your whole life ahead of you. It would be such a shame for it to end so soon. Which reminds me, I forgot to tell you about the second door. How silly of me! Let's say you give us some names, the location where you and your hapless friends have been hiding out—then I would be happy to take off your handcuffs and send you on your way through the second door back onto the street. I'll consider those papers of yours authentic. Young Robert Marchand gets to go home. Imagine how happy your parents would be to have you back. Or, maybe there's a little lady waiting for you? A sweet little fiancée, for example?"

Inspector Vallier glanced up at the clock on the wall and pressed a finger to his ear. "Ticktock, ticktock, you hear that?" he whispered to Robert. "My colleagues won't be long now. You walked into a trap, you know. It wasn't mere chance. Patrols are posted at every crossroads in the vicinity. We know you're hiding out somewhere in those woods. The militia has been hunting relentlessly for weeks now. They will find it, they're very close. With or without your help, it's only a matter of time, a few days at best, before they smoke your friends out. Dying here today would be such a waste, just to delay the inevitable . . . how very silly, how very sad. Think of it this way. You decide to talk, you might actually *spare* your friends' lives. If we're able to find their hideout, we can bring them in quietly. No violence, just arrests. If we manage to surround them, they'll have no choice but to surrender. But if the militia find them during patrol, everyone starts shooting. Same outcome, more bloodshed. If you're clever, you can save your own skin and your friends' lives in the process. Call out when you've made up your mind about what you wish to tell me. You have less than fifteen minutes to decide."

27

ELEANOR-RIGBY

October 2016, Baltimore

The moment George-Harrison walked into the dining area for break-fast, I began talking his ear off about the Stanfields. I had been up until the wee hours of the morning digging, only to come up short, with no leads on the elusive family. I wasn't even able to find the address of their famous Baltimore estate. Thinking back to how Mum tracked down my father in Croydon all those years ago, I went to the front desk and asked for a phone book. The clerk gaped at me as if I had requested some otherworldly, mysterious object.

George-Harrison had barely taken his first sip of coffee when I asked him if he could take me down to city hall.

"Just run away and elope? No way, honey," he joked. "You're going to have to get down on one knee and propose first."

I grinned at his stale joke, promising he'd get a real laugh if he tried a little harder next time. As we parked near city hall, we divided up the tasks so we could move quicker. I would head for the vital records department to find out if Hanna or Robert were still alive, and he'd cover property records to see if he could find any leads on their estate.

"Except if they're already dead, we'll find them in the cemetery, inevitably," George-Harrison offered.

"Good lord. If you keep up this comedy show, it's going to be a very long day . . ."

◆ ◆ ◆

City hall was a perfect example of Second Empire Renaissance architecture, with baroque decoration adorning the structure, a mansard roof, and an imposing dome. I had visited other official state buildings on trips to the US in the past, yet I quickly found myself lost and going around in circles. George-Harrison was equally confounded by the sprawling labyrinth. We decided to split up, each of us knocking on door after door without any luck. After looping past each other three more times in the vast rotunda—a circular space with various corridors extending outwards and leading to the upper levels—we decided to join forces and head up to the second floor, where our luck changed. A woman approached and kindly offered to point us in the right direction. She must have watched us retrace our steps and wander about dejectedly, and realized we could do with a hand. She definitely seemed to know her way around the place.

"Head due south," she instructed, gesturing down over the balustrade. "Take a right at the end, then a left, and you're there."

"And where is 'there' exactly?" asked George-Harrison.

"Vital records. But you'd better hurry up. They close at noon."

"Great, thank you. But how do we even reach that staircase?"

"For that, head due north," she said, turning around. "Straight down that first stairwell, then make a U-turn and continue straight through the rotunda down the middle corridor. That should put you on the right track."

"Thanks. What about property records?" I asked.

"Wait, can I ask a question?" George-Harrison cut in. "Have you ever heard of an old Baltimore family by the name of Stanfield?"

The friendly woman arched an eyebrow and beckoned us to follow her. She led us down the stairs to the ground floor and to the middle of the rotunda—right back where we started. There, six statues stood within alcoves carved into the curved wall. Our new friend led us to one of the alcoves and gestured toward an alabaster statue of a proud-looking man wearing a frock coat and tall hat, his hand resting on the pommel of a cane.

"Frederick Stanfield, born 1842, died 1924. If he's the one you're looking for, maybe you can just read the plaque and save a trip to the records office!" she laughed. "Stanfield was one of the founding fathers of Baltimore, believe it or not. As an architect, he even contributed to the beautiful building in which we now stand. The first plans were submitted just prior to the onset of the Civil War. Construction began in 1867 and took a full eight years to complete. And all this for the meager sum of eight million dollars, which at that time was a massive fortune. It's at least a hundred times more, in today's terms. If I had even a quarter of that, we could fix the entire budget for the year."

"Sorry," I cut in. "But just out of curiosity: Who exactly are you?"

"Stephanie Rawlings-Blake," she replied. My jaw dropped as I realized I was face-to-face with the mayor of Baltimore herself. "Pleased to meet you. And no, I'm not moonlighting as a tour guide, and to tell you the truth, I'm not much of a history buff at all, I just happen to pass by these statues all day long."

After we thanked the mayor from the bottom of our hearts, I asked one last question. "Can you tell me if there are any surviving Stanfields left in Baltimore these days?"

"I have to admit, I have no idea," she replied. "But I might know someone who could help you." She took out her phone and read out a phone number, which I quickly jotted down. "You can find Professor Morrison at Johns Hopkins. He's a sort of 'living memory' around here, the absolute leading authority on Baltimore history. But he's a very busy man, so be sure to call ahead and tell him I sent you. He should be able to help; he already does so many favors for me, one more won't make a difference! He writes all my boring speeches for inaugurations and events like that . . . but don't tell him I said that. Now, sorry to say, I have to leave you. I have a city councilman waiting in my office." With that, the mayor left as discreetly as she had appeared.

"Don't worry, you don't have to bother thanking me," George-Harrison grumbled.

"For what?"

"For having the brilliant idea of asking the mayor about the Stanfields, which may have saved us from wasting an entire day, again."

"Because you knew who she was all along, huh? Well, isn't that rich! For your information, if I hadn't had the bright idea of going to the library in the first place, we wouldn't have uncovered the Stanfield connection at all."

"First of all, you're a total hypocrite. Second, would it really kill you to admit I deserve a thank-you here? And third, why do we keep coming back to these precious Stanfields of yours?"

"If you had actually listened this morning, you'd already know. Hanna and Robert Stanfield were major players when it came to rare and desirable works of art, and were heavily involved in local real estate. They also gave generously to the city. But . . . no one today seems to know a *thing* about them. The only significant proof we've found of their existence came from that article in the *Independent* and a blurb in the *Sun* about a party they held, plus a press release about Robert Stanfield withdrawing his bid for governor. So . . . Mr. Stanfield gives up a run for governor because of a tragedy in his family, but there's no explanation of what this tragedy is. If there's one rule in politics, it's that silence is the most expensive thing money can buy. Maybe that gives you an idea of just who the Stanfields were."

"Fine, the Stanfields were big and powerful. How does that make a difference to us?"

"Well, your mother specifically mentioned a tragic mistake in her letter. Think about it, connect the dots. You don't think there's something there? Of course, if you've got a better lead, I'm all ears."

George-Harrison jingled his car keys. "Okay, Johns Hopkins it is. You can call Professor Morris along the way."

"It's Morrison! And would it really kill you to admit that I'm a damn fine reporter?"

◆ ◆ ◆

The professor agreed to see us in his office later that afternoon. Name-dropping the mayor helped get our foot in the door, but we still encountered a bit of trouble. After the secretary nearly hung up on me, George-Harrison had to snatch the phone straight out of my hands and work his charm to secure the meeting.

We were directed to a lecture hall, where Morrison was just finishing a seminar, and watched from the back as he gathered up his notes and the small group of his students rose from their seats and shuffled out. The professor cleared his throat and stepped down from the lectern, grimacing with each step. He wore a humdrum three-piece suit and had a rim of white hair encircling his scalp, a heavy gray beard hanging from his face. Despite his age, there was still a certain class to the old man. Seeing us approach, the professor let out an exasperated sigh and, with a flippant wave of his eyeglasses, motioned for us to follow him.

The professor's stuffy office smelled of dust and wax. He took a seat at his desk and gestured for the two of us to sit across from him. Then, he opened a drawer, took out a bottle of painkillers, and swallowed two of them dry.

"Goddamn sciatica," he growled. "If you've come seeking pearls of wisdom, I've got one at the ready: better to die young!"

"Well, thank you, I guess," said George-Harrison. "But don't you think we're a bit old to be students?"

"Speak for yourself!" I chimed in.

Morrison leaned forward and stared at us over the rims of his glasses, sizing up his two visitors. "Your friend does have a point," he concluded, rubbing his chin. "If you haven't come seeking help for your dissertation, just what can I do for you?"

"We're here to ask about the Stanfields."

"I see." The professor straightened his back, his face twisting in pain once more. "Often the smallest fragments of history can present a historian with the greatest of challenges. It all begins with cracking open a book, as I'm apt to repeat to my students. If you're interested in learning about Frederick Stanfield's life, why not try the library before wasting my time?"

"The Stanfields we're interested in are Hanna and Robert, as well as the last of the family line," I explained. "We can't find a thing on them. Believe me, I've scoured the internet far and wide, stayed up half the night, and came up with barely a mention."

"Ah, glorious. The internet. How lucky am I to find myself face-to-face with a great historian of tomorrow! She actually went so far as to stay up 'half the night' searching through her precious encyclopedia of nonsense. When are you people going to stop being so daft? *Anyone* can write *anything* in that dismal and intangible catchall. One moron after another vomits words onto the page, posting whatever thoughts come to his head without the smallest shred of integrity. No wonder your great 'web' is such a tangled mess of fantasies and falsehoods. Go ahead. Tomorrow, post about how George Washington was a master tango dancer, and a hundred cretins will start repeating the tall tale. Soon, we'll all be asking Google what time we should take a leak to avoid prostate cancer. In any event, the two of you were sent by some-one to whom I am greatly indebted, thus I have no choice but to help you. But let's try to waste the least amount of time possible, yes? What do you wish to know about the Stanfields?"

"What happened to them, for a start."

"Like anyone who reaches a certain age, they died, the very same fate that will befall the lot of us, sooner or later."

"When did they die?" asked George-Harrison.

"Robert Stanfield died in the eighties, I don't know when, exactly, and his wife not long after that. They found her car on the seafloor, right off the pier, leaving little doubt that the woman's agony had become unbearable, and she had at last given in and taken her own life."

"Can you provide any documentation? Any proof of your claims?" asked George-Harrison. "Or did you just read that on the internet?"

The professor was speechless. It took backbone to put an old grouch like him in his place like that, and George-Harrison suddenly shot up at least ten points in my book.

Morrison glared at him, eyes sharp and beady like a trial lawyer. "My, my, you've got some nerve talking to me like that."

"Must be a lot of that going around . . . judging by how you've treated us from the moment we walked in," George-Harrison retorted, without missing a beat. Another ten points.

"I haven't exactly given you the most cordial greeting, I'll grant you that. Try five minutes with a hip like mine, we'll see how friendly you behave. But, to answer your question, no, I don't have any sort of formal proof. Mind you, there was no streaming video of the First Continental Congress in 1774, yet we can rest easy knowing the founding fathers accomplished great feats during that time in Philadelphia. History is set into stone through deduction and cross-referencing of facts and events. And as far as the late Mrs. Stanfield is concerned, all I can tell you is she summoned all her staff, settled their wages, and left her home, never to return. Unless you think that someone of her stature would go hitchhiking cross-country, I'd say suicide is a safe enough conclusion to draw."

"What was the tragedy that befell the Stanfields?" I asked.

"Make that *tragedies*, plural. First came the trauma of the war. Then the disappearance of their daughter, followed by the loss of Edward, ending their bloodline and the dynasty. Like many mothers, Hanna loved her son very deeply. He was her whole world. In the span of just a few short months, the glory of the Stanfield name was scattered to the wind. Rumors flew about town that the Stanfields had been the victims of a massive theft, and some even made the sordid accusation they had committed insurance fraud after the fact. There were whispers about Edward's 'accident' not being quite so accidental, considering it occurred mere weeks before his own wedding. Finally, the Stanfield gallery canceled an auction at the last minute, leading some to suspect the catalog had been a sham—a veritable faux pas in the art world. Quite a host of rumors flying about for such a small town. The Stanfields led a lavish lifestyle in the heart of high society, and suddenly no one wanted anything to do with them. Their coffers were soon empty. I'm convinced that Hanna Stanfield chose death in the face of solitude and disgrace. In the blink of an eye, she lost everything—family and fortune. Robert was first to go after a fatal heart attack, and there were even some who believed he had been poisoned. A foul lie, masking an even fouler truth—he dropped dead in the arms of his mistress!"

"Why no mention of any of this in the press?"

"As I said, Baltimore is like a small town. While Mrs. Stanfield wasn't loved by all, she certainly had no shortage of friends in the highest of places. I suppose our local journalists and editors had the grace and dignity not to heap more on the back of a family down on its luck, especially one whose matriarch had spoiled the press so thoroughly in her heyday."

"And just what was it they decided to keep quiet about?" I asked.

"All of this happened more than thirty years ago! Just what is your interest in the fate of the Stanfields?"

"It's a long story." I sighed. "You said that history is set into stone through deduction, cross-referencing of facts and events, so I'm just trying to cross-check the story in my own way."

Morrison crossed over to the window and gazed out onto the street. The professor seemed miles away, lost in the not-so-distant past that seemed close enough to touch.

"I crossed paths with the Stanfields from time to time at social gatherings. An academic with any career ambition must venture out and mingle with high society from time to time. But I had never met with them in private, not until I was struck with the idea of publishing a book on the lives of the founding figures of Baltimore, a project I never actually finished. Robert was the only descendant of Frederick Stanfield. I reached out to him and received an invitation to visit. Robert was a quiet man who valued his privacy, but was also very generous. He gave me quite the warm welcome, inviting me into his study and treating me to a glass of incredible Scotch—a bottle of 1926 Macallan, a whisky so rare, there were scarcely ten bottles of it left in the entire world, even back then. It was a once-in-a-lifetime opportunity; the taste was unforgettable.

"We spoke at length, and I eventually gave in to my curiosity and asked a few questions about Robert's past, starting with his wartime experience. Robert had shipped off to fight in France *before* the landings, an exceedingly rare occurrence. Most American soldiers serving in Europe in early '44 were stationed in England. I knew that he and Hanna had met during that tumultuous period, and I secretly dreamt of recounting their story as part of my book. My vision was to demonstrate a continuity between the past glory of the Stanfield family and Robert's own exploits.

"When at last I raised questions about how he and Hanna had met, the lady herself happened to enter the study, and Robert immediately cut the conversation short. Now, getting faithful accounts and asking pointed questions are part of my job, as is grilling my subjects for answers, just as you two are doing now. But I haven't a clue as to the motives behind the couple's secrecy. What I can tell you is that Hanna had a very strong influence over the rest of the family. It took mere moments observing the two of them in that study to see the extent of her authority. Hanna was the empress ruling over all. She called the shots. She even showed me to the door herself that day, both figuratively and literally. Firm yet courteous, she gave a message that was loud and clear: I was not welcome to return. I don't know what else I can tell you. All else is gossip, a tawdry domain which I'm loath to enter."

"So, you visited their house? Where is it?" I asked.

"'House' doesn't quite cover it. It was an estate, one that's long gone. As a leading member of the Baltimore City Historical Society, I, as well as my peers, vehemently protested when the city granted authorization to tear it down. A pack of shameless developers reduced it to rubble, erecting upscale condominiums in its place. This despicable skullduggery is laying to waste our heritage and history, all for the benefit of a select few. This city has become infested with corruption and greed that goes as high as our former mayor, just one more poor fool who flew too close to the sun. Luckily, the new mayor has integrity, luckily for *you*, considering it's that very trait that drove her to send you here to me. On that note, I believe it's high time I returned to my duties."

"First, could you tell me more about the estate?" I insisted.

"It was opulent, richly furnished, lined with canvas masterpieces, and imbued with a grandeur that is, alas, all but forgotten now."

"So, what became of their art collection?"

"Mrs. Stanfield was forced to part with it out of necessity, I suppose. The parting came at a great cost, for the reasons I mentioned earlier. I apologize if this comes as a disappointment, but that collection is long gone. Lost and buried in the sands of time."

Morrison walked us to the door and bid us good luck.

George-Harrison sat behind the wheel in silence for a long time before at last starting the pickup and pulling onto the road. Ten minutes later, I decided to ask where we were headed.

"Well, clearly the Stanfields saw their fair share of tragedy, but so what?" he began. "Most of what he said was useless, except for—"

"You can stop there. You're right, I was wrong. You don't have to gloat. It was a dead end. And what's worse, I don't have a clue where we should head next."

George-Harrison pulled over and stopped the truck in front of a police station. "Except, as I was saying, there was one thing the lovely Professor Morrisman said that fits with our story."

"The theft. When he mentioned them being robbed? That occurred to me as well. But a city of this size has got tragedies and insurance scams to spare."

"Exactly. But that's not what stuck with me. It was the Scotch. The 1926 Macallan."

"What, you're some kind of aficionado?"

"Not at all, and neither is my mother. And yet she had that very bottle of whisky. I remember seeing it, up on the shelf, all through my childhood. Every October, she'd take just the tiniest little glass of it, savoring every drop. I guess that makes sense now, considering how much it's worth. I eventually did ask her what was up with her weird annual ritual, but she never gave me a direct answer."

"Just to play devil's advocate, there must be as many bottles of this type of Scotch in Baltimore as there are thefts and tragedies."

"Not according to the professor, not from 1926. Barely ten of them left at the time, he told us. And he seemed to know what he was talking about. Seems a bit of a stretch for it to be a coincidence that my mother lived in Baltimore and ended up with a bottle. I think it's safe to say, the Macallan on my mother's shelf must have come from Robert Stanfield's own liquor cabinet."

"Could that be the treasure she talked about in the letter?"

"Well, we could look into the actual value of the Scotch, but I doubt that's what she meant. Although that would be hysterical, thinking back on how she treasured it! But seriously . . . I can't help but feel like we're following someone's trail of bread crumbs, and I'd like to know who it is."

"You're not honestly telling me you think running into the mayor was part of some master plan?"

"I wouldn't go that far. But Morris could have been."

"For the last time, it's Morrison!"

"Baltimore's very own 'living memory,' as the mayor put it. Those anonymous letters put the two of us together right in front of a photo of our mothers. That photo led us to the archives of the *Independent*, which put us on the trail to the Stanfields. Sooner or later, we were bound to stumble upon that statue, or at least learn it was out there. Plenty of clues that lead back to that charming professor."

"You really suspect him?"

"Well, why not? Who else would know what really happened at the Stanfield estate?"

"Sure. Okay. And he's obviously not able to get around well, which explains why he'd want us to come all the way here to him. But I don't see how he could have pieced together where you and I fit into all this, much less track us down. What's more, he would have had to know you were desperately hoping to find your father, and so many other intimate details of our lives, down to my sister's name."

"Let's say he knows a little more than he's letting on about whatever was stolen. Let's say he even suspects our mothers of being the perpetrators. If so, that matches what's in the letter, and there's your link. As for the rest, maybe he's not as anti-internet as he says, and he did admit having a knack for pumping people for information."

"You think he's after the treasure? He didn't seem to be the type that's out for money. The only thing more beaten up than his suit was his hairline."

"Don't forget: people who are that passionate aren't always in it for the money. The professor also bragged about being a leading member of the Baltimore Historical Preservation Society, or whatever it was. What if the thing they stole is of great historical value, so he's willing to go to great lengths to get it back?"

"Excellent question. You would have made a great investigative journalist."

"Say, you didn't just pay me a compliment by any chance, did you?" He flashed me a coy look that I had to admit I found downright sexy. And it wasn't the first time I had noticed, to be honest. I wanted to kiss him, right then and there. But I didn't.

Even though I could still hear Maggie's warnings ringing in my ears, I wasn't afraid of George-Harrison anymore—I was more scared of myself. I had no idea where this whole quest might take me, or if I could even see it through to completion. But I did know that my days in Baltimore were numbered. My job wouldn't let me stay here forever. Getting involved with George-Harrison would only complicate things, even if it was ultimately only a fling.

"What are you thinking about?" he asked, right on cue.

"Nothing special, just wondering why we're parked in front of the police station."

"We're here so you can waltz in there, flash your press card, and work your magic on whatever cop comes out to greet you, flirting your way straight into the police archives. With a bit of luck, we might just get our hands on the official police report of the theft, and more specifically, find out just what was stolen."

"And if it's a female cop?"

"In that case, I'll do my best."

"I've already seen you 'do your best' a couple of times, and for someone who claims not to be a ladies' man, you seem to get by just fine."

28

SALLY-ANNE

October 1980, Baltimore

Sally-Anne stepped into the loft and stopped in her tracks. Glass tealights, over twenty in all, had been lined up in a path that led straight to the bedroom. She rolled her eyes and sighed in exasperation. Romantic gestures like this were touching and all, but Sally-Anne felt like her own reaction to them was always forced, and the outpouring of emotion made her feel uneasy. Tonight, she just didn't have the heart to play along. Then, something unexpected caught her eye: shards of broken dishes were scattered across the floor. Sally-Anne sidestepped the sharp ceramic pieces and knocked at the door to the bedroom nook.

May was sitting on the bed in a bathrobe, trails of mascara running down her cheeks and a newspaper in her lap. "I trusted you. My God, did I trust you. How could you do this to me?" she moaned, her voice a mix of disbelief and sadness.

Sally-Anne's mind was racing. She was convinced that May must have discovered the loan rejection and the far reach of her mother's power. She had kept the bank's decision a secret, not out of pride or a desire to deceive, but because she needed to publish the *Independent* as an act of vengeance. It was now time to tell her team that the first issue would also be the last, and that every one of them was officially out of work. Blindsiding her employees certainly wasn't fair, but the rage burning deep in the pit of her stomach made it easy to overlook such things.

"So, you thought breaking all our dishes was going to make things better?"

"I was trying to calm down. It didn't work."

"Was it Edward? Was he the one who told you?"

"Oh, no. Your piece-of-shit brother is far too cowardly for that."

"Tell me something I don't know," replied Sally-Anne, sitting down on the edge of the bed. May's T-shirt showed off her curves, and Sally-Anne suddenly felt desire welling up within her, perhaps intensified by all the tension in the air.

"How could you not tell me?" said May.

"I was trying to protect you."

"To protect me . . . from the humiliation, or just so you could say 'I told you so'? Don't tell me that you're vain enough to be that cruel. You're supposed to hate him, so why in the world would you choose to protect him and let me get screwed over?"

Suddenly unsure, Sally-Anne slid the issue of the *Baltimore Sun* from May's lap and laid her hand down softly on her knee.

"Can you just explain what you're talking about?"

"Enough! Enough lying," May sighed. "Haven't all your lies made enough of a mess already? Don't treat me like a fool."

"You want the truth? We barely have enough money to pay for the paper to go to print. We won't make rent, let alone pay all the wages we owe. I didn't tell you because knowing how honest you are, you never would have let me print the first issue. You would have let everyone go. And you seemed so happy frolicking around with my bastard of a brother, I didn't want to spoil it for you, as crazy as the whole thing has driven me. It was wrong. But I'm begging you to stick with me and see this venture through. We go to print with the first issue, and if you never find it in your heart to forgive me, so be it. We go our separate ways."

May straightened up in bed, her eyes haggard. "Now . . . it's my turn to ask what you're talking about."

The two women looked at each other, angry and confused. Sally-Anne took the first leap.

"I'm talking about my mother's dirty trick, her latest and greatest work: seeing to it that our loan was rejected. What else would I be talking about? We're up to our ears in debt. She wiped her hands of me with a silly little check that doesn't begin to cover our debts. See? We actually needed those dishes. We don't have a cent for new ones. That's all. That's the only secret I was keeping."

May reached past Sally-Anne to grab the copy of the newspaper from the foot of the bed. She held it out, stabbing a finger at the offending text.

> At the end of the month, a masquerade ball will be held at the home of Mr. Robert Stanfield and his wife, Hanna, in honor of their son Edward's engagement to Miss Jennifer Zimmer, daughter of Fitzgerald and Carol Zimmer, and heiress to the bank that bears their name.

"I didn't know! I haven't even been invited," Sally-Anne whispered. "They've cut me out of my own brother's engagement party. And, my God, you had to find out about this through the paper?" She sighed, defeated.

She moved in closer and put her arms around May. "I swear on my life: I had no idea."

May let Sally-Anne rock her softly, their faces cheek to cheek.

"He used me and threw me away . . . like some kind of whore," May sobbed.

Sally-Anne hugged her closer. "It's as though I don't exist to them . . . like I'm something to be ashamed of. It's so humiliating. I can't even say which of us got it worse."

May rose and led Sally-Anne to the door of their room, the glow of the candles still reflecting off the porcelain debris.

"I was cooking a special dinner for your brother. I tried calling him three times. Your butler kindly informed me that Mr. Edward was in a meeting, but would relay my message to him. So, I sat reading the paper while I waited for his call. And that's how I found out he wouldn't be coming. Can you imagine anything so cruel? The only thing worse than the lie is how much of a coward he was. To think that he took me to his island and swore up and down that he loved me. He played me for a fool. I've been a fool. But, I'm begging you, don't say 'I told you so.'"

"It's even worse than you think, worse than him just being a coward. The whole thing was a plot that my mother and Edward hatched together. While my brother drove a wedge between us, my mother sharpened her knives and stabbed me in the back, and you in the heart."

A silence fell over the space, as though the awful reach of Hanna Stanfield's power had extended all the way into the apartment.

"Let's sit down," May said. "There's a nice dinner just sitting there, and we can clear a spot on my desk."

They sat down across from each other. Sally-Anne shook her head. "We can't let this stand," she whispered.

"We got double-crossed and now we're ruined. What choice do we have?"

May thought about the weekend on Kent Island, just days earlier. She had been so happy, but Edward had ruined it. Sally-Anne, meanwhile, was peering across the warehouse at the part that had been transformed into a newsroom. Just days earlier, the *Independent* had been taking its first breaths, but her mother had killed it.

"I'll tell you what we're going to do. We're going to take back what's ours," she said.

"I think I've had my fill of your asshole brother."

"That's not what I meant. I mean the paper."

"You said it yourself: without funding, the paper is finished," May said. She crossed the room and lit the stove burner under a pan of watercress soup.

"My father has a small fortune in bearer bonds in the safe in his study. It's a favorite payment method of art collectors who want to keep some transactions tax-free. Officially, the painting is resold at cost, then all taxable profit is settled this way. No one's any the wiser. The bonds are anonymous. They can be cashed at any bank, without any kind of proof of origin."

"We're not thieves, Sally-Anne. How do you expect us to break into a safe and steal all that money?" May sighed as she poured the warmed soup into a tureen and set it on the desk. It was far from the romantic dinner she had envisioned while slaving away in the kitchen earlier.

"Who said anything about stealing? The Stanfields built an empire on what had been left by my grandfather: his paintings and the legacy of his reputation. I'm the only one who seems to have inherited the man's ethics. He'd be livid if he were here to see how his daughter was acting now. He'd be first in line to help us."

"That's all well and good," said May as she filled their bowls with soup. "Claiming your inheritance wouldn't be stealing, but there's no way your parents are going to give it to you."

"Right. Which means we'll just have to help ourselves."

"If your parents haven't invited you to your own brother's engagement party, what makes you think they'll just let you into their safe?"

"The key is in a cigar box that my dad keeps in his office minibar."

"Great," May said. "So, what? You're going to scale the roof and break into the house in the dead of night to steal the bonds while your parents and their entire staff sleep through the whole thing? Come on. This is real life, not a movie."

"Night would be best. But we won't break in; we'll waltz right in through the front door and do it in style. And then we'll steal the bonds out from under their noses and leave the way we came."

May poured herself a glass of red wine from a bottle of Château-Malartic-Lagravière.

"Wow, a 1970? You weren't messing around!" whistled Sally-Anne. "Well, at the very least, I'm glad I get to drink it instead of my brother."

"You're drunk already, the way you're talking. You don't need another sip."

Ignoring this, Sally-Anne poured herself a glass and raised it in a toast. May downed hers in one swig.

"Okay, enough half-baked revenge plots," May said. "When do we let the team know we can't pay them?"

"We won't even have to; they'll get paid for the first issue and every one after it."

"Enough is enough, Sally-Anne! Don't talk crazy. You're not going to walk out of there with your father's bearer bonds, not if they turn you away at the front door."

"They won't even know who we are. Isn't that the entire point of a masquerade ball? That's when we'll do it."

"The masquerade ball that you aren't invited to!"

"Not yet, but I can fix that. And I'll need you to come along as my date." She laid out the plan, step by step. May would infiltrate the manor and tamper with the guest list. She would be taking an enormous risk.

At first, May categorically refused to even set foot in Edward's lair ever again. She remembered being smuggled out of the service door at dawn like a whore after their weekend on Kent Island. Yet, Sally-Anne proved to be quite adept at convincing her, her powers of persuasion rivaling even those of her mother.

As the night came to an end, May poured the last of the wine, and the two women clinked glasses. There was no turning back.

29

ELEANOR-RIGBY

October 2016, Baltimore

Waltzing into the police station and flashing my press card did not work out as planned. The cop at the front desk just couldn't see why a nature magazine would be so interested in an obscure crime dating all the way back to 1980. He had a point, I had to admit. After losing patience with my thin explanations, he told me I could file a formal request with the appropriate department. I asked how long the process would take, all told.

"It could take a while," he replied. "We're a bit understaffed at present." And with that, the cop buried his nose back in his book, just as we had found him. George-Harrison could tell I was about to explode, and put a gentle arm around my shoulders.

"Chin up, we'll find another way," he said softly. "I promise we will. I know it's sad, but you'll pull through."

"You want sad?" muttered the policeman. "Sad is dragging your feet when you walk to work in the morning, then dragging them twice as slow to get home at night. That's sad."

"True," sighed George-Harrison. "I'm no stranger to that type of sadness. But have you ever been writing a book and felt so stuck? What am I saying? Of course you haven't."

Hook, line, and sinker. The cop looked up from his book.

"Truth is, we're not really here as journalists," George-Harrison continued. "We're novelists, and this whole thing is a major plot point in our story, one we want to be as authentic and reality based as possible. I'm sure you can imagine that having a real police report from that period would add a vital touch of authenticity to our novel."

"What type of novel is it?"

"A thriller."

"Thrillers are the only type of book that really grabs me. My wife only reads romance novels, which is rich, considering romance is what she seems most incapable of in our marriage." Getting all worked up, the cop motioned us closer and leaned in to whisper. "If you agree to name one of your characters after me, maybe I can help you out with this thing, huh? Not necessarily the main character, but somebody with a big role, and one of the good guys! Like a really smooth operator, you follow me? I mean, just imagine my wife listening as I read her passages of a book with *me* in it!"

George-Harrison and the officer sealed the deal with a firm handshake. The cop then peppered us with questions about what exactly it was we were seeking. He disappeared into a room down the hall and emerged a half hour later, a manila folder in hand, all dusty and worn with age. He summarized the details for us out loud, as though the report were an excerpt straight from our nonexistent novel and he were playing stand-in narrator.

"Your burglary took place on October 21, 1980, between the hours of 9 and 11 p.m.," he said, scratching his chin. "It's a cold case. They never found the perp. The events transpired at a party thrown by one Robert Stanfield and his wife. Apparently, the thief mingled with the guests and then robbed the family blind, stealing bonds from the house safe. A hundred fifty thousand dollars, all told, which could be worth as much as 1.5 mil today—and that's a ballpark figure. You gotta be brain-dead to keep that kind of money sitting at home. I mean, it's just not the brightest move, even if people used cash more in those days. Ah, interesting. It says here the lock on the safe was intact. No forced entry. In my opinion—*professional* opinion—the guilty party must have known the premises inside and out. Probably had help from someone on the inside. And what do you know? I see here that all the house employees were questioned, temporary and permanent, including event staff and caterers. There's a good thirty or so eyewitness accounts in here. And as usual, nobody saw or heard a single thing out of the ordinary. Quite the caper. An impressive sleight of hand."

The cop kept reading, nodding eagerly here and there as though he were a sleuth hot on the trail of an elusive master villain. "The theft was first discovered around midnight, when Mrs. Stanfield went to return her jewelry to the safe. Police were called at 12:45 a.m., which probably left just enough time for the victims to recover from the shock and take stock of what had been stolen."

"Jewelry in the safe . . . but she couldn't have been wearing *all* her jewelry," I interjected. "Were any of those items listed as stolen?"

"Nope, not as far as I can see," the officer replied, punctuating his certainty with a firm shake of his head. "Not one item of jewelry reported missing, only the money—those bonds."

"And does that seem normal to you?" asked George-Harrison.

"Normal doesn't happen too often in my line of work. But this I can tell you for sure: this job was done by a pro. He wasn't going to bother with things he couldn't manage to sell. I'm going to let you in on a real insider tip, a nice touch that'll make your story as real as it gets. Maybe even, if you can manage, have my character be the one who makes a speech about it, huh? If possible. A good cop always uses deduction. See these notes here? The eyewitness accounts? I count fifteen employees working full-time with these people. Housekeepers,

231

cooks, butler, private secretary, and even a live-in presser? Just for iron-
ing, I guess. That's wild. I didn't even know that existed. So, you know,
it's not too far a leap to conclude that the . . . what's their name, again?
The, uh, the Stanfields . . . Sorry, lost my train of thought. Ah, right . . .
so, calling the Stanfields a 'wealthy family' would be an understatement.
You still with me, right? I don't gotta slow down? Okay, so. For folks
as rich as them, the lady of the house probably doesn't own even one
piece of run-of-the-mill jewelry. And for a burglar, that's a real snag.
Think: Rolex, pearl necklace, even a reasonably sized diamond ring
can all be pawned relatively easily. But when we're talking jewels with
values pushing five, even six figures? It's impossible to hock that kinda
stuff. Only way to get rid of something that hot is through a specialized
underground network. Stones have to be pulled from their settings,
mostly recut to make them unrecognizable, and then, presto! Back on
the market. But if you don't have those connections, you're out of luck."

"Wow. Have you worked on cases like this before?" I asked.

"No! Never. But like I said, I'm a big reader." Despite his lengthy
and colorful monologue, the bottom line was crystal clear: the thief had
taken only the bonds because everything else in the safe was too tricky
for him to fence.

"Is there anything else that could have been in that safe?" inquired
George-Harrison.

"Guns, maybe? If they had unlicensed firearms in the safe, they'd
be sure to leave that out of the report. Valuable watches can be easier
to fence, but there's no mention of that anywhere in here. Bars of gold,
that can also happen, but they sure are bulky. Just one can weigh over
ten pounds, so it's a little tough to just waltz out discreetly with it
crammed in your pocket. If the Stanfields were younger, or showbiz
types, I would have also thought drugs, but they don't strike me as the
nose candy crowd."

"Aside from illegal firearms or drugs, are there other things people
are reluctant to mention in police reports?"

"Nothing I can think of. More often they overshare. Folks use burglaries as an opportunity to get rich off insurance. They hide their valuables and claim they were robbed. But that's out of our jurisdiction. Companies hire private investigators to flush out that type of scam, and it's usually only a matter of time. Sooner or later, people who play that game slip up and get caught. Lady heads out to dinner wearing a necklace that she reported stolen, or maybe the investigators take a picture with a long telephoto lens of a painting in their living room that they claimed had been lifted."

"But that never happened with the Stanfields?"

"No way of knowing. In general, you get busted for fraud, you negotiate directly with your insurer, and then you're going to pay up, big-time, huge damages, just to stay out of a prison cell. Anyone could come out on top, tables turn, winners become losers, and vice versa. Also, there are cases where folks who got robbed don't bother declaring items that weren't insured."

"What do you mean? Why?" I asked.

"For the rich and powerful, burglary is humiliating. Even if it seems backwards to folks like you and me, some think of it as a sign of weakness. Let's say you had decided to cut corners on insurance and it comes back to bite you in the ass, you come across twice as dumb. So, they leave those things out, just to save face."

"You're saying it is possible something else was stolen that night?" George-Harrison asked.

"Sure, why not? It passes the sniff test, so if it fits for your novel, I say go for it. But whatever you end up using, just make sure it's nothing too difficult to carry. At the same time, don't forget: if the thief had inside help, he could have disappeared with the loot through the kitchen or by the service entrance. But hey, that's your call. You're the writers."

We thanked the officer for his time, and were about to walk out when he called back after us.

"Wait, hold it! How are you gonna hold up your end of the bargain if you don't even have my name?"

I quickly got his name, eager to get the hell out of there.

"Frank Galaggher, with two *g*'s and an *h*. Say, you know what you're gonna call the novel?"

"Hey, maybe we'll call it *The Galaggher Affair*," said George-Harrison with a smile.

"Are you serious?" asked the police officer, on cloud nine.

"Dead serious," said my partner in crime, with enough confidence to leave me stammering and stumbling as we bid the officer goodbye.

◆   ◆   ◆

Watching George-Harrison from the passenger seat, I noticed he had the same driving habit as my father: one hand on the wheel, the other dangling out of the open window.

"Why are you looking at me?" he asked.

"How did you know I was looking at you? You haven't even taken your eyes off the road. Anyway, I wasn't."

"You just enjoy staring at me, is all?"

"I was wondering how you got the idea."

"You mean, about the book?"

"No, about my cousin Bertha! Yes, the book."

"I saw he had a couple of James Ellroy novels on his desk, *Perfidia* and *LAPD '53*, so I took a bit of a gamble. Do you really have a cousin Bertha?"

"You spot a pair of novels on his desk and just cook up that whole scenario? That takes a lot of imagination."

"Is that a bad thing?"

"Not at all."

"So, just technically speaking . . . that's something nice you're saying about me?"

"Yes, I suppose I am."

"I think that may be the nicest thing you've said since we became friends."

"Friends? We hardly know each other."

"I'd say I know quite a bit about you. You're English, a journalist, you have a twin brother and a younger sister. Your dad has a thing for his beat-up old car—I also have a beat-up old car, which you're sitting in right now—and you may or may not have a cousin named Bertha. Jury's still out on that one. That's a start, isn't it?"

"Sure, it's a start. I don't know all that much about you, though. How did you know for sure that the cop would take the bait?"

"Just a hunch . . . Truth is, I had no idea where it would go. I just made something up so we could walk out with our heads held high. It was dumb luck that the guy happened to be bored to death."

"You certainly know how to spin a yarn. I hate lying. The poor fellow is dead set on appearing in a novel that doesn't even exist. And I bet he goes straight home and brags to his wife tonight. Because of us, he'll come across as a total chump."

"Sure. Or maybe we inspired him to finally write his own page-turner. Besides, when you claimed to be there on assignment for your magazine, wasn't that a lie?"

"A white lie."

"Right, of course. White lies, real lies. Not the same thing at all."

"Exactly."

"The woman I was with for nearly five years just up and took off one morning, leaving behind nothing but a tiny little note. The day before, everything was normal. She didn't let on a thing, not a single thing. You really think she made up her mind overnight? So, where does that one fall? White lie or real lie?"

"What did she say? In her note?"

"That I was a bear deep in the woods."

"And what about that, was that a lie?"

235

"I hope so. I hope that's not all I am."

"Well, if you're trying to avoid the bear look, you might want to lose the beard. Why did she leave you?"

"It was the same stuff that drew her in at the start. Our bedroom started to seem too small, and my studio too big. She hated if I even set foot in the kitchen, whereas before all I had to do was put on an apron and she'd get turned on. Suddenly, she didn't want me dozing off while we watched TV. Before, she would let me sleep on her shoulder and run her fingers through my hair."

"Maybe it was more because of the silence, what with the TV and all, that she started to hate the whole thing. Monotony, too. Maybe she really hated what she had become in that world, and there was nothing you could have really done."

"She was upset that I spent too much time in my studio."

"I could see that being quite painful, to be honest."

"My door was always open. All she had to do was to come in for us to stay together. I'm passionate about my work. I didn't know how to live with somebody who didn't care about what I was doing."

"Didn't it occur to you that maybe she wanted you to be as passionate about her as you were about the work?"

"Sure it did. But it was too late."

"Do you regret it?"

"How about you? Are you with somebody?" asked George-Harrison, sidestepping the question.

I sidestepped his. "You know, we've gone really off track with the Stanfields. I just can't picture my mother as some master thief. There's no way that she could have broken into a safe. No way."

"Right. Just to be clear: you didn't exactly answer my question."

"If you were a woman, you'd know that *no answer* is an answer."

"Right. But I'm just a big hairy bear." George-Harrison sighed.

I caved. "To answer your question, just for posterity's sake: no, I am not with anybody."

"Would you have imagined, in your wildest dreams, that your mother and mine could have had a relationship like that?"

"Nope. Not at all."

"Well, that tells me we might not be as far off track as you think. Maybe they did pull off the heist, and maybe it wasn't your mother who broke into the safe."

"What makes you say that?"

"My mom never really had much of a job," George-Harrison explained. "At least nothing steady enough to raise a kid on. We certainly weren't rich, but we had everything we needed."

"She could have set some money aside before having you."

"This is years without work we're talking about here. Years. And the cop did say one thing that confirms it for me: there were bonds in the safe, not cash. And, well, my mother had a nice big stack of bonds. At the start of each summer, she'd cash some in, and then again just before Christmas."

There was nothing to say to that. The facts spoke for themselves: my mother was far from the woman I thought she was. Still, I couldn't bring myself to accept it. And even more troubling: What other lies would I uncover along the way? George-Harrison searched my face for a reaction, letting the silence hang in the air until I at last opened my mouth to reply.

"You never asked her where the bonds came from?"

"I didn't really think about it as a kid. I just remember her telling me she had inherited them."

"Well, our family was barely able to scrape by," I replied. "If we'd learned that Mum was sitting on a stack of bonds, we would have been shocked, to say the least."

"So, that makes her innocent and my mother guilty. Does that come as a relief?"

"Nope. Not at all, actually. My mother—the chemistry teacher, a total do-gooder with these uncompromising values about raising her kids—was really a crazy rebel who pulled off a heist? Honestly, the idea was starting to grow on me."

"God, you are a walking contradiction."

"I'll take walking contradiction over boring any day! Does your mother still have any of those bonds?"

"I cashed the last of them when she went into the home. I guess I should apologize; I should've held on to them, at least shared what was left with you."

"And why should you have done that, if my mother had nothing to do with the heist? Yours took all the risks."

"Not so fast. The fact that your parents had trouble making ends meet only tells us your mother didn't get a cut of the loot. It doesn't mean she didn't take part in the crime itself. Don't forget what the poison-pen said."

"He said that she had walked away from a huge fortune. Maybe it was because yours made off with all of it. Sometimes partners stab each other in the back."

"What a lovely thing to say. But I'm going to have to stop you right there. My mother has always been an incredibly honest woman."

"You're kidding, right? That's your definition of honest? The woman stole over a million dollars out of a safe!"

"He said a hundred and fifty thousand!"

"Which was worth a whole lot more back then! You do realize what you're saying is completely nuts. Your mother pulls off a major heist, keeps my mum's half of the loot, and somehow she's still a saint?"

"Slow down, there's no need to get nasty again. You really think they'd call each other 'my love' if something like that went down?"

"Your mother said that, not mine. I haven't been able to get my hands on my mum's letters."

"So, maybe 'honest' wasn't the best choice. But I can assure you, my mother has always been a loyal and faithful woman."

"Says the kid who never even knew his father!"

George-Harrison shot me an icy glare, then abruptly flicked on the radio and kept his eyes fixed ahead on the road. I waited for the song to finish, then turned the volume back down.

"I'm sorry. I shouldn't have said that. I didn't mean it the way it came out."

"If they gave my mom the wrong change at the cash register, even a dollar extra, she'd return it every time," he said. "When the cleaning lady broke her leg, my mom kept paying her until she could get back on her feet. When I got in trouble at school, the first thing she did after finding out why the fight started was to have the principal tell the other kid's parents they had twenty-four hours to get their brat to apologize, or my mom would come to their house and kick all their asses. I could go on and on, honestly, but just take my word for it: my mother would never be capable of stabbing somebody in the back like that, okay? Believe me."

"Why did you get in a fight?"

"Because when you're ten years old and someone says you've got no dad because your mom sleeps around town, it's a lot easier to talk with your fists than think of a snappy comeback."

"Right . . . I understand."

"No, you don't! You don't understand any of it."

"You're right. I'm an idiot. But you listen to me, George-Harrison: I couldn't care less about the money they stole. Truth is, my first thought about the money was to treat my father to a much-deserved holiday. So I promise you, right here and now: I won't return to London until you find out who your father is."

George-Harrison slowed the car and looked in my direction. His expression changed, and I suddenly felt as though I was staring at the little boy throwing punches in the school playground.

"Why would you do that for me? I thought we barely knew each other?"

I thought of my father. How gentle he could be, the way he was always ready to comfort me when I was feeling down, or how sweet and wise he was whenever I needed cheering up. He was always so involved in my childhood, never lacking patience or time, and wanting nothing but the best for all his children. I couldn't imagine how George-Harrison must have felt to be deprived of that type of figure, and how much pain he must have endured. But I had no idea how to tell him all that.

"We may not know each other that well, but it's a promise just the same. And you never answered my question. Do you miss her?"

"Miss who?"

"Nobody. Forget it. Just concentrate on the road."

I had a thousand thoughts spinning in my head. I guessed it was the same for him. Then, out of nowhere, George-Harrison suddenly blurted out, "Of course! It's so obvious!" He slammed the brakes and steered the pickup to the side of the road.

"They *split* the loot. My mom kept the bonds and yours . . . kept something else."

"What makes you so sure there was something else they stole aside from those bonds?"

"My mother's letter said not to let the 'precious treasure dwell in darkness and fade from memory.' That's enough for me."

"I was thinking about that earlier, around the time when you were telling me not to get nasty again. On that note, you'll have to tell me exactly when I was nasty at all. But I digress. Let's say they did split things up. Knowing Mum, she probably gave up her cut because it was dirty money."

"There you go again. I get it: your mother was a saint. But if that's so true, then the poison-pen would have to be pretty naïve to think that the bonds were some lost treasure that would just pop up untouched after thirty-six years. Unless . . . the poison-pen knows, just like the cop was hinting at, that part of the lost treasure *can't* be cashed in."

30

ROBERT

June 1944, outside Montauban

It was late in the day and Robert had been pedaling nonstop for hours. The pain was nearly unbearable. Ten kilometers earlier, he had been forced to make another stop to vomit on the side of the road. Sitting on the slope, he unbuttoned his shirt and looked over the splotchy fresh bruises across his chest and arms. His eyes were nearly swollen shut, his lips puffed up to twice their normal size. Blood flowed sporadically from his nose, and his whole mouth tasted metallic from the blood from his split lip. Robert's hands were the only part of him left unscathed. They had been bound behind his back, and thus spared the onslaught that the rest of his body had endured for hours on end.

Most of his memories of the torture were hazy, with only small interludes of consciousness. None of that mattered. Robert had neither time for self-pity over what had happened nor the heart to dwell on it. He had only one thought: reach the hunting lodge before the enemy.

Robert at last made it to the foot of the path and threw the tandem into a ditch. He ran the length of the path through the woods, using his last ounce of strength to make the upward climb to the lodge. The loose dirt kept slipping beneath his feet, but he managed to grab hold of branches to keep pushing onward, until the hunting lodge finally came into view at the top of the hill in a haze of smoke.

Everything was calm, far too calm. Robert heard something crackle and crouched down, then made his way cautiously closer to the lodge. When he caught sight of Antoine's corpse sprawled out on the ground in front of the porch, he knew he was too late. The windows had all been shattered by heavy gunfire, the facade riddled with bullet holes. The front door had been obliterated, leaving only a shredded plank of wood swinging from a hinge.

Carnage awaited him inside. The furniture had been torn to shreds in the hail of bullets, and three partisans lay dead on the ground in a horrific state. It was a grisly scene—one had been disemboweled, the other had lost both his legs to a grenade blast. The third could only be identified by his thick build—his face was completely covered by a mask of dirt and blood.

Robert doubled over and dry-heaved, having vomited all the contents of his stomach on the side of the road. Heart pounding, he scanned the space desperately.

"Sam! Hanna!" he shouted. Nothing but dead quiet in response, no signs of life. Robert rushed into their bedroom and froze in the doorway. Sam was slumped backwards over the foot of the bed, his eyes staring blankly into space, his arm dangling with a pistol resting in his hand. A stream of blood trickled from his temple.

Robert knelt before the body and wept as he closed Sam's eyes. Composing himself, he pried the pistol from his friend's lifeless hand and shoved it into his belt. Next, he returned to the porch to scan the woods around the lodge, praying that Hanna made it out alive and was hiding somewhere out there, unlikely as it seemed.

"Hanna!" he shouted. Apart from a crow cawing in the distance, the woods were silent. Robert was terrified at the thought of Hanna being taken by the militiamen, not daring to imagine what might happen to her. He stood motionless for a moment, brought to tears once more as he caught sight of the tree stump where he had sat so often smoking side by side with Sam. The art dealer had told him all about his past, how he had met his wife, how dearly he loved his daughter, his deep passion for art, and his pride at acquiring the precious Hopper masterpiece.

Night fell. Finding himself truly alone now, Robert wondered how many more nights he would last. In just a few hours, the sun would set in Baltimore. He thought of his parents and the comfort of his bedroom on their sprawling estate, all the lavish dinners he had enjoyed there, and the reading room, where his father squandered his fortune in poker games he always lost. Robert remembered finding him one morning in his office, sitting there, drunk, sobbing with rage. He would never forget the shame on his father's face, the look that plunged Robert deep into despair. And he was reminded once more that he was about to die thousands of miles from home because of those poker games.

The thought filled Robert with rage, and the burst of anger gave him a second wind. Sam had taken his own life rather than die at the hands of his enemies, and that act of bravery reminded Robert of the promise he had made. If there was a chance, however slim, that Hanna was still alive, he would find her. With the help of his comrades, he would hunt down Hanna's captors and rescue her, even if it meant taking her place as their prisoner.

"Comrades. What comrades?" Robert mumbled to himself. "The only comrades you had are all lying here, dead, and anyone left alive would be after your hide."

Yet Robert was spurred on by youthful determination. He swore to himself that he'd stay alive long enough to honor the pact he had made with the old art dealer. He would return home a hero, living up to his name, and continue his rise to prominence just as all the men of his family had, save his father. Robert thought of the paintings hidden down in that hole at the back of the cellar. Even if Robert didn't make it home, even if he couldn't save Sam's daughter, the priceless works of art mustn't stay down there, lost for eternity.

The moon had risen in the sky, casting its light over the treetops. Robert, knowing that Sam still lay there in the bedroom, with the corpses of his other friends close by, had not yet found the strength to set foot inside the hunting lodge again. He took a deep breath to steel himself, and decided it was time to head in.

He spotted a banged-up oil lamp on the floor and lit the wick, averting his eyes from the gory scene. He headed straight for the trap-door to the cellar, swung it open, and lowered himself inside.

Robert hung the lamp from one of the ladder's rungs and began shifting aside stacks of crates concealing the tunnel's entrance. As soon as he had made a large enough space to get through, Robert grabbed his lantern and slipped inside.

Just as he was nearing Sam's hiding place, he heard a rustle, followed by heavy breathing from the end of the tunnel where the cases of weapons were stored. Robert gripped the gun firmly in one hand and raised the lantern with the other. The glow of the flame revealed a form huddled against the wall. It was a woman, crouching on the ground. As she raised her haggard face, Robert saw that it was Hanna.

He rushed over to take her in his arms, but she began howling and thrashing about as soon as he touched her. Robert realized he must be unrecognizable in the dark with his face all swollen, and Hanna must have thought he was a militiaman come to force himself on her. He begged her to calm down, and Hanna seemed to recognize the sound of his voice. She curled up in Robert's arms, her entire body trembling as she recounted in a daze what had happened earlier that day . . .

A truckload of armed militiamen had arrived at the foot of the trail in late afternoon. Raoul was stationed at his lookout post nearby and quickly surmised they hadn't come to those woods for mere reconnaissance this time. He ran up to the hunting lodge, warned everyone inside, then grabbed a Sten submachine gun and bravely raced right back out to keep the enemy at bay as long as he could, to buy time for the others to make a run for it.

Sam refused to leave. His legs simply weren't strong enough. The old man begged the Resistance fighters to take Hanna with them, but as soon as Antoine was shot dead outside, everyone realized it was too late, the lodge was completely surrounded. As the partisans opened fire, Alberto, the one built like a bear, sent Sam and Hanna to hide in the cellar. The militiamen were specifically on the hunt for Resistance members, and with a little luck, they might just spare an old man and his daughter. Sam made Hanna enter the narrow passage first, then covered up the entrance with one crate after another. Hanna desperately stuck her hand through, begging her father not to leave her in there alone, but Sam had insisted.

"You must stay alive . . . for me, for your mother, for all the others! Reach for the stars, my darling. Make the most of your life, and never forget that you're Sam Goldstein's daughter. Remember those dreams of peace we shared, all our wonderful trips together, and all that I've taught you. Take the flame I have passed down to you, and light a thousand torches, enough to illuminate the sky. One day you will have children of your own. Tell them about your parents, tell them that your mother and I will always love them. Wherever I'm going, I will be watching over them, just as I've watched over you."

Sam kept telling his daughter he loved her as he finished building the wall of crates to hold her inside. Soon his voice was drowned out by the sound of gunfire and blasts above. He moved the last crate into place, and Hanna's world plunged into darkness.

The gunfire above soon came to an end, and she could hear voices. A man opened the trapdoor and came down to search. Hanna fled to the farthest end of the tunnel and could hear the man barking at his comrades.

"There's nobody down here, nothing but dirt and cobwebs. I'd like to get home before midnight."

"What do we do with the bodies?" asked another from the living room.

"Take their papers," a third replied. "The families will be notified, and they'll come get them. No reason we should have to do the dirty work." Hanna heard snickering above; then the solider climbed back up the ladder, closed the trapdoor, and all was silent.

As her story came to an end, Hanna moaned sorrowfully, wailing like a wounded animal. She rocked back and forth, calling out for her father again and again, her cries filling the cavernous space. Robert feared she might be going mad and knew he had to get her out of there, quickly. He took Hanna by the hand and led her down the tunnel, snuffing out his lantern before they climbed above. "We have to be sure," he said. "They might have left somebody behind to watch over those woods."

Robert was lying. He hoped to spare Hanna the grisly sight of those brave, fallen men who had sacrificed themselves to keep the militiamen from finding her. The two walked through the lodge in darkness. But as soon as they made it out to the porch, Hanna stopped and begged to go see her father. Robert adamantly refused.

"You don't want this," he said in a choked voice. "Please believe me. You'd never be able to unsee it."

They followed the path down into the dark woods. Robert wondered if Hanna would even be able to ride the tandem. But even if she could, he hadn't the faintest clue where to go. Then he remembered Alberto once mentioning guides who smuggled refugees across the Pyrenees mountains. Spain was just over a hundred kilometers away. It would take three days to reach the border on the tandem, maybe less.

Five hundred yards from the hunting lodge, Robert sat Hanna down at the foot of a tree and stared into her eyes.

"I have to go back to the lodge to get some clothes. Mine are soaked through with blood, and if I'm spotted looking like this out on the road, we'll be stopped at the first checkpoint. We need provisions, and most of all, I need to get your papers."

"I don't care about your clothes or those fake papers!" Hanna yelled. "I forbid you to leave me here alone!" Robert clamped his hand over Hanna's mouth to muffle her cries. They weren't far from a road where German patrols could easily be on the prowl.

"I have no choice. I'm on a mission, and I have to get my map with all the local weapon caches. I promised your father I would watch over you if anything ever happened to him, and I'm going to keep that promise. Hanna, look at me. I won't leave you, I swear I won't. You have to trust me. I will come back—it'll be a half hour, at most. Until then, you sit and try to gather your strength. We have a long road ahead of us. Most of all, stay absolutely silent."

Hanna had no choice but to let him go. Robert started the trek back up to the lodge. Once inside, he went to his bedroom and changed into fresh clothes, then went to check the kitchen. All the jars of preserves had been shattered, save one that had rolled under the table. Robert stuffed the jar into a large satchel he found hanging on a nail near the fireplace. Then he climbed down the ladder into the cellar and the darkness swallowed him.

◆　◆　◆

They pedaled until the break of dawn, when Hanna was too exhausted to go further. Robert wasn't faring much better himself. In the distance, through the hazy mist of sunlight glimmering on the plain, they could just discern the outline of a house with a barn beside it. Robert steered the tandem onto the dirt driveway toward the farm, where he hoped they could rest for a few hours and, with a little luck, find food and drink.

◆　◆　◆

Hanna awoke after noon, opening her eyes to see a farmer with a rifle pointed straight at Robert.

"Who are you?" the farmer barked. "Talk. Now."

As Robert rose cautiously to his feet, Hanna spoke for him. "We're not thieves, and we're not here to hurt you. Lower your weapon, I beg of you."

"First, tell me what you're doing in my barn."

"We were traveling through the night, and we needed rest," Hanna continued.

"And what's with your friend? Can't he speak? He hasn't said a single word."

"Why should he, if I tell you all you need to know?"

"If you're traveling at night, it means you're on the run. He's a foreigner, is that it?"

"No," Hanna assured him. "He can't talk. He's mute."

"Ah. Well, maybe I can give his ass a nice little kick and we'll see how mute he is! This fool has had his face pounded into mush. Doesn't take a genius to figure out why and who you two are. I don't want trouble. Not with soldiers, not with partisans. So, gather up your things and get out of here."

"Get out? With my face all pounded into mush?" Robert asked. "We can't travel in broad daylight, it's far too dangerous. Let us stay in here until nightfall, then we'll be on our way."

"American or English?" asked the farmer.

"Foreigner, like you said. That's good enough. And you won't have any trouble with the Resistance as long as you don't make any trouble with the Resistance."

"Ha! He's got balls, your boyfriend," the farmer told Hanna.

"All we're asking is for you to let us stay a few hours," she said. "Pretend you didn't see us. Is that so much to ask?"

"Listen. I'm the one holding the gun, so I'll call the shots. First, no one's going to come threaten me on my own land. If you wanted something to eat or drink, all you had to do was ask. Politely." The farmer lowered his weapon and sized the two up for a moment. "You don't look too dangerous. My wife's prepared lunch and you can join us. But first, go and wash at the well. You're both a total mess."

The water at the pump was so frigid that it stung Robert's wounds and even reopened the gash on his chin. Hanna took a rag from her pocket and put pressure on the cut to stop the bleeding. Robert winced as she pressed on it. "Come on, toughen up," she said.

The farmer and his wife offered both of them clean clothes. Hanna looked like a perfect tomboy in a pair of baggy trousers and a man's shirt. The farmers acted friendly and cordial as the four ate lunch, watching as Robert swallowed down all his stew without any prompting, but noticing Hanna had hardly touched her plate.

"Eat!" the farmer insisted. "Even if you're not hungry, you've got to eat. Where are you two headed anyway?"

"For the Spanish border," replied Robert.

"Well, you won't get far on that silly bicycle."

"What's it like on the roads around here?"

"Quite busy as of late. Between the ones who're fleeing east, those heading northwest to fight with the Allied Forces, and people like you heading due south . . . a whole lot of folks, you see."

"Wait . . . what's this about the Allied Forces?" asked Robert, stunned.

"Well, I'll be damned, have you been living under a rock? Four days ago, they started landing in droves on the beaches of Normandy. It's all over the radio. The Germans aren't giving in, but with the English already at Bayeux and Canadian troops advancing toward Caen, some say this infernal war will soon come to an end."

Upon hearing the news, Robert leapt straight out of his chair and hugged the farmer. Hanna, meanwhile, remained planted in her seat, her eyes welling up with tears. Robert knelt before her and took her hand.

"They were so close to the end, only to die," she lamented. "Papa will never get to see France liberated."

"I'm here for you, Hanna," Robert said softly. "You're going to be all right. I'm taking you home with me."

The farmer's wife motioned to the man to fetch drinks, and he went to the liquor cabinet, coming back with a bottle and glasses.

"So sorry for your trouble, my dear," he grunted. "Drink up. Some pear brandy will do you a world of good."

Hanna helped clear the table after the meal, while Robert was asked to lend the farmer a hand baling hay outside. Robert spent the whole afternoon out in the fields. It was a bit awkward at first, but he quickly got the hang of it, even eliciting a compliment from the gruff farmer. "Not bad for a Yankee!" the man snorted.

Robert recounted the events of the previous day to the farmer out in the fields, describing Hanna's situation and the promise he had made to Sam. At the end of the story, the farmer sighed, eyes full of compassion, and offered his help.

"I'll take you two as far as I can. We'll leave tonight. We'll stow your bike under straw in the back of my truck. Given the time it will take to drive there and back, I'd say I could get you as far as Aurignac, which would put you roughly sixty-five kilometers from the border. But be careful, crossing the Pyrenees is no walk in the park, even at this time of year. In any event, I'll have done my part, and the rest is your problem."

Between the news of the landing and this new development, Robert had been given two glimmers of hope on the same day, at a time when hope was what he needed most. He went back to the farm, washed his face at the well, and ran inside to tell Hanna the news. He found her standing alone in the kitchen.

"I thought you were with the farmer's wife."

"Her name is Germaine and his name is Germain, isn't that completely ridiculous?"

Robert tried to find an American equivalent, but his mind was far too scattered, and Hanna quickly beat him to it.

"Can you imagine a couple named Jess and Jessie?" she mused.

"Why not? If they love each other, who cares?"

"I'm not sensing all that much love in this house."

"I think you're mistaken."

"All I know is they're sure going to love being rid of us. Germaine seemed irritated that I was here. She left without even trying to make conversation."

"Well, maybe she's perceptive and was following your lead. You have to admit you're not the world's most talkative woman."

"I make up for it with other things. Although I don't see what's so special about being a blabbermouth anyway. What time do we leave? This place gives me the creeps."

"As soon as the sun goes down. Germain offered to give us a ride to Aurignac in his truck. It'll save us an entire night on that bicycle."

◆　◆　◆

After coming down with a serious migraine, Germaine didn't reemerge to say goodbye. Her husband apologized on her behalf, saying that she was furious at him for taking such risks for total strangers.

They loaded the tandem into the back of the truck and climbed into the cabin. The lidded headlights weren't especially bright, but they did keep the vehicle discreet at night. The Berliet rattled and jerked its way down the road. With both hands on the wheel, the farmer began to whistle as he drove.

"Your wife is right to be upset," said Hanna. "It must be dangerous on the road these days. I don't know how to thank you."

"It's more than dangerous; it's strictly forbidden. Lucky for you, the Germans and the militiamen like to stuff their faces with only the best. They expect to have their milk and eggs delivered, poultry too. So, if you're a good farmer, you get an *Ausweis* and can move about as you like. Rest assured, my papers are in order. If we get stopped, pretend you're asleep and everything will be fine."

"Be sure to thank your wife for us," Robert insisted.

"Of course, of course, no problem."

The engine made an infernal racket as they drove onward. By L'Isle-Jourdain, Hanna had fallen asleep. They passed Saint-Lys, Sainte-Foy-de-Peyrolières, and Rieumes without the slightest hint of trouble. Robert dozed off as well, lulled by the movement of the truck. Near Savères, the loud sound of shifting gears woke him up with a jolt. The farmer was slowing down in a hurry.

"What's wrong?" Robert asked.

"I think there may be a patrol at the next crossroads. We're still a way off, but I saw some lights on the horizon, and at this time of night, farms would be shuttered up and pitch-black. Just stick with the plan, and everything will be fine. Let the little lady sleep, it's better that way."

Robert glanced over at Hanna, her head resting against the window with her eyes closed and still. And yet Robert could feel her hand slide down his back, closing around his gun and pulling it right out of his belt. As Germain reached for the gearshift, Hanna sat bolt upright and pointed the gun at him.

"Turn off the headlights and pull over!" she ordered in a steely tone that left Robert dumbstruck.

"What is this? Some sort of hustle?" the farmer balked.

"I was about to ask you the same thing. How much were you going to make by turning us in, huh? Twenty francs? Fifty? What's the going price for an American these days? Maybe you could even get a hundred!" Hanna snarled, jabbing the barrel of the gun into the man's cheek.

"The girl's gone insane! Completely mad!"

Germain hit the brakes and pulled over to the side of the road. He raised his hands in surrender, shaking with fear and anger. "Germaine was right all along. I stick out my neck to help you damn foreigners, and this is how I'm repaid? Well, off with you. Run along. What are you waiting for? Take your damn bike and go!"

"You have any idea how to drive this thing?" Hanna asked Robert, who was still frozen in shock.

"Sure, at least . . . I think I can. Driving trucks was part of my training in England."

Hanna turned back to the farmer. "You can get out now," she ordered. When Germain hesitated, Hanna slipped her finger onto the trigger to let him know she meant business.

"I lost my father yesterday after being double-crossed by a rat just like you, so believe me when I say nothing would make me happier right now than blowing your brains out on the side of the road. You've got ten seconds to get the hell out."

Germain cursed under his breath and scrambled out of the truck. Robert quickly took his seat. As the Berliet lumbered away down the road, they could hear Germain shouting after them. "My truck! You goddamn thieves! Come back here with my truck!"

"Head that way," Hanna told Robert, pointing up a winding side road to their left. "And keep the headlights off."

"What in the world are you thinking? The guy was offering us help and you just—"

"That guy's help would've got us killed, believe me. He's a collaborator. Honestly, for a secret agent on a mission, your observational skills could use some work. The farm had nothing but wheat and pigs, not a hen or cow in sight. Just how do you think he bought this truck or got his hands on something as vital as a pass to move about freely? If the man's working the black market, just who do you think he's selling to?"

"How the hell did you put all that together?"

"I've been hiding out a lot longer than you. Survival is a question of staying sharp and always observing. You'll understand soon enough. We stay on the road until dawn. German convoys are easiest to spot by night. During the day, by the time you see them it's already too late. At daybreak, we'll have to switch to that bike of yours. How fast can you go?"

"Forty-five, fifty kilometers an hour, at best."

Hanna grabbed Robert's wrist and checked the time.

"That gives us enough time to cover at least a hundred and fifty kilometers, which should put us pretty close to the border. I can't believe they left you your watch."

"Who?"

"*Who?* The bastards who took you captive, that's who. Someday you'll have to tell me how you managed to get out of there alive."

"Oh, I see," Robert said, darkening. "Next, you'll be telling *me* to run along. What the hell are you insinuating?"

"Not a thing, not a single thing. I was asking sincerely. I'm just interested in hearing what happened to you."

"We got snagged by militiamen who drove us out to a house. Titon and I were separated. They beat us like dogs, trying to get us to talk. Obviously, I didn't say a word, or else I wouldn't have gotten all these pretty little souvenirs." Robert slid up his sleeve to show a series of cigarette burns on his forearm.

"When they figured out I was American, they thought I'd make a nice little gift for the Germans. They threw me in the back of a car. I passed out, so they didn't even bother with a guard, just the driver. When I woke up, we were driving on a country road. I was close enough to grab the guy by the throat. I told him if he didn't stop the car, I'd snap his fucking neck. And that's just what he did."

"And then what did you do?"

"I snapped his fucking neck."

"Well . . . good riddance. One less bastard in the world. You're making me regret letting off that farmer so easily. Not to mention he'll go running straight to that checkpoint and tell them everything. All right, let's focus on the task at hand. Enough talk," Hanna ordered.

As they drove through the night in silence, one part of Robert's story was gnawing at Hanna. How in the world did he manage to recover the tandem? But, of course, it wasn't the only tandem in the world. And in any event, Hanna needed his help and wasn't going to risk offending the one man who could take her to America and save her life.

◆ ◆ ◆

They got lost several times along the way, and even drove straight by Aurignac without realizing. As Hanna searched around for a map, she stumbled upon a pass issued by the militia, thus confirming her suspicions about Germain. She eventually found an old map among the truck's papers and used it to guide their way, flicking on the small light in the truck from time to time as they drove. She wasn't familiar with any of the names of the tiny villages they passed, but knew they would be fine as long as they kept heading south and didn't run into anyone along the way.

The truck reached Saint-Girons around three in the morning. As they entered the village, they caught sight of a German sidecar parked by the side of the road. Luckily, the men on guard were so groggy and slow moving that by the time they made it outside, all they saw were brake lights fading in the distance. And besides, the soldiers would have most likely assumed that only an authorized convoy would be prowling around so late at night.

Robert turned the truck onto a steep, winding road that hugged the side of a mountain as it ascended. The vehicle's clutch struggled with each hairpin bend, until the engine finally gave out not far from the village of Seix. Robert grabbed his satchel and left the tandem behind once and for all, judging that the path ahead would be easier by foot. They shoved Germain's Berliet off the edge of the cliff, watching as the truck plunged into the rocky Ribaute gorges.

After a long and arduous climb, the two weary travelers made it to Seix at the break of dawn. Hanna caught sight of a guesthouse and asked Robert if he had any money.

"Not a cent," he replied, watching as Hanna rolled up a leg of her pants to reveal a thick strip of gauze wrapped around her calf. "Is that a wound? Are you hurt?" he asked.

"No. My father had a talent for predicting the future." Hanna dug under the bandage and pulled out two hundred francs, which she handed to Robert. "Go in and see if they have a room."

"Don't you think that might be risky? With my accent?"

"It would be even riskier if a woman walked in there to do the talking for her husband, but maybe you're right. No choice. We're just going to have to walk straight into the lion's den and hope that this time we get lucky and stumble upon somebody honest."

As it turned out, luck was on their side. Madame Broué, the woman who ran the guesthouse, was more than just honest. Since the onset of the war, she had sheltered refugees fleeing France as they awaited guides to lead them safely into Spain. Madame Broué had never once turned anyone away from her doorstep. As an innkeeper, she was required by law to keep a register, but she simply left all the clandestine visitors off the list. Her selfless acts were even more courageous considering that soldiers would regularly stop by around cocktail hour to check the register. As soon as Hanna and Robert set foot in the guesthouse, Madame Broué took one look at them—defeated expressions on their faces, carrying nothing but a satchel as luggage—and understood everything. Without a single question, she grabbed a key from a hook and led them upstairs to a simple bedroom, with one large bed and a washbasin.

"You'll find the toilet and shower at the end of the hall. You'd be wise to head straight there. You both could use it. Steer clear of the hallways before nine in the morning, and never come downstairs in late afternoon, under any circumstances. You hear me cough from behind the counter? Get back in your room and don't come out until I say so. Lunch is at noon, dinner at seven thirty."

"We can pay for a few days in advance," Hanna offered. "We only need one meal per day; we'll be skipping dinner."

"No, you won't. You'll eat two solid meals. When you cross the border through those mountains, you'll be forced to fast, so you'd best fill up while you're here. As for money, we'll see about that later."

As soon as Madame Broué had closed the door behind her, Hanna headed straight for the bed. She stroked the surface of the blanket, then lay down with a heavy sigh. "My God, I can't remember the last time I slept on cotton sheets," she said dreamily. "You've got to come touch this, it's so soft." Hanna buried her face in one of the pillows and smelled the fabric, savoring the scent. "That smell . . . the smell of *clean* things, I forgot how sweet that smell could be."

"You enjoy it; I can sleep on the floor," Robert said, with the grace of a gentleman.

"You need to rest as badly as I do," Hanna insisted. "You can sleep right here next to me. I don't mind."

"And what if *I* do?" Robert replied mockingly.

In response, Hanna rolled over and playfully whipped the pillow at Robert. He realized it was the first time he had seen the girl smile.

"First, let's take our kind host's advice and go and clean up. There's no way we're getting into these sheets when we're this filthy," she said commandingly.

Hanna took her shower first. The water was absolutely freezing, yet the sensation of it filled her with an unbelievable rush of relief. The past twenty-four straight hours had taken their toll on her. She looked down at her feet, badly bruised and blistered from all the walking. Her legs looked disturbingly thin and malnourished.

They still had a long way to go. France was teeming with dangers, and the passage through the mountains was sure to be harrowing. Yet, the guesthouse was a momentary refuge in which Hanna felt something akin to peace and safety. The thought of a good night's sleep in a real bed gave her hope, restoring her desire to keep pushing onward. The mountain crossing didn't frighten her, because she knew that true freedom and a new life in America awaited her at the end of the journey. After all, some of the best moments of her entire life had been in America, on those unforgettable trips with her family. The mere thought of her parents brought the pain of Hanna's grief back to the surface again. Her eyes were welling up with tears when a knock came at the door.

"Everything all right?" Robert whispered from the other side.

"Yes, I'm fine."

"I was worried you'd passed out. You've been in there forever."

"It's been forever since I had a proper shower, I was just making the most of it. I'll let you have your turn now."

Hanna stepped out of the bathroom wearing only a towel, which clung to her curves and left nothing to the imagination. Robert couldn't help but look, confusing Hanna. She had no idea what to make of it. The only other time she had received this kind of attention was in high school, from a boy her own age for whom she felt absolutely nothing. But Robert? Robert was a man . . .

"What's the matter?" he asked.

"Nothing. It's a narrow hallway and I'm trying to get by."

Robert moved to make space, but their bodies still brushed against each other as she made her way back to the room. By the time he returned from his shower, Hanna was already sleeping soundly. Robert watched her for a long while. Then, as he finally slipped into bed beside her, Hanna let out a heavy sigh and rolled over. She rested her hand on his chest, her eyes still closed.

"Have you ever been with a man?" Robert whispered.

"No," she replied, with the same hushed tone. "Have you ever been with anybody?"

"May I kiss you?"

She at last opened her eyes and let Robert kiss her. She had worried that desire might make him rough, but those fears soon evaporated with his soft and gentle touch. The warmth of his skin and her desire for him overtook her fear. She clung to him fiercely.

◆ ◆ ◆

The rustic dining room at the guesthouse had eight wooden tables for lodgers, and lace curtains at the windows. The innkeeper poured heart and soul into providing guests with a satisfying meal, with a young lady from the village serving as waitress. For lunch, Madame Broué served piperade, a traditional Basque dish, for dinner a Spanish tortilla and potatoes, with shortcake for dessert.

After four days and four nights of rest at the guesthouse, Robert and Hanna had almost fully recovered. Their passionate lovemaking helped, too. Hanna had experienced her first taste of pleasure, and now longed for more. Even if Robert's lips still hurt from the beatings, he didn't deprive his young lover of a single kiss. Every time he held her close, Hanna felt more alive, their fiery passion chasing away all the death around them. More than once she smiled to herself, thinking that her newfound pleasure was taking place in a village called Seix.

One week after their arrival, Madame Broué came knocking at the door of their room and ushered them downstairs to the dining room, where a man stood awaiting them. His name was José, and he was the guide who would lead them into Spain. A secret convoy of ten refugees would set off that night to make the border crossing. The group consisted mostly of university students from Paris hoping to join the French Committee of National Liberation in Algeria. The guide was surprised to learn that Robert hadn't received help from the Comet escape line, the network that helped smuggle foreign pilots back to safety. Robert explained that he had been out of contact with his handlers since his arrival.

"Conditions seem quite favorable tonight; the weather's on our side," the guide told Robert and Hanna. "Believe it or not, weather up in those mountains can be more dangerous than the Krauts. The German patrols have been scaling back ever since the Allied Forces started landing up north. They fear that more will come from the south and they'll get crushed between the two, so they've turned tail and run. Last year, there were more than three thousand of them up on those mountains, prowling around on the hunt for us. The numbers have dropped quite a bit, but we still have to move with caution. Everyone on this trek is young, so we should be able to maintain a brisk pace. We leave at eleven o'clock tonight. Be ready."

Madame Broué provided the two of them with warm clothes for the journey, and when Hanna asked to settle the bill, the innkeeper refused.

"Hold on to every last centime to pay for the border crossing. It normally runs to about two thousand francs per person, but I talked him down to half price. José is a good guide and someone you can trust. He'll get you through to Alós d'Isil. When you see the statue of Eve atop the Romanesque church, you'll know you're home free. Or very nearly . . . You must be careful while in Spain. The French who get caught there end up at the Miranda concentration camp."

The atmosphere at dinner was strange and solemn, and the conversation was kept to barely a whisper. When Madame Broué served the shortcake, the men at the table joined together in a Basque folk song that brought tears to the eyes of all those preparing to brave the crossing.

◆　◆　◆

The Pyrenees proved far more trying than the guide had let on. José pushed the group to the brink of exhaustion, only allowing for stops when someone actually collapsed, at which point they'd make a brief stop for the group to regain its strength. Although it was the middle of summer, they endured subzero temperatures and biting winds. As they trudged through the snow atop the peak of Aneto, Hanna felt that her feet had frozen through, but she persisted with astounding courage. The students in the group hadn't fully recovered from the harsh conditions and lack of nourishment on their long, exhausting journey across France. Despite all this, the members of the group looked out for each other in an amazing show of solidarity. Without fail, every time a climber stumbled on the steep slopes, another was there to help them to their feet.

In the morning, a majestic sun rose over the mountains, leaving everyone breathless. The momentary sense of peace left a lasting impression on the entire group. The climbers pushed on, until the small Romanesque church at last came into view. The guide stopped and pointed out a path leading down into the valley.

"We are now in Spain. I wish each and every one of you safe travels on the road ahead and a long, fruitful life."

He passed around his beret, and everyone emptied their pockets to pay the guide for his hard work. Although the bounty was far less than had been promised, the man accepted his payment without complaint and started back toward France.

Four hours later, a pair of shepherds arrived and approached the group, showing no surprise at the strange ensemble. They invited everyone into their home without question, and gave them polenta and sheep's milk. After the meal and a good night's rest, the group was ready to hit the road again. They parted ways, and Hanna and Robert continued down a paved road on foot. The couple soon managed to hitch a ride aboard a truck full of Spanish laborers, who dropped them off at a guesthouse run by trustworthy allies. The inn even had a phone that Robert used to call the US consulate.

Hanna and Robert slept the entire day. A car came for them around dusk, and they were driven through the night to the US consulate in

Madrid. Over the course of the following week, Robert was debriefed by a liaison officer. After his identity had been verified, he was offered safe passage to Gibraltar. From there, a boat would take him to Tangier, where he'd be able to board a cargo ship that would carry him stateside.

Hanna, the officer informed Robert, wasn't an American citizen and couldn't come home with him. This drove Robert into a blind rage. He adamantly refused to leave without her. The officer apologized but insisted there was nothing he could do. Robert, however, had other ideas.

The next day, the same officer officiated their marriage, and Hanna became an American citizen.

Ten days later, Hanna found herself leaning over the balustrade of a ship, gazing back at the coastline, her past life fading into the distance. Huddled close to her new husband, she thanked him for saving her life.

"You've got it all wrong," Robert replied, overcome with emotion. "We got through this nightmare together. Without you, I would have given up a long time ago. I'm only alive right now because of you."

One of the newlyweds was headed home; the other was leaving home for the unknown. Neither had any luggage, save the satchel that never once left Robert's side throughout the entire journey.

31

ELEANOR-RIGBY

October 2016, Baltimore

As we settled in for lunch, I observed the mixed crowd at the café. A businessman was sitting with eyes glued to his smartphone. A group of teenaged boys huddled close together, interacting only through an online game on the screens of their gadgets. A trio of pregnant women were chatting about baby clothes and buggy brands. A young couple was sitting wordlessly, while an elderly couple had devoured a whole spread of pastries in a show of mischievous indulgence.

George-Harrison had chosen a spot for us at the bar. He scoffed at my restlessness as I polished off a Cobb salad and a Coke.

"You're driving me crazy spinning on the stool like that. What's there to look at here anyway?"

"People?" I shrugged.

"Tell me: What's your first stop when you arrive in a new city? Where do you go to find your angle?" he asked.

"Angle . . . what kind of angle?"

"I mean the angle for your article."

"Hmm. I'd say open-air markets are pretty much the only place where people from all walks of life come together. You wouldn't believe how much you can learn by looking at the stalls and vendors, seeing what people are buying, what they consider valuable."

"I believe it," he said, setting down his empty pint glass. George-Harrison had nearly downed the beer in one swig, and demolished his sandwich in a few massive bites. With most men, I found that type of thing boorish at best and repulsive at worst, but not with George-Harrison.

He definitely had something classy about him—classy in a raw kind of way, without any calculation or premeditation. That struck me as . . . soothing for some reason, or, even more dangerous, disarmingly sincere. Even when he had been upset earlier, George-Harrison's voice had stayed level and calm. My ex, the *Washington Post* reporter, was nothing like him; he never asked a single question about my writing, judging his own work to be much more important. Thinking back, I was blind for so much of the relationship and wasted a lot of time with him. But maybe that was what I really needed then: to tread water in a relationship doomed to fail. That kind of freedom made it easier to keep certain truths at bay.

A girl in a jumper and jeans entered the café, and the screen-addicted teens looked up from their dragons and Vikings to stare. She was stunning, and she knew it. She was ten years younger than me, with a carefree kind of confidence that I could only dream of. I knew I was being stupid, considering how much of a struggle growing up can be. I would have sooner died than relive that period. But I did miss being able to just roll out of bed, throw on anything, and still step out the door looking flawless. As the girl settled down at a table, I couldn't help but wonder if George-Harrison would check her out, too. He didn't even blink, which made me happier than I was ready to admit.

"How about you?" I asked. "How do you tackle a new piece of furniture?"

"I use tools," he said, with a mischievous smile. "But hey, you don't have to ask about my work just to be polite." Wow. *Busted.* What's worse, he also noticed my guilty look at being caught red-handed. "Hey, relax. I'm just messing with you," he said. "Let's see, for starters . . . I envision the blueprint and then sit down to draw."

"If you please, draw me a sheep," I said, in a child's voice, seeing if he would catch the reference to one of my favorite books.

"Sorry, can't help you there. But I can draw a box for the sheep, if you like. And don't worry, I'll be sure to put holes in it so the little fella can breathe."

"So, you're a fan of *The Little Prince*, too. It was the first book I ever really fell in love with," I confided.

"You and a lot of people, I'm sure."

"I know; it's very unoriginal. And how about you?"

"Hmm . . . maybe *Charlie and the Chocolate Factory*? I have to say, I had quite a thing for Willy Wonka. But if I had to choose, I'd say Kipling's poem 'If' was what really floored me when I was a kid."

Of course that poem would strike a nerve with George-Harrison as a child. What boy wouldn't dream of his father reading him those words? I hadn't forgotten my promise to him, but I had so many other things on my mind at that moment.

"I'm sorry," he said. "You're finally taking a stab at being friends, and I'm not really making it very easy on you, am I?"

"Who said that's what I was doing?" I said, lying through my teeth.

"Honestly, I'm sorry," he sighed. "Ever since we met, all we've talked about is our parents and the past. I was wrong to thwart your efforts to change the subject. Do you feel like maybe getting some air? I could go for a walk; I'm really feeling that sandwich."

The normal Eleanor-Rigby would have said that's exactly what you get when you stuff your face so fast. But I didn't. Truth was, I was feeling anything but normal. Being with him was throwing me way off-balance. I grabbed my bag and followed him outside.

We walked the streets in silence, then ducked into a souvenir shop in search of a gift for Michel, but I couldn't find anything my brother would like. Next, I saw a T-shirt shop and wondered if I could still pull that look off even though I wasn't in my twenties anymore. When George-Harrison saw me hesitating in the doorway, he dragged me inside, scouring through rack after rack until he found a couple of options for me to try. I didn't want to shoot him down right away, so I tried them on over the top I was wearing. He shook his head and ducked off to find a few more.

We must have looked like a happy couple out shopping. Back out on the street a bit later, I thought he might even try to take my hand. I don't think I would have minded if he had, to be honest. It had been a very long time since I had gone walking down the street holding hands with a man. The fact in and of itself didn't mean much. But when that kind of thought crosses your mind, you suddenly become convinced that there is something wrong with your life, and perhaps, even something wrong with you. Farther ahead, we came to a junction, just up the road from where we had parked the pickup. George-Harrison took a deep breath and turned to me.

"I'm having a really nice time," he said. "I may be an idiot for telling you that, but I just felt like I had to say it."

"You'd be an idiot if you didn't tell me. I'm . . . having a really nice time myself."

I took stock of the situation. There was a one-in-ten chance that he'd gaze into my eyes and go in for a kiss right then . . .

But he didn't. The odds were against me, and it was high time to put an end to the masquerade. I had even gone as far as to buy one of the T-shirts he had picked out for me. I knew I'd end up wearing it back in London, all alone in front of the TV, wine in hand, raising my glass to my damned freedom.

As soon as my mind drifted to London, I thought of my father. The time had come to question him in earnest. I had a creeping feeling that he knew a lot more than he was letting on. He had to. So, I wandered away from George-Harrison and found some privacy on a nearby bench.

It was only eight o'clock in the evening in Croydon, so there was no risk of waking him up. But after five rings and no answer, I started to worry. When at last my father answered, I could hear boisterous, jolly voices in the background.

"Ray Donovan speaking," my father said, clearing his throat.

"Are you watching TV? I can barely hear you, it's so noisy."

"Nope, I've got company!" he replied. "Maggie and Fred dropped by to see me. It must sound like a bit of a madhouse in here. They brought a couple of friends and some excellent wine—more than one bottle, if you catch my meaning."

"Really? Which friends?"

"A very nice couple. He's in the restaurant business like Fred, and she works in advertising. I don't think you know them. Care to say hello to your sister?"

Maggie hadn't shown even an ounce of interest in my quest since I got to Baltimore. It seemed like she couldn't care less, or at least not enough to merit an international phone call in any event. I had no desire to feign casual conversation with my sister at that moment. Especially since these friends I had never heard of were suddenly making me feel shut out of her life. Who were they anyway? Fred's buddies? Of course, the truth was that I was jealous of my sister for having a social life at all, something I was sorely lacking. The jealousy went hand in hand with shame. Maggie wasn't responsible for my life choices, and it was up to me to live with the consequences. Someday, I'd have to apologize to her for being so mean and unfair. Why should I care if Dad was helping her out here and there? Money never meant a thing to me, and I would swear on all that was *Absolutely Fabulous* and holy, on Saints Edina and Patsy, that I was as selfless a sister as they come.

"Elby? Are you there?" he said.

"Actually, I was hoping to talk to you alone," I finally said. "Would you be able to get somewhere quiet?"

"Sure, hang on, I'll just slip into my room." I heard my father grunt as he sat down on the bed, his knees acting up as usual. "Okay, I'm all yours. Is everything all right, dear?"

"Yeah. Everything's fine."

"What's the weather like over there?"

"It's long-distance, Dad. Forget the weather. I want you to tell me the truth, all right? What was Mum doing in Baltimore?"

I heard my father sigh heavily into the silence that followed.

"So, you leaving in such a hurry wasn't for an assignment after all, was it?"

I couldn't lie to my father, even over the phone. I confessed the truth about the letter and the implication by the mysterious poison-pen that she had committed a robbery. I left out the part about the old photo of Mum kissing George-Harrison's mother. After I had finished explaining, there were a few more moments of silence, followed by another weary sigh, before my father at last began to speak.

"When I said that your mother came *home* to England, it wasn't altogether true," he began. "Her real home was back in the United States. She was born and raised in Baltimore, then sent away to boarding school in England. Your mother was terribly lonely there, until the day we first laid eyes on each other at that pub. The rest you know. We were together for a few years before she decided to reconnect with her family. She spent a good ten years there before coming back to me."

"But Mum didn't have any family. You always told us she grew up in an orphanage."

"Well . . . when you're sent away to a boarding school at twelve, so far from home and entirely against your will, it's a bit like growing up in an orphanage."

"Why lie about all that?"

"Only your mother could answer that, and sadly, it's too late now. Elby, please. I implore you. Don't go digging into your mother's past. You know deep down inside how much she loved you—you even more than your brother and sister. Let her and her past rest in peace. Hold on to your memory of who she was as your mother."

"Dad? You didn't even flinch when I said your own wife had committed a robbery. So, does that mean you knew about it?"

"I will not have you thinking your mother was a thief. It's a bald-faced lie!" my father insisted.

"I've got proof. I spent the whole morning at the police station. I've seen the police report, Dad. Thirty-six years ago, Mum committed a major crime. She robbed a wealthy family blind in their own home. Please stop lying. I'm too old for Santa Claus and Prince Charming. You're the only one I still believe in! Can't you just tell me the truth?"

"My dear girl . . . it wasn't just any wealthy family. It was *her* family, her own."

It was now my turn to be speechless. I took a deep breath.

"You're telling me . . . that Mum was Robert and Hanna Stanfield's daughter?"

"Yes, that's what I'm telling you, essentially. Since you've already got your hands on the police records, you would have uncovered the truth yourself sooner or later. Your mother's maiden name, the one you knew her by, was actually her grandfather's, a man by the name of Sam Goldstein. She claimed it as her own as soon as she returned to England, when we reunited."

"Why change her identity?"

"Because she had left that part of her life far behind her and insisted that you and the other kids never learn the truth under any circumstances."

"But why?"

"To break the curse! She wanted her children to be Donovans, not Stanfields. Never that."

Stanfields. I still couldn't believe it. "What curse? What does that mean?"

"The betrayals, the lying, the souring of any semblance of love . . . the tragedies that plagued the family members and their spouses alike."

"What happened to my grandparents? Why didn't I ever meet them?"

"Those people were not your grandparents. They renounced their own daughter!" my father cried. "They're dead and gone, Elby. You go digging around in their graves, all you'll do is make your mother turn over in hers. Is that understood?"

In all my life, I had never heard my father so angry. His hoarse, raised voice left me dumbstruck. Even at my age, I felt myself shrinking back like a frightened little girl. And then, even worse, my own father hung up on me. Sitting alone on that stupid bench, I burst into tears. After one look at me, George-Harrison came running over and pulled me into his arms.

"What in the world happened?" he asked, a warm, comforting hand on the back of my neck as I curled up and let him hold me. I couldn't hold back the tears, no matter how hard I tried. When at last I could speak, I told George-Harrison about the conversation with my father, my voice broken, my eyes still wet with tears.

Just one phone call had brought my whole world crashing down around me. Mum had told outright lies about her past for the lion's share of her existence, and for all of mine. As rotten as my grandparents may have seemed to her, I might have at least met them, but my mother had made that decision for me. What's more, I had also discovered I was half American. But that wasn't the most stunning revelation from my father's outburst. I now knew that we were more than just Donovans. We were the last of the Stanfields.

George-Harrison gently wiped away my tears and took a long, hard look at me. "I know it's a lot to swallow, everything he told you. But it seems to me you're most bothered by having your own father hang up on you. If you ask me, you should call him back."

"Are you kidding? Not a chance!"

"He's probably just as upset about it as you are. But it's on you to take the first step. It must have taken a hell of a lot out of him, coming clean like that."

I shook my head, but it was clear George-Harrison wasn't going to let me off the hook.

"You know you're lucky to have a father like him. You need to stop acting like a spoiled brat, even though it's kind of cute. I probably would have steered clear of you at school."

"Excuse me? What exactly is that supposed to mean?"

"Nothing, just saying: you must have had all the boys drooling."

"You're full of it!"

My phone vibrated. George-Harrison smiled knowingly and had the good grace to give me some privacy, returning to his truck as I picked up the call.

"What the hell did you do to Dad to put him in such a state?" asked Maggie, coming out swinging. "I got worried when he was gone so long and found him shell-shocked, just sitting on his bed with a crushed look on his face. I mean, really! Even from the other side of the globe, you manage to wreak total havoc on our night!"

I couldn't stomach a dustup with my sister, not now, and I had already made a resolution to stop fighting with my family. Instead, I laid everything out for Maggie, calmly and steadily, the whole saga step by step. Every time I paused at the end of a sentence, I'd hear Maggie sigh and whisper, "Oh, shit." By the end of the tale, she must have said it at least ten times. Then, when I revealed that we—Michel, Maggie, and I—were all descendants of the illustrious Frederick Stanfield and a prestigious American family, the grand finale, my sister let out a more expressive burst of expletives—running the gamut from *fuck fuck fuck* to *son of a fucking bitch*. That was Maggie, through and through.

"Okay! Here's what we're going to do," she said, frantic and excited. "For the umpteenth time, I'll fix things between you and Dad. Give him time to sleep on it, then you call to apologize first thing tomorrow."

"What exactly am I supposed to apologize for? They were the ones who lied to us *our whole lives*! If I hadn't received this stupid letter and come all the way here, Dad would have kept us in the dark forever."

"Right. But they've loved us like crazy our whole lives, too. You are going to apologize because you have the best father in the whole world, the envy of all our friends, and he's probably the most generous person I've ever met. He is essentially perfect, minus the sweet tooth and the ridiculous, inexplicable attachment to that car. When you're lucky enough to have a father like that, you suck it up and swallow your pride!"

Although I was the older sibling, I was already in the midst of my second full-on regression of the day, so I decided to keep my mouth shut and just take it.

"And while I take care of Dad, you go track down that blasted treasure, whatever it is. I don't believe for one second Mum would be stupid enough to give up her cut. It'd be nice to finally move closer to London, and not necessarily to Fred's place, if you follow me. So, I am counting on you, Elby. Get to work. And keep me posted."

"Get to work, *please*. Keep me posted, *please*," I corrected her.

"Tell me: How's your whole Beatles thing coming along?" she asked, meaning George-Harrison.

"It's not."

"That's a relief. Like I've been telling you, he could still be in it just to make off with the loot. I still haven't heard anything to convince me he's not the poison-pen, or that he's not just using you to get closer to the treasure."

"You don't know what you're talking about."

"If there's one subject I'm an expert in, it's men. Talk to you tomorrow, sis."

As I said goodbye to my sister, I realized the truth was out and there was no turning back. I was part of a family I would never meet, people whom I knew nothing about. Out of respect for my mother's memory, I vowed not to look for their final resting places. Visiting their graves would do nothing except make me feel like I was betraying her. However, I was intrigued by Sam Goldstein. My mother had taken his name as her own, so he must have had some redeeming qualities. I was eager to learn more about him. And about the Stanfields, too, to be quite honest.

I approached the pickup to find George-Harrison waiting for me behind the wheel. He gave me a questioning thumbs-up, clearly concerned over whether my father and I had patched things up.

Maggie was dead wrong. One look was all I needed to convince me George-Harrison couldn't be the poison-pen. No way.

"Everything okay?" he asked as he opened the door for me.

"Yes, or at least it will be first thing tomorrow."

"Perfect. Where to now?"

I felt guilty thinking once more that my side of the investigation was advancing so rapidly, while his seemed to be at a standstill. The best I could do was apologize, but he just shrugged it off.

"I've been waiting so long, so what if it's not this week, this month, this year . . . or even this lifetime?"

"Hey, don't talk like that! We're going to find your father. I promised, remember?"

"We'll see. In the meantime, there's still one person I can think of who knows more than he's letting on. So, first thing tomorrow, we head back for round two with Professor Morrison."

I looked straight at him. An old pickup truck parked on a forgettable Baltimore street is probably one of the world's least romantic settings, and yet, right then and there, probably still reeling from my emotional roller-coaster ride, I decided to lean in and kiss George-Harrison.

It was a long, passionate kiss, the type that makes you forget where you are . . . unforgettable and full of tenderness. It didn't seem like a first kiss at all, strangely enough. It was so familiar and natural, it felt like we had known each other forever.

At last, I pulled away, my cheeks flushed and red. "I don't know what came over me," I stammered. George-Harrison started the car without a word, and we drove on for a long while in silence, our hands clasped together.

32

ELEANOR-RIGBY

October 2016, Baltimore

By the end of that day, our kiss seemed like little more than a strange interlude, and George-Harrison was acting like nothing at all had happened between us. All through dinner, I was so quiet, it felt like he was carrying the entire conversation himself. When he finally ran out of other things to talk about, he told me a little about his mother. He seemed to have unending admiration for her. She had been a free spirit who never strayed from her own personal set of values.

"She was always taking on a new cause, the more desperate the better," he said with a warm smile. "I admit, she went too far at times. When I started up carpentry, she forced me to put aside money to replant the trees that would have to be cut down and sacrificed for my livelihood. Which, of course, is total nonsense. Thinning out forests is essential to their preservation. But every time I explained that to her, out came the pamphlets on the sawmills ravaging the Amazon. Protecting the environment, standing up for children, fighting inequality, struggling against authoritarianism and bigotry, jumping to the front lines in the fight for freedom, and defending tolerance . . . she made all the rounds. But her biggest crusade was against corruption. She reserved a special kind of fury for people who lost touch with humanity in their thirst for power and money. I can't count how many times I saw her totally lose it just reading the newspaper. I can even remember the last time, the final outburst before her mind started to go . . . 'Children are slaughtered every day, living under threat of falling artillery shells, starvation, or exhaustion in sweatshops with unspeakable conditions . . . and yet people only run out to the streets to protest when two people who love each other happen to be of the same sex? Those goddamn hypocrites!' Or, at least something like that. The injustice of double standards was another go-to cause for her. 'Try not paying a parking ticket and they come take away your car, but the real criminals, the ones who get punch drunk and gorge themselves on the state coffers, who get paid to do nothing, who rig government contracts just to line their pockets . . . when *they* get caught? Oh, no! All they get is a slap on the wrist and they're free to go. Nobody even cares.' Sometimes I even ask myself if all the outrage is somehow to blame for her losing her mind so young."

As interesting as the conversation was, it still felt like one of the longest nights of my life. I had hoped he would skip dessert, but no luck. I should have known better. I watched the waitress making the rounds, table to table, just wishing I could swap bodies with her. At last, I ducked off to the bathroom, just to buy some time away from him. When I came back, he had already settled the bill and was waiting by the door.

After walking back to the hotel, we stepped out of the elevator onto our floor, and George-Harrison turned to me. "I had a really nice evening, but it seems you didn't. I'm sorry, I think I must have talked too much. See you tomorrow."

And just like that, he left me in the middle of the corridor. I bristled, like a volcano about to erupt. I felt like I could sink right through the floor. I wanted to go pounding at his door, asking if he remembered the adventures his tongue had been on inside my mouth earlier in the day. At least now I knew where we stood, no doubt about it. Starting the next morning, I'd take on the same attitude and act like nothing at all had happened.

I tossed and turned in bed, going over and over the call with my father in my head. In the early hours of the morning, I had a nightmare. I found myself in the Stanfield manor, an exquisite and opulent space full of marble flooring, crystal chandeliers, and wooden walls adorned with gold leaf. I caught a glimpse of myself in a mirror. I had on a maid's uniform, with a striped, fitted-waist blouse and ruffled lace headband holding back my hair. I carried a heavy tray in my hands, so cumbersome that it made me walk unsteadily, as I entered the dining room.

Hanna and Robert Stanfield were seated at opposite sides of a comically long mahogany table brimming with ornate candlesticks and silver cutlery. A child version of my mother was nearby as well, seated with her back as straight as a broomstick. An old man sat across from her, smiling warmly at the young girl. I served the lady of the house, who told me my tray was tipping and warned that she would dock my pay if I spilled a drop on her Persian rug. With an authoritarian flick of the wrist, she ordered me to serve the others. As I worked my way down the table, the stately grandfather winked at me, but the child version of my mother put out her foot and tripped me. I went sprawling and fell straight down onto the rug, eliciting roars of laughter from the entire table.

I awoke in a cold sweat and opened the hotel room window to gaze out at the early-morning sun over the old docks of Baltimore.

◆ ◆ ◆

"Did you sleep all right?" asked George-Harrison at breakfast.

"Like a baby," I replied, hiding behind the menu and avoiding his eyes.

After breakfast, we climbed into George-Harrison's pickup and headed to the university. Morrison made us wait a whole hour, his secretary explaining that he was correcting papers and would receive us as soon as he possibly could. When at last we were granted entry to his office, the man appeared to be in a pretty good mood.

"And what can I do for you two now?" he asked.

"Tell me about Sam Goldstein," I replied, taking the lead this time.

"He was an esteemed art dealer, the father of Hanna Stanfield. But something tells me you already know all that."

"So then, tell us something we don't know."

"This is the second time I've humored you with a meeting, and in case you haven't noticed, I do have other obligations aside from fielding riddles from strangers. So, how about you start by telling me what you've really come here for, and just why you are so interested in this particular family's history."

George-Harrison gently laid his hand on my knee, urging me to proceed with caution. If the professor really was the poison-pen, I'd be walking straight into his trap.

"Out with it now, I'm all ears!" he insisted.

"Hanna Stanfield was my grandmother. I'm Sally-Anne's daughter."

Morrison's eyes widened, and his face froze with shock. He rose from his chair without any sign of pain, as though the sciatica was nothing but a distant memory, and glided speechlessly over to the window. He gazed out over the campus, rubbing his beard.

"If what you say is true, it changes everything," he muttered.

"How so?" asked George-Harrison.

"First and foremost, it changes my level of interest in the two of you, which has gone from nonexistent to piqued. If you truly are a Stanfield, that's another story entirely. I'm certain this new development means we can find common ground."

"Is it money you're after?" I asked.

He flashed me a condescending grin. "You strike me as either plain stupid or plain rude. I certainly hope it's the latter. Otherwise, all of this would be a considerable waste of time. Neither of you seem especially well-off, so if you're hoping for some kind of inheritance, you are out of luck. There's nothing left."

"You also strike me as either plain stupid or plain rude," I replied. "But I'm not quite sure which one I prefer."

"Why, you've got some gall talking to me like that!"

"You started it," I told him.

"Well, how about we start over on the right foot? It just so happens I have a proposition for you."

Morrison admitted to having lied. In truth, he had seen Robert again after the day Hanna sent him away from the estate. He maintained it was only a lie by omission, since there hadn't been any reason to tell us until now.

"While Hanna loved her son most, Robert's soft spot was for Sally-Anne. He suffered greatly when his daughter's love turned to hate. Her exile to the boarding school in England only made matters worse. Robert blamed himself for everything that had transpired, and quickly sank to new depths of loneliness. He was ready to give anything to win back her trust and repair their father-daughter bond, and he would have . . . if only his own wife had not stymied his efforts. But it was always Hanna calling the shots, ruling now more than ever with an iron fist."

"Why did Mum start hating her own dad? Did he abuse her?"

"Robert? He wouldn't have harmed a hair on her head! Not a chance! Everything had changed when she overheard a conversation, one not meant for her ears, especially not at age twelve."

"You talk about Robert like the two of you knew each other well."

"Indeed, we did, eventually. A few months after that first encounter in his study, he paid me a visit. He sat in the very chair you are sitting in now. Having heard about my passionate interest in the Stanfield dynasty, he agreed to let me study the family archives, on the condition that I write a chapter recounting Robert's own story. He desperately needed someone not directly linked to the events to confide in. Someone with an irreproachable degree of credibility."

"Why would he need that?"

"To tell his side of the story. He hoped to win back his daughter with the truth so that she would forgive him and come back into his life. For me, it was an opportunity to advance my work, so of course I accepted. But I also had certain conditions. I would not make any concessions on his behalf. I would tell the facts exactly as they had occurred.

"Robert agreed to my conditions. We met every Wednesday, in this very office. Little by little, he brought me documents to aid my research, each smuggled out of the estate with utter care, so as not to raise Hanna's ire. Our meetings went on over a period of months, during which we became friends. Robert insisted I carry out my work quickly, but between my duties at the university and the impeccable standards of research a historian of my caliber must maintain, it was a long and arduous process. Sadly, just as I was putting the finishing touches on the manuscript, Hanna put a stop to all of it. I cannot fathom what nature of threat she issued, but Robert begged me to pull the plug. Our friendship prevented me from going against his wishes."

"You didn't consider finishing the book after his death?"

"In light of how he died—out with a bang, as they say, allegedly in the arms of his mistress—I did consider it. But beyond the grief that I felt at his loss, I was strictly prohibited from publishing anything. A clause in our agreement granted Robert the right to read the manuscript prior to release. I could do nothing without his consent. It wouldn't have hurt the credibility of my Stanfield book, but the value of my word. A promise is a promise."

"Tell me exactly what my mother overheard that she wasn't supposed to," I insisted.

The professor hesitated, sizing me up for a moment before continuing solemnly. "No, not before conditions have been agreed upon," he said. "I will provide you with the means to find what you're seeking, on the condition you grant *your* consent for my work to be published. Since a Stanfield heir has magically dropped from the sky, I daresay your consent would free me from my promise."

With that, Morrison drew a key on a chain from his waistcoat pocket and unlocked a drawer in the cabinet against the wall. He pulled out a thick folder and laid it down before us.

"It's all there, right in these pages. Read the chapters titled '1944,' '1945,' and '1946,' then come see me, and I'll fill you in on the rest."

With that, he led us to the door and once more wished us luck.

◆　◆　◆

I spent the rest of that day at the Johns Hopkins library, passionately poring over every last word of chapter "1944." Every time I finished a page, I'd hand it straight to George-Harrison and he would read it himself. Through this odd ritual, we discovered the true circumstances that had swept Robert Stanfield out of Baltimore and into a hunting lodge deep in the wilderness of wartime France. We read of his friendship with Sam Goldstein, the clandestine operations with the Resistance, his torture at the hands of the enemy, his narrow escape, and how he heroically protected Hanna as they fled France and then Europe.

After reading late into the afternoon, I was no closer to understanding how Mum had come to hate a man of that caliber, the same man who had rushed to marry a young woman in a Madrid embassy to save her life. By all accounts, my grandfather had kept his word, whisking Sam Goldstein's daughter away to America for a new life by his side.

I turned to the last chapter, eager to discover what befell my grandparents after they stepped off the ship.

33

ROBERT AND HANNA

July 1944 to March 1946, New York

With the war still raging across the ocean, Hanna and Robert watched from the deck of their ship as the Statue of Liberty emerged from the morning fog. While it wasn't the first time either had laid eyes on Lady Liberty, the sight stirred powerful emotions in the newlyweds, sealing their union even more profoundly than their actual wedding day.

After passing through immigration, Robert and Hanna climbed into the back of a taxi that took them straight to The Carlyle, a venerable New York institution with stunning views of Central Park. The couple sat down in the hotel restaurant while their suite was being prepared. Robert ordered breakfast for two, then stepped away to call his parents. He had been unable to get through to them the whole time he was in Madrid, sending only a telegram to let them know he was still alive. Going from that to announcing that they had a new daughter-in-law would be quite a leap. But Robert knew he had to warn them that he'd be returning home with her by his side. He also needed them to wire funds to pay for the hotel and the trip back to Baltimore.

When Robert announced to the family butler that he was on his way home, the servant had no choice but to reveal the truth: Robert's father had fled to Miami after squandering the last of the Stanfield fortune. What was worse, the family estate had been seized by creditors after they had missed too many mortgage payments. All that remained of the staff were one maid and the butler himself.

The news left Robert crushed and humiliated. With the small amount of cash Hanna had left, the couple couldn't afford even the slightest luxury and were forced to leave The Carlyle for a tenement on the corner of Thirty-Seventh Street and Eighth Avenue. The apartment was crammed and shabby, located in the heart of Hell's Kitchen, a poor, Irish neighborhood too dangerous to walk in after dark.

Hanna refused to consider staying there long. She spent her first week in New York combing the classified ads for a better apartment, something modest yet affordable. She found an enclave on the Upper West Side where many European Jews had settled after fleeing Germany in the thirties. There, the owner of a massive townhouse that had been converted into apartments agreed to rent them a ground-floor studio at a reasonable price with no security deposit. The move brought Hanna relief, however short-lived. At least now she had found a neighborhood where she could walk safely, even as far as the park, when time and weather permitted. When she walked past the extravagant buildings on Central Park West, the sight of the broad front gates and impeccable doormen reminded her of her childhood visits to New York. The Dakota stood out above all others. Hanna would gaze up at the windows and dream of the charmed lives of those living within.

As for Robert, he quickly grew disheartened by the harsh homecoming, as he was forced to swallow his pride and slog through one odd job after another. He would leave home early in the morning to make the rounds at the employment agencies, and was lucky if he managed to lock down even the most precarious short-term job. He picked up shifts on the docks or in the stockrooms of clothing stores, until he eventually landed a permanent position driving delivery trucks for a beverage company. He worked for a friendly man who expected hard work and long hours, yet still treated his employees with decency and respect.

Toward the end of fall, Robert was approached by another driver and became entangled in a scheme delivering black-market goods. Robert would keep the keys to the truck on him after his official route had ended, and then, after hours, he would pick up the truck, cross the Hudson River, and drive down to the docks on the Jersey side to load crates of cigarettes and other contraband for distribution.

It was a victimless crime, but it would have come with heavy consequences if he'd ever got caught. Yet the pay outweighed the high risk, a full fifty dollars per truckload. With four runs per weekend, he was at last able to offer Hanna a better life. He could now take her out to dinner on Wednesdays and Saturdays, or even dancing at a West Village jazz club.

One night, Robert came home from work to find Hanna crying at the kitchen stove. She wept soundlessly, as the steam from a pot of fresh vegetable soup rose up into her face. Robert sat down at the table without a word, and after Hanna had set down the tureen and served his dinner, she headed off to bed. Robert followed shortly after, lying in the bed beside her and waiting for his young wife to speak.

"I see how hard you're trying, darling. I don't blame you at all. Rather, I'm indebted to you for everything you've done for me. It's just . . . life here . . . isn't what I thought it would be," she said.

"We're going to be okay," Robert insisted. "We just have to wait it out. If we stay strong and stick together, we're going to make it."

"Stick together?" she sighed. "I already feel like I'm going it alone, almost all the time, every day of the week. And don't think I'm blind to what you've been doing on the weekends; I'm no fool. All I have to do is look out of the window to see who you're cavorting with in the dead of night, and what you're mixed up in. I know a deliveryman's wages would never pay for all those meals out, not to mention the new ice box last month, or that dress you gave me."

"I'm just trying to give you the nice things you deserve."

"I won't wear that dress, Robert. I don't want dirty money, and I don't want to live like this anymore."

Hanna had been spending far too much time walking around posh neighborhoods. She watched the refined, attractive people wearing the most lavish attire and driving around in shiny new cars. She peered through the windows of places she was now barred from entering, gazing at the very people with whom she had spent her entire childhood. The war and the loss of her father had forced Hanna into exile. She was looking in from the outside, wandering about like Alice in Wonderland in search of a secret door that would lead her back to her old life and the world to which she belonged.

"You don't understand, Robert. We're never going to get anywhere with you driving a truck, and I can't stand the thought of you in prison—at least, not unless it's for something worthwhile."

"Are you serious?" asked Robert, astonished.

"Of course not! If you join the Mafia, I'll walk out on you. I only wish we could find a way to get back to France . . ."

"And just what would that change?"

"One day I'll tell you."

Hanna had no idea of the consequences of her words. That one conversation would steer the course of their entire future together, driving Robert further into a life of lies. The absurdity and irony of it all was that every lie was out of love for her.

The end of December 1944 saw Manhattan blanketed in endless snow. On New Year's Eve, Robert promised Hanna he would be back before dinner. She had pushed their budget to the limit on a decadent meal from Schwartz's, their favorite deli on the Upper West Side, splurging on smoked whitefish, pastrami, salmon roe, and sweet challah. She arrived home and set the table, at last ready to put on the dress her husband had given her.

At nightfall, Robert made his last run of the year, arriving to find the docks in total darkness and empty. There was no risk that the police would be patrolling all the way out there on New Year's Eve. The loading of cigarette cartons and crates of booze took place seamlessly. The two longshoremen who helped Robert wished him a happy new year and were on their way. He tied down the tarp, climbed behind the wheel, and turned over the engine. As the truck lumbered between two cranes, a red light appeared in Robert's rearview mirror. A cop car was right on his tail, its siren wailing in the dark night. Robert knew he could play dumb about the cargo, claiming he was a deliveryman putting in some overtime for the holidays. With his spotless record, he risked little more than a night in jail and a slap on the wrist from a judge. But the thought of being held behind bars made Robert panic. He froze, paralyzed by the memory of the only other time he had been held prisoner, and the scars that he still bore from that terrible day.

He slammed on the gas, jerking the wheel. Determined to bury any evidence of wrongdoing, Robert sent the truck roaring straight for the river. He leapt out of the cabin at the last second and rolled, catching just a glimpse of the truck as it plunged into the murky Hudson. The cop car nearly met the same fate, but came to a screeching halt with its front bumper hanging out over the void.

Robert didn't wait for the cop to come to his wits. He scrambled to his feet and fled, disappearing into the labyrinth of stacked cargo.

1945

New York had already rung in the new year by the time Robert arrived home, with skinned elbows and knees, and a fresh set of bruises on his back. Hanna tended to his wounds without uttering a single word. He thought she might explode at any moment, and he'd spent the long two-hour walk through the dark and icy streets preparing for a serious blowup. Yet Hanna seemed strangely calm as she dressed his wounds.

Once Robert was patched up, Hanna sat down across from him and took his hands, the look in her eyes surprisingly gentle and loving.

"I should be furious with you. I was furious around nine o'clock, I was. Around ten, I was even more furious. But by eleven, there was no way I could stay mad a minute longer. I panicked, I was so worried about you. When the clock struck twelve, I made a vow before God and heaven that I wouldn't be mad at all, as long as you came home in one piece. By two in the morning, I was convinced you were dead. But here you are. So, no matter what happened to you, it couldn't be as bad as all the thoughts that ran through my head. Now, listen to me, Robert. Tomorrow, there are two ways this can go. The first, I pack my suitcases and leave. You'll never see me again. The other option is you tell me everything, every last detail of what happened, and I stay. As long as you didn't kill anybody, and you make me a promise that it's the last time you'll ever do anything so stupid."

Robert chose the latter, telling his wife the whole truth and vowing to never again commit a crime. Hanna forgave him.

Robert planned to beg his boss not to turn him in and to promise to pay back the money for the lost truck. But when he arrived at the truck depot two days later, his boss cut in before Robert could even say a word. The man looked like he had seen better days.

"A pair of rotten gangsters stole your truck for black-market stuff! Can you believe that? What's worse, when the cops showed up and caught them in the act, the loons drove the truck straight into the river to save their own hides! I went down there myself yesterday when they dragged it out of the Hudson. It's nothing but a junk heap now. So, as you can imagine, I got hit hard, money-wise. Insurance won't be enough to replace it. There's no easy way to say this, but I got no truck for you to drive, and I can't pay you to sit on your hands. What can I say? I sure am sorry, kid."

With a heavy heart, his boss paid Robert a day's wages as consolation and sent him on his way. Even if he was no longer part of the black-market scheme, Robert still had to find a way to pay for the merchandise he had lost in the Hudson. He doubted that his other "bosses" would be nearly as forgiving. Settling his debts without a car or a job would be no small feat, especially since he'd promised to stay on the straight and narrow. When he got home, Robert bared all the ugly details of the situation to Hanna, who decided to take matters into her own hands. After Robert had acted so recklessly, she knew their survival was entirely up to her. And even if her husband did manage to find an honest job, one working salary wouldn't be nearly enough to settle the debt. Robert was against the notion of his wife going to work, but Hanna told him to go to hell with his old-fashioned ways. Before the war, Hanna had accompanied her father on visits to his wealthy New York clients, many of whom had swooned over a young girl so knowledgeable about art. Hanna was her father's daughter, after all. She had grown up immersed in Sam Goldstein's world and was confident she could carve out a place for herself in the local art scene.

She visited every gallery in the city over the following week. Some of Sam's former clients met with her out of respect, lamenting her father's tragic fate over tea and biscuits. *Such a wonderful man, it's a horrific tragedy . . . but what a relief that you managed to make it out alive . . . so many innocent lives lost . . .* They would run through a whole catalog of catastrophes before inevitably arriving at their own hardship—the struggle to survive in a wartime art market—as explanation for why they simply couldn't do a thing to help her.

And then Hanna went to see John Glover, an English gallery owner who'd had a very close relationship with Sam. He'd opened a gallery in New York in 1935 and decided to make the move there in 1939, right at the onset of the war. Now, he hoped to return to London the moment the ink on the armistice had dried. The weakened Nazi forces were retreating on all fronts, losing battle after battle, and it was only a question of months before Hitler would be forced to surrender. In the meantime, Glover decided to take a chance on Hanna. If she proved herself, he would let the young woman manage his affairs in the United States when he went back to England. Beyond the modest starting salary, Hanna was offered the priceless experience of working side by side with the man himself.

John Glover came to Hanna's aid when she needed it most, which she would never forget. It is rare in life to encounter someone as pure and benevolent as Glover. He was an exceptional man, with a kind soul and a strong sense of humility. Small of stature, Glover had round glasses, a goatee, and an enormous heart.

The gallery owner would come for dinner twice a month at Hanna and Robert's ground-floor apartment in a brownstone on Sixty-Seventh Street. Hanna never felt an ounce of shame hosting him in their threadbare studio apartment. As Robert became friends with the gallery owner as well, Glover once more helped the couple by entrusting him with cross-country deliveries of valuable paintings, vases, and sculptures.

Germany surrendered on May 8, 1945. By the time Japan followed suit and officially brought World War II to a close, Europe had already moved on. Life for the young couple took a turn for the better. Hanna worked tirelessly at the gallery, helping Robert pay back his debt little by little. She took to her new profession with the passion of a fanatic, often traveling to meet clients for the purchase or sale of pieces. All the while, her new mentor kept a watchful but trusting eye on her development. Hanna worked countless hours and gave her all, until the blood, sweat, and tears at last began to pay off. And every day without fail, her walk home across Fifty-Ninth Street to Columbus Circle continued. She would gaze up at that other life she craved so desperately, her eyes tracing the facades of the prestigious buildings overlooking the park.

Robert was aware that his wife longed for something more, and though he never spoke of it, he himself dreamt of his family's lost wealth. It was painful to think he would never become the head of the family that he'd once dreamt of becoming, since his father had recklessly gambled away his birthright. Robert was struck with an idea: What if he found a way to make money from legal deliveries? He already had solid working relationships with clients and suppliers along his legitimate routes. With wartime over, people had a newfound thirst for revelry. The streets of New York were flowing with booze, and yet it was never enough. Robert was inspired to break into the liquor business. Determined to make a killing, he decided to specialize in high-end spirits (bourbon, scotch, brandy), champagne, and rare wines. But to get his business off the ground, he would need to borrow money. Robert made the rounds, only to be refused by bank after bank—the hallowed Stanfield reputation existed only within Maryland's state limits. In New York, Robert was like any other unproven, ambitious young man. He knew of only one person in the world who might trust him enough to take a leap of faith.

◆ ◆ ◆

Robert poured body and soul into his new venture. He found the perfect storefront on Ninety-First Street, with a street-level entrance, an inner courtyard large enough for loading vans, and an old shed for storing inventory. As for Hanna, her whole life revolved around the gallery now. The guarded young girl who had stepped off the boat with a wad of bills hidden beneath a layer of gauze was no more. A resolute woman on a mission had emerged in her place. Intoxicated by her new career and all that went with it, Hanna traveled coast to coast—Boston; Washington, DC; Dallas; Los Angeles; San Francisco—one city blurring into the next. Stepping back inside her tiny, cramped apartment only inspired her to work harder so she could one day leave it.

By the end of fall 1945, Robert's fledgling business had begun to turn a profit, which was no small feat. The young couple saw each other only once a week, on Sundays, when they would make love and sleep the whole day through.

◆　◆　◆

1946

On the second of March, the family butler called with terrible news: Robert's parents had been killed in a car accident in Miami. What's more, they died without a penny to their name, lacking even enough to cover funeral arrangements.

Hanna insisted that she and Robert cover the cost. Even if Robert hadn't forgiven or forgotten, it was imperative a son attend his parents' funeral. In all the time since the couple stepped off that boat, Robert had never spoken a word to his parents. As far as Robert knew, they had died not even knowing that he had married, and Hanna felt guilty for not pushing her husband to patch things up. She had been so focused on building a life for themselves over the past two years that she had forgotten the bonds of family. Now, it was too late. She made all the necessary arrangements for their remains to be returned to Baltimore, where they could be laid to rest in the family vault, the last vestige of the family's former glory.

The couple left for Baltimore two days later. There were very few in attendance at the small funeral in the cemetery chapel. The family butler, seated in the first row, seemed most affected by the loss. Hanna and Robert sat next to the housekeeper in the second row. At the end of the pew was a paunchy man in a three-piece suit and an old-fashioned coat. The sermon was short and to the point, and the officiating priest concluded by offering condolences to the many who would mourn the dearly departed. With only five people in attendance, the words resounded in the chapel like the punch line to a very dark joke.

The funeral came to a close as the coffins were placed in the family vault. Hanna was moved to tears, thinking of her own father. Now more than ever, she felt the need to cross the ocean and stand before his grave to pay her respects. While they were fleeing Europe, Robert insisted that the Resistance would have made sure her father received a proper burial, but there was no way to know for sure.

As they returned to their car, they were approached by the paunchy man from the funeral. After offering his condolences, he told Robert something that affected him even more than the loss of his parents. The Stanfield estate was headed for the auction block to pay off his parents' debts. Robert had but three months to waive his claim of inheritance or be forced to take on those debts himself. Hanna interrupted, asking just how much it would take to hold on to the estate. The banker, as he described himself, said it would take a full five hundred thousand dollars.

Hanna spent the first half of the trip back to New York turning the problem over in her head. As they reached the outskirts of Philadelphia, she took Robert by the hand and told him she might have thought of a way to hold on to the family estate.

"How in the world are we going to scrape together that kind of money in such a short time?" he asked. "If we pay back debts by borrowing more, it just puts us deeper in the hole. Both of us are working like crazy already, my love. Heartbreaking as it is to imagine strangers living in my childhood home, sometimes you have to let go of your dreams and move on."

"Don't give up so easily," Hanna replied. "I wasn't talking about borrowing at all. For my plan to work, I'll need to find a way to get back to France. The rest will be a matter of luck."

Robert thought he was piecing together what Hanna had in mind, but he kept his theories to himself. Night had fallen by the time they got back to the city. After a quick meal, Hanna slipped into bed and huddled close to her husband. Robert had been thinking about her idea nonstop, but fearing the consequences, he had decided he couldn't let her go through with it.

"You don't have to do this," he said, as he turned off the lights. "We can make a future for ourselves. We'll build a new life, one that will make our children proud."

Hanna sat up in bed, deciding all at once it was time to share a secret that had been weighing on her for months now.

"Robert . . . if I haven't gotten pregnant yet, after all the time we've been together . . . darling, I don't think I can have children."

◆ ◆ ◆

Two weeks later, far sooner than she expected, an opportunity emerged for Hanna to carry out her plan. It came in the form of a major client from California, set to arrive in New York. Glover had been on his way to London to close another deal, but felt he should stay to greet the exacting California client personally. When Hanna offered to travel overseas in his place, the art dealer put her on a flight and set her secret plan into motion. It was the first time Hanna had ever flown. Although she had some initial jitters during takeoff, the rest of the trip was unforgettable. The view out the window and the idea of dining above the clouds filled Hanna with pure wonder.

After three days in London, Hanna had completed all her work duties. She called and asked Glover for a few days off, explaining that she was so close to France, it would be a shame not to visit her father's grave. After Hanna's role in closing two astronomical deals in one month, Glover was ready to offer her the moon on a silver platter. He went as far as to sponsor her entire trip, and changed her return ticket so she could fly back directly from Paris.

Hanna caught a train from London, then crossed the Channel by ferry and boarded another train to Paris. After a night at a hotel near the Gare de Lyon, where she left her suitcase, she took one last train to

Montauban. The next leg of the journey Hanna covered by bus. She stopped at two different town halls near the hunting lodge until she had tracked down the address of a blacksmith by the name of Jorge. She hoped his memory would still be fresh. It had only been two years since his brother, Alberto, had perished with the others at the hunting lodge.

She recognized the man instantly as she entered the workshop. When Jorge caught sight of Hanna's face, he dropped his hoof knife to the ground and swept her into his arms, his eyes full of tears.

"Oh, thank God in heaven, you're alive! We looked for you everywhere," the blacksmith gasped. "You made it!"

"Yes, I was one of the lucky ones," Hanna said, doing her best to keep calm and not break down.

"I heard about your father. I'm so sorry for your loss."

"And I'm sorry for yours. I'm only alive today because of what your brother and the others did for me."

For the second time, Hanna recounted the tale of that June afternoon in 1944, and all the horrors that unfolded in those woods just a few kilometers from where they now stood. Jorge gave her a ride out to the cemetery on the back of his motorcycle. He left her alone to pay her respects at her father's grave, then returned and told Hanna all that had transpired following that fateful day at the lodge.

"The next day, around noon, a gendarme came to tell us we could come get the bodies of the dead. Raoul, Javier, Antoine, little Marcel, and my brother, Alberto . . . they're all here," said the blacksmith, gesturing out over the tombstones.

"Along with my father," Hanna added.

"You know . . . they suspected me. They thought I was the one who sold everyone out because I managed to stay alive. Good-for-nothing gossips and their careless accusations. It was only because I had lost my own brother that they were convinced I wasn't the rat. And the American, do you know what became of him?"

"Indeed, I do. He married me, as soon as we crossed the border into Spain," Hanna explained. "And what about Titon? Did you see him again?"

"Never. Perhaps he was the one who turned on the others."

"Perhaps nobody did," Hanna replied. "It's not the only time those butchers spilled blood out in these woods."

"Of course, anything's possible," said Jorge.

"What about the hunting lodge?"

"It's just sitting out there, abandoned. We cleared out the weapons, and I don't believe anyone has set foot inside since. I'm not even sure I'd have the heart to go there myself. I walk by it often, and I always steer clear. The soil up there is still black with their blood. That place is worse than a graveyard."

Hearing this, Hanna knew the next favor she had to ask Jorge would be difficult for him to grant. She wanted him to take her up to the lodge. She needed to set foot in the place where her father died. Only then would her mourning truly be complete.

"All right," replied Jorge after a moment. "Perhaps it would do me good as well. Maybe going together will make us stronger."

They rode his motorcycle to the trailhead, then climbed up the same rocky path that Hanna and Robert had used to flee in the dead of night just two years before. Several times, Hanna grew short of breath and had to stop, the memories making her weak. She would take a deep breath to stop her body from trembling, and then press on.

After what seemed like an eternity, the hunting lodge finally appeared at the top of the hill. No smoke rose from the old stone chimney now. Everything was calm, so much calmer than Hanna could have imagined.

Jorge was the first to cross the threshold. He stood in the exact spot where his brother died, kneeled, and made the sign of the cross. Hanna entered her old bedroom. The wardrobe had been reduced to a heap of rotting plywood, the box-spring mattress nothing but a tangle of rusty spirals. And yet, strangely enough, the chair in which Hanna had sat for hours on end had survived intact, just like Hanna herself. She sat in the chair once more, with her hands in her lap and her eyes drifting out the window into those woods just as she used to, what seemed like a lifetime ago . . .

"Are you all right, Hanna?" asked Jorge, poking his head into the room.

"I think I'd like to see the cellar now," she whispered.

"Are you . . . sure about that?" he asked.

Hanna gave a solemn nod and Jorge pulled up the trapdoor. He sparked his lighter and climbed down first, testing the rungs of the ladder to make sure it wouldn't snap under their weight. Luckily, the stone cellar had kept it dry. Hanna climbed down to join him.

"So, this is where you hid . . . the whole time—"

"Yes," Hanna cut in before he could finish. "I hid down there at the end of the tunnel. Follow me." Taking Jorge's lighter in hand, Hanna took the lead, tracing the length of the tunnel and stopping before her father's hiding place.

"That wooden beam. Give it a nice hard tug, please. It should slide out. Just a few centimeters is all I need."

Surprising as her requests were, Hanna looked so beautiful in the glow of the flickering flame that Jorge would have moved heaven and earth for her at that moment.

"You know, whenever I came up here with provisions or laundry, just getting one single look at you would give me strength. Every time. Knowing you were waiting at the top of the path was the only thing that made the climb worth it."

"I know," Hanna replied. "I've always known. Looking at you gave me strength, too. But that was a long time ago. I'm married now." Jorge shrugged and pulled out the beam to reveal the cavity dug into the wall. Stepping in closer, Hanna gave Jorge back his lighter and asked him to give her some light.

Jorge did as she asked, and Hanna slid her hand into the crevice until her fingers closed around the metal tube. She pulled the precious container out of its hiding place and announced that it was time to leave.

Jorge was not an especially talkative man, but he couldn't resist asking Hanna a few questions as they climbed back down the trail.

"That tube, is that what you came here for?"

"I came to mourn my father," she replied, resting her eyes on the precious cylinder. "This is part of that."

The two arrived at the end of the trail and hopped back on the motorcycle. "Where to now?" the blacksmith asked.

"The station, if you'd be so kind."

As the motorcycle roared down country roads, Hanna gripped Jorge's waist firmly with one hand and clutched the metal tube with the other. The wind biting at her cheeks filled her with a sense of freedom she hadn't felt in ages, as though a great weight had been lifted from her shoulders.

Jorge accompanied her all the way to the platform and stood by her side to await the train. When at last Hanna boarded, he grabbed her hand and stopped her halfway into the train carriage.

"Tell me what's inside that tube," he said.

"My father's personal belongings."

"In that case, I'm glad they stayed hidden in that hole all this time, and that you were able to reclaim them."

"Thank you, Jorge. Thank you for everything."

"You're never coming back, are you?"

"No, never."

"Just passing through. I figured as much when I saw you didn't even bring a bag. Safe travels, Hanna. Goodbye."

Jorge stayed planted on the platform, watching as the train pulled away and Hanna leaned out to blow him a kiss.

Back in Paris, Hanna opened the cylinder and carefully unrolled the canvases on her hotel room bed. Once more, her father had proven wise and farsighted by using the waterproof tube; the paintings were completely undamaged. One by one, Hanna examined each of them, a sense of dread growing in the pit of her stomach as she made a chilling discovery.

There were only nine paintings. One was missing. Hopper's *Girl by the Window* had vanished into thin air.

The next morning, Hanna paid for her hotel room, boarded an Air France Constellation flight to New York, and never looked back.

34

ELEANOR-RIGBY

October 2016, Baltimore

That was it, the end of the chapter. George-Harrison finished just moments later and suggested grabbing a coffee, but all I wanted was to find out the rest of the story and to understand why Morrison hadn't written it down. Why would it end so abruptly? I checked my watch. It was almost six . . . Still a slim chance we'd have time to corner the slippery professor in his office.

"Follow me," I said, my commanding tone catching George-Harrison off guard.

"You're certainly your grandmother's granddaughter," he said, rolling his eyes.

We bolted straight out of the library and sprinted down the campus walkways side by side without slowing for a single moment. If not for our clothes, we could have been mistaken for a pair of runners vying for the finish line, which was how our wild chase actually came to an end. George-Harrison and I ran neck and neck until I spotted a shortcut and split off, leaving him in the dust, with him yelling that I was a cheater. We burst straight into Morrison's office without bothering to knock, out of breath and triumphant. The professor nearly leapt out of his chair, shocked to find us panting and dripping with sweat in his office.

"Somehow, I doubt it was my manuscript that left you two in such a state," he said, wryly.

"No, it's what it was missing! Why would you decide to cut the story off like that, right in the middle of the chapter?" I implored.

"It wasn't a decision at all, as I told you. Hanna strictly forbade Robert to proceed any further with the project. But our friendship did continue thereafter." Morrison glanced at his watch with a sigh. "I'm famished, and eating too late wreaks havoc on my digestion."

"Fine, let's have dinner together," George-Harrison offered. "You choose the spot. Our treat."

"Hmm . . . in that case, might I suggest the Charleston?" Morrison replied, averting his eyes. "It's a fine establishment. Since you seem unable to wait until tomorrow, I'll accept your offer."

◆ ◆ ◆

One glance at the menu and I knew why the professor had been so sheepish about his restaurant choice. The prices nearly made me faint. And there was no way I'd be able to get the meal cleared as an expense, even if I managed to bring my editor Edgar Allan Poe's femur in a take-away bag. But the table was now set, with something in store that was far more valuable than the market-price lobster Morrison had ordered. As soon as the waiter delivered our food and left our table, I fired the opening salvo.

"What happened to the missing painting? What did Hanna do when she got back from Europe?"

"One question at a time, please," the professor replied, as he wrapped a napkin around his neck like a bib.

Morrison devoured over half his lobster without coming up for air. Watching him crack through the shell and lick his own fingertips instantly killed my appetite. George-Harrison seemed fine, though, judging from the way he attacked his T-bone steak.

"When Hanna returned to New York, she told no one about the paintings," the professor began at last. "Not even Robert, who never knew the details of what she'd done in France. Hanna had good reason to hold her tongue. To see her plan to completion, she would have to part with one of the nine remaining paintings without her husband or employer finding out.

"She chose Fragonard's masterful *Happy Accidents of the Swing*, a sixty-by-eighty-centimeter canvas, to which she applied a new and simpler title: *The Swing*. Out of all the paintings of her father's collection, it was the one that Hanna liked the least. She found the rococo painting frivolous, and just a bit sentimental. She didn't tell Glover out of fear that he would want to acquire the piece for himself at market price, whereas she could earn twice as much by selling directly to a collector. And for her plan to succeed, lovely Hanna needed to raise over five hundred thousand dollars. Adhering to a strict code of ethics, she refused to solicit any existing clients of Glover's gallery. For Hanna, that would have crossed the line. She owed the English art dealer total loyalty after all he had done for her, and she would never dream of attempting anything underhanded. Since Sam's name still carried weight amongst his wealthy former clientele in New York, Hanna had other avenues to pursue outside of Glover's circle.

"She set up a Saturday meeting, knowing Robert would be busy carrying out his weekly inventory, and presented the Fragonard to the highly esteemed Perl family. Hanna agreed to leave the painting with them for a few days after receiving initial payment. After closing the deal, she opened a bank account the following week by forging Robert's signature. In those days, married women needed consent from their husbands to open even a basic checking account. She deposited the full six hundred and sixty thousand dollars she had received for the

Fragonard, a sum she achieved only after hard-fought negotiation. She deposited the other eight masterpieces in a bank safe."

"And then what? What did she do next?" I asked.

"Shortly thereafter, she hired a chauffeur to drive her down to Baltimore. She used the payment for the painting to buy back the Stanfield estate from the banks that had seized the property. It was a gift to Robert, but she couldn't tell him about it—not yet—for fear he'd seek to move in straightaway. After all, Hanna had always dreamt of an apartment overlooking Central Park. She refused to settle for withering away in a second-rate city like this, not with her new life close enough to touch.

"In early 1948, Glover wanted to return to his native England and so resolved to sell his New York gallery to the right buyer. He let Hanna know, for the sake of transparency, and the young woman quickly made an offer to become a partner herself. While Hanna was the perfect choice, and he had complete trust in her, Glover knew she couldn't provide any up-front payment, and instead would need to pay for her stake through future art deals. He promised to give the matter some thought. Hanna, fearing she might miss out on a rare opportunity, offered Glover one hundred and fifty thousand dollars in cash, with the promise to pay the rest within two years. Glover was shocked to learn she had such cash on hand, but decided to let the matter lie.

"On the day they signed the papers, he invited her out to dinner to celebrate their partnership. Out of nowhere, in the middle of the meal, he asked her point-blank if she had been behind the sale of the Fragonard to the Perl family. He playfully reminded his speechless young protégée of one of his cardinal rules of the trade: always remember, the world of art dealing is small, and everyone knows everything.

"Glover packed his bags and set off for London. A few months later, the day came at last—one chosen quite deliberately—and Hanna drove Robert to the gallery. He noticed the facade was covered with a tarp. 'I had no idea it was under renovation, you never even told me,' he complained, but his tenor changed immediately when he noticed the look of elation on Hanna's face. She passed her husband the rope holding the tarp in place and told him to pull on it with all his might. It dropped to the ground, revealing the gallery's new name: Stanfield & Glover."

"How did Robert react?" asked George-Harrison.

"He was overcome with emotion. He wasn't well versed in his wife's business, but just seeing the word 'Stanfield' in gold letters across the window was an incredible honor, and he couldn't imagine what she had gone through to make it happen. That Sunday was one of the best days of his life, a date chosen by Hanna because it had been four years to the day since the couple had stepped off that cargo ship from Tangier onto American soil."

"One might have thought he would have suggested using her maiden name for the gallery," I observed. "After all, it was Sam's legacy that allowed Hanna to buy her stake in the gallery."

"Yes, but Robert wasn't aware of that. And at times, generosity means not questioning what is given to you. Even so, Robert did make that very suggestion, but Hanna explained that she wished to develop a career on her own merits, to make her own way. Goldstein was in her past. Stanfield was her future."

"And then?"

"First, allow me a small interlude to peruse the dessert menu. People say the chocolate soufflé here is to die for. Perhaps a nice sweet wine to wash it down, as long as I'm not overstepping my bounds, of course. I must admit all this talking has left me positively parched."

I flagged down the waiter, and George-Harrison made a signal for the sommelier. With his conditions met, Morrison continued.

"The Stanfield & Glover gallery thrived in New York, eclipsing even its sister location in London. The economy in postwar England didn't bounce back quite as assuredly as our own, you see. In late 1948, Hanna and Robert moved into a new home on the top floor of a building at the corner of Seventy-Seventh Street and Fifth Avenue. Hanna had always wanted a view of Central Park, but this was beyond her wildest dreams. The Upper East Side has always been considered swankier than the Upper West, with snobs flocking there in droves, although why, I can't say. Hanna should have been the happiest woman in the world, and yet the city began to choke the life out of her. Robert's own business was growing exponentially. They'd already opened locations in Washington and Boston, with a third on its way in Los Angeles. Hanna barely saw her husband anymore and spent most of her evenings alone in their vast apartment. While once the stuff of dreams, the view out her window at night became a nightmarish ocean of darkness. The situation put their marriage at stake, even though Hanna still loved Robert deeply. She felt that only a drastic change—like having a child—would save their marriage."

"I thought she was unable to bear children."

"As did she, but there are always ways for the wealthy to get around infertility. In July of 1949, in honor of the five-year anniversary of their arrival in New York, Hanna presented Robert with the deed to the family estate in Baltimore, at last ready to make the move. Robert took no offense at her buying the property in secret. Hanna had just given him the keys to the legendary Stanfield estate! It was a dream come true, one he had long since abandoned in defeat. For him, it was a gift born of pure love.

"While the estate was being renovated and restored to its former glory, the couple made arrangements to relocate their entire lives to Baltimore. New York was only two and a half hours by car, and Hanna had staff in place at the gallery to whom she knew she could entrust the business from a distance with total peace of mind. Besides, most of the major deals of that time tended to close outside the city or at major fine art auctions.

"In 1950, around the same time your mother came into the picture and not too long after he moved back to London, Glover's health took a turn for the worse. He was diagnosed with a severe form of pancreatic cancer that would swiftly claim his life. He called Hanna and begged her urgently to pay him a visit, all without revealing anything about his condition. As soon as she arrived in London, Glover informed her that he had decided to retire and offered her the chance to buy him out of the business altogether, with an initial asking price so low that Hanna refused outright. Glover's inventory of art alone was worth double what he was asking for the entire business! Yet, the art dealer reminded Hanna of a second cardinal rule in their trade: the true market value of a piece is only as high as someone is willing to pay. He knew that running a gallery from the other side of the ocean would be a source of unnecessary grief for Hanna, especially since she now had a child and had set down deep roots in Baltimore. The gallery itself meant nothing to Glover. It was just a space he rented, nothing more. He led Hanna down to the safe where he kept his most cherished and valuable works of art, and asked her to make an offer on each and every last painting. In reality, Glover reminded her, as his partner, she already owned half of each painting anyway."

With that, Morrison took his last bite of chocolate soufflé. For a terrible moment, I feared he would leave without revealing the part of the story I had been the most desperate to hear from the very start.

"This sure is intriguing," I cut in. "But can you please tell us what happened between my mother and her parents that caused all those years of bad blood?"

"Patience now, patience. All will be revealed. Hanna took full inventory of Glover's collection at his insistence. Methodical as she was, it was really nothing more than a formality; she already knew every piece in Glover's collection by heart. Hanna herself had maintained Glover's register with utter diligence and precision. Everything between them was open and transparent, without the slightest room for doubt. Every time Glover bought or sold anything, Hanna would know of it immediately. There was never any gray area . . . until all at once, Hanna found herself staring into a world of gray, her eyes landing on a painting that made her heart stop."

"My God . . . the Hopper?" George-Harrison sputtered. I gasped.

"Right you are! *Girl by the Window.* You cannot imagine how shocked Hanna was at the discovery, stumbling upon her father's favorite painting in Glover's safe. If Glover—her partner, her mentor, her confidant—had acquired it through legitimate means, why would he have chosen to keep it hidden from her? There was no coincidence here, no fluke or mere act of chance. It was impossible to think that the *one secret* he kept from Hanna happened to be the piece that meant more than anything to her. She burst into his office in a rage. Glover had seen her upset before, but never like this. His health ailing, the poor man had a hard time making sense of her accusations and found himself completely caught off guard. The fact that Hanna suspected him of wrongdoing upset Glover quite a bit, but he was far too weary to tell her off. Instead, he unleashed the signature British stiff upper lip with a simple question of his own. How could she be so surprised, he had asked, considering it was *her own husband* who had entrusted the painting to Glover in the first place? The look in her eyes was enough for the art dealer to see that the answer was a lot more complicated than he had thought.

"He explained everything, racked with the guilt of unknowingly betraying her trust. A few years earlier, Robert had come to Glover in need of a favor. He desperately needed capital to start his liquor business. While Glover had immediately assured him he would help out in any way, Robert wished to leave something as collateral to prove he would keep his word and repay the loan. The object he chose was *Girl by the Window.* When Robert had paid back the loan in full, naturally Glover wished to return the painting. But for reasons he never fully understood, Robert asked Glover to keep the Hopper in the safe with his collection. Glover didn't ask any further questions, adhering to the third cardinal rule: always be discreet. Glover suggested selling the painting, knowing Robert could have his pick of prospective buyers, but Robert insisted, 'Hanna and I do not wish to sell the painting, not for any price. Not now, not ever.' *'Hanna and I,'* Glover insisted adamantly, longing for Hanna to believe that he never knowingly deceived her. Dumbfounded by the revelations, Hanna lied and apologized, claiming the sight of the painting had so shattered her emotionally that she briefly lost sight of reality.

"That was how they left it. Glover was so crushed by the episode, he couldn't bear keeping any more secrets. He revealed his illness to Hanna then and there. It was pointless for her to actually buy his collection; he was leaving everything to her, and any sum she paid would just come right back to her after his death, which was rapidly approaching. Glover assured Hanna he had more than enough money to attend to all his needs until he passed. Hanna was so overcome with emotion at this latest revelation, she cast aside any lingering questions about the *Girl by the Window*. She paid Glover several more visits over the following months and remained faithfully at his bedside from the very moment he entered hospice care. He died just six days later. Hanna took care of all the arrangements herself. Glover had been like a second father to her, and this new loss affected her deeply. His collection was shipped to the States. The sign in front of the New York gallery was changed in accordance with Glover's last wishes, which he conveyed to Hanna in a letter.

> *"Only art matters, for each work of art is eternal. Those who claim ownership of art are of little importance in the end, since no one can outlive it. Don't you find that to be a delicious little slice of humility? One of the reasons I love and admire you so deeply is that you have never shown even the smallest amount of pride in having works of art within your possession. Like me, you have nothing but love and respect for art and art alone, so it is high time that you reap the rewards for all you have given.*

"In no way should you feel indebted to me, Hanna. You have been a source of light and joy in my life, not to mention an ample source of amusement, as I've always delighted in your many moods—the good and the bad, your uncontrollable laughter and your fits of rage alike. One could say I've led a charmed life. I've met scores of art dealers in my time, but none have ever measured up to you, my dear. From this point forward, I wish to have your name and your name only adorning our New York gallery. The pride I have in my pupil far eclipses how proud I am to have once been her teacher. May your life always be full of all the happiness and beauty that you deserve, my dearest Hanna. Yours sincerely, John Glover.

"Only an Englishman could write something so dignified and restrained. And don't be shocked that I've committed it to memory; I am a historian, after all! Retaining exact quotes is part of my craft.

"But, alas, the hour grows late and there are still many questions to be answered. After Hanna had laid Glover to rest and settled his affairs, it was time for the full consequences of her fateful discovery to come to light. It never crossed Hanna's mind that Robert was in it for money; he would have had countless opportunities to make a fortune off the Hopper. The fact that he had forbidden Glover from ever selling it proved that was never his intention. No, something far more troublesome was at play. Hanna remembered one moment from the night they fled the hunting lodge that had always bothered her: before they set out for Spain, Robert had insisted on going back to the lodge. It now made sense. It wasn't for clothes, or that so-called secret map of weapon depots. No. It was the Hopper painting all along. Hanna could still picture the satchel Robert kept by his side for the entire escape, how he never let it out of his sight, not once during the crossing into Spain or aboard the ship. This led her to one inevitable conclusion: Sam had revealed the hiding place to Robert, and her husband had been lying about everything all along. But that wasn't all. Remember back at the cemetery, when Jorge said that he himself had been suspected of betraying the others? Hanna had asked for news of Titon, Robert's partner on the tandem for that ill-fated mission. She thought of him because of a lingering doubt still gnawing at her, one glaring discrepancy Hanna had observed as they first fled. An important part of Robert's story made no sense. He claimed to have snapped the driver's neck *en route* to the Germans, which would have left him stranded in the middle of a country road. So, how then had Robert managed to recover that tandem?"

"I never thought of that," I admitted. I looked at George-Harrison. "Me neither."

"No, but *she* did," Morrison continued. "And the only logical conclusion to this discrepancy represented a grave dilemma for lovely Hanna. Because if Robert had been lying about the bike, it could only be for one reason: he had lied about his escape . . . because, in truth, it wasn't an escape at all."

"And she didn't try getting to the bottom of it by asking Robert what really happened?"

"At the time, she had good reason not to question the man who was helping to save her life. But now, the truth had turned her life upside down. There was no turning back, and Hanna was never the same again."

"But why not just come out with it and tell him?"

"Because of the ties that bind us. Because at times we need lies, or things left unsaid, to avoid facing certain earth-shattering truths. On the trip over to see Glover on his deathbed, Hanna had been struck by several bouts of nausea. While she initially thought she was unwell out of concern for Glover, it soon became clear . . . that nature had finally given her the one dream she thought would never come true."

"But you said Hanna already had a child—my mother."

"Not quite. I said your mother *came into the picture*, and my choice of words was no accident. They had adopted your mother, Sally-Anne, because Hanna was convinced she was barren. Later, she got pregnant out of the blue. Alas, any joy came hand in hand with deep sorrow. Her future child's father was the very man responsible for her own father's demise. Hanna had no illusions about it: to gain his freedom, Robert must have divulged the location of the hunting lodge, and Sam and the Resistance fighters had paid the ultimate price for his betrayal. One can only imagine the Cornelian dilemma in which the poor woman found herself ensnared! Yet, Hanna wasn't about to forget two of Glover's cardinal rules of the art world: everyone knows everything, and discretion is essential. If the truth were to come out, it would ruin more than just their marriage. It would lay waste to their reputations, tainting their name forever. Bid adieu to the thriving art gallery. No one would even think of doing business with them after such a vile scandal.

"So, Hanna placed the Hopper in a simple art portfolio that she bound with a wax seal and stored away in her husband's safe. She told Robert that the portfolio contained a work to which she was especially attached. She made him swear on the lives of their children never to break that seal. It was a cruel and subtle breed of revenge. Every time Robert opened the safe, his eyes would drift to that portfolio, only to wonder if Hanna had discovered proof of his guilt, or if it was all in his head. Although seemingly untenable, this status quo was maintained over the next eleven years. Of course, Hanna was never again the close, loving wife she had once been. Instead, she saved all her affection for her son. Robert, meanwhile, grew to cherish his daughter most. Sally-Anne, who did not get along with her mother, returned that love unconditionally. Until one fateful day—"

"When she was twelve years old."

"Indeed. It was around that time that she overheard a terrible quarrel between her parents. Sally-Anne learned that her father was having an affair, the first of many mistresses he would accrue over the years. In his defense, Robert was still a handsome man at the time and had long been neglected by Hanna, who was incapable of forgiving all he had done. As humans are wont to do, he sought to love and be loved. On the day in question, insults were hurled from both sides, and the fight escalated. Hanna at last revealed that *Girl by the Window*, the very painting he had taken from the hunting lodge in France, had been locked up for eleven years in Robert's own safe, before also confronting him about his treachery. In the course of one evening, Sally-Anne learned her father was unfaithful and that he was not at all the hero she thought him to be. She saw him for the first time for what he truly was: a man who had done the unthinkable to save himself. Much less could have ignited the fiery rage of adolescence, and this triggered a veritable Molotov cocktail of emotion. Her fury and hatred rippled throughout the entire family.

"Hanna was the enemy for fostering the lie for the worst of reasons. Robert was pure scum, irredeemable. And she hated Edward, too, for being the loved and cherished son, while she was nothing but the black sheep who would never measure up. Hanna feared her daughter would, out of a simple thirst for vengeance, expose the family's shame to anyone who would listen. To prevent this from happening, Hanna had Sally-Anne sent to boarding school in England, where she stayed through early adulthood."

The professor downed the rest of his drink and carefully set the glass down on the tablecloth. "I must say this has been a particularly fine meal. I will leave you now to take care of the bill. We can do this again whenever you like; there's a Chilean sea bass with truffle emulsion that I'd jump at the chance to try. Revisiting the Stanfield story certainly has whetted my appetite to at last complete the definitive family saga. I just hope you will keep your end of the bargain and grant me consent to publish. It was a true honor meeting the last of the Stanfields."

With that, the professor stood, shook our hands, and left.

Back at the hotel, I lay sleeplessly in bed, consumed by the flood of revelations from dinner with the professor.

Strangely, I felt closer to my mother than ever before, closer than we had ever been when she was alive. At last, I had a real sense of what she had endured during her forced exile. To experience such abandonment twice over—first by her real parents and then by her adoptive family—was completely unfathomable. In a way, she had been telling the truth when she described herself as an orphan, or very nearly the truth. But over the course of that long, sleepless night, I understood why she never told us more, and why my father had kept silent as well. It was to protect us. Despite all of that, I still wished she had shared her secret past with us. I would like to think I would have showered her with endless love to make up for all she had missed out on in her youth. And, what now? Did I tell Maggie and Michel the truth, even if doing so would be betraying my mother's memory?

These questions and others weighed heavily on my mind and kept me from getting even an hour of sleep. Had Professor Morrison exaggerated parts of the tale to get the consent he craved so badly for his book? Could he have known my true identity before we met? After all, if the professor wasn't the poison-pen, then who could it be? The worst part was that I felt no closer to grasping just what it was the anonymous puppeteer had been after from the very start.

I vowed I would fulfill my promise starting the next day. It was time to help George-Harrison find the identity of his father.

35

ELEANOR-RIGBY

October 2016, Baltimore

There was a bitter chill in the air the next morning. The city seemed almost gray in the wan light, as puddles of dirty rain gathered on the sidewalks. I can't stand those days in late autumn when the streets are so wind battered, they seem to wither in front of your very eyes.

George-Harrison was waiting for me in front of his pickup truck. He wore an old denim shirt, a leather jacket, and a baseball hat, like a grizzled ballplayer past his prime. Most of all, he seemed to have got out of the wrong side of the bed. He studied my face for a long moment, then sighed and climbed into the driver's seat without a word. As I got into the vehicle, I asked where we were headed.

"You can go wherever you like, I'm going home. Money doesn't grow on trees, and speaking of trees, I have to get back to my work."

"You're giving up now, when we're this close to the end?"

"What *end*? And giving up what? I left to find my father, and ever since I got here, ever since we met, all we've done is uncover secrets about your mother—her struggles and her twisted family history. Fascinating as all this has been, mostly for you, I couldn't afford to stay in this city any longer if I wanted to, twiddling my thumbs without making any progress."

"Don't talk like that. You're right that we've made a lot more headway on my questions than yours. But I'm telling you, it was on my mind just before I fell asleep, and I told myself it was time for us to shift our search in a new direction today."

"And what direction is that? What exactly can we do?" he asked, temper flaring. I had no idea, and because I'm such a god-awful liar, all I could do was mumble excuses, until George-Harrison mercifully cut me off.

"You see what I mean? You don't have a clue, and neither do I. So, let's just leave it at that. It was really nice getting to know you. And just so you know, I'm not a complete idiot or what have you. I haven't forgotten what happened right here in this pickup, however brief it may have been. The way you leaned over and kissed me, and I'm not saying I wouldn't also have wanted to kiss you . . . I mean, I've been wanting to kiss you, too. But you live in London, and I live in a sleepy little town thousands of miles away from your big, beautiful metropolis. So . . . what good would kissing again do? Don't answer, don't even bother. You know there are no good answers. I'm going back home to my life and my job. As for my father, I know why he hasn't shown up. I've known for a long time. So, to hell with the anonymous letter. To hell with your poison-pen. I'm not sure I even care who he is. You ask me, we've wasted enough time on that clown already. And even if it were the professor—who, by the way, and I don't care how eloquent he may be, still eats like a pig—he did all this just to write a stupid book? He can go to hell, too. Him most of all. And here's some advice for you: finish your article and go home. It's the best you can do at this point."

I found myself struck with absolute panic, the type of feeling that twists your insides in knots and makes you want to sink right into the ground. Then, just like that, I suddenly learned how to lie. I pretended not to feel a thing, acting like I thought he was right, that turning and walking out of that pickup made all the sense in the world. I pretended that the idea of never seeing him again would be perfectly fine by me. I nodded and pouted, and didn't say a single word. Unsure how long the Oscar-worthy performance would last and not wanting to push my luck, I leapt straight out of his shitty old pickup truck, proud and resolute . . . so resolute that I didn't even shut the door behind me. It would have made Edina and Patsy proud, or they would have laughed at me and my misplaced confidence.

The pickup started pulling away and I turned back, my eyes full of tears, just in time to see it disappear from view. Not only had that idiot all but thrown me away like an old sock, but I was feeling more alone than I ever had in all my trips around the world. The loneliness cut me to the core, only growing worse at the thought of my amazing father and wonderful siblings back home. I even found myself missing Vera. I was alone in the middle of a rotten city that had brought me nothing but heartache. With nowhere else to go, I turned back to the hotel. Just then, I heard a car honk twice behind me. I turned around.

It was George-Harrison, grouchy as ever. He rolled down the window.

"Run inside. I'll wait while you get your stuff. Just hurry up."

"Just hurry up, *please*!" I corrected him.

"Fine: hurry up! *Right now*, please!"

I was in such a crazy rush that I tossed everything pell-mell into my bag—jumpers, trousers, underwear, back-up shoes, MacBook with charger, toiletry bag, and my tiny travel makeup kit. I paid for the room just as quickly. When I made it back outside, George-Harrison was still there waiting. He grabbed my bag and threw it into the back of the truck.

"So? Where to?" I asked.

"Back where it all started, at least for me. Something we would have tried from the start, had I been more persistent."

"What does that mean?"

"It means we're going to my mother's nursing home. She does have little windows of lucidity—always brief, and extremely rare. But hey, you've had some wild luck so far. Maybe some of it can rub off on me. I don't expect you to come along. If you don't, I'll totally understand. Especially considering everything I said earlier."

"So . . . that whole diatribe was just your way of telling me you want to introduce me to your mum?" I sighed. "All you had to do was ask. Getting to meet my mother's long-lost love? I wouldn't miss it for the world!"

George-Harrison gaped back at me, trying to figure out if I was messing with him. I responded with a look that said pretty clearly, *Yes, you dummy.*

"Well, we've got a solid ten-hour drive ahead of us, so you'd better make yourself comfortable," he grumbled. "Or rather, *try* to make yourself comfortable. Lord knows, in this pickup, it ain't easy."

◆ ◆ ◆

We left Maryland and crossed through New Jersey. As we passed the outer limits of New York, the Manhattan skyline came into view in the distance. I couldn't help but think that one of those buildings had an apartment with a view of Central Park, where my grandparents, two strangers I would never know, once lived.

The whirlwind of the city soon gave way to the forests of Connecticut. The branches of the white oak trees were already bare, but it didn't make the landscape any less stunning. After merging onto a new expressway at Westport, we stopped at a little place for lunch right on the banks of the Saugatuck, where the river rises at high tide with water from the ocean. The geese meandering by the gentle banks of the river had already flown away by the time we finished our meal. Their squadron formed a large V in the sky, pointing south.

"Those guys come from back near where I live," George-Harrison remarked. "Good old Canada geese. When I was a kid, my mother told me that when the geese leave, snow falls from their feathers . . . then they splash into the waters of the southern hemisphere and turn it blue, swallowing liters of it and coming back our way to paint everything in spring colors. It wasn't total make-believe; every year when they take off, you know winter is on its way, and then they come back and bring the nice weather with them."

I looked to the sky at the geese shrinking smaller and smaller in the distance, until they were little more than tiny specks that soon disappeared altogether. I wanted to fly away with them and touch the soft sand on a southern beach, where I could turn off my racing thoughts and bask in the warm glow of the sun.

After filling up somewhere in Massachusetts, George-Harrison asked if I would take a turn behind the wheel.

"Do you know how to drive?"

"Yes. Mind you, back home we drive on the left."

"Well, on the highway it shouldn't make that big of a difference. I've got to take a short break or I'll fall asleep. It'd be a lot safer if we took turns. We've still got a ways to go, after all. We're only halfway."

It wasn't until we crossed over into Vermont that he finally drifted off to sleep. I glanced over at him from time to time as he slept, still keeping an eye on the road. He looked so peaceful. It made me wonder how he managed to stay calm the way he did. That kind of stillness had always eluded me; I needed to be in motion nonstop. I had such a hard time with silence that I sometimes found myself talking just to fill the space. And yet, I no longer felt that need when I was with George-Harrison. It was as if his calm was rubbing off on me. His mere presence made me want to embrace the silence head-on.

We passed by a town called Glover, and I felt a small pang of sadness at the sight. An English art dealer so humble he wanted his name to disappear with him? Imagine how he would have reacted, seeing a whole town bearing his name!

I found that I quite enjoyed driving the pickup. The steering was tough to handle, but the low hum and purr of the engine made me feel like I was in control. And—unlike Dad's Austin, which nearly scraped the tarmac—the truck was high up off the ground. I checked my reflection in the rearview mirror, smiling at myself like an idiot in the silent car. At least, for once, I didn't look all that bad. Maybe life was nice up in the True North. Vast lakes, endless forests, open spaces, wild animals—somehow, everything seemed so wholesome up here. Once more, I could hear Maggie's voice telling me that I watched too much TV.

The last remnants of daylight burst out over a mackerel sky. Night was on its way, the treetops darkening as we climbed further north. I opened the window and filled my lungs with air so pure and fresh it was intoxicating. As I fumbled to turn on the headlights, George-Harrison reached out and hit the switch on the dashboard without even opening his eyes.

"You're not too tired?" he asked, groaning as he woke up.

"I think I could go all night. I'm really enjoying myself."

"Luckily, we don't have that far to go. Won't be long before the Canadian border. We can cross over just after Stanstead. At this time of night, there shouldn't be much of a wait. Once we're in Canada, we have less than an hour to go."

The officers at the border checked our passports. We had nothing to declare at customs, and my backpack interested them even less than George-Harrison's little suitcase. Two passport stamps later, we had crossed over into Quebec. George-Harrison directed me onward, glancing quickly at the clock on the dashboard.

"Still time to stop over at the dep," he said.

"Depp . . . as in Johnny?" I asked.

"You wish!" he laughed. "Dep as in *dépanneur*. It's what we call convenience stores around here. I don't have a thing in the fridge at home, and they're open late."

"I thought we were going to see your mother."

"We'll have to head over there tomorrow. It's too late tonight, so let's make a pit stop at my place, there's plenty of room. I've had my fill of hotels."

"Didn't you say something about your bedroom being tiny?"

"And my studio too big, right you are . . . but I can take a hint. I made sure to tweak the space a little after Melanie left. And don't worry—even if I *am* a bear, it's not like I'm going to drag you off to some cave out in the middle of the woods."

"I wasn't worried!"

"Well, maybe a little," George-Harrison said with a playful grin.

We made a stop at his *dépanneur*, which was little more than a block of concrete next to a lamppost, with all the charm of a cemetery. George-Harrison seemed like a regular, judging by the firm handshake the guy gave him on the way in and the help we got with our groceries on the way out. I was ravenously hungry, and grabbed items off the shelves without restraint as I walked the narrow aisles. George-Harrison watched all the while, giving me a little side smile that made it clear what was on his mind.

We drove farther into the pitch-black night, until George-Harrison pointed me down a small dirt road. I couldn't see a cave, but we were definitely heading out to the middle of the woods. Soon we arrived at a clearing at the end of the road, where I could make out George-Harrison's studio in the moonlight. It was nothing like I had imagined. His ex-girlfriend's claim that it was "too big" was a gross understatement—it was massive! More of a hangar than a studio, it had a surface punctuated by large windows with metal frames, with a high sloping roof hanging over the sides. George-Harrison grabbed a sleek little garage-door opener out of the glove box. With the push of a button, the entire structure lit up and the garage door opened in front of us.

"Pretty modern, huh?" he said. I pulled into the garage, and the surprises just kept on coming. I realized that George-Harrison's entire home was actually *within* the hangar itself. The elegant chalet stood on stilts, with the wooden facade painted a pretty shade of blue. It had a charming deck with a thick railing wrapped all around it, beyond which I could see a table and chairs.

"My bedroom used to be up on the second level of the studio. When she left, I took it apart and built this house in its place."

"Right. That's what you mean by 'tweaked the space a little'? At least now I know you're not the type to exaggerate."

"I may have gone a bit overboard. Knowing she was gone for good made me want to keep building the space up more and more every summer, and I guess I never really stopped."

"What was that, revenge?"

"Something like that. It's pretty damn stupid considering she'll never even see it."

"Well, you definitely didn't improve your chances by building it *inside* the hangar. You could at least send her a picture, you know. If I were you, I'm not sure I'd be able to resist."

"Seriously?"

"We can even do better than that. How about a selfie with me in it? That'd show her." That made George-Harrison burst out laughing. "It is kind of weird, though," I admitted, glancing about.

"What's weird?"

"Most houses are built outside."

"This way, in winter I don't have to shovel snow just to get out my front door."

"And what about taking your dog for a walk?"

"I don't have a dog."

"Oh, come on, admit it. It's like paradise for a recluse!"

"Or paradise, period. You don't think it's nice?"

"Nice? The fact that you're a nutcase?"

"The *house*! You don't think the house is nice?"

"I do. I also think it's nice that you're a nutcase."

George-Harrison took my bag and ducked into the chalet. When he returned, he set the table for us out on the front porch. We wouldn't be dining under the stars, but the weather—if you could call it that, since we were inside—was nice enough. The scent of wood wafted through the entire studio, only adding to the feeling that we were out in the middle of nowhere. But not in a bad way.

We were both exhausted from the long drive and decided to call it an early night. George-Harrison set me up in the guest room. It had an understated aesthetic and was decorated in shockingly good taste, far more refined than my place in London. Melanie was an idiot—a man with such style couldn't possibly be a bear.

◆ ◆ ◆

The next day, before George-Harrison could stop me, I jumped behind the wheel of the pickup. He did protest that it was his car, but I reminded him that he had done all the driving in Baltimore, and it was only fair. He seemed to get a kick out of my childish and stubborn behavior. We took to the road once more.

After two hours of driving with George-Harrison as my copilot, we passed through a wrought-iron gate and continued down a gravel road toward an elegant residence perched on a hill. The park surrounding the place was empty, the weather far too cold for the residents to venture out for a stroll.

"It's not exactly Hyde Park, is it?" George-Harrison said.

"Have you ever been to London?"

"No. I only really know it from movies, but I did check it out a bit online, you know, back when we were in Baltimore."

"Really? You don't say. Why would you do that?"

"Just out of curiosity."

I parked beneath an ornate awning and the two of us entered the residence.

◆ ◆ ◆

As we walked into the reading room, I quickly recognized May from the picture at Sailor's Hideaway, although presently she was far less jubilant. She sat staring sourly at an old woman playing a game of solitaire at a nearby table, as if upset that she hadn't been invited to join in. May's skin had been marked by the passage of time, but the twinkle in her eyes was just as bright as it was in the photo on the wall. The sight of her made my heart swell in ways I hadn't anticipated. This woman loved my mother, and my mother loved her. May knew things about my mum that I would never understand. It made me think of an old African proverb. *When an old person dies, it's as though a library has burnt to the ground.* I longed to discover the volumes May still carried around with her, even if she herself had long since forgotten them.

"You brought your girlfriend!" she cried, rising to her feet to greet us. "I'm so glad the two of you patched things up. I knew you couldn't stay mad at each other forever. I can't even remember what you were fighting about in the first place, so it couldn't have been that serious!"

George-Harrison was mortified. I let him stew in it for a couple of seconds before coming to his rescue. I reached out to shake her hand, but May pulled me in close for a hug and spoke right in my ear. "While I have you here, let me just say that it's not my fault if my son is such an enormous pain in the ass," she whispered, pressing her cheek against mine. Her skin was soft as anything, and she had a surprisingly strong grip for her age. I picked up the scent of ambergris, which I immediately recognized from the fragrance that Mum had worn every Sunday.

"Is that . . . *Jicky*? Your perfume?"

May gaped back at me, peering right into my eyes. "Why ask, if you already know?" she said, turning back toward her son.

I decided to give them some time alone and told them I was going to take a walk around the grounds.

"If you're planning on smoking a cigarette, be subtle about it! They confiscate every last smoke, the bastards. Not for your health, God knows, but just to keep them for themselves! So, how is school going, son?" she asked. "Are they giving you lots of homework?"

I stepped outside, but it was far too chilly, and besides, I wasn't a smoker. Slipping back into the reading room, I settled down at a table near an old man with his nose buried in a book. Whatever he was reading must have been very funny, since he chuckled several times as he read. After a few minutes passed, I realized that he hadn't turned the page. Not even once. The realization was far more chilling than even the cold outside. I could see May and George-Harrison talking on the other side of the room. The conversation seemed sporadic, but in truth I wasn't spying to try and figure out what they were talking about. I was gazing at George-Harrison in awe. He was so patient and loving, the way he seemed to hang on her every word, however nonsensical. I almost wanted to lose my memory so someone would show the same affection toward me.

The old man beside me burst out laughing once more, but this time, his guffaw quickly transformed into a hacking cough. All at once, the man's face turned cherry red. He leapt to his feet, retching, and then collapsed to the ground.

The care worker on call in the reading room rushed in to help, but soon became totally overwhelmed and paralyzed with panic. The other residents watched with giddy curiosity, more affected by witnessing something out of the ordinary than by the fact that one of their peers was fighting for his life. Suddenly, George-Harrison pushed past the panicking care worker and leaned down over the suffocating man. He shoved two fingers into his mouth to open his airways. The man let out a gasp and his breath steadied. Though still incapacitated, he seemed out of immediate danger, with the color returning to his cheeks. But he had yet to open his eyes, and he didn't respond when George-Harrison gently shook him.

"Mr. Gauthier, can you hear me? Squeeze my hand if you can hear me." The old man gave George-Harrison's hand a weak little squeeze.

"I'll call an ambulance," said the care worker.

"There's no time," George-Harrison insisted. "It'll take them half an hour to get here, and he needs to get to the hospital sooner than that. I'll drive him. Grab some blankets; we can put him in the back of my truck."

A young attendant who had been serving cookies nearby offered to take him in her own car, a station wagon, so the poor man could at least stay warm. Two other staff members arrived soon after to lend a helping hand. When Mr. Gauthier was all set up in the back of the station wagon, George-Harrison announced that he was coming along, too. I wanted to go as well, feeling partially responsible since the poor guy had collapsed before my very eyes, but the stupid station wagon only had one other seat available, and George-Harrison said I should stay behind.

I watched from beneath the awning as they exited the wrought-iron gate, hugging myself to stay warm as the headlights faded from view.

When I returned to the reading room, everything was back to normal. Residents were carrying on as if nothing had happened, or else they had already forgotten the whole episode. The woman next to May had returned to her game of solitaire, while others were content watching TV or simply staring into the distance. May peered straight at me with an odd look, crooking her finger and beckoning me closer. I sat down beside her.

"It really is something getting to meet you, you know," she said with a smile. "You look so much like her. It's uncanny. Like a ghost from the distant past. She's gone, isn't she?"

"Yes. She's gone."

"What a god-awful tragedy. I should have been first to go. But, oh well. She always knew how to make a dramatic exit."

"It wasn't intentional, and it really wasn't dramatic either, at least not the way you mean," I replied, leaping to my mother's defense out of pure instinct.

"You're right, of course. But once upon a time, it was another story. And that's what ruined us. We almost got away, we could have, but she wouldn't hear of it, all because of what was in here," she murmured, absentmindedly rubbing her stomach. "You're not planning on stealing him away from me, are you? Because I can tell you I would never let that happen."

"Steal who?"

"Don't play dumb with me, girl. I'm talking about my son, my only child."

"You said you almost got away . . . away from what?"

"From the god-awful mess your mother got us into. That's why you're here, isn't it? You came to find out . . . where she hid it?"

My breath quickened.

"I don't have a clue what you're talking about."

"You're full of it! But you look so much like her, I don't mind. She may be gone, but I'm still in love with her, even after all these years. I'm going to let you in on a secret, as long as it stays between us. I absolutely forbid you to say a single word to anyone . . ."

George-Harrison had been hoping my luck would rub off on him, but apparently it was still only confined to me. I had no way of knowing how long she would stay lucid. I remembered him saying these little interludes were as rare as they were brief. There was no time to think it over. So, I made a promise I had no intention of keeping. May reached out and took my hands in her own, drawing a deep breath and smiling warmly.

All at once, her face lit up, as though the photo from Sailor's Hideaway were coming to life before my very eyes.

"I took some insane risks to get those invitations," she began. "But that was nothing compared to the night of the ball. It was a night of reckoning. Fitting, a masquerade ball . . . like the grand finale to a thirty-six-year-old spectacle—a show full of lies. But it won't be long now . . . before everything comes to light . . ."

36

ELEANOR-RIGBY

October 2016, Eastern Townships, Quebec

Something strange had come over May, like an inner voice awakening after years of lying dormant. She spoke like a perfect narrator, whisking me away to a Baltimore evening, back to late October 1980 . . .

"Our chauffeur we hired for the night pulled up beneath the awning and we stepped out of the car, the procession of elegant vehicles continuing after us like clockwork. Those lucky enough to be invited that evening were huddled out front awaiting entry, with a pair of hostesses at the door in matching uniforms collecting invitations and checking names. I was wearing a long skirt, a man's tuxedo shirt under a formal coat, a top hat, and a mask. Sally-Anne was decked out in a domino-style wraparound dress, with a dark mask and hood that hid her face. We had chosen our flowing costumes carefully; they had to let us move about freely, yet still be large enough to conceal what we planned to walk off with.

"Your mother flashed our invitations, those precious golden tickets that had been so risky to obtain, though how and where they came from I can't recall. Times and dates don't come so easily these days.

"We entered the great hall of the manor, a vast space lit by massive chandeliers. A red-rope barrier blocked off attendees from the grand staircase that stretched upward before us. A wrought-iron balustrade ran the whole length of the upper-level hallway, with a spectacular glass ceiling looming over everything. We joined the flow of guests into the enormous ballroom, where a sumptuous buffet was laid out beneath ornate windows. Everything was exquisite and larger-than-life. A six-piece ensemble was playing on a stage beside a stone fireplace, performing an endless rotation of minuets, rondos, and serenades. It was a spectacle the like of which I had never seen, and I took in every detail with pure wonder. A strapping young man dressed as a jester was kissing a countess's hand across the room, while a Confederate soldier clinked glasses with a Hindu sorcerer, and an enemy Union soldier mingled with Cleopatra. George Washington was already good and tipsy, with no signs of slowing down anytime soon. A Huguenot poured champagne into a flute until it bubbled over onto the tablecloth. A prince straight out of *Arabian Nights* fondled Juliet, while her Romeo was nowhere to be found. A fakir stuffed his face with foie gras, while a hook-nosed wizard looked thoroughly ridiculous as he tried to keep his mound of caviar from spilling off his blini. It was endless. A Pinocchio and a Marie Antoinette chatted between clowns, Caesar kept scratching his forehead under an itchy laurel wreath, and Abraham Lincoln was French-kissing an exotic concubine. Anything was possible with those masks, and nothing was forbidden.

"A beautiful young singer joined the ensemble onstage, and her powerful voice left the whole room awestruck. Sally-Anne and I used the diversion to make our way to the study. We went through a secret door and up a small spiral staircase. As she led me down the second-floor hallway, we had to hug the wall to avoid being seen by the horde of guests mingling below. We walked straight by the same office I had waited in one day while pretending to have an appointment with the sex-obsessed secretary, but that's a whole other story, one I can tell someday if you like. Farther down the hall, we arrived at Robert Stanfield's study, and I played lookout while Sally-Anne slipped inside. I can still hear her telling me, 'Stay as far back in the shadows as you can, or the guests will see you. All it takes is one person glancing up to admire the chandelier and we're toast. You see anyone coming, you hide in the study with me. I'll take care of everything, darling. I'll be back in a flash. Don't worry.' But I was worried, and I desperately wanted to pull the plug. I begged Sally-Anne not to go in, insisting that it wasn't too late to back out. We didn't need that money. We could find another way. But Sally-Anne was ready to see it through to the bitter end, all for that damn newspaper that she loved more than anything—even me. Worse still, your mother was out for revenge. You listen to me, girl: never let yourself act out of rage, or you'll have to face the consequences sooner or later. But that night, I was determined to be Sally-Anne's good little soldier.

"I could catch little glimpses of her through the crack in the door as she eased open the minibar, took out her father's cigar box, and dug through it until she found the key to the safe. What happened next changed everything and altered the course of our lives. I've never stopped thinking about it; a few minutes earlier or later, and everything would have turned out differently. You wouldn't even be here today, that much I can tell you.

"My memory may not be so sharp nowadays, but I can still picture every last detail of that masquerade ball. Some things you just don't forget . . .

"Now, where was I? Ah, yes. I heard footsteps and glanced cautiously out over the railing. A costumed guest had ducked under the red rope and was climbing the grand staircase. He would reach the second floor at any moment. I rapped lightly on the door to the study to warn Sally-Anne, and could hear her fumbling for the light switch. The room went dark. She opened the door a crack and tugged at my hand, trying to pull me into the shadows to hide with her. But I stayed firmly in place, as though in a trance. Looking back now, maybe I would have done it differently. But in that moment, I was determined to protect her. Instead of hiding by her side, I broke free of her grip, gently closed the door, and marched right up to meet the masked stranger in his Venetian carnival costume. I was praying he was no more than a guest who had wandered past the barrier and up those stairs looking for a telephone. I considered using the very same excuse myself, if need be. But before I could say a word, the stranger demanded to know what I was doing there, his voice full of authority.

"It was a voice I knew all too well. *Edward.* Yet I stayed calm—dead calm—suddenly consumed by my own thirst for revenge. After all, the entire spectacle, the masquerade ball in all its wonder and monstrosity, was in his honor. I was struck with an idea, the perfect way to mark the occasion. I would give Edward a gift that would haunt him until the end of his days.

"He opened his mouth to speak again, but I silenced him, holding a finger to his lips. I could tell in that moment that he longed to know just who was smiling at him from behind that mask. He informed me that this wing of the manor was strictly off-limits to guests, but kindly offered to give me a private tour, should I desire one. I couldn't answer without giving myself away, and it was far too soon for that, so I simply whispered 'yes' and took him by the hand. I led him past the office where I had waited for Miss Verdier. We entered a small study and I shut the door behind us. I should say that there was no chance he had mistaken me for his wife-to-be; her costume was completely different. Edward knew exactly what he was doing.

"I shoved him back roughly into an armchair, to his great amusement. He let his hands fall to his sides, careful to show no resistance. I unbuttoned his pants and slipped my hand inside, feeling his desire intensify. I knew just what he liked. But I wasn't going to stop there. I wanted to have him *fully*, one last time. I lifted up my skirt and straddled him. Understand, men have come and gone in my life, some

I walked out on, and others walked out on me. With Edward, it was different. Judge me all you like. I don't care what you think. There's no better feeling in life than making love to a man you both love *and* hate. I had to take it slow, to make sure he lasted long enough to buy Sally-Anne the time she needed to finish next door. She could probably hear everything through those walls, but I wanted to be sure. I didn't hold back one bit. It wasn't only because Sally-Anne had cheated on me with Keith, or because I was only there that night for her. I was also lashing out at her and her parents for wanting Edward to marry one of 'his own kind' instead of a poor girl like me. I was getting revenge on him and the entire world by fucking him at his own engagement party, forever tarnishing the night in his memory.

"When it was over, he wanted to see my face, but I refused. Instead, I asked in a full voice, not whispering, 'Did you enjoy my engagement gift?' and watched Edward go white with shock. You should have seen the look on his face, a mix of amazement and fear, fear that I would waltz right back down that fancy staircase, take the soloist's place onstage, and sing loudly about Edward's sinful ways for all to hear . . . I kissed him tenderly and caressed his cheek, insisting he had nothing to be afraid of. His future wife might not realize what kind of man he was for a long time to come. But every time Edward told her he loved her, he would remember that he had cheated on her the very night of their engagement party.

"I told him to go to her now so none of the guests would see us walking down the staircase together. I promised to leave discreetly. He wouldn't see me for the rest of the night, or ever again. With that, Edward straightened out his clothes and furiously stormed off.

"After ensuring the coast was clear, I went to join Sally-Anne in the study. Without a word, she tied a cape around her body to conceal our stolen treasure, closed the safe, and returned the key to the cigar box.

"I asked if she had gotten what she came for, but she shot the same question back at me. We both knew what had gone on in those two adjoining rooms—we had robbed the Stanfields blind, each in our own way.

"On the way out, Sally-Anne brazenly swiped a bottle of Scotch and slipped it under my cape as the final touch. It was an amazing whisky we would enjoy later that night as we toasted our victory. Sally-Anne was already drunk off the realization that the *Independent*'s future was secure. With what we had stolen from that safe, we could launch the paper and ensure its survival for several years, no matter the profit margin.

"With the party in full swing, the getaway was smooth and easy, our driver waiting for us outside. Before we knew it, we were home at the loft. It was over. The deed was done."

May fell silent, looking lost and staring out in the void. Her face withered back to its normal age. I could tell there was nothing else I would learn that day and feared she might not even know who I was, until she sighed wearily and told me once more how much I looked like my mother. Then, without hesitation, May rose and snatched the deck of cards from her neighbor, shuffled the deck, and asked if I knew how to play poker. Indeed, I did . . . or so I thought.

I proceeded to lose a hundred dollars in a matter of minutes. When George-Harrison returned, his mother discreetly slipped the money into her pocket. She greeted her son as though she hadn't seen him in weeks, telling him how nice he was for paying his mother a visit.

George-Harrison announced that Mr. Gauthier had died before they had made it to the hospital.

"I called it! You didn't believe me, but I told you he wouldn't make it through the year!" May exclaimed with a hint of joy.

We spent the whole afternoon by her side, with her mind far away throughout. At about three in the afternoon, the sky cleared, and George-Harrison took his mother for a walk around the grounds. I took advantage of the time alone and tried to sort my head. Once more, I had uncovered a new wave of revelations, but once more they were all about my mother. We were no closer to learning who George-Harrison's father was. I had no idea how to break the news that I hadn't used May's moments of lucidity to ask about his father. Especially in light of the promise I had made.

When the two returned, I looked at George-Harrison regretfully, sending the message that my lucky streak had ended and the visit had been fruitless. After the three of us had chatted for a while over a cup of tea, George-Harrison told his mother it was time for us to leave. May hugged her son and then turned to me.

"Oh, Melanie, I can't tell you how glad I am you two got back together!" she said. "You really do make a lovely couple."

As we crossed the parking lot toward the pickup, I told George-Harrison I had to run back to the reading room to get my phone, which I must have forgotten. It was a lie.

I found May sitting in the same spot, holding a cold cup of tea in front of her, her glazed eyes fixed on the chair where Mr. Gauthier had been sitting that very morning. Taking a cue from our poker game, I strode up to her and went all-in.

"I have no idea if you're still in there, but if you can hear me, you need to listen to me. It's my turn to give you some advice: you won't be around forever. Don't take your secret to the grave. Not knowing who his father is is tearing George-Harrison apart, and I can't bear to watch him suffer. Can't you see what you're putting him through? Haven't all these secrets caused enough pain and sadness? How can you still think some things are better left unsaid?"

May turned to me, her eyes sharp and full of spite. "Lovely sentiments, dear. But I'm not dead yet, thank you very much. You think that he'd be happier knowing that his father died years ago, and it was his mother's fault? Some things *are* better left unsaid. So, if that's all you've got to say, girl, you can go on your way now. I don't like you keeping my son waiting."

"Where are all the letters my mother wrote to you? Do you still have them?" I insisted.

May slapped my hand softly, as though scolding an impetuous child. "There are no letters from your mother! It was one-sided, except once, when we were making arrangements to meet. Your mother thought even writing to me would be like cheating on her husband. She chose to turn the page and move on. The only exception came at my insistence, when your family went to Spain on vacation . . . You must have been about fourteen years old . . ."

I could still remember that holiday perfectly. My parents only took us abroad three times. Once we went to Stockholm, where Maggie never stopped complaining about the cold. Then there was Paris, where my parents ended up flat broke after Michel went overboard with the pastries. Then came Madrid, which so enchanted me that I vowed to travel the world as soon as I was old enough. May sipped at her tea and continued.

"Six months before the trip, I wrote your mother to tell her I was sick. It was just a small lump they had taken out of my breast, but it could have been quite serious. I began wondering who would be there to raise my son if anything ever happened to me, and I thought of your mother. Words alone would never convince her, so I thought it might be different if we met face-to-face . . . although maybe that was all just an excuse to lay eyes on her one last time, to see her family in the flesh. She agreed to come, that we could *see* each other, but not meet or interact in any way.

"On the Sunday of your visit, you went walking in Retiro Park. Right there on the front steps of the Crystal Palace, facing the reflecting pool, I saw you sitting with your mother, father, brother, and sister. You were a beautiful family. George-Harrison and I sat on the stairs just to your left. I think it may have brought me more pain than joy, but for those few short minutes, it was like leaping into the past. That one moment was well worth the trip. That trip also has a special place in my heart because it was one of my son's happiest childhood memories. Your mother and I exchanged a smile that told me all I would ever need to know.

"Soon after, your family rose to leave, and I saw that Sally-Anne had left a notebook behind on the steps. It was her diary; the same one she had kept since her boarding school days. In it lay the whole Baltimore saga—from the moment we met as young journalists, to our move into the loft. She described all our friends, Keith with the most detail. Reading it was like reliving those crazy days leading up to the *Independent*, and the wild nights at Sailor's Hideaway . . . all our hopes, dreams, and heartaches. Your mother even wrote about the famous ball, and all that happened after . . . everything, until the very day she left for England. After that? Nothing. She hadn't written a single word about her new life."

"Why did she go running away to London, and why did she never come back?"

"I have neither the time nor the desire to talk about that. There's nothing left of those days; it's all gone. So, why bother? Take my advice, girl. Leave the past behind you. There's no reason to let it torment you. You were lucky to have such wonderful parents. Hold on to your mother as you remember her. Sally-Anne as I knew her was an entirely different woman."

"Where is the diary?" I insisted. "Do you still have it? May?"

But it was too late. Once more, May's eyes had taken on that faraway look. I could tell it was a lost cause as she abruptly flipped off an elderly woman at a nearby table, then turned back to me, laughing.

"Let me tell you why my son became a carpenter. I had a crush on an antiques dealer, and I could tell he felt the same for me. I was alone, he was unhappily married. Two broken people trying to fix things by giving the other what they lacked. As a child, George-Harrison spent quite a lot of time with the man, almost every day after school. Pierre was there for us when no one else was. He was like a godfather to

George-Harrison, taught him everything he knew. That suited me just fine, even if I could see a certain irony to the whole thing. You see, there had been a carpenter in my life once before, a good man, perhaps the best I've ever known. He came to see me shortly after George-Harrison was born, hoping I'd drop everything and run away with him. I acted like a fool. I still regret it. But it was far too late anyway. Don't say a thing to George-Harrison. He always thought carpentry was his own choice, and he'd be outraged at thinking his mother, of all people, had any influence over him. After all, he is just a man. Okay. You run along now, dear. I've told you more than enough, and if you can't connect the dots now, then you must be even thicker than you look."

"Are you the one who wrote those letters to us?"

"Get out of here! I have to take my bath, and you're not my nurse, last time I checked. Wait just a minute! Are you telling me you're my new nurse? They can't just switch nurses without telling me! This place is a dump! Any more of this crap, I'm going to complain, I swear I will."

This time she was gone for good. Despite my mixed feelings for the woman, I gave May a hug goodbye, perhaps just to enjoy that comforting, familiar perfume one last time.

I stood outside George-Harrison's pickup and took a deep breath before getting inside. I was at a total loss. Not only did I have to break the news that his long-lost father was dead, but I was betraying May's trust by telling him. I didn't know where to start.

"Did you solve the mystery?" he asked.

"What? What do you mean?" I stammered.

"The case of the missing cell phone. Did you work it out? It's been over ten minutes, I was starting to worry."

I swallowed. "Drive. We have to talk."

37

ELEANOR-RIGBY

October 2016, Magog

It was getting dark as we pulled out of the retirement home, with the air outside even colder than the night before. I knew I could have stayed silent. But if I had learned one thing from my quest so far, it was that secrets could be poisonous. Completing the task ahead of me would be no small feat. I knew I had to tread lightly from the start. And telling George-Harrison would only be the beginning. Sooner or later, I'd have to reveal everything to Michel and Maggie as well, and I had no idea how to do that without going against my mother's wishes. But for the time being, I had to face the problem sitting next to me in the driver's seat.

When at last I managed to tell George-Harrison that his father had died years before and that May had implied she had something to do with his death, his unfazed, stoic reaction was the last thing I was expecting. He simply kept driving, stone-faced and quiet. I told him how sorry I was for his loss, and how guilty I felt about exposing May's deep, dark secret. Still nothing. George-Harrison sat biting his lip with incredible reserve.

"I guess I should be sad," he finally said. "Strange as it sounds, I'm more relieved than anything else. What used to hurt most was thinking that he didn't care about meeting me, that he was ignoring my existence altogether, like his own son was . . . unimportant. At least now, he has a foolproof alibi. You can't really blame him for not showing up."

May hadn't mentioned exactly *when* George-Harrison's father died, but I didn't see any point in emphasizing that now.

"When she told you she had killed him, did it seem like she was still thinking straight?" he asked.

"That's not what your mother said, not exactly. She told me it was her fault. It's not the same thing."

"It sure sounds like the same thing to me," he said, the bitterness at last coming through in his voice.

"It's not! We don't know a thing about how he died. It could have been a car accident, and she feels it's her fault because she wasn't there."

"It's pretty naïve and hopeful, jumping to her defense like that."

"That's not it at all. It's just . . . I could see how much she loved him."

"What difference does that make? A crime of passion is somehow more forgivable?"

"It doesn't change anything for you to know you were created by two people who loved each other?"

"I see how hard you're trying, I really do. It means lot to me, a hell of a lot, but slow down a little bit. She also was in love with a guy named John, a guy named Tom, a guy named Henry . . ."

"A guy named Pierre," I added, and instantly regretted it.

"Wait, what about Pierre?"

"She also had a thing for a guy named Pierre, an antiques dealer."

"I know who the guy is, damn it!"

"And you know that . . . that they . . ."

"Of course I know! And you can spare me your pity. I've known forever. The way they would brush up against each other, the way they acted when she dropped me off or picked me up at his shop, or whenever he came to our place. Whenever he saw her, he would always caress her hand ever so softly. Then he'd give her a very friendly kiss when saying goodbye, right near her lips. It's the type of thing a kid doesn't miss. But I didn't care. Out of all the men she was with, he was the only one who never . . . you know, treated me with pity, like he felt sorry for me. Quite the contrary. Whenever he talked about Mom, he made it sound like I was lucky to have her all to myself. He didn't act all guilty and sheepish. It was a breath of fresh air. All Pierre ever did was take care of me, with enough decency to never act like a substitute father. Having him around was . . . reassuring. But why'd you mention him?"

"Because I have a hunch he knows a lot more than he's ever told you. Maybe more than just a hunch."

George-Harrison reached out and cranked up the volume on the radio, letting me know he had heard enough for one night. A whole half hour passed without a word. Finally, as we arrived in Magog, he turned the volume back down.

"There's one thing gnawing at me. If our poison-pen knows every last thing about the two of us, wouldn't he already know my father was dead? So, why write to me in the first place?"

That sent chills down my spine. The first logical explanation that came to mind was that the poison-pen *couldn't* tell George-Harrison, so instead he had tried to steer him toward uncovering the truth on his own. But I kept that to myself, not wanting to add another layer. I had already done enough damage for one night.

George-Harrison pulled the truck into his studio. Just being back inside the hangar lifted my spirits, for maybe the first time that day. It was chilly, and the cold had somehow penetrated the walls, so George-Harrison turned on a space heater while we ate dinner. Though he tried to hide it, I could tell that the sadness and loneliness were consuming him. Seeing him like that broke my heart. Even with my own family waiting for me back in London, I knew I had to face the truth.

There was something I had been denying desperately ever since George-Harrison nearly left me on the sidewalk in Baltimore. The intense panic I felt at that moment wasn't out of fear of being left alone; I was afraid of being apart from him. After all we had been through, I wasn't going to let secrets and hypocrisy stand in the way of my happiness ever again.

I waited until he had been in bed for a while, then went into his room and nestled in between the sheets, pressing myself close against him. George-Harrison turned and took me in his arms. It would have felt wrong to make love for the first time on the day George-Harrison had learned his father was dead. Instead, we floated together in our own little bubble, more tender than any mere joining of bodies.

◆　◆　◆

We spent the next day together in the hangar. George-Harrison was running behind on a job, and I got a kick out of watching a master at work. As he carved out the legs for a chest of drawers, I found the lathe especially fascinating. The way the wood whistled as the chips flew made it seem like a musical instrument, and watching the spirals take shape was utterly mesmerizing. It was beautiful to see someone so passionate about their craft. A little later, George-Harrison assembled the whole piece, explaining that the key was to sculpt the tenons so they fit perfectly into each mortise. While I thought he was pushing it with all the jargon, I played along and pretended to be fascinated by all the details. He studied the chest carefully from every angle until he was satisfied with the results. I gave him a hand loading it into his pickup, then agreed to come along and help unload it at the antiques shop.

As we stepped inside, Pierre Tremblay looked up from his newspaper and leapt to his feet, greeting us warmly. The man was positively over the moon about meeting me. I could tell by the kind, warm look in his eyes that it wasn't every day "GH" brought someone to meet him. However, his face fell when he saw the chest of drawers. He shook his head in disappointment, pouting and telling us to just leave it in the back.

"Really? You're not going to put it out front in the window?" asked George-Harrison, feigning surprise. Pierre grumbled something about leaving it in the corner overnight until he made up his mind, then George-Harrison asked the antiques dealer to join us for dinner. They chose La Mère Denise so I could feast my eyes on their "authentic" antique eighteenth-century bookcase. The forgery was undeniably impressive, even to the untrained eye. Seeing George-Harrison's talent filled me with a sense of pride, however silly that sounds.

Pierre Tremblay recommended the bouillabaisse from the Magdalen Islands, which he thought would pair perfectly with a dry white wine from Les Brome—a local Quebecois winemaker, he noted with home-town pride. After a warm toast, Pierre leaned in to George-Harrison and raised the delicate subject of the chest of drawers, chalking the whole thing up to a misunderstanding.

"I know you're not going to want to hear this, GH," he said. "But I think I asked you for an antique sled, not a chest of drawers."

"Indeed, you did," George-Harrison shot back. "And I asked *you* for any leads on my father, only about a thousand times. Since you never had any, or at least none you were willing to share, I had to go out and do some digging of my own. Which took a very long time. Nobody can be in two places at once, as they say. So, it was either hit the road or work on your sled. So, the sled had to wait, you see. Count yourself lucky. I started that old chest of drawers a while back, and spent all day today putting the finishing touches on it so I wouldn't come empty-handed."

"I see," Pierre grunted. "So, the whole dinner invitation, introducing me to this fine young lady . . . was just a trap?"

"What good would that be, since you don't know anything?"

"Easy now," Pierre cautioned. "Don't make a scene and get all nasty in the middle of a restaurant. I never told you anything because I wasn't allowed to. I made a promise. And a promise is a promise, as they say."

"What exactly did you promise?"

"Not to say a word, GH. Not while she's still around."

"But she's not really still 'around,' now is she, Pierre? The woman you made that promise to is gone; she doesn't even know who she is most of the time."

"I will not have you talk about your mother like that."

"It's sad but true, and you know it. You've seen it yourself, many times over. You think I'm blind? You didn't think I'd recognize all the furniture you brought out there to spruce up her bedroom? Bedside table, pedestal table next to the door, Victorian armchair by the window . . . You've gone to see her enough times to bring a whole bedroom set."

"Well, *somebody* had to go."

"Don't play the guilt card. I'm sure she prefers getting attention from you over me any day. Now, I'm asking you to do exactly what you should have done from the minute I told you about that letter, and tell me what you know."

"What I know? First, you tell me: What's any of this got to do with your new friend here?"

"Eleanor-Rigby is Sally-Anne Stanfield's daughter," George-Harrison responded, calm and steady as always.

Pierre's face gave him away, leaving no doubt that he knew of my mother. George-Harrison summarized everything we had learned since the last time he had seen Pierre, before the trip even started. By the time he had finished recounting the tale, Pierre agreed to fill in the missing pieces.

"On the night of the heist, after the deed was done, your mothers went back to their loft apartment. They stashed away what they had stolen and met up with their buddies on the Baltimore waterfront.

Apparently, it was a night to remember. While all others in attendance thought they were celebrating the inaugural issue of the *Independent*, your mothers were celebrating their heist, which was somewhat ironic considering what would happen the day after that first issue hit the newsstands." He shivered at the thought. "The police were extremely thorough and diligent with their investigation, but the only fingerprints they found on the safe were Robert's and Hanna's. With no proof of forced entry, they could only come up with two hypotheses. One: it was an inside job; the thief was an employee. Two: the whole thing was a sham. The Stanfields were already very wealthy, so the idea of them committing insurance fraud seemed far-fetched. Hanna Stanfield was more afraid of a scandal than losing money, especially since her livelihood was built around her reputation. Highly renowned art collectors entrusted her with rare works of art. Imagine what they would think when they heard that a priceless painting had been stolen right out of her own home! So, of course, she didn't say a word about it to the police."

Pierre stopped short at the sight of our stunned faces. "What? What did I say?" he asked, but George-Harrison and I were both in a state of absolute shock. The puzzle pieces all seemed to fit, and the anonymous letter began to make sense. Before Pierre could continue, George-Harrison asked what happened to the painting, but the antiques dealer just shrugged.

"All I know is that your mothers had a terrible falling-out over that painting, not because of the insane value of the thing, but because it was of such importance to Hanna Stanfield. As I understand, it had belonged to her father, and Hanna was more attached to that one painting than the rest of her entire collection combined. That may be the very reason Sally-Anne stole it, or so May suspected.

"She didn't commit the robbery because she wanted to keep the *Independent* from going under, but out of revenge, plain and simple. When put on the spot, Sally-Anne swore up and down that she had no idea the painting was there, that she had just stumbled upon it in the safe and grabbed it without thinking. But May didn't buy that, not for a second. She was infuriated at having been manipulated and used. The problem was, she wasn't the only one. And that's where poetic justice comes in. If Sally-Anne hadn't been so bold as to publish that article blatantly smearing her family's name in the first—and, as it turned out, last—issue of the *Independent*, putting her own initial on it like a point of pride, Edward would have never figured out who had written it. But the damage was already done. Her brother instantly pieced things together and thought that he had been played for a fool. Up until that point, he had thought that May had done what she did only out of . . . well . . ."

"Well, what?" George-Harrison pressed him.

"Forget it. It's none of your business, kid. Let's just say that the article convinced Edward that May had ulterior motives for coming to the masquerade ball that night, aside from simply spoiling his engagement. Their . . . encounter had been up on the second floor, right next to the scene of the crime. So, when he read that stupid article and saw how far his sister would go to get revenge on her own family, the pieces fell into place. All the time he had been . . . 'talking' with May . . . Sally-Anne had been robbing her own mother, snatching the thing Hanna loved most in the world right out from under her nose. You understand? Is that all clear enough for you?"

"Yes, crystal clear," I cut in. I had spared George-Harrison some of the more sordid details of his mother's retelling, and was relieved that Pierre had the good grace to do the same. "Tell us what happened to the painting," I said.

"No one knows. Sally-Anne kept May completely in the dark, and I know May never had the painting in her possession."

"How could she keep May in the dark if the two of them were living in the same apartment?"

"Well . . . they didn't stay up in that loft very long. Edward Stanfield was so convinced of his sister's guilt, he set out to thwart her plans and retrieve what she had stolen. You have to understand, Edward loved his mother very deeply. While it did hurt Hanna's pride to have a small fortune in bonds stolen from her, the loss of the painting left her crushed, inconsolable. So, Edward decided to follow Sally-Anne and May. For days, he spied on them coming and going, everything. While the two busied themselves with the next issue of the newspaper, he staked them out, watching them through the window, sitting in his mother's car so he wouldn't be recognized. He even followed May to the bank, watching the entire time without her ever knowing. He saw her cash in a bearer bond to pay some suppliers and that was that: he had proof of their guilt, and it was irrefutable.

"Edward soon made another startling discovery. As May left the bank, she doubled over and puked her guts out onto the sidewalk. He thought maybe it was her nerves. But then it happened again, as soon as she stepped out of the taxi she had taken home. It didn't take a genius to put two and two together. No sooner had she entered the loft than Edward jumped out of his mother's car, climbed that tall flight of steps all the way to the very top, and began pounding on their door. What came next was absolutely horrible.

"Edward threatened to turn them over to the cops if the two thieves didn't immediately return what they had stolen. The bank teller would testify about May cashing in the bond, and they'd both end up behind bars. May didn't bother waiting for Sally-Anne's response. She ran off to get the rest of the bonds. But the moment Edward demanded that Sally-Anne also return the painting, May finally understood what had happened. The argument raged out of control. Sally-Anne hurled insults at Edward, while May was furious with Sally-Anne. In short, it was a scorched-earth free-for-all. When Sally-Anne refused to return the painting, Edward asked what would become of May's baby if its mother was rotting in a prison cell. Sally-Anne had no idea May was pregnant, and finding out like that was unimaginably painful. There was a brief, shocked silence. Each one of them was visibly shaken by the statement— Edward, because May didn't deny it; May, for being exposed in front of her accomplice; and Sally-Anne, who had just pieced together who the father of May's child was. At that point, Sally-Anne gave in and returned the painting to Edward."

"Wait! Just wait," George-Harrison cut in, forcing the words out with trembling lips. "Was Edward shaken because . . . because *he* was the father?"

"Yes, that's what I'm saying," sighed Pierre.

"Why? Why have you never told me this? Why wait all these long years?"

"Because of what happened next," said Pierre, avoiding George-Harrison's eyes. "But listen to me: think long and hard before I go on. Even if learning the truth might make you understand and forgive me, even if you finally see why your mother kept it from you all your life . . . the next part changes everything. Forever."

"I'm ready, Pierre. I know she killed him."

"You don't know a thing, kid. So, I repeat: think long and hard. Because there's no turning back."

I took George-Harrison's hand in my own, gripping it so tightly that his knuckles went white. I knew beyond a shadow of a doubt it would be best to stop the conversation there, for George-Harrison's sake. But who, at that point, wouldn't have wanted to know the truth?

George-Harrison nodded gravely at Pierre, and the old man at last continued the tale.

"As Edward walked out of the door to the loft, that god-awful son of a bitch just couldn't leave well enough alone. Excuse my language, but he was rotten to his very core. It wasn't enough that he had gotten what he came for; he couldn't resist making one last threat from out there on the landing, this one the most deplorable of all." The antiques dealer swallowed, then continued. "Edward threatened to rat them both out, unless May aborted the pregnancy. And he didn't stop there. 'My *sister*,' he said, with an air of disgust, 'is an orphan, nothing but a phony Stanfield.' And after all Sally-Anne had done, he promised that she wouldn't even be that for very much longer. And he sure as hell wasn't going to let some bastard child ruin his marriage and tarnish his good name. To his mind, that heartless son of a bitch's ultimatum was an act of mercy. Spare the child a life of welfare and food stamps while his mother rotted in prison . . . Better the child was never brought into the world to begin with . . .

"Sally-Anne may have had her faults, but she wasn't going to stand by and let May take that. She lunged at her brother, screaming at him out there on the landing, and hit him over and over again with all her might. Edward was stunned. He lost his balance . . . and fell straight down those steps, all one hundred and twenty of them. Sally-Anne always called those stairs a death trap. Her brother snapped his neck on the way down . . . He was dead before he hit the bottom."

Saddened and concerned, Pierre at last looked to George-Harrison, with nothing but kindness in his eyes. George-Harrison couldn't get a single word out. Pierre reached out and touched his hand.

"I can understand if you're angry at me, kid," he asked.

George-Harrison finally met his eyes. "I may never have had a father, and maybe that's for the best. But I've got one hell of a mother. And I have you, Pierre. That's already a lot, right there. Far too much for me to be anything but grateful."

After Pierre paid the bill, the three of us walked back to his shop and gathered in front of George-Harrison's truck. We were just starting to say our goodbyes when Pierre beckoned us to follow him into his office, where he drew out an old spiral notepad from a desk drawer. It was little more than a common school notebook.

"I've never read a single word, I swear. It was your mother who gave it to me," he told George-Harrison. "But I believe . . . it belonged to yours," Pierre said, turning and handing the notebook to me.

"Take it," he said. "I've had enough secrets for one lifetime."

◆ ◆ ◆

George-Harrison drove his pickup through the pitch-dark of a moonless night, headed for home. I sat watching the headlights stream down the highway, holding my mother's diary tightly on my lap. I didn't have the heart to crack it open. Not yet.

38

ELEANOR-RIGBY

October 2016, Magog

I spent the night snuggled up to George-Harrison while he slept, or at least pretended to sleep. I thought that might be the case, that he had his eyes closed to give me my privacy while still staying close by my side, should I need him.

I read my mother's diary start to finish, rediscovering the whole story in her own words: the terrible suffering she endured at the boarding school in England; the tortured, sleepless nights she spent at the dormitory; and the onslaught of loneliness and abandonment she felt day after day. There was also joy in those pages. I read about her meeting my father in a pub with the Beatles singing "All You Need Is Love" as the perfect soundtrack. The first chapter of their relationship seemed like a three-year stretch where she came close to finding true happiness. I could understand why she had to return to Baltimore, driven by hope and a need to reconnect with her family. I discovered her life as a journalist, full of adventure and freedom, the two things she lived for above all else. I was amazed at how similar we were at the same period of our lives, both seekers venturing to the far ends of the earth while never even truly knowing our own parents. I revisited all that I had learned of my mother from the beginning of this journey: her total commitment to journalism, the harsh struggles she had faced, and the madness that she got caught up in.

I read all through the night. Around the break of dawn, I reached the end of the diary and discovered, to my surprise, a worn envelope between the last few pages. I turned to George-Harrison—knowing full well I might be in love with him already—and woke him up. I had decided to read him the last few pages. After all, my mother's final entry was addressed in part to May herself.

October 27, 1980
This will be my final entry.

I think back to that fateful day when we went rushing down those stairs, all but certain we would find my brother dead at the bottom. But May saw he was still breathing, however faintly. It wasn't too late; there was still hope. We jumped into my mother's car and drove Edward to the hospital. Mere moments after they came to take him away on a stretcher, we ran for the hills like the thieves we were. In the middle of the night, I called to find out how he was, and the doctors told us there wasn't much hope. He had a broken neck and it was a miracle that he was still breathing, with machines the only things keeping him alive. In the blink of an eye, we went from idealistic thieves to hardened, violent criminals, even if it all was by accident.

We went down to the waterfront at dawn and drove my mother's car straight off the docks. We stood together, watching it sink down and disappear into the frigid waters. No one knew that he had come to see us, and the car was the only evidence that could link us to the crime. Later on, around midday, I got the call from my mother.

She ordered me to come to her side immediately, so I climbed onto the old Triumph for one last ride.

My mother was there at the hospital waiting for me. She had watched over my brother through the night. I wanted to see him, but she wouldn't allow it. I planned to confess right then and there, no matter the consequences, and return the painting that she loved so dearly, which would only come as a small consolation, of course. But my mother never gave me the chance.

She ordered me to stay quiet and listen.

"Go. Leave the country and never come back. Leave now, before it's too late. I lost my son last night. I don't want to lose my daughter to a life in prison. Don't look so surprised. I know everything; I'm your mother. When the nurses told me that two women had brought Edward to the hospital, I feared the worst. All it took was one look at you, and now I see everything. Remember, on the phone: I told you to come to my side, but I didn't say where I was. And yet, here you are. You'll have to get rid of my car, if you haven't already."

With that, my mother left, dignified in her heartache, leaving me shattered and alone in her wake.

After the hospital, I stopped by the loft, but May wasn't there. I decided to go to the bank to cash the check that my mother had given me to buy me off and put me in my place. At the bank, I ran into Rhonda's husband and had him open a safety-deposit box in my name. I knew my mother's precious Girl by the Window *would be safe there. He had me fill out the papers, no questions asked. I refuse to take the painting with me. Despite how beautiful that girl is, I can't look at her any longer without thinking about what the painting has done to our lives, without thinking of my brother . . .*

After leaving the bank, I went to buy a plane ticket and put what money I had left into an envelope. I will leave it on the nightstand for May to help her cross the border into Canada, in hopes she'll find a fresh start with the new life that awaits her there.

◆ ◆ ◆

This is the last time that I will write to you, my love.

I went back to the loft a second time and found you there waiting for me. I told you of my decision. We spoke at length, and then shed tears without saying a word. You packed your bag and then mine.

I left while you were still sleeping. I didn't have the heart to lie to you and say we might see each other again one day, and I simply couldn't bear the thought of having to say goodbye for good.

I left all the bonds on the nightstand so you could build a new life from the ashes of the one I had destroyed. The child you now carry, my love, may not be of my own blood, but he carries with him part of my story, a past I've now left behind. The day will come when you will need to tell your child the truth.

Don't worry about me, my love. There's someone I know in London who I can count on, or at least I hope so. I think you know who he is. It's his fault you had to listen to those Beatles records around the clock, which I know must have been torture for such a huge Stones fan.

This is the last time I'll be able to write to you. I don't want any more secrets or lies, or any more cheating. If the

man in that faraway land can bring himself to forgive
me for being away such a long time, I will devote my life
to his happiness, giving him every last ounce of love I still
have left in my heart.

I hope that you, too, will have a happy life together.
Fill your child's life with the joy I know you can bring.
Some of the best moments of my life have been spent by
your side. No matter what becomes of us, you will be in
my heart for the rest of my days.

Sally-Anne

It was the very last page in the diary. Day was breaking. George-Harrison handed me a sweater and jeans, and the two of us went out for a walk in the forest.

39

ELEANOR-RIGBY

October 2016, Magog

I called to check up on Michel, missing him more than ever at that moment. I managed to slip in a question, asking if Mum had ever mentioned a bank where she might have hidden a painting. Michel was confounded, finding the whole thing nonsensical. Why store a painting in a safe, when it was meant to be hung on the wall? My explanations just weren't up to snuff. He asked if I'd be back soon, and I told him I would come as soon as I could. Then, Michel asked if I had found what I was looking for. Yes and no, I told him, smiling as I looked to George-Harrison. Maybe, as it turned out, I had found what I *wasn't* looking for. Michel confirmed he had read that such things were known to occur. Many scientific discoveries were a simple matter of chance. Although chance, in and of itself, was not scientific at all, he clarified. Michel then told me there were two people visiting the library, and with that kind of "crowd," he should probably get back to work. He promised he'd send Maggie and Dad my love, then made me swear that I'd call up and do it myself anyway.

George-Harrison stood waiting for me in front of the pickup. We closed up his studio and hit the road again, making it to the outskirts of Baltimore by nightfall.

First thing the next day, we paid Professor Morrison a visit and upheld our end of the bargain. We filled him in on all we had discovered—or at least all the news that was fit to print, since the rest was just for us. We tried asking subtly if he had any leads for tracking down the bank my mother might have used to store the painting. Morrison didn't even blink an eye at the question, taking on his normal crabby disposition and shoving his manuscript at us like we were fools.

"See for yourselves! It's written right in here, if you had bothered to pay attention. The Stanfields were major stockholders on the board of the Corporate Bank of Baltimore, an establishment still in existence today, I believe. I trust you'll be able to procure the yellow pages and look it up yourselves? Now, once more: Do I truly have your consent to publish this book?"

"Yes, as long as you can answer one final question," I told him.

"Well then, for goodness' sake, ask away!" he said, flustered.

"Are you the one who wrote the anonymous letters?"

In response, Morrison pointed toward the door.

"Out! Just get out. You two are absolutely out of your minds!"

We arrived at the bank and were received by a cold, no-nonsense teller. Before he could confirm or deny the existence of the safety-deposit box, we had to prove that we were the rightful owners. I tried in vain to explain that it had belonged to my mother, who had recently passed away, but the man wouldn't budge. He asked for proof that I was the legitimate next of kin. As soon as I showed him my passport, everything spiraled into a Kafkaesque merry-go-round. My last name was Donovan . . . Mum had opened the safety-deposit box under her maiden name . . . which she'd changed when she moved to England . . . Even if Dad had sent me an original copy of their marriage certificate, it wouldn't have been enough to convince the overzealous gatekeeper.

Finally, clearly wanting to get rid of us, the teller explained that the only person with the authority to override the bank's strict rules was the branch president and CEO, who only stopped in twice a week and wouldn't be back until the day after tomorrow. It was pointless in any event, he added. After all, Mr. Clark was a Mormon, and Mormons never bent the rules, not even a tiny bit.

"Sorry, did you say Mr. Clark?"

"Why, are you hard of hearing?" sighed the teller.

Knowing we had no time to waste, I begged and pleaded with the teller to get a message to Mr. Clark that Sally-Anne Stanfield's daughter was in town. I told him to remind the bank president that his wife—or at least his wife at the time—had worked closely with my mother to launch a weekly paper, and that my mother had entrusted him with a painting of a girl sitting by a window. I was convinced it was enough to land us a meeting, at the very least. I left my number with the teller, as well as the address of our hotel, and even offered to leave my passport. The man waved away my offer, immovable as ever, but took the scrap of paper and promised to pass along the message, as long as I agreed to vacate the premises immediately.

"I just don't think it's going to work," said George-Harrison as we finally walked out of that horrible bank. "I mean, especially considering the boss is a Mormon."

"Say that again! Repeat what you just said."

George-Harrison balked. "What? I didn't mean to offend anyone! I've got nothing against Mormons."

I leaned in and kissed him, leaving him totally clueless as to what caused my sudden burst of energy. What he said had reminded me of a conversation between Maggie and my dad, when my sister was cooking up an excuse for sneaking around his apartment.

"Mormons wouldn't call the work of other Mormons into question!" I whispered, breathing fast.

"Slow down, you're not making any sense."

"Mormons! They're obsessed with genealogy. There's a whole genealogical center in Utah they founded at the end of the nineteenth century. But they didn't stop there! They continued into Europe and managed to convince nearly every major country to provide them with all these vital records for their studies. To this day, they've still got millions upon millions of records on microfilm, all stored in safes hidden away in the mountains."

"How the hell do you know all this?"

"It's my job. For whatever reason, my father used the Mormons at some point to get info on our family tree. He was careful to only show me the part with him and my mother in it, but I'm sure I can get the rest if I go straight to the source . . . The point is, Mr. Clark would accept my family tree, since it uses research done by Mormons!"

I found what I was looking for on the internet in no time. The Mormons had gone completely modern. All I had to do was enter my info and my parents' names on their genealogy website, and I nearly instantly obtained the family tree that would serve as proof of my lineage. I had planned to march straight back to that teller with the document to give him a piece of my mind, when I got a call from Mr. Clark's secretary.

The branch president had agreed to meet with us the next day, at twelve o'clock sharp.

◆ ◆ ◆

I couldn't tell which was oldest: the president, the furniture in his office, or his secretary.

As we settled into a pair of cracked-leather armchairs, I took a closer look at our host. Impeccably dressed in a three-piece suit and bow tie,

Mr. Clark wore rectangular glasses that rested on the tip of his nose, and had a bald head and white mustache. He looked like a well-dressed version of Geppetto, which I found sweet. Despite his charming appearance, the man kept a poker face throughout my entire explanation, leaning down and closely inspecting the documents I had brought. He studied my family tree with utmost care and attention, muttering "I see" on three different occasions, while George-Harrison and I awaited his verdict with bated breath.

"This . . . is quite a complicated matter," he finally said.

"What's so complicated about it?" asked George-Harrison.

"Strictly speaking, a family tree does not constitute an official document. Yet, this one does attest to your roots. The safety-deposit box in question hasn't been opened for thirty-six years. In just a few months, it would have been declared abandoned, and its contents seized by the bank. You can imagine my surprise at this visit from someone claiming it."

"But aren't you holding proof of my hereditary rights in your hand right now? I'm Sally-Anne Stanfield's daughter."

"That much is clear, I grant you that. You do also look a lot like her, I must say."

"You remember my mother, after all these years?"

"Do you have any idea how many years my wife resented me for not having approved your mother's loan? Or the countless times she told me I should have stood up to my board of directors, insisting that their fears had been unwarranted? You have no idea how many years your mother cast a cloud—albeit indirectly—over my entire existence. Probably best I don't give you the actual number."

"Then you know the truth, you know what happened."

"I know that she fled the country after her brother's accident, abandoning her mother to go live abroad. Like anyone who had a relationship with the Stanfields, I was dismayed to learn all this."

"Did you know Hanna?"

I picked up the slightest twitch in his face at the name.

"She was a lovely woman," he said. "Never willing to listen to those doctors. Hanna . . . was a saint, as I live and breathe."

"Listen to them about what?"

"About pulling the plug on her son, about turning off the machines that kept him alive. To ensure that Edward received the best possible care, she sold all her paintings, one by one, with the legendary Stanfield estate following soon thereafter. She lost most of her fortune. She eventually moved into a modest little apartment, all by herself, spending her days watching over her son at the clinic and waiting for a miracle that never came. Technology grew more and more sophisticated, yet nothing could bring Edward back to life. She sacrificed everything for him, and when he finally died, it wasn't long before poor Hanna followed suit."

"How long did Edward last?"

"At least ten years. Maybe longer." Mr. Clark lifted up his glasses, dabbed at his forehead with his handkerchief, and coughed.

"Let's get back to what you came here for. You are aware this document proves your brother and sister are also Miss Stanfield's rightful heirs? Or rather—your mother's, I should say."

"Indeed, I am."

"The rental contract expressly stipulates that only she or one of her children be allowed access to the safety-deposit box."

Mr. Clark took my family tree in his hands, along with the contract itself, and handed both to his secretary. She had been listening the whole time, with the door to her adjoining office cracked open. It was as though Mr. Clark wanted a witness to prove he hadn't broken any rules, that he had remained a faithful servant of the bank over which he presided. The secretary returned a short while later, nodding to Mr. Clark to let him know everything was in order.

"Well, then. Shall we?" sighed Mr. Clark.

Reaching the safety-deposit box involved an elevator taken straight from an old film noir. As we descended lower and lower at a snail's pace,

I noticed George-Harrison admiring the elevator, studying the ornate wood marquetry, the grate, and the wooden crank, most likely imagining all the steps it would take to create an exact replica.

The safe-deposit vault was vast and impressive. Mr. Clark asked us to kindly wait outside with his secretary. The old woman gave us a warm smile, the first we had seen from her. Mr. Clark returned a short while later carrying an art portfolio with a protective cover. He laid the portfolio down on a table at the center of the space and backed away from it.

"I'll let you open it. I'm merely the custodian."

We cautiously approached, as though there were some sort of sacred relic hidden within. In a way, there was.

George-Harrison untied the strings sealing the portfolio, and I lifted the flap to reveal the *Girl by the Window* in all her timeless beauty. The light streaming onto her face was so realistic, it seemed like daylight itself had been captured upon the canvas.

The sight reminded me of another young woman looking out of a different window as her father smoked cigarettes with a young American liaison officer. All of it came back to me at once, just as though it were part of my own past: the harrowing escape through the mountains, all those who helped them along the way, the warm-hearted English art dealer who took a chance on a young protégée. I could see the claustrophobic view out of the window of their tenement on Thirty-Seventh Street dissolving into the stunning view from their apartment window on the Upper East Side. The arrival of my mother, their adopted daughter, and the birth of their son . . . all the many lives whose fates were bound to the Hopper masterpiece, Sam Goldstein's very favorite work of art.

After a moment, Mr. Clark and the secretary discreetly approached to admire the painting as well. They both seemed equally in awe as they took in the young girl captured on canvas.

"Do you plan to take it today?" whispered Mr. Clark.

"No," I replied softly. "It's far safer here."

"In that case, let's keep this simple. I'll transfer the contract to your name and add today's date; that way you can leave with a copy in hand. If you'd be so kind as to wait in the lobby just a few minutes, my secretary will bring it to you."

We came back to ground level via the same elevator and said goodbye to Mr. Clark. He climbed back inside the ornate elevator, and this time took it all the way back to the top floor.

After ten minutes or so, the secretary arrived carrying a sealed envelope. As she handed it over, she urged me to never lose the document, explaining that it was the very first time Mr. Clark had taken such extraordinary measures in all his long career, and she doubted he would ever break the rules again. The kind old woman then smiled at us a second time, and took her leave to go back to work.

◆ ◆ ◆

We chose Sailor's Hideaway for lunch—not as some intense pilgrimage for our mothers' sake, but more to revisit the location of our "first date." During the meal, George-Harrison asked what I planned to do with the painting.

"I plan to give it to you. You're the rightful owner. You're the only one with Sam and Hanna Goldstein's blood running through your veins. My mother was adopted, remember?"

"I almost forgot—but I couldn't be more thrilled about it!"

"I didn't realize you were so eager to get your hands on that painting."

"I'm not. It's an absolute masterpiece, don't get me wrong, but I don't give a damn about all that. As far as I'm concerned, adopted or not, your mother was still their daughter, and she was the rightful heiress."

"I'm lost. So, why is that such great news?"

"Because it means you and I are not related, in any way. Which is great news for both of us, because there is no way in hell I'm letting you go back to England, unless you want to take me with you."

I had no plans of leaving him, although I had to admit I would have gone so far as to board the plane just to make him beg me to stay.

"I know," I replied, a slight tremble in my voice.

"Sure you do. You know everything," he said, seeing right through me. "Except for one thing, the one mystery we may never crack: Just who is our poison-pen?"

◆ ◆ ◆

As we climbed into the pickup, I reached into my pocket and drew out the document that Mr. Clark's secretary had given me. My eyes immediately locked on to my own name, handwritten on the front of the envelope. The handwriting . . . full of rich curves and delicate edges, as though it had been written a century ago. No one wrote like that anymore, yet I was sure I recognized it.

Just like that, the final pieces fell into place. I began to laugh and cry at the same time. We stopped at a red light, and I handed the envelope to George-Harrison.

"Morrison was wrong! Hanna didn't commit suicide. Her car, remember? It was *her* car our mothers sank off the pier, to get rid of the evidence . . ."

"You lost me."

"The poison-pen was Hanna, and Hanna . . . is Mr. Clark's secretary!"

40

Mr. Clark's office, one hour earlier

"Well? Are you satisfied?" Mr. Clark asked as he walked Hanna to the front door of the bank.

"As a matter of fact, I am. My father's painting will see the light of day once more. I have kept my promise to him, to always keep it in our family and never sell it. And, as an added bonus, I was able to stare into the faces of two of my grandchildren, however briefly. Even you have to admit: it was well worth a couple of trips to the post office, even if one of them was all the way in Canada. You know you will always have my eternal gratitude for all you've done."

"And why not just reveal who you are now, Hanna?"

"After all that they have gone through to discover the truth, if they want to come back and meet me, they know where to find me."

Hanna said goodbye and made her way toward the bus stop. Mr. Clark watched as she marched away, as dignified and graceful as ever.

EPILOGUE

On January 1, 2017, Ray Donovan started a strict diet with the aim of fitting into his dinner jacket.

On April 2, 2017, Eleanor-Rigby and George-Harrison married in Croydon. It was a beautiful ceremony. Maggie dumped Fred and went back to college, determined this time to become a lawyer, although next year she would shift gears once more to pursue a career as a veterinarian.

The night of the wedding, Vera and Michel announced that they were moving to Brighton together. Michel had read that fresh sea air was far healthier than city air for pregnant women. A logical choice.

Seated in the back row as Eleanor-Rigby and George-Harrison took their vows was Hanna Stanfield—attending incognito, more or less. During her stay in England, she also went to pay her respects at her daughter's grave. Having now laid eyes on all her living descendants, she left with a smile on her face.

On April 20, 2017, Professor Morrison published a book titled *The Last of the Stanfields*, which would go on to become a smash hit . . . at least among the handful of his peers who received a copy.

Today, Eleanor-Rigby and George-Harrison live together in Magog. The house that George-Harrison built has been relocated outside the hangar.

As for May, she lived long enough to meet her first grandson. Sam is a remarkable baby boy, not least of all because he may be the only child in history to have a masterpiece by none other than Edward Hopper hanging in his bedroom.

Sometimes, just before falling asleep, he says good night to the young woman looking out the window.

ACKNOWLEDGMENTS

Pauline, Louis, Georges, and Cléa.

Raymond, Danièle, and Lorraine.

Susanna Lea.

Emmanuelle Hardouin.

Cécile Boyer-Runge, Antoine Caro.

Daniel Wasserman.

Caroline Babulle, Élisabeth Villeneuve, Arié Sberro, Sylvie Bardeau, Lydie Leroy, Joël Renaudat, Céline Chiflet, the whole team at Éditions Robert Laffont.

Pauline Normand, Marie-Ève Provost, Jean Bouchard.

Léonard Anthony, Sébastien Canot, Danielle Melconian, Mark Kessler, Xavière Jarty, Julien Saltet de Sablet d'Estières.

Laura Mamelok, Noa Rosen, Devon Halliday, Kerry Glencorse.

Brigitte Forissier, Sarah Altenloh.

Lorenzo.

And special thanks to the Beatles for . . . "Eleanor Rigby." (© Lennon-McCartney)

www.marclevy.info

www.laffont.fr

www.versilio.com

ABOUT THE AUTHOR

With more than forty million books sold, Marc Levy is the most-read French author alive today. He's written nineteen novels to date, including *P.S. from Paris, All Those Things We Never Said, The Children of Freedom,* and *Replay.*

Originally written for his son, his first novel, *If Only It Were True,* was later adapted for the big screen as *Just Like Heaven,* starring Reese Witherspoon and Mark Ruffalo. Since then, Levy has not only won the hearts of European readers, he's won over audiences around the globe. More than one and a half million of his books have been sold in China alone, and his novels have been published in forty-nine languages. He lives in New York City. Readers can learn more about Levy and follow his work at www.marclevy.info.